A QUESTION OF FASHION

"I really hate the thought of going back to London," Camilla said. "Beginning next week, there'll be precious few peaceful moments, I assure you!"

Jean nodded. "I know. The season begins next week. The only time I'll see you will be when you're surrounded by crowds of people." Suddenly he reached out to finger the tiny lace cap atop Camilla's curls. "Why do you always wear that thing—or something very similar—even when you're wearing a bonnet? Your sister never wears a cap."

"My sister isn't married."

"Neither are you."

"Don't be silly," said Camilla rather breathlessly. Jean had moved closer to her on the blanket. His hard thigh in the tight buckskin was pressing against her leg. "I'm a widow, so it's the same thing. And married women wear caps, I have no idea why. It's the custom."

"Being a widow isn't the same thing as being married, but now isn't the time to argue," Jean murmured. He whisked the little lace cap from her head. "There. Now I can see your beautiful hair. I could see it even better if it were down around your shoulders . . ."

Resting his weight on one arm, he leaned forward, running the fingers of his free hand through her hair, gently tugging at the hairpins that kept her curls in place.

"Jean, stop that," Camilla exclaimed, trying to pull his hand away. "My abigail spent half an hour this morning arranging my coiffure."

"Shush." Imprisoning her hand, Jean buried his face in the tumbled masses of her hair. "You smell like flowers. *Tu m'enivres,"* he whispered. His lips caressed the sensitive skin of her neck, gradually moving to her cheeks and eyelids. Camilla's entire body felt aflame . . .

A Memorable Collection of Regency Romances

BY ANTHEA MALCOLM AND VALERIE KING

THE COUNTERFEIT HEART   (3425, $3.95/$4.95)
by Anthea Malcolm

Nicola Crawford was hardly surprised when her cousin's betrothed disappeared on some mysterious quest. Anyone engaged to such an unromantic, but handsome man was bound to run off sooner or later. Nicola could never entrust her heart to such a conventional, but so deucedly handsome man. . . .

THE COURTING OF PHILIPPA   (2714, $3.95/$4.95)
by Anthea Malcolm

Miss Philippa was a very successful author of romantic novels. Thus she was chagrined to be snubbed by the handsome writer Henry Ashton whose own books she admired. And when she learned he considered love stories completely beneath his notice, she vowed to teach him a thing or two about the subject of love. . . .

THE WIDOW'S GAMBIT   (2357, $3.50/$4.50)
by Anthea Malcolm

The eldest of the orphaned Neville sisters needed a chaperone for a London season. So the ever-resourceful Livia added several years to her age, invented a deceased husband, and became the respectable Widow Royce. She was certain she'd never regret abandoning her girlhood until she met dashing Nicholas Warwick. . . .

A DARING WAGER   (2558, $3.95/$4.95)
by Valerie King

Ellie Dearborne's penchant for gaming had finally led her to ruin. It seemed like such a lark, wagering her devious cousin George that she would obtain the snuffboxes of three of society's most dashing peers in one month's time. She could easily succeed, too, were it not for that exasperating Lord Ravenworth. . . .

THE WILLFUL WIDOW   (3323, $3.95/$4.95)
by Valerie King

The lovely young widow, Mrs. Henrietta Harte, was not all inclined to pursue the sort of romantic folly the persistent King Brandish had in mind. She had to concentrate on marrying off her penniless sisters and managing her spendthrift mama. Surely Mr. Brandish could fit in with her plans somehow . . .

Available wherever paperbacks are sold, or order direct from the Publisher. Send cover price plus 50¢ per copy for mailing and handling to Zebra Books, Dept. 3912, 475 Park Avenue South, New York, N.Y. 10016. Residents of New York and Tennessee must include sales tax. DO NOT SEND CASH. For a free Zebra/ Pinnacle catalog please write to the above address.

An Uncommon Affair

Lois Stewart

ZEBRA BOOKS
KENSINGTON PUBLISHING CORP.

ZEBRA BOOKS

are published by

Kensington Publishing Corp.
475 Park Avenue South
New York, NY 10016

First printing: September, 1992

Printed in the United States of America

Prologue

I'm a kidnapper.

The horrifying thought occurred to Camilla Rayburn as her post chaise neared its second stop at Chippenham, not two hours into her journey from Bath to London.

But of course the accusation she'd made against herself was ridiculous. Wasn't it? How could anyone believe she was abducting Dorcas? Hadn't her younger sister fairly leapt at the suggestion that she should come to live with Camilla in London?

And yet . . . Uneasy qualms continued to haunt Camilla as she stole a sideways look at her sister on the seat beside her. Dorcas's face looked so excited, so expectant, so—so *young*. She was only seventeen, after all. Had Camilla really done the right thing? Her thoughts drifted back to the tear-smudged, cryptic scrawl that had sent her rushing to Bath from her home in London four days previously.

"I desperately need your help," Dorcas had written. "I can't cope by myself. Please, Camilla, will you come?"

Chapter One

The post chaise swept down from the crest of the hill in a final steeply sloping descent into the city of Bath, nestled in its circle of hills.

Camilla's eyes began to sparkle as she glimpsed the first familiar landmarks of the city in which she'd grown up: Camden Crescent, the Upper Assembly Rooms, the Circus, all off to her left, and ahead to the right the lovely arches of Pulteney Bridge. She'd paid only a few brief visits to Bath since her marriage four years previously, and she'd almost forgotten how beautiful the city was, how elegant and orderly. It was such a civilized place, with its pleasingly proportioned houses of luminous light colored gray and amber limestone, crisscrossed with neatly paved streets and interspersed with pleasure gardens and delightful promenades. Camilla thought to herself with a little smile that Bath wore a welcoming air even in the dank chill of an early March day. The daffodils were already blooming, their graceful yellow bells dancing in a stiff breeze that held a hint of snow.

The post chaise made a right turn onto George Street, proceeded down Gay Street and came to a halt in front of a handsome Palladian house in Queen Square. The postilion opened the door and let down the steps. As Camilla stepped down to the pavement, followed by her abigail, she reflected that the convenience of being delivered to her door was well worth the handsome tip she was about to give to the yellow-jacketed postilion. The comfort of traveling by post rather than by stagecoach had been worth every penny of the added expense, even for someone like herself who had to watch every shilling.

The postilion placed her portmanteau and valise on the pavement and drove off to the posting inn near the Abbey. Camilla walked up the steps of the house and lifted the knocker.

The young housemaid who answered the door was unfamiliar to her. "Yes, ma'am?" the girl said politely. She looked curiously at Camilla's luggage, rather as if she suspected the visitor had come to the wrong house.

"I'm Mrs. Rayburn. I'm here to visit Mrs. Vernon." When the housemaid's plain little face showed no sign of recognition, Camilla added, "I'm Mrs. Vernon's stepdaughter. Will you tell her, please, that I'm here?"

As Camilla entered the small but well-appointed drawing room of the house a moment later, a trim figure rose from a chair by the fireplace and walked toward her. "My dear Camilla, what a surprise," said Francine Vernon, giving her stepdaughter a languid peck on the cheek. "What brings you to Bath?"

"Really, Mama, what a question! I wanted to see you and Dorcas, of course."

"You've managed to restrain your eagerness to see us for well over a year, as I recall," said Francine dryly, motioning her stepdaughter to a chair. "The last time you were here was on the occasion of your father's funeral."

Francine Vernon was a slender, dark-haired woman of thirty-seven, whose still considerable good looks were marred by a nervous, brittle manner and deep lines of discontent carved beside her mouth. Camilla disliked her intensely. The dislike was mutual. Though she'd been only four years old at the time, Camilla had a distinct memory of the hostility she'd sensed in Francine during their very first meeting, when Camilla's father had introduced the pretty young woman to his daughter as his future wife. Francine's jealousy and resentment of her stepdaughter had been obvious from the beginning.

"I marvel you could tear yourself away from your grand

social life in London to come visit us provincials," Francine remarked with a barb in her voice, after she had rung the bell to summon the maidservant and had ordered a tea tray.

Camilla removed her gloves and took off her bonnet. "It's only the beginning of March, Mama," she said composedly. "Town is very thin of company. The season won't start for two months. And you forget, I think, that I'm a widow with a limited income. I don't live a grand life. On the contrary. Most people would consider my daily routine very quiet, almost dull."

"Not by any means as quiet and dull as the daily routine of other widows I could name," retorted Francine. "At least you have the opportunity to live in London."

Camilla sighed to herself. It was a familiar plaint. Francine had always longed to take an elegant house in London during the season, and it had never been possible on her husband's income.

"Actually, Mama, I believe you vastly overrate London. Driving into Bath today, I was reminded all over again what a pleasant city it is to live in."

"Oh, don't talk fustian," snapped Francine. "You'd sing a different tune, I daresay, if you were trapped in this backwater for the rest of your life."

Camilla sighed again. Memories of the uncomfortable years she'd spent in this house with her discontented stepmother were flooding over her. How had her father endured Francine's daily litany of complaints down through the years?

Although he was descended from a distinguished family, Thomas Vernon, Camilla's father, had not been wealthy. The younger son of an earl, he'd been obliged to make his own way in the world. Retiring from the Navy with the prestigious rank of admiral but with only a modest pension, he'd come to live in Bath with his motherless child. Francine was the daughter of a local merchant. She'd definitely married above her station, and the discrepancy between her husband's position and her own had never ceased to rankle. Over the years her bitterness had increased when she real-

9

ized she would never achieve her dream of being a part of the London social scene.

After the birth of her own daughter, Dorcas, Francine had begun to nurse still another grudge. She firmly believed, and deeply resented, the notion that Camilla enjoyed more advantages than Dorcas. Camilla was due to inherit a small but respectable income from her mother when she turned eighteen or when she married. Camilla had also enjoyed a lavish coming out season in London, thanks to the generosity of her godfather. Thomas Vernon had argued in vain that no injustice toward Dorcas was involved. Francine didn't believe him. Relations with her stepmother had finally become so strained that Camilla had rushed into an impulsive, unsatisfactory marriage with dashing Philip Rayburn.

"Well, my dear, how long are we to enjoy your company?" asked Francine as she poured herself a second cup of tea. "I only hope you won't die of boredom here."

Before Camilla could answer, her half sister burst into the room, a spot of color high on either cheek. Dorcas was small and slight, looking even younger than her seventeen years, but otherwise she much resembled her taller sister. Both had dark gold hair, deep blue eyes and delicately modeled features.

Dorcas froze on the threshold in momentary surprise, then rushed to Camilla, who had risen from her chair. "Oh, I'm so glad to see you," Dorcas exclaimed shakily, throwing her arms around Camilla. A moment later she put her lips to Camilla's ear, breathing in a barely audible whisper, "You — you didn't tell Mama I wrote to you?"

"What do you take me for, you goose, a talebearer?" Camilla murmured.

"What's this now, secrets?" inquired Francine, with the sugary smile that always seemed to have a hint of vinegar around the edges.

"Come, now, Mama, how could we have any secrets?" protested Camilla. "Dorcas and I haven't seen each other for months."

Francine's eyes were fixed on Dorcas. "You look overset, lovey. Is something wrong? Didn't you enjoy your walk with Susanna Orcutt? Such a lovely girl," Francine added in an aside to Camilla. "Her father's a retired general, and her mother is a connection of the Feltons of Bowness Hall."

"Susanna and I had a lovely walk, except that we were forced to cut it a little short," Dorcas said hurriedly. "Mr. Stinchcombe caught us up in Gay Street and insisted on driving us home."

Francine beamed. "Isn't that just like Mr. Stinchcombe? He's so kind." To Camilla she added with an air of importance, "Mr. Octavius Stinchcombe is a new acquaintance. For many years he was a resident of Barbados, managing his valuable estates there. But now he's come home to Bath, where he was born. He's bought a handsome estate not far from the city, and plans to take part in all the activities of Bath."

Francine turned back to Dorcas, saying, "But I don't understand why Mr. Stinchcombe should be still in Bath. Only last week he told us he'd be making a short visit to friends near Bristol."

"He was on his way to Bristol in his traveling carriage, Mama," replied Dorcas shortly.

Camilla looked from Dorcas's flushed face to Francine's complacent-looking features, and began to glean an inkling of the truth, but it wasn't until the following day that she could speak to Dorcas alone. Their evening was fully occupied. Francine had invited friends to a card party. She pressed both Camilla and Dorcas into service when two of her guests sent their belated regrets, and Camilla tumbled wearily into bed well after midnight, without having had the opportunity for a private word with Dorcas.

On the following morning, Camilla and her sister, dressed in warm pelisses, scarves and gloves against a raw, biting wind, went for a stroll in the Crescent Fields — the long slope of land below the lovely graceful sweep of the Royal Crescent. Thanks to the inclement weather, there were few other strollers about, except for an occasional nursemaid with her

11

charges. Camilla and Dorcas didn't need to fear being over-heard.

"It's so good to see you," said Dorcas, her eyes shining. "It seems ages since we've been together. I've missed you."

A wave of guilt swept over Camilla. Despite the difference in their ages, she and Dorcas had been very close when they were growing up, although Camilla had often felt more like an alternate mother, or a young aunt, than a sister. She should have made more of an effort to keep in contact with Dorcas these past few years, Camilla acknowledged. She shouldn't have allowed her antipathy to her stepmother to cast a shadow over her relations with her sister.

She squeezed Dorcas's arm. "I've missed you too, love. I promise I'll try to visit more often in the future. Now, then, out with it. What did you mean in your letter, that you were desperate for help?"

Dorcas's eyes filmed with tears. "Oh, Camilla, I feel so guilty, dragging you here all the way from London, but I didn't know where else to turn." Hesitating for a moment, Dorcas blurted, "Mama wants me to marry Mr. Stinch-combe."

Unsurprised, Camilla inquired, "That's the gentleman she was talking about last night? The man who has the valu-able estates in Barbados?"

Dorcas nodded, her expressive face clouded with gloom.

"This Mr. Stinchcombe has made you a formal offer?"

Dorcas nodded again.

"And you don't fancy him?"

"Oh, he's pleasant enough, but . . . Camilla, he's *old* and fat and he *wheezes* when he walks. Rather than marry him, I'd as lief remain on the shelf, a hopeless spinster, for the rest of my life!"

Temporarily reserving judgment—after all, a seventeen-year-old might regard a gentleman of thirty as ancient—Camilla asked cautiously, "Just how old *is* Mr. Stinchcombe?"

"Mama says he's a 'young fifty,' but I think he's older than that. *Much* older!"

"Oh." Camilla paused. So Dorcas wasn't merely enacting a Cheltenham tragedy. She had grounds for her unhappiness. After a moment, Camilla said, "Tell me about it."

"Well, there's not much to tell. I met Mr. Stinchcombe in the Pump Room about a month ago. He'd become acquainted with old Mrs. Finchley—you remember her, don't you? She lives in Laura Place, and her granddaughter is a special friend of mine—and so Mr. Stinchcombe asked Mrs. Finchley to introduce him to Mama and me. Within a week—a *week,* Camilla—he asked Mama for my hand."

"I see. And Mama's been pressuring you to accept his suit?"

"Yes. Mama says Mr. Stinchcombe is a great catch. She says I'll be a fine lady, established for life. You see, he's offered to settle a great deal of money on me, and . . ." Dorcas's voice trailed off uncertainly. Finally she resumed, "And he's also offered to give Mama a handsome allowance."

Oh, the devil, thought Camilla. Mr. Stinchcombe must be a clever man. He was dangling an irresistible carrot in front of Francine. With a large sum of money in her hands, and with Dorcass *off* her hands, Francine would be free to travel, to buy fashionable new clothes, even, perhaps, to attempt an *entrée* into the London *ton.*

Aloud, Camilla said, "We're not living in the Middle ages, Dorcas. Mama can't force you to the altar against your will. If you don't wish to marry Mr. Stinchcombe, say so, firmly, and then keep to your decision."

Dorcas heaved a discouraged sigh. "Oh, I know you're right, but . . . Mama is so *set* on my marrying Mr. Stinchcombe. She says I'll never receive such an advantageous offer again."

Camilla was silent for a moment. Even if this marriage was truly so distasteful to Dorcas, Camilla doubted that her sister would be able to hold out for very long against her mother. Sweet and yielding of disposition, eager to please, Dorcas had always found it difficult to assert herself. It had probably required a great effort of will even to send her call for help to Camilla. And Francine . . . Camilla shook her head. Francine had the tenacity of a bull mastiff when it came to matters affecting her personal wishes and comfort!

At last Camilla said, "Would you like me to speak to Mama, Dorcas? Mind, I can't promise I'll be able to change her mind."

"Oh, yes, please." Dorcas's eyes shone with relief. "Mama can't help but listen to you. You're so much older than I am, you have so much experience of the world."

Camilla thought uneasily that Dorcas was relying entirely too much on her sister's powers of persuasion. Francine was almost certain to resent any interference from her stepdaughter.

Hiding her concern, Camilla said with a teasing smile, "I had no idea I appeared so old to you, Dorcas. I've just turned twenty-two, you know."

"Oh!" Dorcas reddened. "I didn't mean—of *course*, you're not old, Camilla . . ."

Before Dorcas could finish her floundering reply, a large dog escaped from the insecure grasp of a small boy and bounded into Camilla, entangling her with his trailing leash and causing her to fall heavily to the ground, which was damp and soggy after several days of rain. A fellow stroller rushed up to pull Camilla to her feet and free both her and the dog from the encumbering leash.

"Are you hurt, *madame?* May I be of assistance?"

Shaking herself out of her brief dazed surprise, Camilla looked at her rescuer. He was a tall, powerful man with curling dark hair, a bronzed skin, and intensely black eyes. Handsome in a rather rough way, she thought. Her eyes, accustomed to the cosmopolitan perfection of dress of the London dandies, registered immediately that the man was wearing an unfashionable cloak rather than a trim many-caped greatcoat. He was also wearing breeches and inexpertly polished top boots rather than the more usual town morning dress of pantaloons and Hessians.

"No, thank you. I don't need any further help. You've

done quite enough, sir," she said politely, and turned back to Dorcas.

"Wait." The man reached out a hand to detain her. A confident smile on his handsome, well-shaped mouth, he said, "Are you sure you're not feeling faint? Perhaps I should escort you home."

His smile faded as Camilla jerked her arm from his grasp and fixed him with a cold, unfriendly glance. She wasn't accustomed to such familiarity from strange men. Who was this fellow, anyway? A country bumpkin from the hinterlands, perhaps, his manners as crude as his dress was unfashionable? But no, that deep resonant voice had an accent. Quite a strong accent. The man was a foreigner. French, at a guess. Possibly different standards of conduct prevailed on the Continent. Camilla had never been to France—the country was off limits to Englishmen since the resumption of the war with Napoleon.

She said, chin in the air, "No, I don't require an escort. Thank you again for your help. Good day, sir." She walked away without a backward glance.

When she and Dorcas arrived back in Queen Square, Francine was quick to notice the grass stains on Camilla's pelisse. "I do hope it will clean," she fretted. "I daresay you paid the earth for it," she added, looking closely at the pelisse of pale violet velvet, trimmed with Egyptian crepe and antique lace. "I hear people exclaiming over what fine shops we have in Bath, but I'm sure they can't touch the shops in London."

At the familiar note of discontent in Francine's voice, Camilla suppressed an irritated retort. "Actually, Mama, I rescued this pelisse from the back of my wardrobe, and my abigail made it look like new again with a bit of fresh trim. You must know I can't afford to buy a completely new wardrobe every year on my income. I heartily recommend to you refurbishing your old garments. You have no idea how much money you'll save!"

Francine looked singularly unimpressed with the advice.

That evening after dinner, Dorcas put on a rather unconvincing show of fatigue and went to bed early, leaving Camilla to talk undisturbed with her stepmother.

"You'll forgive me, my dear, but I hardly think this is your concern," said Francine in an offended voice when Camilla broached the subject of Mr. Stinchcombe.

"Dorcas is my sister, Mama. I want her to be happy."

"And you don't think her own mother wants her to be happy? I'm doing my utmost to ensure that she's provided for, with a fine home and a devoted husband."

"But Dorcas has told me she doesn't care for Mr. Stinchcombe. Don't you think he's rather old for her?"

"Dorcas doesn't know her own mind. She doesn't realize she needs the support and guidance of a mature man. You must have noticed yourself that she tends to be rather timid and flighty. She'll care enough for Mr. Stinchcombe, you'll see, after they're married."

Since Francine showed no sign of yielding, Camilla tried another tack. "I'd like to ask a favor, Mama. I'll be returning to London in a few days—"

"You're leaving Bath so soon? I quite expected you to stay for several weeks," Francine interrupted. She sounded injured. Although she couldn't possibly have derived any pleasure from her stepdaughter's presence, it was obvious that she regarded the shortness of Camilla's stay as a personal slight.

"I must go," Camilla replied. "I'm engaged to dine with friends on Saturday. I promise I'll return for another visit as soon as I can. Meanwhile, I'd feel so much easier in my mind if you promised to do something for me."

"And what would that be?"

"I'd like you to ask this Mr. Stinchcombe to refrain from pressing his suit for—oh, say, six months. That would give Dorcas a little respite. At the end of that time, she'd at least know her own mind better."

Rather to Camilla's surprise, Francine seemed to be seriously considering the suggestion. Finally she said, in the tone of one making a generous concession, "I declare, you may have hit on something, Camilla. Heaven knows, I

16

wouldn't wish to rush my darling Darcas into something she might regret. I'll discuss the matter with Mr. Stinchcombe."

Done, thought an exultant Camilla. Who could know what might happen in six months? Young as she was, Dorcas had already attracted one eligible suitor—eligible in Francine's opinion, at least. Possibly, during the next few months, Dorcas might meet a younger man who appealed to her, someone with a tidy fortune who would also appeal to her mother.

"Now, don't tell me *that's* a refurbished garment, for I wouldn't believe you," declared Francine with an admiring glance tinged with envy, as Camilla walked into the drawing room wearing a dress of pale green *crêpe lisse* trimmed with lace and tiny yellow roses. Her dark gold curls were drawn to the crown of her head beneath a frivolous headdress of roses and bows of green satin ribbon.

"No, the gown is new, or at least not previously worn," Camilla replied, smiling. "It was also a real bargain. Mme. Labelle, whose clothes are usually far too dear for my purse, had made the dress for a lady who'd suddenly become widowed, so she returned the gown to the shop. Fortunately, it fit me perfectly. *Madame* practically paid me to take it off her hands."

It was Camilla's last evening in Bath. She was to accompany Francine and Dorcas to a ball in the Upper Assembly Rooms. A hired carriage took them up Gay Street, around the Circus and into adjacent Bennett Street. They might easily have walked the short distance, but this would have offended Francine's sensibilities. She didn't keep her own carriage, partly because of the expense, but mostly because a carriage was really unnecessary in Bath's compact center, at least in the daytime.

A wave of nostalgia swept over Camilla as she entered the central vestibule of the Upper Rooms and paused in the Great Octagon Room with its luminous Gainsborough portrait and its exquisite chandeliers of Whitefriars crystal.

She'd attended so many enjoyable functions here while her father was still alive, and before she went off to London and marriage with Philip.

Despite the chilly weather, the rooms radiating off the central vestibule were comfortably filled. As soon as they entered the ballroom, a young man came up to Dorcas and led her into the country dance that was forming. A moment later a stout, middle-aged gentleman greeted Francine with a low bow.

Francine's eyes lighted up. "La, sir, I hardly expected you back from your visit to Bristol so soon."

"My dear Mrs. Vernon, I found Bristol confoundedly dull, and I missed the company of my good friends in Bath, so back I came," said the gentleman. He cast a politely inquiring glance at Camilla.

Francine took Camilla's arm. "My dear, may I present to you Mr. Octavius Stinchcombe? My daughter, sir, Mrs. Rayburn."

Mr. Stinchcombe bowed to Camilla, and then turned to Francine with a beaming smile to say, "Allow me to congratulate you, Mrs. Vernon. I had no idea that *both* your daughters were so beautiful. Like the mother of the Gracchi, you're fortunate in possessing not just one, but two, jewels of great price."

Mr. Stinchcombe's labored classical allusion failed to impress Camilla. Looking at him closely, she concluded that Dorcas's objections to the man had been, if anything, understated. Mr. Stinchcombe wasn't just stout, he verged on the obese. Camilla had heard the faint creak of his stays as he bowed. He also wore a dusting of rouge on his cheeks, which Camilla could not like, although she was aware that many of the younger dandies favored the practice. And Dorcas had been quite right, a "young fifty" Mr. Stinchcombe was not. He appeared much older.

Francine said to Camilla with a meaningful stare, "My dear, would you mind very much if Mr. Stinchcombe and I leave you for a few moments, while we go off to the tea room for a private little chat?"

"No, not at all." Watching the pair walk off together, Camilla felt a sense of relief. Francine seemed to be keeping her promise, and more promptly than Camilla could have expected. Her stepmother surely was about to ask Mr. Stinchcombe to desist from pressing his suit on Dorcas for the next six months.

Camilla gazed out over the line of dancers, spotting her sister with her partner. Dorcas was obviously enjoying herself. Camilla reflected with satisfaction that her trip to Bath had been well worth the effort. Dorcas had become almost a different person, more like the carefree young girl she deserved to be, since Camilla had told her in confidence, several days ago, that Francine had agreed to rein in Mr. Stinchcombe's matrimonial pursuit.

An old acquaintance, one of Bath's perennial bachelors, came up to ask Camilla for the next dance. The Master of Ceremonies introduced several young men who promptly asked her to dance also. At the end of a lively Scottish reel, as she was coming off the floor with a partner, Mr. Stinchcombe, too, put in his request for a dance.

Extending his arm to her, Stinchcombe said genially, "Mrs. Rayburn, I must confess I'm no great dabster on the dance floor. I know you won't object if, instead of dancing, we sit down in the tea room, or perhaps the card room, where we can have a comfortable coze. I'm sure you agree we should learn to know each other better." Then he flicked her a conspiratorial wink.

Camilla didn't understand the wink. It made her feel vaguely uneasy.

Seated opposite Camilla at a table in the tea room, Mr. Stinchcombe gave an order to a hovering waiter and then leaned forward on his elbows, speaking in a low, confidential tone. "I'm so pleased you came to Bath, Mrs. Rayburn. Had you not come, I should have felt obliged to journey to London to meet you!"

"Really? Why would you do that?"

Mr. Stinchcombe's rather beady eyes filled with reproach. "Mrs. Rayburn! Surely you realize that an honorable man like myself could not fail to make myself known to all the relations of my future wife. As Miss Dorcas's sister, you have the right, nay, the duty, to meet me and inquire into my prospects and my ability to provide for her."

Camilla said in surprise, "I beg your pardon, sir. So far as I'm aware, it's not at all certain that a marriage between you and my sister will take place."

"Of course it's certain," exclaimed Mr. Stinchcombe, frowning. "Save for signing the contracts and the actual ceremony, Miss Dorcas and I are as good as married. As a matter of fact, her good mother and I have composed an announcement of the coming nuptials that will appear in the Bath newspapers within the week."

"But . . . I understood my stepmother was going to advise you tonight to postpone any idea of marriage for six months."

Mr. Stinchcombe looked blank. "You must have misunderstood. No, no, Mrs. Vernon spoke to me only about the betrothal announcement. She feels, and I concur, that it's unwise to postpone the wedding date indefinitely. The delay could cause great embarrassment for Miss Dorcas. Folk might think I wasn't serious in my courtship!"

Camilla stood up abruptly. "Pray excuse me," she muttered to Mr. Stinchcombe, and headed toward the door of the tea room, where, a moment before, she'd caught a glimpse of a hovering Francine. By the time Camilla reached the door, her stepmother had disappeared. Camilla walked through the Great Octagon Room and the card room, and finally located Francine sitting in the midst of a group of dowagers at the side of the ballroom. Francine gave Camilla a hunted look, but made no move to leave her companions.

She's barricaded herself behind those old ladies so I can't reach her for a reckoning, Camilla reflected savagely. Well, no matter. She can't avoid me when we go home tonight. However, the thought of confronting Francine gave Camilla little comfort as she left the ballroom to pace agitatedly up and down the long vestibule of the assembly rooms. There was no need to ask her stepmother for explanations. Camilla already knew the answers. Francine had never had any intention of asking Mr. Stinchcombe to delay his marriage plans. She'd agreed to do so merely to keep Camilla pacified until she left Bath. Once Camilla was out of sight and hearing in London, Francine could do as she liked. Apparently it hadn't occurred to her that Mr. Stinchcombe would let the cat out of the bag by engaging Camilla in a private conversation to discuss his coming marriage.

And what a diabolical scheme Francine had invented to ensure that Dorcas would marry her elderly suitor! Once the betrothal had been formally announced in the newspapers, Francine could be virtually certain that gentle, biddable Dorcas would never find the courage to cry off and thereby brand herself a shameless jilt.

Oblivious to the swarms of people passing by her in the vestibule, Camilla pounded her hands together in frustration. Was there nothing that could be done?

"Would you care to dance, *madame?*"

Camilla looked up at the man blocking her way. Blinking her eyes to clear her mind, she became aware of a familiar face. It was the foreign gentleman who had attempted to strike up an acquaintance with her in Crescent Fields several days ago. Even in her distress, fashion-conscious Camilla noted that he was no more suitably dressed than he'd been at their last encounter. He was wearing leather breeches and topboots instead of silk breeches and stockings and low slippers, and his double-breasted coat, with its exaggerated padding at the top of the sleeves and its skimpy coattails, was not only years out of date, but could never have been regarded as proper evening attire.

She said impatiently, "No, I thank you, sir. I don't wish to dance."

He moved closer, forcing her to take a backward step. "You can't really mean that," he protested. "I've been standing in the ballroom, watching you dancing with one partner after the other. You were born to dance." He put light, caressing fingers on her arm, at the point where her long kid gloves just failed to meet her sleeves. For a moment she could have sworn she saw electric sparks igniting in the depths of his dark eyes. The narrow band of bare skin on her upper arm felt abnormally sensitive. He murmured, his accent growing more pronounced, "Won't you take pity on a passing stranger who doesn't know anybody in this town?"

The accumulated strains and vexations of the evening caught up with Camilla. Her eyes flashing a blue fire, she exclaimed, "The standards of the Bath assembly rooms have obviously sadly deteriorated since I was last here, my good sir. Even a few years ago, a man who failed to dress and act like a gentleman would never have gained admittance. When you paid your subscription fee, someone should have advised you that you may not ask a lady to dance unless you have been first introduced by the Master of Ceremonies!"

The man stepped back, the disturbing electric sparks dying out of his eyes, which had turned to hard, expressionless ebony. "I hardly think I'll put the Master of Ceremonies to such trouble, *madame*," he drawled. "I doubt the experience would be worth the effort."

With a slight bow, he walked away, leaving Camilla trembling with rage. What kind of a savage was he to speak to her like that? Gradually anger turned to mortification. Never in her ladylike, well-ordered existence had she been guilty of such an outburst in public. She must have sounded like a fishwife! It didn't matter that the foreigner had richly deserved her rebuke. She'd let down her own standards of conduct.

She looked up to see Dorcas walking out of the ballroom on the arm of an attentive-looking young man. Both of them were smiling. Camilla's eyes narrowed. Dorcas had been right. Desperate measures were necessary.

The jolting of the post chaise was much worse on this stretch of the road, Camilla observed. Perhaps the turnpike trusts on this part of the London to Bath road had failed to make the necessary repairs. Or perhaps the road seemed unnecessarily rough only because she and Dorcas had been sitting in weary discomfort inside the vehicle for over five hours.

Camilla glanced at her sister in concern. Dorcas sat huddled limply against the squabs, her face pale and drawn. "Aren't you feeling well, love?"

"It's nothing." Dorcas attempted a smile. "Have you forgotten what a poor traveler I've always been? Remember Nurse forcing me to drink all those glasses of Aunt Tabitha's gooseberry wine in order to calm my stomach? I'll begin feeling more the thing the moment this chaise stops in front of your London house." She swallowed hard. "Camilla, what if Mama should come after us?"

The unexpected question startled Camilla. She replied firmly, "Mama won't do that." And, in fact, she was reasonably sure she'd spiked Francine's guns. After their return from the assembly rooms last night, she hadn't remonstrated to her stepmother about Dorcas and Mr. Stinchcombe. Instead, she'd waited until Francine had left the house on Queen Square this afternoon to meet her friends in the Pump Room, and then, after a frenzy of packing, Camilla and Dorcas had climbed into the post chaise for the journey to London. Behind her, Camilla had left a brief note. "I've taken Dorcas to stay with me for the six months grace period we agreed upon."

Camilla considered that she'd presented her stepmother with a *fait accompli*. Francine could hardly object to the arrangement without revealing her own duplicity. Dorcas was safe for six months.

But Camilla had underestimated Francine Vernon.

As they approached Newbury, fifty odd miles and some six hours from London, Camilla had decided to give Dorcas's sensitive stomach a respite from the swaying and jolting of the post chaise. It was already eleven o'clock in the evening. They would stay the night at the George and Pelican in Speenhamland, in the northern part of the town of Newbury, and resume their journey to London in the morning.

Tucking Dorcas into bed herself — Camilla's abigail hadn't accompanied them, since the post chaise seated only two passengers; the maidservant would follow them in the mail coach — Camilla went downstairs for a late supper in one of the private dining rooms of the inn. She'd consumed part of a plump capon and most of a dish of boiled eels, and was pouring herself a second glass of an excellent Madeira when her stepmother burst into the room. From the disheveled state of her dress, it was obvious she'd left Bath in a tearing hurry.

"Viper!" Francine spat at Camilla. "Unnatural female! You've stolen my child!" She glanced around the parlor. "Where is she? What have you done with her?"

Camilla stood up. "Oh, don't talk fustian. Dorcas is upstairs sleeping. You know she becomes ill during long carriage rides." Camilla eyed her stepmother calmly. "You've wasted your time and your energy chasing after us. As I told you in my note, I'm taking Dorcas to live with me for a while to give her a little breathing room while she makes up her mind about her future. After all, Mama, we did agree, you and I, that Dorcas should have six months to consider if she really wishes to marry Mr. Stinchcombe."

Francine opened her mouth and slowly closed it again.

Checkmate, thought Camilla.

After a moment's pause, however, Francine recovered herself. She said resentfully, "Don't think you're bubbling me. I know what you're about." A cajoling note crept into her voice. "My dear Camilla, there's no reason why we should be up in the boughs with each other. What about a compromise? Mr. Stinchcombe offered me as his future mama-in-law an allowance of one thousand pounds a year. A nest egg for my future. I'm sure no one else will lift a finger to save me from the poorhouse! Well, then, supposing you give me — oh, shall we say twenty thousand pounds in a lump sum? In return, I'd be willing to relinquish Dorcas's care into your hands."

Camilla looked at Francine with contempt. It was obvious, from the ease with which the sum had tripped off Francine's lips, that her stepmother had carefully calculated the size of her demand. Twenty thousand pounds invested in the Funds would return an income of approximately one thousand pounds a year, the exact amount of the allowance Mr. Stinchcombe had promised her stepmother.

"I'm not in the business of buying and selling human beings, Mama."

"Don't you play the virtuous innocent with me," Francine exclaimed angrily. "You were willing enough to sever a helpless child from her loving mother, leaving me to a lonely old age. Will you, or will you not, give me my rightful due?"

"Aside from any other objections I might have, you must know that I don't have twenty thousand pounds of disposable capital. I live on a fixed income."

Francine pounced on the remark, apparently reading into it a softening on Camilla's part. "You could find the money," she said eagerly. "You could sell some of your investments in the Funds. And you have wealthy friends. There's your godfather, he's rich as Croesus. He'd never miss twenty thousand pounds."

Camilla's eyes flashed. "If I found twenty thousand pounds lying on the street in front of me, I wouldn't give it to you, Mama. I told you, I won't buy Dorcas from you."

Flushing an ugly red, Francine snapped, "Then I'm taking my daughter back to Bath with me. Which room is she in? You won't tell me? Don't fancy that will stop me. I'll ask the landlord." She turned to leave the room.

"Don't bother to talk to the landlord, Mama," Camilla called out after her. "I'm reasonably certain you're not carrying any proof with you that you're Dorcas's mother. If you persist in going to the landlord, I'll simply inform him that you're Dorcas's poor, crazed former governess who can't bear to see her darling leaving home. We'll see which one of us will be believed."

Francine whirled about, apparently losing the last remnant of her self-control. She rushed at Camilla, screaming, "You've been a thorn in my side since you were four years old! I wish you'd never been born!" She lashed out at her stepdaughter with clawing hands, attempting to rake Camilla's face and hair.

After an initial moment of shock, Camilla managed to confine Francine's wildly flailing arms. "Mama, have you gone queer in your attic? For God's sake, stop this."

But Francine was past listening to reason. She struggled frantically to free herself, all the while screeching obscenities strange to Camilla's sheltered ears, the meaning of which she could only guess.

She looked up in relief as the door of the parlor opened, expecting to see the landlord or one of the servants, drawn to the room by Francine's screams. However embarrassing the situation might be, Camilla could use a man's help to calm her stepmother. But it wasn't the landlord, or any of his hirelings, who stalked across the room and separated the two women, holding them effortlessly apart, each at the end of a long powerful arm.

She gasped, as she recognized the dark foreigner who had twice accosted her in Bath. "What are you doing here?"

"Like you, *madame,* I'm traveling from Bath. It seems I'm also preventing you ladies from committing mayhem on each other," said the man with a look of cool amusement.

"Please release me," said Camilla stiffly.

He removed his hand from her arm and turned an inquiring glance on her stepmother. The shock of his sudden intervention had dampened Francine's belligerence. "Let me go," she muttered sulkily. To Camilla she said, "For the last time, are you going to send Dorcas home with me?"

"No. I'll bring her back to you in the autumn."

"Don't think you've heard the last of this. I'm going now, but I'll see that you pay for what you've done — kidnapping, and assault, and alienation of affections. You'll wish you'd never crossed swords with me." Swinging on her heel, Francine walked through the door of the parlor and slammed it so hard behind her that the floorboards shivered.

"Friend of yours?" the stranger inquired, the amusement growing in his dark eyes.

"She's my — No. Would you please go, sir? This is a private parlor."

The stranger's face hardened. "In a moment. First I'd like an answer to a question. The last time we met, you accused me of not knowing how to act like a gentleman. Will you now tell me if the scene I just witnessed is a fair example of how ladies of quality behave toward each other?"

"Oh-h-h!" Camilla exclaimed in a voice shaking with outrage, "Leave the room immediately, before I call the landlord to evict you!"

Instead of complying, he wrapped his arms around her and crushed his lips against hers in a bruising kiss. For a moment she panicked, overcome by a familiar feeling of repulsion at the touch of a rapacious male. Then the repulsion faded, replaced by an electric surge of sensual awareness. Without willing it, she relaxed against the stranger's lean muscled body, responding to the insistent pressure of his mouth.

He dropped his arms and stepped back from her. His lips curved in a sardonic smile. "*Voilà,* I knew we had something in common. We like to kiss each other." He walked to the door, turning to say, "I bid you a regretful goodnight, *madame.* I'm pressed for time, much as I'd like to — er — further explore our mutual feelings."

A much-tried Camilla did something she'd never done before. She picked up a plate from the table and hurled it at the stranger. The plate shattered harmlessly against the closing door.

Chapter Two

His face alight with excitement, Miles Wingate lifted his hands from the keys of the pianoforte and jumped to his feet, exclaiming, "It's splendid, Camilla. The second movement's a gem!"

"What? Oh—I'm happy you like it," replied Camilla rather lamely. Standing beside the pianoforte while Miles played her sonata, she'd allowed her mind to wander. Normally, of course, she'd have been concentrating on his playing with bated breath, waiting for his judgment on a work that had taken her two years to complete. This afternoon, however, she'd been unable to keep her thoughts from the letter she'd received that morning from the solicitor in Bath.

Noting Miles's faintly disappointed expression, she forced her mind away from the letter and said warmly, "I'm more than happy you like the sonata. I'm ecstatic! I not only respect your musical taste—I know you'll always give me your honest opinion."

Miles flushed faintly with pleasure. "Well, I may be the first to congratulate you, but I assure you I shan't be the last!" His eyes widened. "Camilla! Why don't we ask the Academy of Music to perform the piece?"

"Oh . . ." Camilla drew a deep, wondering breath. She and Miles were both subscribers to the respected musical society, which gave public concerts during the season at the Crown and Anchor tavern. "I know the Academy occasionally plays works by contemporary composers, but . . . Do you really think the members would consider a sonata composed by a female?"

"My eye and Betty Martin, they will if I have anything to say about it!"

Camilla smiled. "You're such a good friend, Miles. What would I do without you?"

Miles Wingate was a slender, erect man of medium height, with pleasant, open features and steady gray eyes. Thirty years old, he was a member of an old but untitled family, with a substantial income that allowed him to live as he pleased, either in his comfortable rooms at the Albany in London, or at his country estate in Hampshire. He had always formed a part of the small, congenial circle of acquaintances that Camilla had gathered around her during the years of her widowhood. They all shared her interests in music and the other arts, but Miles had become her close personal friend.

"Are you troubled about something, Camilla?" he asked now. "You seem — oh, I don't know — distracted. Is it your sister? What a charming girl she is, by the way. She resembles you so much." Miles had met Dorcas earlier in the afternoon, on his arrival at the house on Park Street. "I'm sure you're delighted to have her with you," he went on. "However, she'll certainly be an added responsibility for you. That is, if you plan to sponsor her coming out."

Camilla's brows drew together in a troubled frown. "You know my situation. I'd like nothing better than to bring Dorcas out, but I can't possibly afford the expense of a London season for her, more's the pity. I couldn't begin to buy the clothes the child would need, for one thing. And this house is far too small to host an affair of any size." Camilla sighed. "I hope Dorcas won't be bored to tears during her stay with me."

"I'd challenge anyone to be bored in your company," Miles declared loyally.

Camilla smiled. "Thank you for your kind words, sir,

29

but you must admit you're prejudiced!"

He didn't return her smile. "Camilla, I don't like to see you troubled about anything. Especially not about money. I'd gladly lend you any amount you needed—"

"I know that," Camilla interrupted him. "And I thank you. But you know I couldn't accept a loan from you. For one thing, I'd never be able to repay you."

"And for another, you refuse to be under obligation to anyone," said Miles ruefully. "I'm all too familiar with your scruples." He cleared his throat. "If we were married, there wouldn't be any question of obligation. I'd have the right and the duty, and yes, the great joy, of taking care of all your needs."

"Oh, Miles." Camilla shook her head at him. Regularly, every month or six weeks for the past year, Miles had made her a formal offer of marriage. Just as regularly, she'd refused him. "If I were to marry anyone, it would certainly be you, but . . ."

Miles hunched his shoulders. "You needn't bother to give me your reasons for refusing my latest offer. I've heard them so often, I know them by heart. Let me see, now. You're a recent widow. It's too soon to think of re-marriage. Actually, of course, it's been three years since your husband died, hasn't it, Camilla? But, in any case, you don't wish to marry again. You like your independence. You like living in your own house, free to come and go as you please. Have I forgotten anything?"

"Miles, I'm sorry. You know how much I value your friendship—"

"And you'd rather have me as a friend than as a lover," he finished. He broke into a sudden smile, in which Camilla could discern not a trace of bitterness or self-pity. "Don't look so guilty," he told her. "You can't help your feelings. Certainly I can't help mine! I'll propose again next month. Possibly even sooner. Who knows, you might change your mind if I'm persistent enough!" He bent his head to brush her cheek in a light kiss. "Goodbye,

Camilla. I have an engagement with Harry Oates, and I'm already late."

"Are you off to cup a wafer at Manton's, or possibly to go a round with Gentleman Jackson?" teased Camilla.

"Actually, I'm going to Boodle's to have a try at breaking their faro bank," said Miles calmly. "Harry Oates tells me I need to indulge in a little dissipation. Thank you for allowing me to be the first to play your sonata. I'll see you tomorrow evening?"

For a few moments after Miles had left, Camilla stood staring at the closed door of the drawing room, an amused smile on her lips. It was so completely ludicrous to think of correct, conventional Miles indulging in any degree of dissipation! The smile faded, as she thought of his renewed offer of marriage. There'd been times—and this was one of them—when she'd felt tempted to accept his proposal. Kind, gentle, considerate, he'd delight in removing all of her burdens from her shoulders. If she were married to him, she could snap her fingers at the letter from the solicitor in Bath.

Yes, and she could also say goodbye to her cherished independence, Camilla reminded herself. Sighing, she left the drawing room and walked slowly down the narrow hallway to the tiny room she used as a study. She sat down in front of her desk and picked up the Bath solicitor's letter. She read it again, for at least the dozenth time, although a rereading was quite unnecessary. Though it was written in dry legalistic language, its meaning was crystal clear.

If Mrs. Philip Rayburn of Number 72, Park Street, London, did not immediately return the person of Miss Dorcas Vernon to her mother's protection in Bath, Mrs. Thomas Vernon was prepared to order her solicitor to institute proceedings against Mrs. Rayburn, resulting in possible legal and social unpleasantness. The solicitor, a Mr. Edward Stanton, was her humble and obedient servant, etc., and begged for the honor of an immediate reply.

Camilla leaned back in her chair, collecting her

thoughts. She had to do something, and that immediately. She realized now that she'd been foolishly optimistic to believe Francine would accept her daughter's removal to London. Obviously Francine wasn't going to give up that easily. She wanted either her daughter's custody or her pound of flesh in the form of the twenty thousand pounds. Probably she had no real preference for either one of the alternatives! Dorcas represented merely a source of income to her. Unfortunately, for all of Francine's lack of maternal feeling, she had the power of the law behind her if she cared to invoke it. She *was* Dorcas's mother.

Coming to a quick decision, Camilla reached for a piece of writing paper and a pen. Her only recourse was to give her stepmother the blood money. And much as she hated to be under a sense of obligation, she must swallow her pride and ask for the loan of the twenty thousand pounds. As she dipped her pen into the ink, a maidservant — actually, her only servant, aside from Cook and her abigail — opened the door to announce, "Lord Sheringham to see you, ma'am."

"Uncle Nigel," Camilla exclaimed in delight, jumping up from her chair. She rushed to throw her arms around the tall gentleman who had entered the room. "I was just about to write to you. I had no idea you were in town. I thought you were still in Northamptonshire."

The Earl of Sheringham returned his goddaughter's embrace. "What were you writing to me about?" he asked with a fond smile.

"First things first, Uncle Nigel." Camilla turned to the maidservant. "Lizzie, bring Lord Sheringham a glass of Madeira."

"Well, my dear?" said the earl a little later, looking at Camilla over the rim of his glass.

Camilla smiled at him affectionately. He was a handsome man still, even in his sixties, she reflected. He'd changed little over the years. The thick hair was gray now, and there were a few lines in the lean planed face. However, the tall figure was erect and graceful as ever, and the earl would never lose his air of elegance or his ability to project an effortless charm.

Once, long before Camilla's birth, the young Nigel Hilliard, the future Earl of Sheringham, had fallen in love with Lady Evadne Montgomery. She'd chosen to marry Thomas Vernon, a younger son with few prospects, who joined the Navy and eventually became an admiral. Nigel had married someone else, and had had children of his own, but he'd willingly, even joyfully, consented to stand as godfather to Thomas and Evadne Vernon's baby daughter. Over the years, Camilla and her "Uncle Nigel" had developed a closeness that was more like the relationship between father and child. The earl had no daughters of his own, and in many ways he'd taken the place of Camilla's father during the Navy man's frequent absences at sea.

After the death of Philip Rayburn, Camilla's young husband, Nigel had been a tower of strength to her. In fact, she owed the very roof over her head to his generosity. Philip Rayburn had left Camilla penniless, save for the income from a small legacy bequeathed to her by her mother. The earl had insisted on buying this house for her, thereby enabling her to continue living in London in modest independence.

"Well?" said the earl again, as the silence deepened. "You look very serious, Camilla. Do you have a problem? Is that why you were writing to me?"

"Uncle Nigel," Camilla blurted, "I need twenty thousand pounds."

He raised a thin, well-shaped eyebrow. "Is that all? Don't trouble your pretty head about it. How soon do you require the money?"

Camilla threw up her hands, her face flooding with embarrassed color. "I *hate* to ask you for money. You've already done so much for me . . ."

"You've allowed me to do precious little for you," the earl replied firmly. "It's no sacrifice for me to give you the money, as you must know. I'll never miss it."

Camilla thought that was probably true. In addition to a

large income from his estates, her godfather enjoyed an even larger income from the vast coal and iron properties he'd inherited from his mother, a Lancashire heiress.

"I don't like to pry—well, I'll admit it, I'm an inquisitive old man!—but I'd really like to know why you suddenly need twenty thousand pounds," said Nigel with an interested, faintly amused air. "It's so unlike you to be in low water. I rather doubt you've been speculating on 'Change, or wasting your blunt at the track."

Camilla suddenly felt more at ease. She laughed, saying, "You know me too well. I daresay I'll always be a penny pincher." Sobering, she told the earl about Dorcas and Mr. Stinchcombe and Francine's offer to exchange her daughter for cash.

"Dreadful, common women," he commented. "I never could understand how your father came to marry her, especially after . . ." His voice trailed off. Camilla knew he was thinking of his first love, her mother.

Nigel shook himself out of his reverie. He said sympathetically, "What a lowering experience for you. You say your stepmother actually attacked you physically?"

"Yes, it was rather unpleasant," Camilla murmured, but she wasn't thinking of Francine. Quite unbidden, the memory of the rakish Frenchman from the Bath road had leapt into her mind, and not for the first time, if she was honest with herself. Once again, she found herself reliving the pressure of the man's tautly muscled body against her own, and the enticing, urgent temptation of his kiss. She hadn't felt so aroused by a man in years. She disliked and resented the feeling. Why did she keep thinking about him?

"What is it, Camilla?"

"Nothing, nothing at all. I was just being silly."

"Sure? Well, then, let's make plans," said Nigel. "We'll pay off that vampire of a woman immediately, of course. Let my solicitor see to the details. He'll draw up a document making you Dorcas's guardian in exchange for the twenty thousand pounds."

"Oh, I never thought to make my position legal."

"You're an innocent. After your stepmother had squandered the twenty thousand, she'd have no compunction about coming back to you with another demand. Blackmailers return again and again to suck their victims dry. In this case, once Mrs. Vernon signs over Dorcas's guardianship to you, she'll have no further hold over you. Good, that's settled. Now then, you'll want to give your sister a coming out. Send the bills for her new clothes to me. And you'll of course use the facilities of Sheringham House for any balls and dinners you see fit to give."

"No, Uncle Nigel. I can't let you do this. Dorcas has no claim on you at all."

"Nonsense. During the Season I'll be rattling around in a vast empty town house big enough for a regiment. And I'm a lonely man. I'll enjoy seeing young faces and hearing young voices around me. I'll enjoy seeing *you* taking your rightful place in society, my dear. These past few years you've been living almost like a hermit." He cast a disparaging glance around the tiny study. "This house, for instance. You should have allowed me to buy you that place in Cavendish Square that caught my fancy. Old Waverly's house. It would have suited you perfectly. This house is scarcely large enough for a respectable merchant's family. As a matter of fact, I believe you have several tradesmen among your neighbors."

Camilla laughed at his disdainful expression. "Quite right, Uncle Nigel. Mr. Rodgers next door is the proprietor of a thriving jewelry shop in Piccadilly. He's far more prosperous than I'll ever be! However, I assure you I love my house. It exactly suits my needs."

"H'mph. Your needs, indeed! You live far too modestly. You give little dinners for your musical friends, you attend an occasional concert at the Academy of Music, you go once a year to see the new pictures at the Royal Academy. What kind of a life is that for a beautiful young woman of twenty-two?"

"I'm content, Uncle Nigel."

35

"Well, you shouldn't be," he retorted. His voice softened. "Sometimes you remind me of a snow maiden, going through life without feeling anything, without *wanting* to feel anything. You should be married, my dear, with a husband who adores you, and a houseful of children."

Camilla shook her head. "I was married once. That was enough. I don't want to marry again."

"But not every man is a wastrel like Philip—" The earl broke off. "I'm sorry. I shouldn't have said that. None of my affair. Well, it's understood, then? You'll do me the great honor of allowing me to sponsor your sister's coming out?"

"I—" Camilla stifled her protest. In refusing her godfather's offer, was she merely indulging her own prickly pride? Dorcas would treasure a London coming out for the rest of her life. She might even meet a far more eligible suitor than she would ever encounter in her sister's restricted circle. At last Camilla said, "I know I shouldn't let you do this, but yes. Dorcas and I accept with pleasure."

"Famous." The earl beamed. He added offhandedly, "Naturally, I'll expect a favor in return."

Camilla gazed at her godfather in surprise. His mood had suddenly changed. He looked grimly serious. "I'd be happy to do anything you asked me. You must know that."

Hesitating, as if he didn't quite know how to begin, the earl said at last, "You know I'm almost the last of my line."

Camilla nodded. The earl's elder son had died in infancy. His second son had had a fatal hunting accident in his teens. A nephew, the only child of his late brother, had died last year at the age of forty, unmarried. Camilla observed, "I remember your telling me that the next heir was a distant cousin whom you'd never met."

"Not merely the next heir. My *only* heir. When I die, and if this cousin also dies without issue, the Hilliards of Woodford Priory, and the earldom of Sheringham, will become extinct. It would be a tragedy. The first Nigel Hilliard, you know, came to England with the Conqueror. We've held title to our lands in Northamptonshire since the twelfth century. We've been at Woodford Priory since the time of the Dissolution. Seven hundred years of service to crown and country, and soon it may come to an end."

Bewildered, Camilla said slowly, "I don't understand. Why should the Hilliard line come to an end? You have an heir. Unless he's an old man who's past the age of siring children—"

The earl cut her off. "John Stephen Hilliard is about twenty-eight years old. No doubt he *will* marry and have children. His age isn't the problem."

"Well, then?"

"The problem is that he doesn't wish to be my heir."

Camilla's bewilderment increased. "But it's not possible, is it, for Mr. Hilliard to renounce the Sheringham title?"

"No, he can't escape becoming the tenth Earl of Sheringham, not unless he predeceases me, which seems unlikely. However, there's no law that requires him to come to England to take up residence at Sheringham House or at Woodford Priory."

"Come to England? Where's he living now, then?"

"In Canada. Lower Canada, to be precise. The colony was divided into two provinces some years ago. But that's of no interest to you. You see, John Hilliard is the son of my cousin Stephen, who went out to Canada as a young man and died there at an early age, after marrying a young woman of the province and fathering a son, John Stephen. The child was reared by his mother's family, who've been resident in Canada for many generations. He regards himself as a Canadian, not an Englishman."

"That's understandable, I suppose. I must say, though, that I find it hard to believe a man with English blood in his veins could possibly think of himself as anything but an Englishman!"

The earl gave a bark of laughter. "That's an English admiral's daughter talking!" His amusement quickly faded. "Unfortunately, my young cousin doesn't share your patriotic views."

"You've been writing to him, I gather."

"Yes. It wasn't easy to locate him. Actually, I didn't even know he existed. I was trying to find his father. I assumed—or at least I hoped—that my cousin Stephen Hilliard was still alive, although I'd had no news of him after he went out to Canada. Some months ago, when I learned that, although Stephen was dead, he'd sired a son, I wrote to my young cousin immediately, informing him that he was my heir, and inviting him to visit me." The earl shook his head, an expression of disbelief flitting over his face. "You can imagine my shock when the boy wrote back that he wasn't interested in becoming an English peer. He'd made a life for himself in Canada, he said, and he preferred to remain there."

A frown appeared on Camilla's forehead. "But that's ridiculous. Mr. Hilliard hasn't given the matter proper thought. If he should succeed to the title, I presume he'd arrange to leave his affairs over here in the hands of a steward. Doesn't he realize that the estate would go to wrack and ruin without the active supervision of a resident owner? And what about his duties in the House of Lords?"

"Exactly. The line of the Hilliards of Woodford would go on, but the family would cease to have any significance in England. An end to seven hundred years of history."

"Did you point that out to him?"

The earl shrugged. "Oh, yes. Apparently he doesn't care. He tells me he dislikes me so much that he doesn't wish to have any association with me or the estate."

"But why would he say such a thing? He's never even met you."

"He believes I broke his father's heart and spirit by driving him into a hard exile in Canada. That's what his father told him, and that's what he believes."

"But it's not true," said Camilla hotly. "You've never been unjust to anyone in your life."

Hesitating, the earl said slowly, "No, it's not true, but I

38

understand how Stephen Hilliard had persuaded himself it was true. Camilla, I've never spoken of what I'm about to say to anyone. I want your promise that you'll never speak of it, either."

"Of course."

"Well, Stephen and I actually didn't know each other very well while we were growing up. He belonged to a junior branch of the Hilliard family, not a very prosperous one, I fear. He was quite wild as a youth, but in the beginning I didn't consider him any wilder than most young men. No wilder than myself, for that matter! He did get into the hands of the cent-per-centers on several occasions—he was an inveterate gambler, though he had almost no card sense—and I paid his debts twice, warning him I wouldn't do it a third time. So when he again crossed over into Dun territory, he didn't apply to me. He forged an old aunt's name and made off with her small fortune, leaving her destitute. When I found out about it, I replaced the money and offered to pay Stephen's debts again, provided he left England for Canada and promised never to come back. He accepted my offer. Well, what else could he do? I made him sign a confession of embezzlement. I still have it."

"So Stephen Hilliard told his son a false version of the story, defaming you," said Camilla indignantly, "and now the son is punishing you for injuring his father by refusing to come to England to take up his rightful position. It's the most infamous thing I've ever heard of. Uncle Nigel, you must set this John Stephen Hilliard straight. Tell him about his father."

"No, I won't—can't—do that. It's obvious the young man idolized his father. How can I destroy that love? Supposing, that is, that John Hilliard were to believe my story, which he probably wouldn't."

"That's like you," Camilla said softly. "So what will happen now? Do you think you can change Mr. Hilliard's mind?"

"That, my dear, rather depends on you. Remember I

told you I wanted a favor from you?"

Camilla felt an odd flicker of apprehension. "What kind of a favor?"

"Well, I finally prevailed on John Hilliard's sense of fair play," said the earl with a faint smile. "He's agreed to come to England for a trial visit. He's given me no promises. After he's met me and inspected the estates, he'll then decide about making a permanent move from Canada. He should arrive in this country soon."

The earl paused, cocking his head at Camilla. "You asked me if I thought I could change John Hilliard's mind about living in England. No, I don't, but I think *you* can. Remember that favor I asked of you? When he arrives, I want you to make friends with him. Offer to show him the sights of London, introduce him to your own friends. Do whatever you must to persuade him to do his duty to his family."

Camilla exclaimed in dismay, "I couldn't possibly do that. For one thing, you overestimate my powers of persuasion."

"Coming it too strong, my girl. Many's the time I've observed you making micefeet out of impressionable males. I recall, during your coming out year—"

"Uncle Nigel!" Camilla turned red from embarrassment and annoyance. "I was never a flirt."

"Forgive me. Of course you weren't."

"And what's more," said Camilla, unappeased, "it wouldn't be honest, making friends with Mr. Hilliard under false pretenses. Supposing he misunderstood my attentions? Supposing he assumed I had a—er—a *tendre* for him? Why, he might even propose marriage!"

"So?" said the earl tranquilly. "You know I'd like to see you well married. Which you certainly would be, as the future Countess of Sheringham. Well, Camilla? Will you do this for me? One favor in exchange for another?"

Her godfather's tone was light, almost playful, but Camilla could hear clearly the underlying note of strain. She understood him so well. He was alone now, and at the end of his life, and his one remaining desire was to see his line continue on his ancestral estates.

Camilla drew a deep breath. Yes, she cringed at the thought of playing Delilah to Mr. John Stephen Hilliard's Samson, but shouldn't she put her feelings of distaste aside? Didn't she owe the earl a debt of gratitude for all his many kindnesses over the years? He'd spoken of exchanging one favor for another. She knew very well that he wouldn't hold her to the bargain. If she refused to charm and cajole John Hilliard into remaining in England, her godfather would accept her decision. He wouldn't dream of breaking his promise to give her the twenty thousand pounds to buy off Dorcas's mother.

She rose and walked over to the earl's chair. Giving him an impulsive hug, she said, "I'll do the best I can, Uncle Nigel. I only hope that John Hilliard never realizes that I'm his Judas goat!"

Chapter Three

"Turn around, my dear. Slowly," said the Earl of Sheringham.

Dorcas revolved in front of the earl and Camilla as she modeled a robe of delicate white lace over a petticoat of sheer pale blue silk, embroidered in seed pearls.

The earl gave an approving nod. "Perfect. Quite perfect, indeed, for your coming out ball, Dorcas. The other gowns you selected were most becoming, also."

"It's all Camilla's doing," said Dorcas. "She has such exquisite taste. Even Mama always said that—" Dorcas stopped short, looking intensely embarrassed.

"Never mind, Dorcas," Camilla told her. "Uncle Nigel is quite familiar with Mama's opinion of me."

Dorcas still looked embarrassed. Snatching at another subject, she said hastily, "Lord Sheringham, this is my first opportunity to thank you for your generosity. In fact, you've been much too generous. Camilla's bought me so many lovely new dresses. More than I'll ever be able to wear."

"Oh, but you will, I assure you. You'll have so many invitations for each night of the Season that you'll be obliged to pick and choose between them! And there's no need to thank me. It gives me great pleasure to see a beautiful girl beautifully dressed."

Dorcas appeared so overwhelmed by the compliment that the earl mercifully turned his attention to Camilla.

He said with a teasing smile, "I've heard no mention of purchases for yourself. Do you mean to say you found nothing to tempt you in the shops?"

Dorcas piped up, "Oh, but she did. The most exquisite aërophane crepe in a shade between coral and apricot. I begged Camilla to buy a length of the material and have it made up into a tunic dress. But she said she didn't need any new gowns."

The earl shook his head at Camilla. "For an intelligent woman, you can be positively bird-witted," he complained. "Certainly you need a new gown, several, in fact. You'll be acting as my hostess for several events during the season, recall. I expect you do to me credit. Have Mme. Labelle, or whoever is the current most fashionable *modiste,* make you several new creations, and charge them to my account."

"Uncle Nigel—"

"No arguments," said the earl. He smiled at Dorcas. "Thank you for calling this matter to my attention."

After Dorcas had left the room to change out of her finery, Camilla shook her finger at her godfather. "You're a rogue, Uncle Nigel. When you offered to sponsor Dorcas's coming out, you never said a word about buying *me* a new wardrobe also."

"Naturally not. I'm a devious old man. I preferred to postpone your protests as long as possible," retorted the earl. He patted Camilla's shoulder. "You'll do me proud, both of you. Incidentally, my dear, I like your sister. She's a lovely little creature. Reminds me a great deal of you at that age, though I'd venture a guess that she's made of softer fiber than you are."

"Oh, I know Dorcas appears a little shy and unsure of herself, but that's hardly surprising. Remember, she's been under Mama's thumb all her life."

"You grew up in Francine Vernon's care, and she didn't break *your* spirit."

A shadow crossed Camilla's face. "Perhaps not, but I

43

might not have rushed so hastily into marriage with Philip if I hadn't wanted to get away from Francine."

"Well, I'm very happy to inform you that Francine Vernon will never cause difficulties for you and Dorcas again. Yesterday my solicitor received documents signed by your stepmother making you Dorcas's guardian."

"Really? I never thought Dorcas's affairs would be settled so soon. It's been only three weeks since I—"

"Since you kidnapped your sister," the earl interrupted her, his eyes twinkling. "Your stepmother signed the papers with great alacrity. I daresay she wanted to be sure you wouldn't change your mind about giving her the twenty thousand pounds."

"Carlton House to a Charley's shelter, Mama was more concerned about the money than she was about her daughter."

"Oh, I won't dispute that statement! By the way, do you think Dorcas would like to be a guest of the Prince of Wales at Carlton House? I'd be happy to speak to His Royal Highness's aide, Colonel MacMahon, about it."

Camilla smiled. "I fancy Dorcas would be *most* impressed to receive an invitation to meet the Prince. I only hope she won't be disillusioned. I hear His Royal Highness is fatter than ever."

"Doubtless he'll be so charming, and she'll be so starry-eyed, that she'll never notice his obesity," retorted the earl. "Now, what about Almack's? I presume you'll want to obtain vouchers for Dorcas. If I can be of any help there—"

"Thank you, but I have it in hand. Fortunately, Lady Jersey is already in town. I called on her several days ago. She was most gracious. She assured me she'd be happy to recommend Dorcas to the committee of patronesses."

"I'm not surprised. Sally Jersey was always an amiable soul." The earl rose. "I'm off to see my tailor. Weston informs me that I urgently need several new coats." He looked down at Camilla with a suddenly anxious expression. "My dear, I told you I was a devious man. I didn't come to see you this morning merely to inspect Dorcas's new wardrobe, or even to bring you the news that you're now your sister's guardian. Camilla, I'm here to call in my vouchers. My cousin, John Hilliard, has finally arrived in London. He sent me a note from Fenton's Hotel that he proposes to call at Sheringham House this afternoon at four o'clock. I'd like you to be there."

"Oh, Uncle Nigel, I'm not sure . . ." Camilla paused. Much as she longed to do so, she couldn't bring herself to tell her godfather she'd changed her mind about charming the next Earl of Sheringham into accepting his family responsibilities. Sighing, she said, "Yes, all right. I'll come to Hanover Square at four o'clock." A thought struck her. "Mr. Hilliard is staying at a hotel?"

The earl shrugged. "I invited him to be my guest at Sheringham House, naturally. He refused. Not a very auspicious beginning to our association, eh?" He took her hand and raised it to his lips. "Until this afternoon, then. And thank you, from the bottom of my heart."

After her godfather's departure, Camilla settled into a chair, immersed in gloomy thoughts. She felt in her very bones that nothing good would come of this meeting with John Hilliard. Her godfather's scheme smacked of near seduction. Well, not that, of course—Camilla colored at the thought—but one could hardly blame Mr. Hilliard for thinking her some kind of ladybird if he ever found out about the deception!

"Camilla? I'm not interrupting you?"

Camilla looked up to see Miles Wingate hesitating on the threshold of the drawing room.

"No, of course not, Miles. Come in. I'm happy to see you. What have you got there?" Camilla asked, looking curiously at the stack of books under her friend's arm.

"Well, you remember I told Dorcas that my mother had several collections of old English folk songs," said

45

Miles, advancing into the room. "Unfortunately, I couldn't recall what had happened to the collections after my mother's death. Yesterday, I finally located the music in a trunk in the storeroom of the Albany." Miles put the books down on a table and abstracted one volume from the pile. "Look at this," he said eagerly, turning to a page in the book. "My mother loved playing and singing this ballad. I think it would suit Dorcas's voice beautifully."

Camilla hummed a few bars of the song. "Yes, I think it would suit Dorcas's voice, since she doesn't have great range."

"Well, no, but she does have a true voice of great sweetness. To tell the truth, I'd as lief hear Dorcas sing as listen to Mme. Albani at the Italian Opera."

"Did I hear someone taking my name in vain?" Dorcas inquired as she came into the room.

"I found that ballad I was telling you about," said Miles. "If you like it, you might want to sing it at Camilla's musical evening. Shall we have a try at it?"

Watching and listening as Miles accompanied Dorcas at the pianoforte, Camilla gradually made an interesting discovery. She'd been so busy these past few weeks with the arrangements for her sister's coming out that she hadn't noticed that Miles and Dorcas were becoming quite such good friends. Miles had long been such a frequent visitor to the house on Park Street, and she'd grown so accustomed to relying on his helpfulness and concern, that Camilla had accepted Miles's kindness to Dorcas as an extension of his attentions to herself.

Since Dorcas's arrival, Miles had taken to calling at the house every morning, accompanying the sisters on shopping expeditions, taking Dorcas in his carriage for rides in the park or on excursions to the Tower or to the Egyptian Hall. Camilla had felt nothing but gratitude. The arrangement gave her a little free time to herself that was very welcome. Much as she loved Dorcas, it sometimes felt a little wearing to spend every waking moment in the company of a shy and insecure and inexperienced young girl.

But now! Camilla observed Miles's tender little smile when he glanced up from the keyboard at Dorcas, and the bemused expression in Dorcas's soft blue eyes when she looked at Miles, and the way neither of them seemed to be aware of another presence in the room. Camilla drew her own conclusions. Possibly Dorcas didn't yet suspect that Miles was becoming anything more to her than her sister's kindly older friend, but Miles, experienced man of the world that he was, must surely have begun to question his own heart.

And why not, Camilla asked herself. Miles would be an excellent *parti* for Dorcas. He was handsome and well born, and old enough to be a steadying influence on a seventeen-year-old bride. The possessor of a fine income and a snug property in Hampshire, he would see that Dorcas never wanted for anything. Above all, he was generous and loyal. He would never fail Dorcas.

Camilla felt the tiniest twinge of—No, it wasn't jealousy exactly, knowing that she no longer ranked first with Miles. She'd never been in love with him, there'd never been the slightest possibility that she'd accept one of his offers of marriage, and yet . . . Miles's devotion had been a constant in her life. Now there would be a void.

"Bravo!" she exclaimed when the song came to an end. "Or should it be brava? Well, never mind. Dorcas, you definitely must sing that ballad at my musical evening."

"Oh, I don't know if I could . . ." The blush that came so easily to Dorcas colored her cheeks. "Well, if Miles promises to play my accompaniment . . ."

"Of course he will. And now that these musical matters have been settled, Miles, I must ask you to excuse us. Dorcas and I have shopping to do. Unless, that is, you'd care to drive us to Oxford Street in your carriage?"

"Shopping?" said Dorcas, aghast. "Not for me, surely? What more could I want or need?"

"Lots of things. Uncle Nigel wants you turned out in the first style of elegance," Camilla replied with a grin. "Gloves, shoes, fans. Another pelisse, a bonnet or two. St—" Camilla broke off with a cough. She'd grown used to saying whatever came into her head in front of Miles, but it would certainly be the outside of enough to mention stays or other articles of intimate apparel in his presence!

"Well . . ." Dorcas sounded doubtful, but she made no further protest. Camilla smothered a smile. Since her arrival in London, Dorcas's favorite diversion had been her visits to Oxford Street. To give her her due, she would have been perfectly happy merely to window-shop. Though Bath had a provincial reputation for fine shopping, it could offer nothing like the long, broad thoroughfare with its double row of handsome lamps, its standing room for carriages, and its myriad of shops offering every conceivable object that a customer could desire.

Today, as always, Dorcas blissfully enjoyed her excursion to Oxford Street. Trailed dutifully by Miles—who, to Camilla's constant amazement, seemed genuinely interested in feminine fripperies—they went from shop to shop, selecting an opera hood with garlands of roses and lilies of the valley, a pearl-embroidered bandeau for the hair, numerous pairs of long white kid gloves for evening, walking shoes of kid or jean, evening slippers of satin or kid, a parasol in the popular pagoda shape.

At one point, when Dorcas admired a jeweled watch, intended to be worn dangling at the waist, and then resolutely decided against it on the grounds that Lord Sheringham had already been far too generous, Miles opened his mouth and then closed it again without saying anything. Camilla could almost read his mind. The watch was far too expensive a gift for a gentleman to give to a young woman he had just met, and to whom he was unrelated, but Camilla could see the yearning in Miles's eyes. She suspected he would contrive to find some excuse to present the watch to Dorcas as the Season progressed.

The shopping expedition eventually shifted from Oxford Street to an almost equally tempting stretch of New Bond Street, where Miles insisted on buying each sister a charming nosegay and a large box of exotic sweetmeats from the prestigious confectionery shop of Richard Robinson.

However, after several more purchases, including three bonnets, a number of shawls and a particularly fetching spencer of canary-colored sarcenet, Camilla exclaimed in dismay, "We'll never fit into your carriage, Miles, with all these parcels."

"Don't worry about that. We don't mind a squeeze, do we, Dorcas?"

"Well, I do mind," Camilla retorted, "and heaven help you if these bonnets get crushed." She glanced at the little gold watch pinned to the bodice of her pelisse. "Heavens, I had no idea it was so late. I have an engagement to take tea with my godfather at four o'clock. Why don't you drive Dorcas and the parcels home and leave me here on New Bond Street? I can easily while away a half an hour or so in the shops, and Hanover Square is only a few minutes' walk from here."

"Leave you unattended in public? I wouldn't hear of it."

Camilla threw up her hands. "Oh, Miles, you're such a high stickler! I'm a thoroughly respectable widow, not a green young girl. Nobody will think the worse of me if I spend a few minutes alone in the shops and then walk a short distance to Hanover Square. And I'm sure my godfather will send me home in one of his carriages."

Having wrestled successfully with Miles's scruples, Camilla waved him and Dorcas off in the carriage. Then, marking time until her engagement at Sheringham House, she strolled along New Bond Street, stopping occasionally in one or another of the shops. In a music shop she was happy to find a newly published sonata in F Sharp by the German composer, Beethoven, and a book of Bach preludes and fugues for the harpsichord to replace her own well-worn copy. In a nearby book store she dipped into an oddly titled volume, *Sense and Sensibility,* by A Lady of Quality. Refreshingly, it contained no references to terrifying ghosts or ruined castles or long-lost heirs shut up in gloomy dungeons. Indeed, the book seemed to be about respectable people of good family, very much like herself. Camilla decided to buy the book.

As she was paying for her purchase, she glanced at the clock on the wall of the shop and noted with dismay that it was already four o'clock and she was late for her engagement with her godfather. What was worse, she noted as she looked out the window of the shop that the skies had darkened while she was in the bookstore, and now she could hear a rolling barrage of thunder and see ominous flashes of lightning on the horizon. Hastily she collected her parcels and dashed out the door of the shop just as the first drops of a torrential downpour started falling. She collided with a tall gentleman passing by on the street, who said politely, "Pray allow me to be of service, *madame,*" and held an umbrella over her head.

"Oh, I beg your pardon for running into you like that," Camilla gasped. "I fear I wasn't watching where I was going." As the rain splashed down with increasing vigor, she instinctively edged a little closer to the man under the sheltering umbrella. Peering up at his face, she said, smiling, "Thank you for sharing —" She broke off. "You!" she exclaimed. "What are you doing here?" She shrank away from him, pressing herself against the door of the shop with its very inadequate overhang.

He shifted the umbrella slightly so that it still protected her from the rain. "What am I doing here, *madame?* The same as you, *bien entendu.* Shopping."

The mocking smile on his lips made Camilla's blood boil. He was baiting her, just as he'd baited her in the posting inn in Newbury, when he'd dragged her and Francine apart and as much as accused her of behaving like a common scold. "You had no right to follow me," she stormed, instantly realizing she was making a goose-cap of herself.

"Follow you? But no, *madame.* Is this not a free country? Is it not permitted that I walk along New Bond Street?"

She ground her teeth, longing to give this obnoxious foreigner a humbling set-down. Unfortunately, she couldn't think of a sufficiently crushing retort. "Oh, never mind," she muttered. Out of the corner of her eye she saw a hackney cab advancing down the street, its outline nearly obliterated by curtains of slashing rain. "Please get out of my way, sir. I must catch that cab."

"Allow me, *madame.*"

Before Camilla quite knew what he was about, the stranger grabbed her hand and dragged her along with him into the street, holding the umbrella rather sketchily over the both of them. Narrowly escaping being run down by a vehicle coming from the opposite direction, he flagged down the hackney. When the carriage stopped, the Frenchman wrenched open the door of the cab, let down the steps and motioned Camilla to get in.

"Thank you," she said, stiffly. She climbed into the carriage and settled herself on the seat. It was infuriating to be beholden to this man. A split second later she gasped as he got into the hackney after her, folding the umbrella as he did so.

For a moment outrage closed her throat. Then she spluttered, "What's the meaning of this intrusion, sir?"

"Intrusion? This is my cab, *madame.* Out of the kindness of my heart I'm prepared to share it with you."

Beside herself with rage, Camilla reached for the handle of the door on her side of the carriage. Then common sense prevailed. She'd be drenched to the skin in moments if she left the hackney now.

"Where to, guv?" called the driver.

The Frenchman edged his head around the still opened door of the carriage to speak to the coachman. "We'll take the lady to her destination first." He turned to Camilla. "Where do you wish to go, *madame?*"

Camilla bit her lip. "Number 24, Hanover Square," she muttered. "It's not far from here." She added with a flash of spite, "We needn't inflict ourselves on each other's company for more than a few minutes."

He stared at her. "No, indeed." He relayed the direction to the driver, pulled the door shut, and sank back against the squabs.

During the short drive to Sheringham House, the Frenchman sat in silence, making no effort at conversation. She was pleased, but puzzled. In their several encounters to date, he'd persisted in his attempts to engage her in a flirtation; now he wasn't taking advantage of his captive audience. He didn't even look at her. Which suited her perfectly, of course.

Soon the hackney made the turn from Brook Street into Hanover Square, stopping in front of a large four-story, red and gray brick house on the west side. Facing the house across the railed garden was the familiar facade of the Hanover Square Rooms, where Camilla frequently attended concerts.

The driver opened the door and let down the steps. For a moment Camilla forgot her own lacerated feelings. The coachman was a pathetic sight, his hat a sodden mess, his greatcoat plastered limply to his body.

Her unwelcome escort jumped down to the pavement, unfurling the umbrella and extending his hand to help her down. She resisted the impulse to refuse his help. It was still raining heavily. She still needed the umbrella.

He walked beside her up the steps of Number 24, holding the umbrella above her head. When they reached the portico, she stepped under it and lifted the knocker. She reached into her reticule. "How much do I owe you for my share of the fare?"

"Think nothing of it, *madame*."

Camilla's lips tightened. She thrust a shilling into his hand, saying curtly, "Thank you. I don't require any further assistance. You may go."

He didn't move.

"Now, see here, I won't stand for this harassment," Camilla was saying angrily, when the door opened. Her godfather's butler said politely, "Good afternoon, Mrs. Rayburn." He looked past her to the Frenchman with an inquiring lift of his eyebrows.

"The name is Hilliard," said the quiet, accented voice. "Jean-Étienne Hilliard. I believe *Milord* Sheringham is expecting me."

In stunned silence, Camilla walked past the butler into the vestibule and followed him up the stairs to the drawing room. Close behind her came the Frenchman. Her legs almost too weak to support her, Camilla sank into a chair in the drawing room. The Frenchman sat down opposite her. She stared at him incredulously. After the butler left them alone, she cleared her throat, saying, "Are you really John Stephen Hilliard, the Earl of Sheringham's heir?"

"Yes. Though my family has always called me Jean-Étienne. Or plain Jean. My mother was French Canadian."

Of course. His father had died when his son was very young. The boy had probably spoken French almost exclusively while he was growing up in the care of his mother's family. It explained the French accent. But not the other things . . . An oddly provocative thought crossed Camilla's mind. She reviewed quickly the little she knew about Canada. The death of General Wolfe.

Fur traders. Fishing fleets. Indian wars. She said suddenly, "You don't look English at all."

"No. Fortunately, I resemble the members of my mother's family."

She looked closely at the raven black hair, worn much too long over his collar, at the dark, bronzed skin, at the coal black eyes, and blurted, "Do you have Indian blood, Mr. Hilliard?"

"I do." The dark eyes lighted with a sardonic amusement. "My grandmother was a princess of the Cree tribe."

Before Camilla could recover from her shock, the Earl of Sheringham came into the drawing room, extending his hand to his cousin. "John. I'm happy to see you at last."

"Sir." Hilliard stepped back, his slight bow barely softening the effect of his deliberate avoidance of the earl's handshake. "I don't use the name of John. Most people call me Jean."

For a brief moment, the earl's face registered his shock at Jean's appearance, his hurt at the younger man's refusal to take his hand. Camilla's heart ached for him. Then Lord Sheringham said composedly, "Jean it will be." He sat down, glancing from Jean to Camilla. "Do you two know each other? Jean, this is my goddaughter, Camilla Rayburn. Mrs. Rayburn."

"We—er—introduced ourselves," said Jean. He added with a stiff politeness, "You and your husband live in London, Mrs. Rayburn?"

"My husband is dead, Mr. Hilliard." Camilla's eyes narrowed. Had she imagined the faint expression of relief on Jean Hilliard's face when he learned that she was a widow?

"I'm sorry to hear that," said Jean, even more stiffly.

"Thank you for your concern, Mr. Hilliard, but I've been a widow for some time."

The earl eyed Jean thoughtfully. "Frankly, I'd expected

to see you in London weeks ago. I was beginning to fear that your ship was wrecked. I understand there are icebergs in the Atlantic at this time of year. Or possibly that you'd been waylaid by footpads after you arrived in England. But I daresay you took passage on a later ship."

Her godfather's remark stirred a vagrant thought that had been hovering in the back of Camilla's mind. If, almost three weeks ago, she and Jean Hilliard had met at Newbury on the London to Bath road, why had it taken so long for him to reach London?

Hilliard shook his head. "No, I embarked from Montreal on my scheduled ship. But after I docked in Bristol I decided to do a little sightseeing before going on to London. I stopped in Bath, for instance. A charming place." He flicked a look at Camilla. "When I got to a town called Newbury—not especially charming, but it had its points of interest"—again he glanced at Camilla—"I headed north for a look at your new industrial areas. There's a remarkable iron bridge at Telford, have you seen it? The coal fields and the iron foundries and the textile mills around Manchester and Birmingham are remarkable, too. I understand they call it the Black Country? I also had a look at some sheep farms in Yorkshire. Very fine animals you have up there. I think they might thrive in our harsh climate back home."

The man had no manners, no sense of consideration, Camilla thought resentfully. But then, she already knew that, didn't she? Obviously it hadn't occurred to him to write a line to the earl, explaining that he'd be delayed. Or perhaps it had occurred to him, and he'd deliberately set out to indicate how little he cared for Uncle Nigel's feelings.

If her godfather was hurt, he didn't show it. "I'm glad you saw something of the country," he observed. "The more you see of it, the easier it will be for you to come to your final decision about remaining in England."

"I've already made my final decision, sir. I intend to return to Canada."

"But—" Lord Sheringham couldn't conceal his shock. "We made a bargain. You were to come to England, meet with me personally, visit the family estates, sample the social life, then make up your mind about staying here."

Jean Hilliard shook his head. "No, sir. You're mistaken. Or you were guilty of wishful thinking. I made no such bargain. I'm a Canadian. I'll always be a Canadian."

Camilla couldn't restrain herself. "Why *did* you come here, then, Mr. Hilliard?"

He replied coolly, "Why, to investigate what financial advantages, if any, existed for me in England."

The earl frowned. "But you know what your financial advantages will be. When you succeed me, you'll be a wealthy man."

"Will, sir. Future tense. I need money now. You see, I'm a businessman. I'm in the fur trade. Some years ago I started a fur trading company with my cousins. Unfortunately, we didn't have enough working capital. So far we've failed to turn a decent profit."

"Oh, if that's all." The earl sounded relieved. "I'll be happy to lend you whatever sum you require. Don't give it another thought."

"I don't want a loan from you," Hilliard snapped, in a voice suddenly dripping with ice. "I don't want money with strings attached. I came here to look into the possibility of securing a loan on my future prospects. Didn't you tell me in one of your letters that you owned thousands of acres? And that the price of agricultural land was soaring because of the war with Napoleon? I call that a handsome collateral!"

Lord Sheringham turned a dull red. "I forbid it. I won't run the risk of having even one acre of my land fall into the hands of the cent-per-centers."

Shrugging, Hilliard said coldly, "Precious little you'll have to say about it after you're dead. When I succeed to your earldom, I intend to sell up every last acre and take the proceeds back with me to Canada."

"You can't do that. Woodford Priory is entailed!"

"Entailed on whom? Didn't you also tell me I'm the last of the Hilliards? I can do what I like with the damned place after you're gone."

"Perhaps I can't stop you from selling my lands after I'm dead," said the earl in a trembling voice, "but let me remind you that my estate revenues represent only a fraction of my income. I have an enormous fortune in coal and iron mines, and I'm under no obligation to leave you a penny of it."

"I don't want your blunt. I don't want any part of *you*. However, I've no scruples about enjoying the profits from liquidating your estates when you receive your notice to quit, because I'll merely be collecting on a debt you've long owed my father. Call it blood money. If you hadn't driven him out of England, he might still be alive today."

Camilla burst out, "You've no right to speak to my godfather like that. If you had the slightest instincts of a gentlemen . . ."

"But then, as you've so often pointed out, I'm not a gentleman," snapped Jean Hilliard. "What's more, I'll thank you, *madame*, not to interfere in my affairs."

Rising, he picked up the umbrella he'd propped beside his chair, and settled on his head his unfashionable low-crowned hat. "I'd like to inspect the estate at Woodford Priory as soon as possible," he told the earl. "Pray send word to my hotel informing me when it will be convenient for me to do so. Good day, sir, *madame*." He stalked out of the drawing room.

Her fists clenched, Camilla said in a voice shaking with anger, "What an insufferable boor! Uncle Nigel, don't concern yourself with this man. Let him go back to Canada. I know you couldn't bear to watch a savage like that lording it over Woodford Priory as the next Earl of Sheringham. It would break your heart."

Looking old and tired, the earl said quietly, "My feelings have nothing to do with the matter, Camilla. Jean-Étienne Hilliard *is* the next Earl of Sheringham."

Chapter Four

"Camilla, do I look presentable?"

Camilla turned away from the pianoforte, where she was arranging music on the stand, to took at Dorcas, standing in the doorway of the drawing room. Dorcas was wearing one of her new gowns, a round dress of white net over a petticoat of pink satin, trimmed at the hem with flounces of lace caught up with seed pearls. Her soft curls were confined by a white bandeau embroidered with pearls.

Noting the expression of nervous strain on her sister's face, Camilla exclaimed, "Presentable! Dorcas, you goose, you must know you look positively enchanting!"

Appearing only partially reassured, Dorcas said shyly, "You really mean it? I want so much for your friends to think well of me."

"Well, of course they will," said Camilla stoutly. She quite understood her sister's nervousness. This evening's concert in Camilla's drawing room would be Dorcas's first formal engagement in London. Camilla had taken her to tea with Lord Sheringham and with Lady Jersey, and they'd gone to the theater with Miles, but tonight for the first time Dorcas would be meeting a group of Camilla's friends.

The maid ushered Miles Wingate into the drawing room. "You asked me to come early, Camilla, so here I am," he announced cheerfully. He paused, staring at

Dorcas. "You look so beautiful," he murmured. His heart was in his eyes. It was obvious that, momentarily at least, he'd forgotten that he and Dorcas weren't alone.

Dorcas blushed scarlet with pleasure. In moments the strained expression faded completely from her face. She remained calm even when Miles brought up the subject of the song that she'd be singing tonight for Camilla's guests. Dorcas had been fretting about *that* for days. "Let's rehearse the song one last time, to make sure you haven't forgotten the words," Miles suggested, and Dorcas agreed without the slightest trace of apprehension.

Well, thought Camilla with amusement. Probably Dorcas herself didn't realize it yet, but Miles had replaced Camilla as the principal source of Dorcas's reassurance and well-being.

As Miles played through the song and Dorcas hummed along softly, Camilla's thoughts wandered. In her own way, she felt as nervous as Dorcas. Tonight, for the very first time, her sonata would be performed in public. For the occasion she'd invited, not only her close circle of friends, but a pair of far more important guests, Lord and Lady Montfort. Lord Montfort was one of the most prominent members of the Academy of Music. If he liked her sonata, he might recommend that the piece be performed at one of the Academy's concerts.

Her mind still wandering, Camilla wondered if Jean Hilliard would put in an appearance tonight. Very much against her will, she'd sent him a note of invitation. "Dear Mr. Hilliard," she'd written, "I'd like to wipe the slate clean and start afresh with our acquaintance. After all, we're related—or as near as makes no difference!—and we ought to learn to know each other, don't you think? Please come to a musical evening at my house on Park Street on Friday evening."

She'd felt like a hypocrite writing those words. She didn't want to have anything more to do with Jean Hilliard after he'd treated Uncle Nigel so shabbily, threatening to sell off the ancient acres that the earl loved so much. Better by far that the man return to Canada, as she'd told Lord Sheringham, than for him to be forced to watch such a savage presiding over the demesne of Woodford Priory. But Uncle Nigel, hurt and despondent though he was, had refused to give up on Jean Hilliard.

"He *is* the next Earl of Sheringham," the earl had insisted. "We can't change that, Camilla. And he *must* stay in England. He hates me, he doesn't want to have anything to do with me, but he's attracted to you, that's obvious. I saw the way he looked at you. Won't you help me? Won't you try to be his friend? Would you consider inviting him to your musical evening?"

Camilla couldn't refuse the earl. She'd sent off the invitation, comforting herself with the thought that Jean Hilliard most probably wouldn't accept it. After all, even if it was true, as Uncle Nigel believed, that Hilliard was attracted to her, her every encounter with the loutish Canadian had been unmitigated disaster. Surely, by this time, Jean Hilliard himself would have realized that a friendship between them was impossible.

Camilla's guests were arriving. Most of them were the amateur musicians of her small social circle, who all knew each other. After greeting her at the door, they took their seats in the chairs ranged closely together around the sides of the room.

The Earl of Sheringham strolled into the drawing room, elegant as always in his restrained black evening clothes. "You look charming, my dear," he remarked with an approving look at Camilla's tunic gown of apricot-colored aërophane crepe over an underfrock of gold tissue.

"It's all your doing," she teased her godfather. "This is the fabric Dorcas told you about. You insisted that I should buy a length of it and have it made up into a gown at your expense. And so I did, and I assure you the gown was *very* expensive!"

"And worth every shilling of it," the earl rejoined. "I'm quite anticipating a triumph, tonight, you know. Tomorrow the whole town will be talking of nothing but the newest talented composer, and a female, at that!" Lord Sheringham glanced about the room. In a low voice, he added, "Did you send an invitation to Jean Hilliard?"

"Yes, I did, Uncle Nigel." Camilla's lip curled. "Naturally, he hasn't seen fit to acknowledge the invitation, either to accept it or to reject it." Seeing the faint shadow of disappointment on her godfather's face, she said hastily, "Perhaps he'll come. It's quite early yet. And don't worry. If Mr. Hilliard *does* decide to honor us with his company, I promise I won't be rude to him."

"Good girl," the earl murmured, and went off to take his seat.

Soon almost every chair in Camilla's tiny drawing room was occupied. Lord and Lady Montfort arrived. They were social acquaintances, rather than personal friends, and Camilla suspected that they might not have accepted an invitation to her little house in unfashionable Park Street if she hadn't been related to the Earl of Sheringham.

Lady Montfort was a woman with thin, repressed looking features that were matched by the thin, angular stiffness of her body. "So, my dear Mrs. Rayburn, I understand we're to have the pleasure of hearing one of your own compositions," she said with a vinegary smile that indicated quite clearly to Camilla her ladyship's opinion of gently bred females dabbling in the arts.

However, Lord Montfort, that pillar of the Academy of Music, more than made up for his wife's lack of enthusiasm. He was a stout, jovial-looking man who fixed Camilla with an enthusiastic stare and held on to her hand rather longer than necessary. "A sonata, eh? Famous!" he exclaimed. "I look forward immensely to hearing it, Mrs. Rayburn."

"Thank you. I hope my composition lives up to your expectations." As gently as she could, Camilla detached her hand from Lord Montfort's grasp and directed him and his wife to two of the last remaining chairs.

Camilla glanced at the tiny jeweled watch pinned to her bodice. Eight o'clock. Time to begin the concert. In any case, her guest list was complete, or nearly so. Subconsciously, she was thinking, "Thank God, Jean Hilliard's decided not to come," when the tall powerful figure of that gentleman loomed in the doorway of the drawing room.

Gentleman! she jeered mentally. There was nothing gentlemanly about Jean Hilliard. He was wearing the same clothes in which he'd appeared at the assembly rooms in Bath: leather breeches and topboots and that dreadful unfashionable coat, instead of the silk breeches, stockings, low slippers and impeccable coat that graced her godfather's elegant form. His thick black hair was longer and shaggier than ever.

But then he smiled at her. It was an intimate smile, and it had the effect of shutting out every other person in the room. "Mrs. Rayburn, it was kind of you to invite me. This is the first social function I've attended since I arrived in London."

For a moment Camilla forgot about his unsuitable clothes. She even overlooked the rather overpowering whiff of spirits that clung to his person. Blue ruin? Port? Madeira? Had he felt it necessary to fortify himself before he arrived on Park Street? No matter. She was only aware of the strong current of sexual magnetism that seemed to be flowing between them. His black eyes traveled deliberately down her person, from her tawny curls beneath the coquettish wisp of lace cap to the slender curves barely suggested by the folds of the delicate aërophane crepe, and ignited with an ebony flame that seared her even as it enticed her.

Camilla took a deep breath. "Mr. Hilliard, I'm so happy to see you. Lord Sheringham is here. I'm sure one of my guests will be happy to move to another seat so that you can sit with him."

The black eyes cooled and became hooded. "That won't be necessary, Mrs. Rayburn. That chair over there

63

will be quite satisfactory." He sauntered over to a vacant chair beside Lady Montfort. Camilla noticed uncomfortably that the murmur of conversation in the room had died away. The eyes of most of her guests were fixed curiously on Jean. He stood out like a sore thumb in this assembly of the *ton,* of course. But if he was aware of the silent scrutiny of so many eyes, he gave no indication of it.

"Good evening," Jean said affably to Lady Montfort. His deep voice carried across the room, and his accent seemed stronger than ever. "I'm Jean-Étienne Hilliard. What's your name?"

Lady Montfort's eyes widened in affronted surprise at the familiarity of Jean's greeting. She looked down her long nose at his dreadful garments in fastidious disapproval. Perhaps, thought Camilla, her ladyship's refined nostrils had caught the raw odor of spirits.

"Hilliard?" said Lady Montfort, in the same tone she might have used to describe a noxious insect. "I don't believe I know—"

From across the room, the earl's quiet voice cut in. "Hilliard, as you may recall, Lady Montfort, is my family name. Mr. Hilliard is my heir. He's recently arrived from Canada."

Jean flicked the earl an expressionless glance and looked away. Lady Montfort said stiffly, "How do you do, Mr. Hilliard."

Eyeing Jean's carefully blank face, Camilla felt a strong surge of apprehension, which she tried to ignore. *Nothing* must happen to spoil this evening. She'd worked far too long and too hard for the opportunity to have her sonata performed. She stepped up to the pianoforte. "Thank you all for coming to my musical evening. We'll begin with Miss Timson, who will sing "Che farò senza Euridice" from *Orfeo ed Euridice.*

Miss Timson had a well-trained voice. She sang the aria beautifully. Too beautifully, perhaps. It was Dorcas's turn next. For a moment Camilla deeply regretted asking her sister to sing. Dorcas stood rooted to the floor, chalk-faced, petrified with stage fright. Camilla's heart ached for her. It was asking too much of a shy young girl at her first London social engagement to be expected to follow Miss Timson's polished performance.

Then Miles took Dorcas's hand and bent his head to whisper in her ear. In seconds the rosy color reappeared in her cheeks, she smiled shyly, and she walked with Miles to the pianoforte. He played a few bars of introduction to the lovely Elizabethan song, "All in the Garden Green," which she then sang so sweetly and tenderly that the room burst into applause when she finished.

Miles beamed with proprietary pride. Camilla overheard him assuring Dorcas, "I *knew* you could do it!"

Dorcas glowed with pleasure at the compliment. Miss Timson looked a trifle haggled, as well she might. She had a voice of near-professional caliber, and yet the audience had responded to Dorcas's simple ballad with more genuine enthusiasm than they'd accorded Miss Timson.

Next, Lord Oscar Vane played a Paganini caprice for unaccompanied violin, and then it was time for Camilla's sonata. She sat down near the door, clasping her ice-cold hands tensely together in her lap, while Miles settled himself at the instrument. Camilla tried to listen to Miles's playing with a sense of detachment, pretending that some other composer had written the sonata, but she failed utterly. During the allegro she thought she detected a flicker of approval on Lord Montfort's intent face, and her spirits soared. The andante sounded even better than the allegro. That is, it did so until close to the end of the movement, when Miles's soft slow notes were interrupted by a rhythmic sawing noise.

Camilla glared at Jean Hilliard. He'd fallen asleep in his chair—doubtless as a result of inbibing too much blue ruin or Madeira—and he was now snoring softly. She had a sudden primitive urge to seize him by his thick dark hair and shake him violently into wakefulness. How dared he spoil the performance of her sonata? Moments later, mercifully, the fast rollicking notes of the final rondo drowned out the sound of his snoring. A prolonged burst of applause at the conclusion of the sonata awakened him abruptly. He opened his eyes, looking around blankly as if he were uncertain about where he was.

Camilla turned her back on him as her friends began crowding around her to congratulate her. In his enthusiasm, Lord Montfort seized both her hands, declaring, "Magnificent, Mrs. Rayburn! Your andante reminded me just a little bit of the slow movement from one of that fellow Beethoven's sonatas—the one in D Major, as I recall. Not that your piece wasn't entirely original," he added hastily. "It was splendid, simply splendid!"

Camilla unobtrusively retrieved her hand from the enraptured Lord Montfort. She and Miles exchanged hopeful glances. If any man could persuade the Academy of Music to perform her sonata, it was Lord Montfort.

Into a momentary pause in the conversation came the sound of Lady Montfort's carrying voice, saying with a poisonous sweetness, "We're told that 'Music has charms to soothe a savage breast,' Mr. Hilliard. Could it be so in your case?" She tittered. "Something, certainly, caused you to doze off during the performance of Mrs. Rayburn's sonata."

With a deep feeling of foreboding, Camilla turned to face Jean and Lady Montfort. Raising his eyebrow, Jean inquired, "Did you have any special reason for using the word *savage*, Lady Montfort?" His voice was slightly slurred now. Evidently the blue ruin was catching up with him.

"Why, er—no. I had no special reason for using the word *savage*," said Lady Montfort. "I was merely quoting from the poem. 'The Mourning Bride,' you know, by William Congreve."

"No, I don't know," replied Jean bluntly. "I never heard of William Congreve. I see, however, that I gave you too much credit. I thought you were being very perceptive when you talked about savages. For your information, my grandmother was an Indian. A *savage,* if you will."

From somewhere behind her, Camilla heard a muttered comment. "Uncouth Colonial!'

Bright spots of angry color showed on Lady Montfort's angular cheeks. "Pray enlighten me, Mr. Hilliard," she snapped. "Do all residents of Canada share your evident lack of appreciation for cultural subjects like music? Or is such lack of appreciation limited to people of native ancestry?"

Jean rose from his chair, baring his teeth in a smile that made Camilla's blood run cold. *"Au contraire, madame,"* he said in a purring voice to Lady Montfort. "We French Canadians are *very* fond of music. Allow me to show you." He stalked over to the pianoforte, where Lord Oscar had left his violin on top of the instrument after playing the Paganini caprice. Jean picked up the violin, ran the bow across the strings and expertly adjusted several of the pegs. "Nice sounding fiddle," he remarked to Lord Oscar.

Camilla blenched. Lord Oscar's "nice sounding fiddle" was an Amati, and he looked distinctly nervous at the sight of his rare and prized instrument in Jean's casual hands.

Jean tucked the violin under his chin and began to play a lively tune, tapping his foot vigorously to mark the rhythm. Soon he was singing in French to his own accompaniment. Camilla could make out only a few words. Her French was more academic than fluent. Besides, Jean's French had an odd twang to it.

Jean finished his song, lowered his bow and placed it beside the violin on the top of the pianoforte. He turned to face his audience. Not a sound greeted him. Camilla's guests stared back at him with blank faces.

He appeared not to notice the lack of response to his playing. Fixing his gaze on Lady Montfort, he said, "As you can see, *madame,* we French Canadians do indeed like music. That was an old canoeing song. My mother's family were *coureurs de bois* — fur trappers and traders who roamed the wilderness — long ago, when Québec was still French. Before the English stole the province from us."

Lady Montfort's eyes glittered with anger at the deliberate provocation in Jean's tone. Apparently deciding to give as good as she got, she observed, "Indeed, Mr. Hilliard. I daresay your song was most charming, but unfortunately I couldn't understand the words very well. I was educated in Paris, you see. Perhaps French Canadians speak a variant dialect of French? Oh, I caught a few words here and there. Something about a fox, and a beaver?"

"Quite right. That was a love song. An animal love song, *bien entendu*."

"A love song?"

Jean proceeded to translate the words of the song to Lady Montfort in careful detail. The tale was hilarious. It was also vulgar in the extreme. Before Jean could finish, Lady Montfort jumped up from her chair, her face flaming, and said to her husband, "I wish to leave, please. Goodnight, Mrs. Rayburn. I would like to thank you for your hospitality, but I find I can't." She swept out of the room, her husband following helplessly behind. Within minutes, the other guests had made their subdued farewells, most of them refusing to meet Camilla's eyes. Only Miles, Dorcas and the earl remained behind with Camilla. And Jean Hilliard, of course. He stood slightly apart from the others, his black eyes expressionless in his dark face.

The earl was pale. "That was unforgivable behavior," he said to Jean. "No other gentleman of my acquaintance could have been guilty of it."

The black eyes glinted. "You are, of course, free to think anything you like, sir. I should remind you, however, that you and I have different standards."

"Now, see here, Hilliard," Miles spluttered.

As he took an impulsive step forward, Camilla put a hand on his arm. "Go home, Miles. You, too, Uncle Nigel. Dorcas, please go up to bed. I'd like to speak to Mr. Hilliard privately."

Her pert little face distressed, Dorcas gave Camilla a hasty kiss on the cheek and scuttled out of the room. After a long indecisive pause, the earl walked slowly to the door. Miles struggled with himself even longer, but finally he patted Camilla on the shoulder and followed the earl out of the room, leaving her to face Jean Hilliard alone.

The dark eyes bored into hers. "Well, Mrs. Rayburn? You wished to speak to me?" The bronze face was impassive.

Camilla burst out angrily. "Did you enjoy turning my musical evening into a disaster?"

"Is that what I did?"

"You must know you did! This was the first public performance of my sonata. Well, the first semipublic performance, at any rate. It's a piece I've been working on and polishing for years. Lord Montfort is a member of the Academy of Music, and I was hoping that, if he liked the sonata, he'd recommend a performance by the Academy. And then you disrupted Miles's playing by falling asleep and snoring, and after that you made matters even worse by playing and singing that vulgar French Canadian song, and after *that* you deliberately scandalized Lady Montfort by telling her that dreadful story. She'll probably think I encouraged your disgraceful behavior, because she knows I'm Uncle Nigel's goddaughter, and you're his heir. How likely is it now, do you think, that Lord Montfort will feel inclined to recommend my sonata to the Academy of Music?"

After a pause, Jean said, "I'm sorry if I spoiled your evening. If I'd known about your sonata . . . But when I came here tonight I had no idea the occasion was so important to you."

Camilla was unappeased by the apology, if that was

what it was. "Ignorance doesn't excuse bad manners," she snapped. "It was unpardonable, the way you talked to Lady Montfort."

Hilliard's face blazed with a sudden anger. "Oh, is it bad manners we're discussing now? Do you consider Lady Montfort an expert on the subject?"

Camilla bit her lip. Lady Montfort *had* been rude and overbearing. Perhaps it would have been too much to expect Jean to overlook the lady's slurring remarks about his ancestry. But no, there was no excuse for his behavior. Camilla's temper flared again. He had no right to shock Lady Montfort with that dreadfully vulgar story.

Jean broke into her thoughts. "Why did you ask me here tonight, Mrs. Rayburn? You didn't seem overjoyed to see me. And certainly I have nothing in common with your fine society friends."

"Why . . . I told you in my note. We're related, or nearly so, and we ought to be better acquainted."

Jean put out his hands to grasp her shoulders. Gasping with surprise, Camilla tried to free herself, but she couldn't dislodge those steely fingers.

"You invited me to your 'musical evening' only because Lord Sheringham asked you to do so, isn't that right?" Jean's voice was hard and angry.

"I—yes." What was the point of denying something that must be so obvious? Jean Hilliard might be an uncouth provincial, but he was no fool.

He released her shoulders, pushing her back with such force that she nearly fell. "Tell Lord Sheringham, Mrs. Rayburn, that I can't be bribed into staying in England by the promise of female companionship, not even the companionship of his goddaughter. Oh, I admit the opportunity to know you better might have appealed to me. That was before I discovered you were as frigid as an Atlantic iceberg!"

Chapter Five

"No," said Camilla.

Her godfather looked at her reproachfully. "You promised me you'd help me, Camilla. And this is such a little thing, merely to spend a few days at Woodford Priory."

"It's not such a little thing, when it means I'd be trapped in Jean Hilliard's company for those few days," Camilla retorted.

It was the day after the infamous musical evening. The Earl of Sheringham had come to the house on Park Street to announce that he'd invited Jean Hilliard for a visit of inspection to the Northamptonshire estates, and Jean had accepted the invitation for the coming Saturday.

"But you needn't be exclusively in Jean's company," the earl protested. "After what happened here last night, I can see it might be a trifle awkward for you . . . So I've decided to invite Dorcas, and that friend of yours, Miles Wingate, to join our party. They'll certainly help to occupy some of Jean's time."

The earl paused, his eyes darkening with concentration. "I don't like to press you, Camilla," he said at last, "but this visit by Jean Hilliard to Woodford Priory may be crucial. Seeing the ancestral estate might awaken his family loyalties. He might well be impressed enough to agree to stay on in England. So I'd like to make the visit as pleasant as possible for him. You could help me do that."

Camilla glanced around her little drawing room, which presented its customary appearance, now that all the extra chairs had been removed from around the sides of the room. Her brows drew together in an angry frown as she recalled how Jean Hilliard had turned her musical evening into a debacle. She was still smarting, too, from his ill-tempered accusation that she was as frigid as an iceberg. Recalling *that* remark, her blood started to boil. Again.

"Uncle Nigel, I know I promised to make friends with Jean Hilliard, and I've truly done my best, but the man's impossible. I think you should give him up as a lost cause. He's a boor, a savage. Even if you persuade him to stay in England, he'll never in a million years learn to act like a civilized English gentleman."

The earl gave Camilla a thoughtful, curious look. "It's not like you to dislike anyone so strongly on such short acquaintance," he observed. "Oh, granted that Jean behaved disgracefully last night, but then he had some cause, don't you agree? Lady Montford wasn't being exactly conciliatory, either. Won't you give him another chance?"

"He's already had more chances than he deserves," Camilla retorted.

"I don't follow you, my dear. To my knowledge, you've met Jean exactly twice, when he came to Sheringham House on his arrival in London, and again last night at your house."

"Oh." With a slight shock, Camilla realized that her godfather didn't know she'd already encountered Jean Hilliard before their meeting at Sheringham House.

"Well, my dear?"

"As it happens, I've known Jean Hilliard for some time."

"But where—why—?"

"It was in Bath. Actually, you could say he did me a

service. You recall that Francine physically attacked me in that inn on the Bath road? Well, Mr. Hilliard came into the room and dragged Francine away from me before she could inflict any real damage."

"Well, then? It seems to me you should be grateful to Jean."

"I don't feel in the least grateful to him. He was—he was . . ." Camilla's lips pressed tightly together in an angry line as she remembered Jean's provocatively insulting remarks and the kiss he'd forced on her. "I didn't know who he was, of course," she went on. "I didn't *want* to know his name. He was, quite simply, the rudest man I'd ever met."

His brows drawing together, the earl demanded, "Camilla, did Jean force his attentions on you?"

She looked away, biting her lip. Jean *had* "forced his attentions on her," but the phrase didn't really describe their encounter. Not exactly. Well, he'd backed off when she discouraged him, hadn't he?

"You don't need to answer me, Camilla. I can see how the land lies. Well, that settles the matter," the earl snapped. He rose, saying, "Naturally, I won't ask you to pay a visit to Woodford Priory while Jean Hilliard is there. In fact, I promise you I'll never inflict my cousin's company on you again. Goodbye, my dear."

The earl's decisive tone contrasted with the faintly dejected sag in his shoulders. As he walked to the door, Camilla said impulsively, "Wait, Uncle Nigel. I've changed my mind. I'll come to Woodford Priory."

"But if Jean—"

"If he makes any advances, I can certainly cope with him. I've done so before!" And enjoyed it too, came the unbidden thought into Camilla's mind. She recoiled with distaste. Where did these errant thoughts come from?

Standing in front of her house with her godfather, Dorcas, and Miles Wingate, Camilla gazed admiringly at the earl's traveling carriage—with the Sheringham crest on the doors—which was drawn up in front of her door, ready to carry its passengers to Woodford Priory. The carriage was as elegant as her godfather's person, his house, and the rest of his belongings, thought Camilla with a little smile. A second carriage would follow along behind them, transporting the earl's and Miles's valets, Camilla's maid and the luggage. Miles's curricle and pair, attended by his tiger, waited nearby.

"By Jove, sir, those tits look like sweet-goers," said Miles, as he examined the four perfectly matched bays in the earl's team.

"Thank you. Yes, I fancy they're real blood-and-bones," said the earl with a hint of complacency. "Bought 'em off young Ingolsby for a song, when he got into low water." Camilla, standing beside her godfather on the trottoir, suppressed a grin. Lord Sheringham had always prided himself on his taste in horseflesh. "Well, shall we be off?" said the earl.

"But—Lord Sheringham, what about Mr. Hilliard? Isn't he coming with us?" asked Dorcas.

"He'll be along. Come, Camilla."

The groom handed Camilla up the steps of the carriage, and her godfather settled into a seat beside her. Miles then helped Dorcas into his curricle, his tiger leaped into the seat behind his master, and the cavalcade started down Park Street.

"Mr. Wingate seems very pleased to be driving Dorcas in his curricle," the earl observed with a faint air of amusement. "I thought he was your beau, Camilla."

"Not any more, Uncle Nigel. I think Miles lost his heart to Dorcas the first time he laid eyes on her."

"You don't seem concerned. There's no denying young Wingate would be a suitable *parti* for you." The earl's voice held a questioning note.

"I like Miles very much, but not enough to marry him." Camilla gave her godfather a direct look. "As I've told you more than once, I don't intend to marry again.

I'll be very happy if Miles and Dorcas make a match of it." She raised an inquiring eyebrow. "Now, then, what's this about Jean Hilliard? Miles drove his curricle today because he was afraid your carriage would be too crowded with five passengers. Are we stopping at your cousin's hotel to pick him up? Or has he decided against coming to Woodford Priory after all?"

The earl's face darkened. "Oh, indeed, he's coming. He sent word that he preferred to make his own way to the Priory."

Camilla stared at her godfather. "But that means he'll be obliged to travel by stagecoach, or by the mail coach, or possibly by chaise and four, which would be very expensive. Why would he put himself to such inconvenience when he could be riding in your very comfortable, well-spuing carriage?"

Lord Sheringham shrugged, his face bleak. "I fear you must ask him, my dear."

If that isn't just like Jean Hilliard, thought Camilla in exasperation. He'd do anything to frustrate Uncle Nigel, even if it meant cutting off his own nose to spite his face. She hoped he was having a wearying, uncomfortable journey. It would serve him right.

The six-hour drive was a familiar one for Camilla. So many times since her marriage to Philip she'd traveled from London through Middlesex and Buckinghamshire and on into Northamptonshire to visit Lord Sheringham at Woodford Priory. And before that, of course, during her childhood, she'd often made the long trip from Bath to her godfather's estate.

In the late afternoon, the carriage left the turnpike for a rural road meandering through an undulating landscape of hedgerows and well-tilled fields and rich pastures, interspersed with stretches of thick forest. Finally they passed through impressive gates in a high wall surrounding a large wooded park. At the end of a long winding drive one all at once beheld the breathtaking classic facade of Woodford Priory, situated on a slight eminence, with the River Nene flowing placidly in front of it. The house consisted of a great central block modeled after a Roman triumphal arch, with four pavilions radiating outward from it. Lord Sheringham's father, the eighth earl, had built the mansion on the foundations of earlier medieval and Elizabethan buildings, after his return from his grand tour and after his marriage to a fabulously wealthy Lancashire coal and mining heiress.

Dorcas's eyes widened as she walked up the entrance steps and entered the Marble Hall, an enormous room with a skylight, lined with tall alabaster columns alternating with copies of statues from Greece and Rome. "The architect conceived of this room as a kind of Roman atrium," Camilla murmured to Dorcas. "Uncle Nigel's father wanted to make his house a copy of a real Roman villa."

"It's—it's magnificent," murmured an impressed Dorcas.

Camilla chuckled. "But not very homey, is that what you're thinking? As a matter of fact, all the rooms on this floor are rather awe-inspiring. They're meant to be used for state entertaining. But don't worry. You'll find your bedchamber will be quite comfortable, with no statues or bas-reliefs, and the south pavilion of the house is a private wing containing rooms of considerably more modest proportions, where the family spends much of its time."

At seven o'clock, after a refreshing nap and a cup of tea, Camilla made a leisurely toilet. Then, going to Dorcas's room, she found her sister fully dressed, and the two girls went downstairs to the drawing room in the private pavilion, where they joined the earl and Miles in a glass of Madeira.

Glass in hand, Dorcas inquired after a few moments, "I wonder what's keeping Mr. Hilliard? Do you suppose he came by the mail coach?"

Miles shook his head. "He'd have been here by this time, surely. The mails all leave London at eight in the

76

evening."

The earl consulted his watch, frowning. "If he had traveled by post chaise, he'd have arrived long since. And he should certainly have been here by now, if he came by coach. I'm told the day coaches start from the coaching inns at unearthly hours of the morning. There could have been an accident, I daresay. I understand some of these coach drivers are drunkards."

His voice trailed off. He and Camilla exchanged glances. Had Jean Hilliard decided not to come to Woodford Priory after all? Camilla decided angrily that if the Canadian upstart again failed her godfather, she would personally find a way to feed Jean's heart to the vultures.

A dignified butler appeared in the doorway. "Mr. Hilliard is here, my lord."

The earl rose and walked toward the center of the room, hand extended. "Good evening, Jean. Welcome to Woodford Priory. Did you have a pleasant journey?"

"Pleasant enough," Jean said shortly, disengaging his hand from the earl's clasp as quickly as possible without appearing positively rude. He bowed to Miles and the two girls, his eyes lingering on Camilla.

Camilla nodded to Jean, feeling a surge of malicious amusement. He'd probably be too stubborn to admit it, but he'd obviously had a far from pleasant journey. His unfashionable cloak was rumpled and dusty, and his face was drawn with weariness.

"How did you travel, Mr. Hilliard?" she asked with an assumed interest. "By post chaise and four? By stage-coach?"

Jean shot her a quick look. Had he caught a faintly jeering note in her voice? Accepting a glass of Madeira from the earl, he sat down and took several sips of the wine before he answered Camilla. He said coolly, "I took a coach from the Bull and Mouth in St. Martins-le-Grand to Northampton, Mrs. Rayburn. We made very good time. The driver said his average speed was seven miles an hour. It's your roads, of course, that make such speeds possible. Some day, I hope, we'll have as good roads in Québec."

To Camilla, his account sounded entirely too smooth. "When did you leave London, Mr. Hilliard?" she said innocently.

His lips tightened. "At six this morning."

"But then you should have arrived in Northampton no later than two this afternoon," observed Miles in surprise. "And Northampton is—"

"Northampton is exactly ten miles from Woodford Priory," Jean finished. A faint color appeared in his bronze cheeks. "I hired a curricle to drive out here, and I got lost. Lost," he repeated venomously. "I've been driving around these country lanes for hours. I can make my way without roads from Montreal all the way to Hudson's Bay, and I get lost in this little corner of England." He sounded so chagrined that Camilla almost felt sorry for him.

The earl refilled his glass and said soothingly, "I daresay you misunderstood the directions they gave you at the livery stable. Our people here in Northamptonshire speak with a strong accent. It's sometimes difficult for foreign visitors to understand them."

Jean tossed the earl an appraising look. "Perhaps so," he muttered. After a second glass of Madeira, he appeared to have recovered his usual brash self-confidence. Over dinner, he questioned the earl about the estate. "This looks like good farming country, sir. You're growing wheat and barley, mostly, I observed. You appear to raise a lot of cattle, too."

The earl nodded. "Yes, although we actually fatten more cattle than we breed."

"How much land do you have here?"

"A hundred and forty thousand acres. That includes woodland and waste, of course."

Jean did a hasty mental calculation. "One hundred and sixty-eight thousand arpents. A sizeable property, sir."

The earl replied coolly, "As I told you in my letters." After a short pause, he added, "I presume you noticed that we have considerable forest on the estate. Northampshire is famous for its ash trees, of course, and we have quite a number of very ancient oaks. Would you care to go hunting while you're here? We have a large herd of deer, and my keepers tell me we actually have a few wildcats, which are very rare now, I'm told, outside of Scotland."

"Hunting?" Jean shook his head. "Not unless you're in need of venison. In that case I'd be happy to bag a few deer for you. As for the wildcats—which I assume are the same as our Canadian lynx—I see little point in shooting them. Their fur is useless commercially. In Canada, we deal almost exclusively in beaver."

Lord Sheringham stared at Jean with an expression of such complete incomprehension that Camilla put her napkin to her face to hide a grin of helpless amusement. Poor Uncle Nigel. He was so much the sportsman that he couldn't understand a man like Jean Hilliard, who looked at all animals from the standpoint of pure practicality. If Jean didn't need food, or if he couldn't use an animal's pelt in trade, he wasn't interested in hunting. Camilla wondered idly if he rode—this part of Northamptonshire was famous hunting country—and how he felt about foxes.

After dinner, and a brief stay in the dining room to drink a glass of port with his male guests, Lord Sheringham proposed an inspection tour of the house. Leading out of the Marble Hall was the Saloon, an immense circular domed room modeled, the earl informed Jean, after the Pantheon in Rome. The other rooms to both sides of the Marble Hall and the Saloon—a music room, dining room, library, picture gallery—were similar in scale and decoration, with elaborate coffered ceilings, carpets that echoed the pattern of the ceilings, and walls adorned with marvelously carved and gilded paneling.

Occasionally Camilla stole a look at Jean as they walked through the rooms. His face was completely expressionless. If he was impressed by all this splendor, he gave no indication of it.

The earl spent considerable time in the picture gallery. The earliest portrait was rather primitively executed, depicting a man in full armor. "The twelfth Baron Hilliard," the earl told Jean. "Another Nigel. He fought at Agincourt." A little farther along the row of pictures, the earl pointed to the portrait of a tall man in a small, soft-crowned hat, a doublet and a loose, flowing gown. "The first Earl of Sheringham," he announced. "He saved Henry Tudor's life on Bosworth Field. Henry VII was properly grateful when he became king, and created him an earl." Still farther along was the portrait of another tall man in a voluminous periwig and a full-skirted coat. "The seventh earl," reported Nigel. "He fought with Marlborough at Malplaquet." The last portrait in the row was of a young Nigel, in the curled bagwig, velvet coat and tight breeches of the eighties of the last century.

Camilla drew a sudden quick breath. She'd never noticed before the strong family resemblance in all the Hilliard portraits, despite the differences in clothing and hair styles. Born centuries apart, Uncle Nigel and the first earl could almost have been brothers. And Jean—black hair, coal black eyes and dark skin aside—he was clearly a Hilliard, too.

Whether or not Jean recognized the family resemblance, his thoughts were obviously on another subject. Turning away from the portraits, he remarked abruptly to the earl, "This is a very large house. It must be very expensive to maintain, and apparently you live here for only a few months of the year. How do you justify the extravagance?"

Miles and Dorcas gasped at Jean. Lord Sheringham swallowed hard. "Extravagance?" he repeated weakly. "I never thought . . . Well, of course, the house *is* expensive to maintain. After all, it's the finest specimen of pure

Palladian architecture in England. And though I'm in residence for only a short time during the autumn and the spring. I entertain extensively for the county while I'm here."

"Why?"

"Why do I entertain?" The earl looked incredulous. "Because it's expected of me, that's why. I'm the Lord Lieutenant of the county. I have certain standards to keep up. You'll do the same, when you succeed to the title. I'm assuming that the Crown will appoint you Lord Lieutenant in my stead, as the most important landowner in the county."

Jean shook his head. "You're forgetting something, sir," he said curtly. "I'll be living in Montreal, if and when I succeed you. The Crown is hardly likely to appoint me Lord Lieutenant." As Lord Sheringham's face fell, Jean gestured at the long expanses of the picture gallery. "As for this house, I consider it a dead weight against the estate. It's more like a museum, or a—a mausoleum than a residence! I advise you to cut your losses and shut the place up, except perhaps for the private pavilion. You'll save a fortune."

The earl looked stunned, as if someone had hit him suddenly in the pit of his stomach. Camilla ached for him. He'd always been so proud of the Priory, long considered one of the major showplaces of the English countryside. Obviously he'd hoped—expected—that Jean would be impressed by the house as a symbol of the Hilliard family's importance in the county. Instead, Jean had reacted like the tradesman he essentially was. He saw the Priory as a useless extravagance, eating up the revenues that he might later have the opportunity to use for one of his business ventures in Canada.

She heard herself saying sharply, "Uncle Nigel happens to think that some things are more important than money, Mr. Hilliard."

"As do I, Mrs. Rayburn. Things like the right to choose where one wishes to live, and the freedom to speak one's mind."

Camilla stared into Jean Hilliard's mocking eyes and resisted the impulse to slap his face.

It had been a very long day—a very long two days, as a matter of fact. Immediately after breakfast yesterday morning, the earl had begun his young cousin's tour of inspection of his future property. Camilla and Jean rode with the earl in his carriage, Dorcas with Miles in the curricle. That first day they'd driven along hedgerow-lined narrow lanes through mile after mile of prosperous farmland and pasture. They'd visited the main village of Woodford, where the townspeople had greeted the earl with beaming smiles and low bows. Stopping at the home farm, they'd been pressed to take glasses of gooseberry wine and fresh-baked scones in the housewife's neat parlor, where the tenant farmer had enthusiastically picked Jean's brains about methods of growing grain in Canada.

Today the party had spent considerable time in the county town of Northampton, in which there were so many reminders of the close association of the Hilliard family with the history of the town and the county. The free grammar school, founded in 1493, had been endowed by an early Countess of Sheringham. In the spacious marketplace, the towering statue of the Duke of Marlborough was a gift to the town from the eighth earl. Near the ruins of the old castle, itself an ancient stronghold of the Hilliards, was the gaunt Norman hulk of the church of St. Blaise, in which most of the memorials belonged to the earl's family, including several splendid tombs topped by effigies of knights who had gone to the Crusades.

Now, in late afternoon, the earl and his guests had stopped south of the town to examine an elaborate Gothic structure known as the Queen's Cross, one of the few remaining Eleanor crosses erected by King Edward I to mark the various resting places of his wife's funeral cortege as it wended its way to her burial place in Westminster.

Jean Hilliard, it seemed to Camilla, had become increasingly silent as the day progressed. He took a long look at the graceful arches of the Eleanor cross, then remarked to the earl with an edge to his voice, "I daresay one of your ancestors was a member of the queen's funeral train?"

"Well, as a matter of fact, the seventh baron thought it only respectful to join the funeral party. After all, he'd accompanied the king to Palestine on a Crusade in 1268."

"That's what I thought," Jean muttered, turning away.

Camilla dressed carefully for dinner that night, in a gown of softly sprigged coral muslin, with a coquettish lace cap perched atop her tawny curls. It would be her last night at Woodford Priory until at least the end of the Season. Jean had insisted on returning to London the following day, and there seemed little point in remaining at the Priory if he wasn't present. The whole purpose of the visit had been to reveal to him the glories of his heritage.

Unfortunately, it didn't appear that Jean had been much impressed by his stay in Northamptonshire, Camilla mused as she descended the stairs to the family wing. Nor had she seen any sign that he'd relaxed his hostility to Lord Sheringham.

When she entered the drawing room, the earl was standing at the window, looking out into the formal garden. He turned to greet her, his face drawn and somber.

"Well, Uncle Nigel, we had a busy day," she said with an assumed cheerfulness.

"And a futile one, I fear. Camilla, do you think this visit has changed Jean's mind about staying in England?"

"No," she replied reluctantly. Her voice took on an angry note. "You never had a chance, Uncle Nigel. I think he deliberately closed his mind to everything you said and did."

The earl nodded. "That's what I thought, too."

"I'm sorry I didn't give you more help. I know you hoped I'd be able to influence him during this visit, but there weren't many opportunities to speak privately with him."

"Don't apologize, Camilla. You did your best. At least you were civil, which is more than I can say for Jean at times."

The earl broke off as Jean entered the room. He nodded curtly to Camilla and her godfather. The man's impossible, thought Camilla irritably. He has no small talk at all. In her world, polite small talk was the lubricant that greased the wheels of civilization.

After dinner, Dorcas proposed a walk in the gardens. "It's such a lovely evening, and the grounds of the house are the only part of the estate Mr. Hilliard hasn't seen yet."

"A splendid idea," said the earl promptly. "You four young people go along. The day's been a little strenuous for an old man. I believe I'll retire early."

The earl's motives were transparent, at least to Camilla. He still believed she could soften Jean's attitude toward him and the estate, and he undoubtedly hoped that she'd make an opportunity to be alone with Jean during their evening stroll. Camilla sighed. Very well, she'd make one last effort, for all the good it would do.

The early spring twilight was drawing in as the two couples entered the formal gardens. They sauntered slowly down the Long Walk, past the topiary trees and the neat beds of early spring flowers, and admired the statues and fountains in Lord Sheringham's newly designed Italian Garden. However, when Dorcas expressed a wish to explore the maze, Camilla said to Jean in a low voice, "Would you like to walk in the park? The ruins of the old priory are quite interesting. For one thing, the monastic buildings occupied the site long before the Hilliards built their first house here."

Obviously the invitation took Jean by surprise. It was the first overture she'd made to him since their meeting on the Bath road, except for the invitation to that disastrous musical evening. After a brief hesitation, he nodded, saying, "Why—yes. I'd like to see the priory."

Miles and Dorcas had gone on ahead to the maze, chattering animatedly to each other. They never noticed that their companions weren't following them. Camilla and Jean slipped out of a gate in the wall surrounding the gardens.

The park at Woodford Prior was more heavily wooded than the parks of other great houses, with many centuries-old oaks and magnificent ashes. Camilla and Jean walked in silence beneath the trees. Camilla wondered at herself. She'd invited Jean to go off in the park with her so she could talk to him about his duties to the estate, but suddenly she couldn't think of anything to say. Inexplicably, she was tongue-tied. She, the mistress of salon small talk! Apparently Jean felt tongue-tied, too.

It was quite dark beneath the trees, and the winding path was so narrow that they frequently brushed against each other. At one point her fleecy shawl caught on a dead branch. Jean disentangled the shawl and carefully arranged it around her shoulders. She shivered as his fingers brushed against the delicate skin of her neck. She remembered the electrifying effect of the touch of his fingers on her throat from their encounter at the Bath Assembly Rooms, when he'd attempted to persuade her to dance with him. His hands weren't the smooth hands of a gentleman like Miles, or her godfather. They were calloused, the hands of a man who'd engaged in manual labor. Somehow, the roughness of his hands made his touch all the more enticing.

"You're shivering, Mrs. Rayburn. Are you cold?" Jean asked quickly. "Would you prefer to go back to the house?"

"No, I'm fine, thank you. The ruins are just ahead."

The trees thinned out and the starkly lovely arches of

85

the cloister came into view, outlined against the last rays of light slanting across the rippling waves of the river that flowed placidly past the ruins. Camilla had always loved the solitude and peace of the site. She'd come here often after her husband's death, when her world had seemed to be disintegrating, and she couldn't bear the company of friends and family.

There wasn't much left to see of the priory. Only the two remaining walls of the cloister, a part of the monks' refectory, a solitary cross. Jean wandered around the ruins, coming back to Camilla to say, "It's beautiful. I don't know why I think so, it just is." He added wryly, "I know. You needn't tell me. It's one more place with a centuries-old association with the Hilliard family." He was silent for a moment, then said abruptly, "Mrs. Rayburn, I owe you an apology."

Camilla lifted astonished eyes to him. In the fading twilight, she sensed, rather than saw, his faint flush.

"I disrupted your musical evening," he went on doggedly. "I didn't mean to do it. I meant to be on my best behavior, but I should have known better than to drink so much blue ruin before I came to your house. I was— well, to tell the truth, I was a little nervous about meeting your friends. And afterward . . ." He looked away from her. "I said something to you I wish I hadn't said. It wasn't true."

Between them, the phrase, "frigid as an iceberg," hovered unspoken.

Camilla couldn't understand what was happening to her. Shards of ice seemed to be melting away from her heart. "Mr. Hilliard, you weren't the only one at fault," she heard herself saying. "My guests weren't very polite to you." She swallowed. "I wasn't, either." Holding out her hand, she said impulsively, "Shall we let bygones be bygones?"

Hesitating, Jean stared down at her for a long moment. Then he reached out to clasp her hand between both of his. "Make a fresh start, you mean?"

She nodded.

He went on, "Does this mean we might be friends one day?"

"Why—yes, if you wish."

"Oh, I wish." He suddenly seemed to realize he was still holding her hand, and hastily released it.

Camilla could almost hear her godfather murmuring in her ear. She realized that this was the time to strike out in his behalf. "But Mr. Hilliard, it will be rather difficult to be friends if I'm on one side of the ocean, and you're on the other, don't you think?"

"Oh." Jean seemed startled.

Camilla pressed her advantage. "Isn't it possible you've decided too hastily about returning to Canada? Why not stay in England for, say, three months, until the end of the London Season? By that time, the end of July, you might find your attitude toward my godfather's plans for you had changed. You might even find you liked English society."

Jean smiled grimly. "Come now, you know as well as I do that even if I wanted to enter English society, I wouldn't be accepted. I may have been foxed the night of your musical evening, but there was nothing wrong with my ears. I heard the remarks your friends were whispering. 'Savage. Uncivilized manners. Uncouth Colonial.' "

"If I sponsored you, you'd be accepted," she said coolly.

He studied her. "And why would you do that?"

She didn't make the mistake of lying to him. "For my godfather's sake. He wants so much for you to stay in England." Pausing briefly, she added, "And for friendship's sake, too, if you will. Haven't we agreed to let bygones be bygones?"

For several moments he stood in rigid silence. Had she permanently antagonized him? At last he said, "You say you'd sponsor me. What does that mean?"

"I'd introduce you to my friends. I'd entertain for you." She added daringly, "I'd help you choose a new

87

wardrobe."

He gazed down at his unfortunate coat. "What's wrong with my clothes?"

"Everything."

A moment of hard-breathing silence followed. Then he burst out laughing. "You promise to make me a swell like that fellow I've heard so much about — what's his name? — Beau Brummell?"

"Oh, you'll be at least as elegant as the Beau. He's getting a mite long in the tooth, you know."

"And you'll show me how to get on with the *ton?*"

"Yes."

"Then we have a bargain, Mrs. Rayburn. I'll stay on in England for three months, and during that time I'll do my best to try to understand this peculiar country, and to come to terms with your godfather." Extending his hand, he said, "My ancestors used to smoke a peace pipe when they concluded treaties, but supposing we simply shake hands."

As she felt her fingers enclosed in that strong, rough clasp, Camilla had a moment of panic. How deeply had she committed herself? Would it be dangerous to become personally involved with Jean Hilliard?

Chapter Six

The little maid ushered Miles Wingate into the drawing room, where Camilla and Dorcas were sitting, bonneted and gloved and dressed for the street.

"One of the surest ways to a gentleman's heart is never to keep him waiting," Miles remarked, grinning. "You two are shining examples of that virtue. Shall we go? It's rather a long drive to Windsor."

"You'll have to make do with my company today, Miles. Camilla has another engagement," said Dorcas, with a demure look that said quite plainly she knew Miles would have no objection to an excursion for two. "Camilla is going shopping with Mr. Hilliard."

"Good God," exclaimed Miles blankly. "How did this come about, Camilla? I was certain you detested the man, and with good reason. He's no gentleman. At Woodford Priory a few days ago, you and Hilliard were barely on speaking terms. What's more, I understood he was planning to return to Canada almost immediately."

Camilla cleared her throat. "Mr. Hilliard has changed his mind about leaving England. He plans to stay on for the Season. As for my disliking him, Miles—well, actually, we've become quite friendly. He's asked for my advice in buying a new wardrobe."

Rolling his eyes, Miles retorted, "The good Lord knows he could use advice about his wardrobe!" He looked at

Camilla, frowning. "You know I wouldn't dream of interfering in your affairs—"

"What a bouncer, Miles! You're always giving me the benefit of your excellent advice," said Camilla, teasingly.

Miles acknowledged the barb with a good-natured grin. Then, becoming serious, he went on, "This is just a guess, Camilla . . . Has your godfather asked you to be civil to Hilliard, hoping you'll be able to persuade the fellow to remain in England?" He paused, gazing at Camilla inquiringly.

She hesitated. After a moment she said, "Miles, you know me too well. Look, you and Dorcas, you're not to say a word about this to anyone else, but yes, my godfather has asked me to be friendly with Mr. Hilliard. For some reason, Uncle Nigel seems to feel that I might have some influence . . ." Camilla shrugged. "In any case, I've agreed to introduce Mr. Hilliard to the *ton*. We'll see what happens."

"We will, indeed." Miles's expressive face showed plainly what he thought of the scheme. However, he said, "You forget that London is a man's town. I think I can be of some help to you. I'll be happy to put Hilliard up for membership in my clubs, and I'll take him around to Gentleman Jackson's Saloon and Manton's Shooting Gallery and Daffy's Club, and all the other places where females can't go."

"Miles, that's a splendid idea. Thank you."

He cut her off, looking embarrassed. "It's nothing, nothing at all. Happy to oblige. Goodbye, Camilla. Dorcas, it's time to go, if we're to get to Windsor before noon."

The next few days might be rather embarrassing, Camilla thought uneasily, after her sister and Miles had left. Miles wouldn't be the only person to question a sudden friendship with Jean Hilliard. Most of her closest friends had witnessed Jean's ramshackle behavior at her musical evening, and they would certainly wonder why she was becoming intimate with him. Well, time would tell. In the long run, she thought cynically, society might be willing to overlook a number of flaws in a man who was the heir to one of the greatest earldoms in England.

Jean arrived a few minutes later, precisely on time. Glancing at her bonnet and pelisse, he said, with a faintly relieved air, "You're ready to go. I—ah—I thought you might have changed your mind about our shopping excursion."

"Why would you think that?"

Shrugging, he said, "It's a female privilege, isn't it, changing one's mind?"

He sounded ill at ease, a little unsure of himself. Camilla recognized the feeling. She felt much the same herself. Their pact of friendship was so new, so different from the prickly hostility of their earlier acquaintance. She really didn't know how to act toward him. Trying for a light tone, she said, "Why, no, Mr. Hilliard, I haven't changed my mind about our shopping expedition. I enjoy spending money, especially when it isn't my own."

Jean laughed, and the moment of awkwardness passed. He said impulsively, "Could I ask a favor?"

"Yes, of course." Camilla was mystified. "What is it?"

"Well . . . It's this Mr. Hilliard thing. I'm not used to so much formality. Couldn't you call me Jean?"

"Why, certainly—Jean. And won't you call me Camilla?"

"Camilla," Jean repeated dreamily, letting the name roll off his tongue as if he were savoring a delicious sweetmeat. "It's a beautiful name. Back home in Québec, you'd be *Camille*, did you know that? I think I like Camilla better." He cleared his throat, as if he was suddenly aware that he was sounding like a gawky schoolboy, and changed the subject. "Shall we be off? We don't want to miss any bargains."

Camilla laughed. "Bargains? My dear Jean, I'll not take you to any establishment that offers bargains. We're out to make you into a pink of the *ton*. Only the most fashionable and most expensive shops will do." She laughed again at the faintly apprehensive expression that appeared on Jean's face.

As she emerged from her front door, Camilla paused on the steps, looking intently at the carriage waiting in the street in front of the house. "But that's my godfather's town carriage," she said in surprise. "I thought you were . . ." Her voice trailed away into embarrassed silence.

"You thought I'd be too stiff-necked to accept my cousin's offer of his carriage," Jean said, obviously enjoying her discomfiture. "Actually, I was thinking of you."

"Me!"

"Yes. I've ridden in too many of your London hackneys. I didn't want to subject you to broken springs and the smell of moldy hay." Jean handed Camilla into the carriage and climbed in after her. After the footman had put up the steps and closed the door and the carriage was in motion, he added casually, "I think you'll be pleased to know that I've also accepted your godfather's invitation to stay at Sheringham House."

Camilla gazed at him, too astonished to speak.

Obviously enjoying her reaction, he went on, "As a businessman, I have to watch my expenses, and Sheringham House will provide much cheaper accommodations than Fenton's Hotel." After a moment, he added, "And besides, I did promise, you recall, that I'd do my best to become better acquainted with the earl. That will be much easier to do if we're living in the same house, don't you agree?"

"Oh, yes, I do. What a splendid idea, Jean." Camilla was touched and pleased. Jean was certainly doing his best to observe his side of their odd bargain. Aloud, she said, "How are you and Uncle Nigel getting along?"

Jean shrugged. "Tolerably well, I'd say. As a matter of fact, we don't see much of each other. The earl told me to treat the house as my own, to come and go as I pleased. That's what I've been doing."

It didn't sound like a very cordial relationship, but at least it was a beginning, Camilla thought. If she were a betting person, she'd lay her blunt on her godfather. Few people could resist his charm.

The carriage stopped in front of Weston's fashionable tailoring establishment on Old Bond Street. As Camilla and Jean entered the shop, the proprietor glanced from one of them to the other, and his welcoming smile faded. "Yes?" he said coldly.

Camilla could guess what Mr. Weston was thinking. Undoubtedly he'd never before met a gentleman dressed in such regrettable clothes. Ergo, he'd automatically decided that Jean wasn't a gentleman. And since ladies of quality didn't normally patronize tailoring shops, Mr. Weston probably regarded her as Jean's fancy piece, genteel-looking, to be sure, but a ladybird nevertheless.

"Good morning, sir," Camilla greeted the proprietor composedly. "I'm Mrs. Philip Rayburn. My late husband was one of your customers. I believe my godfather, Lord Sheringham, has also patronized your establishment."

Mr. Weston's supercilious expression changed instantly. He was all smiles as he said, "Indeed, Mrs. Rayburn. I was honored by your husband's patronage. Er—how can I be of service to you?"

Camilla motioned to Jean. "This is my friend, Mr. Hilliard. He's newly arrived from Canada, and is in need of a new wardrobe. Since he's unfamiliar with the London shops, I've offered to be his guide."

"But of course." The tailor snapped his fingers at a hovering clerk. "Show Mr. Hilliard to the fitting rooms and take his measurements."

When Jean had gone off with the clerk, Camilla said casually, "Mr. Hilliard is the Earl of Sheringham's heir. At present, he's the guest of the earl at Sheringham House in Hanover Square."

"Ah!" Mr. Weston nodded in complete understanding. A valuable bit of information had been tactfully offered, and gratefully received. The tailor need have no worries about the payment of his new customer's account.

After Jean had been measured, there were important decisions to be made. Should his coats be single-breasted or double-breasted? Made of light material or superfine? In what colors? Velvet collars or no? And how many capes to his greatcoat? How about his waistcoats? Did he prefer striped toilinette or kerseymere? Should the vents on his new pantaloons be closed with buttons or running strings?

Gazing in bewilderment at the swatches of superfine — dark blue, light blue, black, dark green, light green, maroon, scarlet — from which he was expected to choose materials for his coats, Jean finally said, "I'll take those two, the light blue and the maroon."

"But Jean," Camilla protested, "you'll need at least six coats, including one in black or dark blue for evening wear."

"Six!" Jean looked horrified. "How could I possibly need six coats?"

"Easily," said Camilla. "Eight might be better."

"Six will be fine," Jean said hastily to Mr. Weston, and made his color choices.

"My staff will begin work on these garments immediately, Mr. Hilliard," said the tailor, beaming at the size of the order. "At least one of your coats will be ready for a fitting by the end of the week."

As he and Camilla drove away from Weston's premises on Old Bond Street, Jean said feelingly, "I had no idea it would be so complicated to buy a few clothes."

"We've only started, you know," replied Camilla with a wicked smile. "You need shirts, cravats, stocks, gloves. We'll go to Harboro and Acock on Cockspur Street for those. And boots. Hoby is the best bootmaker, according to Uncle Nigel. And a hat or hats, of course."

Jean shot her a jaundiced look. "If I hadn't just had that session with the tailor, I'd think you were bamboozling me. Back in Québec, it would never have occurred to me that one man could need such an extensive wardrobe." He turned thoughtful. "Camilla, is it usual for a lady to accompany a gentleman to his tailor? I thought that fellow Weston was looking at you

94

very fishily before you introduced yourself."

"Well, no, it's not usual. In fact, it isn't done. I suppose. However, I daresay nobody will criticize me in this instance. After all, I *am* your cousin, after a fashion, and I'm a widow, besides. Widows can do what they like, within reason, of course."

"I see. Ah—how long have you been a widow?"

Camilla said briefly, "Philip died three years ago."

"Do you—do you still miss him?"

She gave him a level look. "I'm finished with my grieving. Time has a way of healing wounds, you know."

He must have heard the brittle note in her voice, and realized he was treading on uncertain ground. Quickly changing the subject, he said, "Odd, that fellow Weston never said a word about billing me. He doesn't even know where I live."

"Oh, I told him you were living with Uncle Nigel at Sheringham House. He'll send his bill there."

"Good. To my account, of course." When Camilla didn't answer immediately, Jean said suspiciously, "You didn't tell Weston to send the bill to your godfather, did you?"

"No," Camilla said, quickly. Too quickly, even though, in one sense, her answer was perfectly true.

Jean's brows drew together in an ominous scowl. "A little matter of omission? You didn't tell him *not* to send the bill to the earl, is that it? Camilla, what in God's name made you think I'd let the Earl of Sheringham buy my clothes? I pay my own way."

Camilla thought quickly. From various remarks Jean had made about his financial difficulties with his fur trading company in Canada, she doubted that he'd come to England with a very full purse. And from her own experience with her husband Philip's tailoring bills, she knew that the cost of outfitting a candidate for the London *ton* could be ruinous.

In a matter-of-fact voice, she asked, "Do you have any

idea what a fashionable London tailor like Weston charges for a coat?" She named a sum. Jean's eyes widened in disbelief. She rushed to the attack. "Isn't it a fact that you wouldn't be buying a new wardrobe if you weren't staying in London? And isn't it also a fact you're staying in London to oblige my godfather? Well, then, why shouldn't the earl pay for your clothes?"

A slow smile spread across Jean's face. "You talk like a businessman, Camilla. In other words, my new wardrobe, in a sense, represents a business expense for Lord Sheringham, and it's his duty to pay for it."

"Precisely."

Jean burst out laughing. "Camilla, you wretch, I can see you driving a wicked bargain with some hapless shopkeeper. Very well, you've convinced me. I'll graciously consent to allow the earl to buy my new clothes, and I hope he's properly grateful for the privilege."

As they went from shop to shop, Jean made no further objections to the size of the wardrobe he was expected to acquire, until he dug in his heels at Lock's in St. James's Street. "No," he said explosively, when he was shown several handsome specimens of the hatter's art.

"But Jean, you must have a new hat," exclaimed Camilla, with a disparaging look at Jean's disreputable headgear.

"Not a beaver hat," he growled. "They're much too expensive." He glared at the clerk. "It's highway robbery, in fact it's extortion, what you're charging for these hats. When I think of how little I receive for each beaver pelt I trap . . . Where do you get your skins, and how much do you pay for them?"

"Why, from the Hudson's Bay Company showrooms in Fenchurch Street, sir," replied the nervous clerk. He named a figure.

Jean blinked. Then he reached across the counter to seize the clerk's hand. "Pray accept my apologies. I should have known who the real villains were. God knows I've rapped heads often enough with those thieves from Hudson's Bay. They tried to put me out of business, you know. Claimed my company had no right to trade in their territory." He picked up one of the beaver hats at random and jammed it on his head, without bothering to glance into the mirror on the counter. "I'll take this one."

The clerk was so unnerved by the actions of his odd customer that it took him several seconds to recover his composure and complete the sale. Camilla hardly knew whether to laugh or to sink through the floor in humiliation. She squirmed at the thought of what her friends in the *ton* would have said if they'd witnessed the incident. Perhaps she'd bitten off more than she could chew when she'd offered to introduce Jean to society. Perhaps he wasn't capable of becoming a gentleman of the *ton*. He was so accustomed to speaking his mind, and his view of life was so different from that of Camilla and her friends — he might never lose the raw edges of his provincial manners.

The next few days were a revelation to Camilla, as she and Jean explored London. For one thing, she'd apparently underestimated his capacity to learn and to adapt. He had a very quick mind, and his outbursts against one aspect or another of the London scene became noticeably fewer and less vehement. Then, too, Camilla gradually realized with considerable astonishment that she was seeing the city through the fresh eyes of a stranger.

Jean wasn't interested in the usual run of sightseeing. Westminster Abbey, the House of Commons, the Tower of London, the Royal Academy, all left him singularly unimpressed. What he really wanted to see was the mercantile city, the center of trade and commerce.

They went down to the wharves, to the Pool below London Bridge, packed with every variety of oceangoing ship, East Indiamen, tea clippers, whalers, schooners of every description. They gaped at the great granite portals of the newly-built East India dock. They visited the porticoed Bank of England, and the colonnades of the Royal Exchange, where traders from every nation on earth were offering their wares. They even spent some time in the coffee shops clustered in the courts and alleys behind the Royal Exchange, where traders and auctioneers met to conclude their deals.

As they were standing one afternoon in admiration before the six great Ionic columns fronting East India House, Camilla chanced to mention that she knew one of the directors of the East India Company.

"Could you introduce me?" Jean asked eagerly.

"Why—yes. But Jean, why on earth would you want to meet Sir Thurston Gardiner? I assure you, he's rather a dull sort of person."

"Because he's a person who knows how to make money. I could learn something from a man like that."

"Careful, Jean," Camilla said with a teasing smile. "You'll be a peer of the realm one day. You can't let yourself be too closely connected with trade."

"Why not?" He was scowling at her. "What's wrong with trade? It's the lifeblood of any nation. Napoleon called you English a nation of shopkeepers. He meant it as an insult. I call it a compliment."

"Why . . ." Camilla floundered. "It's just that a gentleman doesn't engage in trade . . ."

"Then I'm no gentleman, is that what you're saying?"

"No, of course I'm not saying that. Jean . . ."

"Perhaps it's just as well that we know where we stand, Camilla," said Jean coldly. "It's growing late. You'll want to return to Park Street."

Several days later, Miles Wingate arrived at Camilla's house to escort her and Dorcas to tea with the Earl of Sheringham.

"Well, where did you and Hilliard go today?" asked Miles with an indulgent smile. "There can't be a corner of London that you two haven't seen."

Camilla said pensively, "Actually, I haven't seen Jean lately. I think I offended him when I warned him—just funning, of course! — against becoming too interested in trade."

Miles threw up his hands. "Camilla, *I* think the man's impossible! I told him the other day that I'd proposed him for membership in White's and Boodle's, and do you know what he said? 'What do they do in these clubs?' I explained to him that membership was more a social cachet than anything else, but that gambling was a principal activity. He said, 'In that case, I don't see much point in belonging to these clubs. Gambling's a waste of time and money.' Well, now, Camilla, I ask you, don't you think Hilliard should be a little more grateful? I was trying to do him a favor, you know."

Camilla was silent for a long moment. At last she said slowly, "Perhaps it's not such a great honor after all, Miles, to belong to White's. I agree with Jean, gambling is no great thing."

Miles looked bewildered. "But, Camilla —"

"It's time to go, Miles."

At Sheringham House, Camilla and Miles and Dorcas entered the drawing room in the midst of an ongoing argument between the earl and Jean.

"No," Jean declared with finality. "I won't have it. I don't need a valet. I've managed to dress myself since I was in leading strings."

Camilla's eyes widened as she gazed at a changed Jean. Mr. Weston had been true to his word. He'd delivered a superbly tailored coat and waistcoat and pantaloons in less than a week's time. At some time too, during the past few days, Jean had visited a hairdresser. Quite simply, he looked magnificent. His thick curling locks were dressed in a becoming Brutus coiffure that emphasized the lean handsome planes of his face and his clear dark complexion. The superbly tailored coat and fitted pantaloons set off his tall, powerful, yet graceful, form.

"Jean," Camilla exclaimed involuntarily. "You look superb! It's you who enhance Mr. Weston's clothes, not the other way around."

He hesitated for a moment, apparently still suffering from a sense of offended dignity left over from their near quarrel of a few days earlier. Then he flashed her a rather sheepish smile. "Thank you. I think that fellow Weston did rather well by me. But," he continued, turning back to the earl, "I don't need a valet."

The earl said, "Who tied your cravat, Jean?"

Jean glanced at the intricate starched folds of his cravat. He said defensively, "Your valet helped me, as you know perfectly well. You told him to do it."

"Well, then. Are you prepared to spend a half hour or more each day, creasing and tying squares of linen into an Osbaldeston, or a Mahratta? Wouldn't it make more sense to hire a valet?"

"Jean," said Camilla in a small voice. "Don't blame my godfather. It was my idea to hire a valet."

"Oh." Jean stared at her from beneath drawn brows, his expression unreadable.

A dapper little man named Curtis decided the issue. Announced by the butler, he paused just inside the door of the drawing room to peer inquiringly at the occupants of the room. "Lord Sheringham?"

The earl inclined his head slightly. He motioned to Jean. "My cousin, Mr. Hilliard."

The man Curtis walked over to Jean, eyed him searchingly from the crown of his head to his brand-new Hessians, and then circled him slowly for another long look.

Unnerved by the silent scrutiny, Jean growled, "What the devil do y'think you're doing?"

The man drew himself up to the fullest limit of his meager height. "Sir, I'm Emmanuel Curtis, your new valet. Mind, I wasn't sure I could accept the position when I came here. I have my standards, and I find little satisfaction in dressing a gentleman who is obese, or who has badly shaped legs, or inelegant hands, or an overly short neck. But you, sir"—the valet gave Jean an admiring look—"you, sir, have no defects at all. It will be a pleasure to dress you."

Chapter Seven

Several weeks later, on a pleasant spring morning, Camilla sat at her desk in her small morning room, leafing through the thick stack of invitations that had just arrived in the morning post. It was the end of April, the season was about to begin, and already she and Dorcas had more invitations than they could accept.

Camilla settled back in her chair and marveled at the changes that had taken place in her quiet life since that day in March, when she'd gone to Bath to rescue Dorcas from her scheming mother. Soon she'd be caught up in the hectic activities of Dorcas's coming out, when her days were already so full that she scarcely had time to draw her breath.

Her rift with Jean, if one could call it that, had quickly mended. During the past few weeks, she'd seen him almost daily, usually in the company of Miles and Dorcas. The four of them had roamed the environs of London, visiting places like Kew Gardens, Chiswick, Richmond, Hampton Court, Greenwich, which were familiar to Miles and Camilla, but were new and novel to Jean and Dorcas. Today they were making a longer excursion. The Earl of Sheringham had invited the foursome to spend the weekend with him at his seaside villa in Kent.

The housemaid, Lizzie, interrupted her thoughts. "Mr. Wingate is here, ma'am."

Camilla pushed her correspondence into a neat pile and went to the drawing room. Miles rose as she entered, saying in mock complaint, "My word, Camilla, your foyer is piled so high with portmanteaus that it's difficult to pick one's way through them. You'd think you and Dorcas were planning a season in the Antipodes, rather than a few days in the country."

"Next you'll be telling me you've left home with one tiny valise," Camilla retorted.

He grinned at her. *"Touché.* My valet, like Jean's new man, has his standards. He won't let me go off for a country visit with little more than the clothes on my back." Hesitating briefly, Miles cast a quick look at the door of the drawing room, as if to assure himself that they were alone. He said quickly, "Camilla, I came early, hoping to have a chance to talk to you privately. You see, since Dorcas has no father, and her mother is . . ." He shrugged. "We both know what Mrs. Vernon is. In any case, you're Dorcas's guardian—"

Camilla interrupted him. "Are you applying to me for Dorcas's hand, Miles?"

He looked uncomfortable. "Yes, I am. I daresay you'll think me a frippery sort of fellow. It was only a few weeks ago that I was asking you for *your* hand."

"And I refused you, remember, because I knew we wouldn't suit. Miles, I'd be very happy to see you and Dorcas engaged."

Miles's face lit up, and he opened his mouth to speak.

Lifting her hand, Camilla said, "But not for a while yet. Not until the end of the Season."

"But Camilla—"

"Miles, listen to me. Dorcas is very young, and I don't want her rushed off her feet, even by someone I like and trust as much as you. If you'll just think about it, you'll remember that Dorcas wouldn't be living with me in London if my stepmother hadn't tried to drive her into a hasty marriage with that dreadful Mr. Stinchcombe. Let her enjoy her London Season. Let her have the opportunity to meet a number of eligible young men."

"Yes, and one of them might well cut me out," Miles said ruefully. "Dorcas is so lovely, so wonderful in every way."

Camilla felt a flicker of amusement. Miles was certainly a lovesick suitor. She said calmly, "If another man cuts you out, then you and Dorcas were simply not meant for each other."

"Well, I intend to do my best to prove to Dorcas that we *are* meant for each other," Miles exclaimed. After a moment he looked at Camilla with a sheepish expression. "Sorry to be difficult, my dear. I know you're right. I want to do what's best for Dorcas. Of course she should have a little more experience of the world before she chooses a husband." He cocked his head at Camilla. "Speaking of betrothals, what about you and Hilliard? I'd lay you a monkey that your godfather wouldn't be at all averse to seeing you as the next Countess of Sheringham."

"Don't be ridiculous," Camilla said sharply. "Jean and I are simply friends." She changed the subject. "Incidentally, I've never thanked you for showing Jean about town. He tells me you've been taking him to all your haunts."

Miles began to laugh. "No thanks necessary. It's been very diverting."

With a sense of foreboding, Camilla inquired, "What do you mean, diverting?"

"Oh, well, it's just that Hilliard can't seem to avoid putting his foot in his mouth. For example, we were at Tattersall's one day with a friend of mine, Dick Lincoln, and Dick spent hundreds of guineas on a pair of hunters. Jean informed Dick he'd wasted his blunt, that no animal was worth that kind of money. Poor Dick, he was too polite to say anything, but he turned a bright red. Another time Hilliard and I were at Manton's Shooting Gallery, where he put on a virtuoso display of marksmanship, cupping every wafer. Lord Bloodworth, one of the greatest shots in England, complimented Jean, who, instead of accepting the compliment graciously, told Bloodworth he didn't think much of English standards of marksmanship. In Québec, Jean said, any stripling can shoot out the eyes of a fly."

Suddenly Miles doubled over in a fresh paroxysm of laughter. "Yesterday Hilliard outdid himself," he gasped.

"He was boxing a round with Gentleman Jackson and sent the champion to the floor. It was an accident, of course. Had to have been. No one plants a leveler on Jackson. Anyway, when I remonstrated with Hilliard, telling him it wasn't good form to lay a hand on Jackson, unless the champion permitted it, Hilliard looked at me as if I were speaking gibberish. He said Jackson shouldn't box if he wasn't prepared to be milled down."

Miles so evidently considered that Jean had committed a social blunder that Camilla didn't argue with him, even though the offense seemed illogical to her feminine mind. Why shouldn't Jean floor the champion if he had the ability to do so?

"I tell you what, Camilla," Miles went on, his amusement fading, "Hilliard had best learn to keep his opinions to himself, if he hopes to make friends in the *ton*."

In one part of her mind, Camilla knew that Miles was right. Jean *was* incorrigible. He simple couldn't, or wouldn't, control his tongue. And yet, there were times when his candor, his lack of subterfuge, were very refreshing. At the very least, he wasn't like anybody else!

She glanced out the window, observing that a line of carriages and fourgons had drawn up in front of her house, behind Miles's curricle and the vehicle carrying his valet and his luggage. Rather to her surprise, Jean was climbing out of another curricle, and her godfather had just descended from a traveling carriage. Soon Jean entered the drawing room, followed by the earl.

By this stage of Jean's stay in London, all the tradesmen had made heroic efforts, and his complete new wardrobe had been delivered. Today he wore his maroon coat. He looked impossibly handsome, his coat and pantaloons fitting like a second skin, every strand of curling hair in place, his cravat impeccably tied. Some, if not most, of the credit must belong to his new valet, of course, but even so, Brummell himself wouldn't have disdained to walk up St. James's Street beside him.

"I've never seen you drive a curricle before," Camilla remarked to Jean. "Did you do a great deal of driving in Canada?"

"Hardly any," said Jean cheerfully. "I traveled mostly by canoe, or on horseback. However, when your godfather remarked that his curricle was gathering dust in his stables, and offered me the opportunity to drive it, I jumped at the chance."

Before he could stop himself, Miles exclaimed disapprovingly, "Look here, Hilliard, if you've never handled the ribbons on a curricle, do you really think you should be driving Lord Sheringham's grays?"

Jean stiffened slightly, and Camilla held her breath. Then, relaxing, Jean drawled, "Oh, I'm not entirely without experience, Wingate. In Québec, I occasionally drove a sleigh in the wintertime. We had a pair of huge old animals that didn't mind deep snow. And once or twice my grandfather allowed me to drive his ox cart."

The derision in Jean's tone was quite clear. Miles's face darkened, and the earl hastened to intervene, though he couldn't keep a faint quiver of amusement out of his voice. "I suggested to Jean, Camilla, that you and he ride down to Kent in the curricle. You could describe the landmarks to him."

"You'll have to buy me a new bonnet if it rains," Camilla warned. Uncle Nigel was so transparent. Now that he and Jean seemed to have achieved a wary equilibrium, the earl was pursuing his second goal of pairing off Camilla with his heir. Though how he could think that a ten-hour journey in an open carriage would be conducive to romance . . .

Camilla's eyes widened. Jean had taken an enamelled snuffbox out of his pocket, and now he inhaled a delicate pinch of snuff up each nostril. Instantly he began choking so hard that he had to stumble to a chair and sit down. When he could speak, he glared at Camilla, saying, "Why did you advise me to try taking snuff? A man would have to be out of his mind to use the hellish stuff!"

"I merely told you that knowing how to use snuff gracefully was the mark of a polished man about town," said

Camilla defensively. "Jean! Is this the first time you've ever inhaled snuff?"

Jean nodded, looking foolish. "Yesterday I went to that tobacconist you mentioned—Fribourg and Treyer?—and ordered one of their mixtures, and then I bought a snuffbox to put it in, but I never practiced using the stuff. It looked simple enough," he muttered.

Camilla exchanged glances with her godfather, and after a moment the pair collapsed in helpless laughter. Even Miles, still very much on his offended dignity, joined them. Jean glowered at all of them. At length, wiping his eyes, the earl recovered himself so as to say, "Well, at least you haven't entirely wasted your blunt, Jean. Even if you never inhale another pinch of snuff, you can use that handsome snuffbox as an accessory."

A reluctant grin curved Jean's lips. "What a kind thought, sir. A real consolation for making such a complete jackass of myself. Thank you very much."

The earl bowed. "A pleasure, my boy." He consulted his watch. "We should go. We have a long drive ahead of us."

"I'll fetch Dorcas. I daresay she's still prinking," Camilla said. After she had tapped at Dorcas's door, she stopped in her own bedchamber. She lifted from a shelf in her wardrobe a lacquered box in which she kept miscellaneous small treasures, and took out a small object that she tucked into her reticule.

As he and Camilla in the curricle swung in behind the earl's traveling carriage, Jean turned his head to glance at the string of vehicles following them. "*Mon Dieu,* we're like an army on the march, complete with baggage train," he remarked in a tone of disbelief. "We're only five of us, we'll be staying in Kent for less than a week, and yet we're setting out with a carriage, two curricles, three baggage fourgons and five personal servants." He shook his head. "I fear it's a little too rich for me. I'm not accustomed to such luxury."

"Well, for your information, I'm not accustomed to such luxury, either," Camilla retorted, "but I certainly intend to enjoy it."

Jean chuckled. "I like being with you, Camilla. You're the first female I ever met with a real sense of humor."

Suddenly it struck Camilla that she'd been so concerned about Jean's occasional lapses into bad manners that she'd overlooked his genuine sense of fun. More than that, he could laugh at himself. This morning, he'd good-naturedly derided his driving skills, mentioning his experience with his grandfather's ox cart, and he'd joked with Uncle Nigel over his failure to use snuff properly.

During the first part of their drive, Camilla, mindful of Jean's lack of experience in London traffic, kept a sharp eye on his performance. After he'd guided the team safely along Piccadilly and across Westminster Bridge into Southwark, however, she began to relax. Perhaps he didn't have Miles's nearly flawless skill with the ribbons, but so far he was proving a safe and competent driver. He might even develop into a very good one some day, with his keen eyes, powerful arms and intense concentration.

In the courtyard of The Bull at Shooter's Hill, where they made their first stop to change horses, Camilla turned to him and said simply, "Bravo."

The black eyes twinkled. "Riding along beside me in fear of life and limb, were you, Camilla? Own up, now. Did you think I might overturn you?"

"Certainly not. At least, not after you avoided a collision with that brewer's dray in Charing Cross. *That* put my heart in my mouth." Camilla reached into her reticule and pulled out a small object wrapped in a scrap of linen. "I'd like you to have this."

Jean stared down at the gold snuffbox, which was topped with a lacelike ivory carving of a tiger hunt, complete with a tiny elephant bearing a howdah.

"It belonged to my father," Camilla told him. "He bought it in Bombay, during his service with the fleet on the India Station."

"Camilla . . ." Jean looked at her helplessly. "This is beautiful, but I can't accept it. For one thing, I don't even use snuff, as you saw for yourself this morning. For another, the box is a family heirloom. It should stay in your family."

"Dorcas is my only family. I don't have any male relatives. I think Papa would enjoy knowing that one of my friends was using his snuffbox. You needn't sniff snuff yourself, you know. Do what Uncle Nigel suggested. Use the box as an accessory to your costume."

Hesitating only a moment longer, Jean reached for her hand and gripped it tightly. "Thank you," he said softly. "I'd be pleased to accept a gift from a friend." He released her hand in slight confusion when Miles drew up beside them in his curricle.

"Dorcas and I beat you here by a good ten minutes, Hilliard," said Miles, in high good humor. "We've already changed horses, and we're ready to go on."

"Miles!" Dorcas exclaimed excitedly. "Why don't we race Camilla and Jean to the next stage? It would be such a lark."

Narrowing his eyes, Miles said after a brief pause, "Why not a race all the way to Sandgate? That's the last stop before we turn off for Lord Sheringham's villa, which is several miles beyond the town. How do you feel about it, Hilliard? Are you on? We could make the race even more interesting with a small wager. Say, ten pounds?"

Miles's voice had an odd intonation. Camilla took alarm. "Don't waste your blunt, Jean," she murmured. "You couldn't expect to beat Miles. He's a member of the Four-in-Hand Club."

The black eyes sparked. "Really? Is this Four-in-Hand Club such a great thing, then?" Jean smiled at Miles. "Done, Wingate. Ten pounds I reach this Sandgate place before you do."

Watching Miles drive his team out of the courtyard of the inn, Jean remarked, "You'll have to be my guide as to distances and posting stops, Camilla. This territory is new to me."

"Jean, give up this shatterbrained notion," Camilla urged. "It could be downright dangerous for you, with your limited driving experience, to attempt to race a curricle and four along the London to Folkestone road, one of the busiest highways in the country."

"I've already accepted Wingate's challenge, Camilla," Jean said curtly. "If you're concerned for your safety, I suggest we wait here until your godfather arrives in his carriage. I'm sure he'll be happy to have your company on the journey to Sandgate."

Camilla threw up her hands in exasperation. "No, thank you! I started off with you, I'll stay with you. But just remember this: if we have an accident, my blood will be on your hands."

As the hostlers completed harnessing the new team to the curricle, Camilla entertained dark thoughts about Miles. It wasn't like her old friend deliberately to entice someone into an unequal contest. Why had he done it? Earlier today, he'd questioned Jean's ability to drive the earl's blood cattle, and Jean, with his needlelike riposte, had made him look a little foolish. Had Miles decided to even the score by challenging Jean to a contest he couldn't win?

Afterward, Camilla couldn't recall the details of that drive except as a nightmarish blur. She never got the opportunity to point out to Jean the curious shallow pits on Dartford Heath, or the buildings of the King's arsenal in Rochester, or the Gothic Archbishop's Palace in Maidstone. Nor did Jean pay the slightest attention to the beguiling scents wafting from the Kentish cherry, apple and pear orchards. He was blind to everything except his driving.

Her heart in her mouth, Camilla watched helplessly as Jean dashed around a slow-moving carriage and eased in front of it, just in time to avoid an oncoming phaeton. She watched him feather-edge a blind corner, and take a hill at a splitting pace, checking at exactly the right moment at a sudden bend in the road. It was only when he'd skillfully avoided a collision near Ashford with a lumbering two-wheeled cart, drawn by oxen and loaded with hops, that she relaxed her feverish grip on the side of the curricle. It finally dawned on Camilla that what Jean lacked in driving finesse he more than made up for in iron nerve and superb coordination.

It was a close race. Between Shooter's Hill and Sandgate, the two curricles were usually in sight of each other all the way, with Miles either a few hundred yards ahead or a short distance behind. Nearing the last stop at Sandgate, Jean definitely had the lead. It had been some time since he'd even glimpsed Miles. Jean slowed his team and drove sedately into the courtyard of the Crown Inn. As the hostlers and the inn servants swarmed around them, Camilla remarked, "You've won the race, Jean. Congratulations!"

Jean chuckled. "That was handsome of you. More than once during the last few hours, I think you'd willingly have strangled me. I'm sorry if I gave you any anxious moments, Camilla."

"Not at all. I quite enjoyed being nearly crowded off the road into a flock of sheep. And it was interesting to speculate on how delicious and refreshing a cup of tea might have tasted, or a bite of cold ham, if we'd stopped in one of those inns along the way."

Jean laughed so hard that tears came into his eyes. "Poor Camilla," he gasped at last. "Not only did I put you in danger of losing life or limb, but I nearly starved you as well." He climbed out of the curricle. "Come along. We'll have that cup of tea you've been yearning for."

Miles and Dorcas joined them inside the inn a few minutes later. To Camilla's relief, Miles's face reflected only his usual sunny good temper. He handed Jean a ten-pound note, saying, "My hat's off to you, Hilliard. You've the makings of a first-rate fiddler. I'll put you up for the next opening in the Four-in-Hand Club, if you like. Mind, I think I had a good chance to beat you if I hadn't been boxed in between those two chaises the other side of Maidstone. Cow-handed drivers, both of them."

"I think you're right. It was nip and tuck up to that point. There's no doubt I had a bit of luck," Jean admitted. He extended his hand, and Miles took it with a broad smile.

The four young people were enjoying a leisurely cold supper in a private parlor when Lord Sheringham strolled into the room. He raised his quizzing glass to examine the sun-reddened cheeks and windblown bonnets of his god-daughter and Dorcas, and remarked, "At each posting stop where I changed horses, the innkeepers and the hostlers could talk of nothing but the great race between the two swells in the curricles. Next time you come to Kent, my dear Camilla, I daresay you and Dorcas will choose to ride with an elderly gentleman who prefers comfort to excitement."

It was so early that the dew was still heavy on the shrubs and the flowering borders. None of the servants had been stirring when Camilla had slipped out of Ashcombe Manor and into the gardens behind the house.

Savoring the utter stillness and peace of her surroundings, Camilla wandered slowly along the immaculately kept paths of the garden. Occasionally she paused to sniff the intoxicating scent of sweet violets, or bent to admire a bed of multicolored primula, before settling on a stone bench overlooking the winding path leading down to the beach. Through the screen of trees, she could just glimpse the sparkling waters of the little cove.

"You're an early riser, Camilla."

She turned her head to watch Jean coming down the path toward her. "You, too."

He hesitated. "Would you rather be alone?"

"No, not at all. I'm no solitary. It's just that I woke up early and couldn't get back to sleep, so I decided to come out for a walk in the gardens." She motioned to the bench. "Sit down."

Jean breathed deeply. "It smells good here. I like this garden better than the one at Woodford Priory. It's smaller, more human." He glanced back at the house, a modest two-story building topped with a gracefully incongruous little cupola. "I like the house better, too. And what a glorious view from my window! You didn't tell me that Lord Sheringham's villa was situated right on the Channel. We got here so late last night that it was too dark to see our surroundings."

Camilla smiled. "I agree with you. I really think I like Ashcombe Manor the best of all Uncle Nigel's houses."

Looking startled, Jean inquired, "You mean the earl has other houses in addition to Woodford Priory, Sheringham House in London, and this place in Kent?"

"Why, yes. He has a hunting box near Grantham, and he still owns his grandfather's house in Manchester. His mother was a Lancashire coal heiress, you know. Then there's the property in Aberdeenshire where he goes for the salmon fishing—"

Jean cut her off. "That's enough. Lord, your godfather must own half the real estate in England!" The words were light, but the tone wasn't. His lips were set in a straight line.

"It will all belong to you one day, Jean."

"Don't remind me," he muttered.

Camilla said hesitantly, "Tell me, are you sorry you agreed to stay in England for the Season? Do you still dislike Uncle Nigel as much?"

For several moments, Jean stared off into the distance without speaking. At last he said, "No, I'm not sorry. You were right. I'd have been very shortsighted to return to Canada without knowing what the situation really was like here. As for your godfather . . . We're civilized toward each other. That's progress, isn't it?" He smiled suddenly. "One thing I'm decidedly *not* sorry about is gaining the opportunity to know you better." His voice changed and deepened. "You're looking very lovely this morning. I think that deep rose shade is your color."

"Thank you," said Camilla lightly. "You're very well turned out yourself," she added, looking at his tight-fitting buckskin breeches and riding boots.

Jean grimaced. "Curtis informed me this was the correct dress for the country. Would you believe it, that valet of mine wouldn't let me out of the bedchamber this morning until I'd tied my cravat properly. Ruined ten cravats before I satisfied Curtis. 'The Gordian Knot,' he calls this arrangement." Jean's brows drew together in a ferocious frown. "I'll tell you what, Camilla, some day I'm going to get back at you for saddling me with Curtis. The man's a dictator. I'm not a person to him. I'm a mannequin that he dresses up to display his handiwork to the world!"

Camilla knew perfectly well that Lord Sheringham had arranged this Kentish excursion primarily to throw her and Jean together. Having done his duty by accompanying them as a chaperone, however, he washed his hands of his guests. "I know you won't mind if I leave you to your own devices," he announced that first morning at breakfast. "You young people don't need my company to enjoy yourselves."

The earl divided his time at Ashcombe Manor between his library and gossipy sessions with old cronies in the area. His young guests were more active. They paid a visit to the fishing community in the little village of Lynharbor near the villa, where Miles gave it as his acid opinion that the locals did more smuggling than fishing. The foursome also explored Walmer Castle in Deal and prowled the old streets of Dover.

Standing on the Western Heights opposite Dover Castle, Jean stared at the waters of the Channel far below. "It's hard to believe that France is over there, only twenty-two miles away," he mused. *"Dieu,* I'd love to go there."

"Wingate," he appealed suddenly to Miles, "didn't you say that the fishermen in Lynharbor were probably smugglers? D'you think they'd take me across with them on one of their smuggling runs?"

"Good God, Hilliard, why would you want to risk your neck by going to France? We've been at war with the Frogs for almost twenty years."

"Well, I have relatives there. I'd like to meet them. I'm told my first cousin once removed, Sylvestre Benoit, has an important post in the customs in the Calais district."

Puzzled, Camilla remarked, "But Jean, didn't you tell me your family went out to Canada well over a century ago? How could you still have close relatives in France?"

"My Uncle Pierre got into — er — difficulties with the authorities about fifteen years ago. Something to do with who owned what beaver traps." Jean grinned. "My family and friends often have disputes about the ownership of beaver traps. Anyway, Uncle Pierre decided it might be healthier to leave the country. He went to France, married there and decided to stay. We still hear from him occasionally."

"Well, Hilliard, I fear you'll have to restrain your commendable desire to meet your family members until after we've beaten Napoleon and you can travel to France legally," said Miles dryly.

Camilla began to laugh. "Jean, I can just see you trying to persuade the Lynharbor fishermen to take you on one of their smuggling runs across the Channel. They'd suspect you of being an excise man in disguise. They'd never believe you wanted to go to France just to meet your cousin!"

The earl's young guests spent their last afternoon at Ashcombe Manor at the little cove below the house, enjoying a picnic supper. Lord Sheringham politely declined an invitation to join them, declaring he was too old to risk finding ants and other animate objects in his food.

Having eaten their fill of capon, ham, roast beef and assorted jellies and sweetmeats, Miles and Dorcas strolled down to the beach, with the avowed intention of searching for shells. Camilla and Jean remained behind, seated comfortably on a blanket beneath a sheltering tree.

With a gamine smile, Camilla removed her gypsy straw hat and tossed it on the grass. "There, that's better. I've never really liked hats, and I don't see why I should wear one on a picnic." She took the glass of wine Jean had just poured for her and sipped at it slowly. "It's been a lovely, peaceful three days," she said, sighing. "I really hate the thought of going back to London. Beginning next week, there'll be precious few peaceful moments, I assure you!"

Jean nodded. "I know. The Season starts next week. I won't be seeing as much of you, will I, Camilla?"

"Of course you will. I told you I'd introduce you to the

ton. I've seen to it that you'll receive invitations to most of the parties that Dorcas and I will be attending."

"It won't be the same thing, will it? The only times I'll see you will be when you're surrounded by crowds of people." Suddenly Jean reached out to finger the tiny lace cap atop Camilla's curls. "Why do you always wear that thing—or something very similar—even when you're wearing a bonnet? Dorcas never wears a cap."

"Dorcas isn't married."

"Neither are you."

"Don't be silly," said Camilla rather breathlessly. Jean had moved closer to her on the blanket. His hard thigh in the tight buckskin breeches was pressing against her leg. "I'm a widow, so it's the same thing. And married women wear caps, I have no idea why. It's the custom."

"Being a widow isn't the same thing as being married, but now isn't the time to argue," Jean murmured. He whisked the little lace cap from her head. "There. Now I can see your beautiful hair. I could see it even better if it were down around your shoulders . . ." Resting his weight on one arm, he leaned forward, running the fingers of his free hand through her hair, gently tugging at the hairpins that kept her curls in place.

"Jean, stop that," Camilla exclaimed, trying to pull his hand away. "My abigail spent half an hour this morning arranging my coiffure."

"Shush." Imprisoning her hand, Jean buried his face in the tumbled masses of her hair. "You smell like flowers. *Tu m'enivres,"* he whispered. His lips caressed the sensitive skin of her neck, gradually moving to her cheeks and eyelids, leaving a trail of delicate butterfly kisses. Camilla's entire body felt aflame. When, finally, his mouth settled on hers, gently but greedily drinking in the sweetness of her lips, she relaxed against him, responding to the growing urgency of his kiss.

"Oh, God, Camilla, I've been wanting to do this for so long," he murmured, his lips fluttering against hers. In a sudden, fluid movement he sank back against the blanket, pulling her down with him so that their bodies melded together. His arms tightened around her. "You feel wonderful. You feel perfect," he said huskily. "Camilla, I—damnation, what's the matter with you?" he gasped, as she shoved herself away from him.

She broke his hold and scrambled to her feet. As she tried to rearrange her disheveled hair with shaking fingers, he came up to her, extending his hand with several hairpins on his open palm. She snatched at the hairpins and began jabbing them haphazardly into her hair, finishing by jamming her straw bonnet onto her head.

Having watched her silently for several minutes, Jean at length said quietly, "What's wrong, Camilla?"

Her face flaming, she looked away. "You shouldn't have kissed me."

"Why not? I like kissing you. I thought you liked—"

She cut him off. "Jean, please listen to me," she said with a fierce intensity. "I don't want a lover. I don't want any romantic entanglements in my life. It's nothing to do with you, it's . . ." She shook her head. "I'd like to be your friend. I can't be anything else. If that's not enough . . ."

Jean stared at her for a long moment. Then he smiled. "Oh, it's enough, Camilla." He reached for her hand, bending his head to plant a soft kiss in her palm. The black eyes glinted with a dangerous light. "It's enough for now."

Chapter Eight

Jean muttered an extremely vulgar oath in French. "I prefer to arrange my own hair, Curtis."

"Yes, sir, of course, sir," said the valet soothingly. Standing behind Jean at the dressing table, Curtis produced, apparently out of thin air, a small pair of scissors, which he used to snip a fraction of an inch from a lock of hair on the crown of Jean's head. "There you are, sir. Quite perfect."

"You're sure of that, are you, Curtis?"

"Oh, indeed, sir. Now then, if you'll just stand up—"

The valet walked around Jean, examining every inch of the tall form, from the dark blue coat with the gilt buttons to the chaste waistcoat in white marcella to the tight-fitting white breeches and white silk stockings down to the shoes with their glittering buckles. Giving a satisfied nod, he handed Jean his bicorne hat and gloves. "You're attending Lady Ellington's ball tonight, I believe, sir?"

"Yes," said Jean morosely. "I can't say I'm looking forward to it. My friend, Mrs. Rayburn, tells me it will be a frightful squeeze."

The valet's face lighted up. "Oh, indeed, sir. I understand her ladyship always invites twice as many guests as her house will comfortably accommodate. The ball will certainly be one of the early successes of the Season."

Jean stared fixedly at the valet. It was a mystery to him how Curtis always seemed to have the latest *on dit* of the *ton* at his fingertips. "And you call that type of affair an enjoyable social occasion?"

Curtis looked shocked. "But sir, one doesn't attend these affairs to be *entertained*. One goes to be *seen*."

Dorcas nervously fingered the single strand of pearls that Camilla had insisted on loaning her. "I don't think I can go to the ball. I'm not feeling well."

Camilla looked closely at her sister. Dorcas did seem a little pale. "Do you have the headache?"

"Yes. No. Actually, it's my stomach. I have cramps." Dorcas glanced at the door of the drawing room. "Oh—Miles."

Miles stopped short on the threshold of the room. "Dorcas, you look so lovely," he breathed.

A soft blush suffused Dorcas's cheeks, matching the shade of her gown of pale pink silk gauze caught up at the hem with tiny bouquets of white roses. "You really think so?" she asked shyly.

"I know so. Hilliard," he appealed to Jean, who had just been ushered into the drawing room, "tell Dorcas how perfectly beautiful she looks."

Jean's eyes twinkled. "Was there any doubt of it? You'll put every other female in the shade," he assured Dorcas. "Except your sister, of course."

Camilla could feel the color mounting in her own cheeks. She hadn't been alone with Jean since he'd attempted to make love to her on the beach below Ashcombe Manor. She'd driven back to London in her godfather's carriage rather than in Jean's curricle, and, though he'd called on Park Street since their return from Kent, she'd made an excuse not to receive him. She needed more time before she saw him again. And she still hadn't decided whether to ask him about the whereabouts of the little lace cap he'd removed from her head on that occasion at the beach. She'd missed it when she returned to her bedchamber that evening. She was sure he had it, but it might be embarrassing to ask him about it, reviving unwelcome memories of that amorous interlude.

She studied Jean surreptitiously as he bantered with her

sister and Miles, remembering the shaggy-haired, badly dressed provincial she'd first met in Bath. No amount of careless grooming, of course, could really take away from the effect of those magnetic dark eyes, that handsome bronze-skinned face, the sinewy grace of that tall, powerful figure. But, while Jean had always been undeniably good-looking, now he was magnificent.

"Dorcas, I give you fair warning that I expect to have at least three dances with you," said Miles, as he helped her arrange a scarf of embroidered white China crepe around her shoulders.

"I promise I'll show you my card before I allow anyone else to scribble a mark on it," she said with a pleased smile. They went out the door arm in arm. Camilla shook her head. So much for Dorcas's indisposition of a few minutes ago, which obviously had been caused by nervous anxiety at the prospect of attending her first formal engagement of the London Season. Miles had made short work of *that*, thank goodness!

"A penny for your thoughts, Camilla."

Somewhat startled, she looked up to find Jean standing very close to her with her shawl of Lyons silk in his hands. "My thoughts aren't worth a penny," she said lightly. She took the shawl from him and draped it over her arms. "Shall we go? Miles and Dorcas are waiting."

"Why wouldn't you see me yesterday, Camilla?" he murmured as they walked down the front steps of the house. "I wanted to show you how diligently I've been practicing being friendly. That's what you wanted me to do, isn't it? Prove to you how much I wanted to be your friend, rather than your — er — lover."

Camilla broke into a laugh. "Jean, you wretch." The constraint she'd been feeling melted away.

"I aim to please." Jean squeezed her hand that he'd tucked under his arm.

Lady Ellington's ball was indeed a squeeze. It was difficult to pass from room to room, or to go up or down the stairs. Miles's fears of being cut out of Dorcas's company by eager dancing partners proved groundless. The rooms were so crowded that most people gave up on the idea of greeting their old friends, or of being introduced to new friends. Even so, Camilla observed that Jean's tall lithe darkness did not go unnoticed, especially by female eyes.

Only on the dance floor was there any freedom of movement. Camilla danced the first group of country dances with Jean. When she walked off the floor with him after a strenuous Scottish reel, she said breathlessly, "I had no idea you could dance so well, Jean."

"Well, now, I don't care to boast, but we French Canadians are famous for our dancing ability." He bent his head toward her, saying in a low voice, "I have other good points, too, that you haven't allowed me to touch upon."

Camilla shook her head, trying to look severe. "Jean, that's enough."

A laughing voice broke into their conversation. "Mrs. Rayburn, how pleasant to see you," said Lady Jersey. The pretty, elegant woman looked expectantly at Jean.

Camilla introduced the famed patroness of Almack's. "Lady Jersey, Mr. Hilliard."

"Oh, I've heard all about you, Mr. Hilliard," said Sally Jersey with an arch smile. "You're Lord Sheringham's heir, come all the way from Canada. Now, then, I simply must introduce you to some young ladies who would dearly love to know more about the colonies. And who, incidentally, are very good dancers!" She turned to Camilla. "Mrs. Rayburn, I assure you I'm not leaving you partnerless. Here's an old friend who very much wants to renew your acquaintance." Lady Jersey motioned to a man who had been standing behind her, unnoticed, a short distance away. She placed her hand on Jean's arm. "Come along, Mr. Hilliard," she said, ruthlessly propelling him away.

Camilla looked into the eyes of the man who had been standing behind Lady Jersey, and froze. "Sir Aubrey," she gasped.

He was a tall, slender man in his middle thirties, fair-haired, with thin, classically handsome features and very

120

light gray eyes that had all the warmth of sunlight on ice. He walked with a decided limp. Pausing in front of Camilla, he raked her with a long, intrusive stare from those cold gray eyes.

"Well, my dear Camilla, we meet again."

Camilla said between stiff lips, "I didn't know you'd come back to England. I thought you were still on the Continent."

"I returned to London from the Sublime Porte last week. Camilla, I want to talk to you. Alone."

"No. We've nothing to talk about."

"Oh, I beg to differ with you. We have a great deal to talk about. Fortunately Lady Jersey, dear old friend that she is, quite understood when I told her I wanted to be alone with you. Clever lady, she made it possible for us to have a *tête-à-tête* by getting rid of that swarthy-looking fellow who was monopolizing your company. Who is he, Camilla? Another of your devoted admirers?"

"Sir Aubrey, I don't wish to talk to you. Certainly not here. It's much too crowded."

Sir Aubrey Elvaston extended his hand to wrap his fingers around Camilla's wrist in an iron grip. "I've gone to a great deal of trouble to arrange a private place for our chat. I bribed one of Lady Ellington's footmen to persuade the card players to vacate the library, and then to lock the door after them and give me the key."

Without calling undesirable attention to herself, Camilla knew she couldn't engage in a public struggle to remove her wrist from Elvaston's vice-like fingers. "Please release my hand," she muttered. "I don't want to go with you."

"I fear you have little choice." Elvaston tucked her hand under his arm, retaining his grip on her wrist, and began walking slowly with her across the crowded dance floor to the door of the ballroom.

Camilla unwillingly went along with him. Sir Aubrey was right. If she wished to avoid the makings of a titillating scandal, she had no choice but to accompany him. After all, she reassured herself, nothing could really happen to her in Lady Ellington's library.

They proceeded very slowly through the crush of people coming up and down the staircase, and even more slowly along the crowded corridor on the ground floor leading to the library. Even under less crowded conditions, Camilla reflected, their progress would have been slow. Sir Aubrey's limp was so pronounced that he couldn't walk fast. The injury to his leg several years ago must have been far more serious than she'd realized.

Sir Aubrey unlocked the library door and ruthlessly shoved Camilla ahead of him into the room. As he turned to relock the door behind them, Camilla wrenched her arm away from him. She walked to the far side of the library and stood rubbing her wrist, which ached from the cruel pressure of Sir Aubrey's fingers.

"What do you want?" she demanded when he swung around to face her.

"At the moment, nothing. Merely the opportunity to chat. Later . . ." He shrugged. He was obviously enjoying himself. "Later, the possibilities are endless. We have a great deal of unfinished business between us, Camilla."

In a trembling voice, Camilla said, "We have nothing between us. After what happened that night three years ago, you can't believe that I'd want to see you, or have any contact with you, ever again."

The smile of malicious amusement left Elvaston's lips. "And *you* can't believe, my dear Camilla, that I'd allow you to escape the consequences of what you did to me." His mouth twisted as he looked down at his crippled leg. "You owe me a debt. I plan to collect it."

Camilla shrank back against the desk behind her. "You can't mean . . ."

"I mean exactly that. I want what you refused to give me three years ago. And this time, my dear, I promise you I won't go away empty-handed."

Someone pounded on the other side of the door, and rattled the door handle.

"Go away," Sir Aubrey called.

A familiar voice on the other side of the door growled,

"Camilla? Are you in there? Are you all right?"

"Dear, dear," said Sir Aubrey, lifting his eyebrows. "Would that be your swarthy-looking dancing partner, Camilla? He sounds quite solicitous, if a bit rough-mannered. Well, we don't wish for any unpleasant gossip, do we?" He limped slowly to the door, turned the key, and opened it.

Jean stormed into the library. He came to an abrupt halt when he observed that Camilla and Sir Aubrey were separated by the length of the room. "Has this fellow been annoying you, Camilla?" he asked, scowling.

Elvaston took out his quizzing glass and leisurely surveyed Jean through the lens. "My good man, you're quite abroad," he drawled. "There's no question of my 'annoying' Mrs. Rayburn. She and I are very old friends." He bowed to Camilla. "You'll be hearing from me soon, my dear."

As soon as the door had closed behind Elvaston, Jean walked over to Camilla, looking down at her with a troubled frown. "What's wrong? You're white as a ghost, and you're trembling as if you had the ague. Who is that fellow? I saw him practically drag you out of the ballroom, and as soon as I could escape from that witch of a woman—Lady Jersey, is that her name? Would you believe it, she wanted me to sign the dance cards of a regiment of females—I went down to the ground floor, looking into all the rooms, and then, finally, I came to this door, and it was locked."

"So, naturally, you pounded on it," said Camilla, trying not very successfully to smile. "It's nothing, Jean, really. Sir Aubrey Elvaston is a man I used to know, long ago. He was a friend of my husband. Sir Aubrey's in the diplomatic service, and some years ago he was posted to the Sublime Porte in Constantinople. I didn't know he was back in England, and to tell you the truth, I'd as lief he'd stayed in Turkey. As I said, he was Philip's friend. I—I never cared for him."

"That's it?" said Jean incredulously. "The man forces you into a room with him, locks the door, and it's nothing?"

Camilla struggled for control, and lost the contest. Her eyes filled with scalding tears, and she couldn't speak. When

123

Jean swept her into his arms, she relaxed against his broad chest, feeling the same vast, warm sense of comfort she'd felt years ago in her nanny's arms, when her old nurse had soothed some childish grief like her father's departure on another long sea voyage.

Gradually, however, as she grew calmer, she became aware of the enormous difference between Jean's embrace and old nurse's. There was no resemblance at all between Jean's hard, tautly muscled body and Nanny's billowy curves, and her nurse's heart had never pounded beneath her cheek with such an insistent, powerful beat.

Jean stirred, slipping one hand beneath her chin so that he could see her face. *"Camille, ma Camille, je ne te résiste pas,"* he whispered, and claimed her mouth in a hungry, devouring kiss while his arms tightened around her until their bodies melded together in an intimate joining. Every nerve in Camilla's body seemed to have come clamorously alive, and deep inside her she felt a throbbing sensation so acute that it was exquisitely, enticingly painful.

Still holding her closely, Jean at last lifted his head, his dark eyes glowing with a consuming flame. *"Je te désire,"* he said huskily. "Say it back to me, Camilla. You know French well enough. Tell me you want me—"

With his warm, clinging lips no longer holding her senses captive, Camilla's mind cleared. "No, Jean, let me go," she panted, trying to pull herself free.

His hold tightened. "Camilla, *chère,* you don't mean that—"

Panic set in. She fought him, flailing frantically at his chest with her fists. His arms fell away. They faced each other in a hard-breathing silence.

At last Jean said, "Are you going to tell me what this is about, Camilla?"

She swallowed hard. She felt drained and exhausted by the storm of powerful emotions that had swept over her since her first sight of Aubrey Elvaston earlier this evening: anger and fear, and an irrational ravening physical desire to be clasped on Jean's arms. She muttered, "I told you I didn't want—that—from you. I told you I just wanted to be friends." He moved slightly, inadvertently, and she warned him in a shaking voice, "Don't come near me, don't touch me."

Jean was pale with rage beneath the dark bronze of his skin. "Oh, I'm not going to force you," he said contemptuously. "I've never forced a woman in my life. But don't think you've fooled me, even if you've fooled yourself. I'm well aware you responded to me tonight. You responded to me the other times I've kissed you, too, at that inn on the Bath road, and a few days ago, at your godfather's villa. I've no idea why you blow hot and cold like this. You act like some virginal schoolgirl who's never felt a man's arm's around her before. But you've been married, Camilla. Didn't you let your husband touch you? Whatever your problem is, this I do know: tonight you wanted me as much as I wanted you."

Camilla gasped. Never in her life had anyone spoken to her so crudely, so hurtfully. Overwrought, past rational thought, she raised her hand and struck him as hard as she could across his face. "I wish I'd never met you. I never want to see you again."

Jean's eyes were blazing, but he made no move to come near her. Instead, not saying a word, he gave a jerky bow and strode out of the room.

Jean stirred. He had a throbbing headache, and something sharp was probing into his back. He was also very cold. He opened his eyes and looked about him groggily. In the faint light coming from the windows of the house behind him, he could see that he was lying in the gutter, half in, half out of the street. The sharp object at his back was a large rock.

He pulled himself up and sat on the curbing, his head in his hands, his elbows braced on his knees. He didn't know where he was, or how he'd gotten here. Gradually he began piecing together snatches of memory.

He'd left Lady Ellington's house in a mood of impotent

rage, bent on relieving in some way the physical and emotional pressures that had built up inside him. He needed a drink, first of all, but, though he walked up St. James's Street, past White's and Boodle's, clubs to which Miles Wingate had nominated him, he passed them by. Tonight he had no stomach for the likes of Camilla's aristocratic friends in the *ton*. Instead, he hailed a hackney cab and had himself taken to a gaming hell that Miles had specifically warned him against, on Jermyn Street.

He couldn't remember very much of what had happened in the gaming hell. As his dazed mind began to clear, he realized he was now sitting in the street directly in front of the establishment. He'd had some wine in the gaming club, quite a lot of wine, as a matter of fact, which shouldn't have been a problem. He had a very hard head for spirits. He'd gambled a bit. He recalled doing very well indeed with a main of eight. After that, however, his memories grew hazy, except for snatches of an intensely acrimonious altercation with one of the croupiers at the hazard table.

It was coming back to him now. He'd accused the croupier of using a pair of barred dice. Shortly after that, two of the pugilistic-looking employees of the gaming hell had dragged him out the door and had thrown him into the street. Jean reached into the pocket of his coat. His money case, of course, was gone.

Burying his face in his hands again, Jean began muttering disconsolately to himself in French. "Hellish, Godforsaken country. Why did I ever come here? Why didn't I stay in Canada, where people are civilized? England! If I could, I'd help Napoleon invade the damned place and bury it, including every sniveling, miserable member of the *ton*."

"I think you go a little too far, *mon ami*," said an amused voice in an oddly accented French.

Jean looked up to find a well-dressed gentleman bending over him. Wincing at the pain caused by the sudden movement of his head, he asked brusquely, "Who are you?"

The stranger smiled. "You might call me a friend in need, *monsieur*. It seems to me you are badly in need of friendly assistance."

Before Jean, still befogged, quite knew what was happening to him, the strange gentleman had directed his grooms to help Jean into a waiting town carriage. After a short drive, the same grooms helped Jean out of the carriage and up the steps of a substantial house. Later he learned that the house was in New Court, St. Swithin's Lane, a stone's throw from the Stock Exchange.

Over an hour later, after Jean had consumed innumerable cups of scalding hot coffee and a substantial supper of beefsteak and boiled oysters, he sat in a comfortable chair in what appeared to be a library or an office, gazing at his benefactor, who sat behind a large desk. His host was a man in his early thirties, red-haired, somewhat stout, thoroughly undistinguished in his appearance except for a pair of shrewd, intensely observant eyes.

"I'd like to thank you, sir, for rescuing me," Jean said, rather shamefacedly. "I was a fool to go to that gaming hell. A friend certainly advised me against it. I was robbed there, and I think I may have been drugged."

"Oh, almost certainly you were drugged, *monsieur*. The establishment is a notorious hell. So why, then, *did* you go there?"

Jean shrugged. "For a very stupid reason. I had a quarrel with — with someone."

"I see." There was little expression in the accented voice, but the shrewd eyes twinkled. "That sort of thing happens to all of us at times, especially when we're young. *Monsieur*, we haven't introduced ourselves."

"My name is Hilliard. Jean-Étienne Hilliard."

"Ah, Lord Sheringham's newly arrived heir from Canada."

"You know me?" Jean exclaimed in surprise.

"I know *of* you, *monsieur*. I know *of* a great many people in this city." The stranger smiled. "Judging by what you were saying when I found you in the gutter in front of that gambling den, you and I are kindred spirits. We live in London, but neither of us really feels a part of it. For myself, I'm not only a foreigner, I'm engaged in trade, and, worst of all, I'm Jewish. Permit me to introduce myself. My name is Nathan Rothschild."

Jean sat up straight, ignoring the protest from his aching head. "The banker to royalty?"

"Bankers, *mon ami*. I have numerous brothers, who are working in most of the capitals of Europe. You are interested in banking?"

"I'm interested in money," said Jean bluntly. "I wouldn't be in this infernal country today if I'd had more of it."

"Oh? And how was that?"

"Well . . . Do you know anything about the fur trade in Canada, *monsieur?*"

"A little. The Hudson's Bay Company has a monopoly of all the natural resources, including fur, in the area known as Rupert's Land, I believe."

"Exactly. So, when some cousins and I formed our own company several years ago, with the object of exploring opportunities in the fur trade in the Pacific Slope, farther west, we needed permission from the Hudson's Bay Company to cross the Hudson's Strait if we were to have any possibility of turning a profit. The Company refused. Its directors didn't want anyone interfering with their own plans for the area. Of course, our small company was only one of several fur trading concerns from Québec in the same predicament."

Nathan Rothschild said dryly, "I understand there was considerable violence on both sides. Burning of trading posts, armed clashes, that sort of thing. Very difficult to make a profit under those circumstances, I would think."

Jean eyed his host with respect. "You know a great deal, *monsieur.*"

"It's business. I make it a point to know about business. All kinds of business. You never know when odd bits of information might be useful."

Grinning, Jean said, "I wish there were more like you in this world, *monsieur.* Well, to get on with my story, my company was losing money, obviously. So when I heard unexpectedly that I was Lord Sheringham's heir, I came to England to see if I could raise money on my future prospects."

Rothschild nodded. "Most bankers would be willing to advance you money as Lord Sheringham's heir. His estates and his coal and iron properties are gilt-edged in value. But Mr. Hilliard, one day, perhaps fairly soon, you'll be Earl of Sheringham. Why would you want to borrow money on your inheritance to invest in Canada?"

"Because I intended to go back to Québec and live there permanently, even after I have succeeded to the title," Jean muttered, his face turning bleak. "I wasn't on good terms with the earl, and I didn't care for all those swells in what they call the *ton*. When I first came here, they treated me like—they actually called me—an uncouth Colonial. But then Cam—someone—persuaded me to stay on for a bit, to learn to know the country a little better."

"And?"

Jean glanced down at his stained, rumpled garments. "Well, as of tonight, I wouldn't call my efforts very successful." He rose, saying, "I won't intrude on you any longer at this hour, sir. Thank you for bringing me here. Otherwise, the Charleys might have found me, very dead, in the gutter in the morning."

The banker rose in turn. "I know your pockets are to let after your experience in the gaming hell. Allow me to lend you some money to hail a hackney. Or, better yet, let me send you home in my carriage." He extended his hand. "I like your spirit, Mr. Hilliard. We have a good deal in common, I think. Come back and see me. We might have supper one night."

"Thank you, I'd like that." Only half in jest, Jean said, "You wouldn't consider starting a branch bank in Montreal with me in charge, I suppose? I don't know anything about banking, of course, but I'm a quick learner, so my friends tell me."

Rothschild shook his head, smiling. "No offense meant, but I couldn't do that. For one thing, you're not Jewish. What's even more important, you're not a member of the

Rothschild family."

"I understand perfectly," Jean assured him. "When my cousins and I started up our company in Montreal, we thought long and hard before we admitted an outsider, a Scotsman named Cameron. Of course, his grandmother was French Canadian. That did make a difference."

Nathan Rothschild laughed outright. "Oh, I knew you were a man after my own heart. Come to supper on Friday."

Ten minutes later, Jean dismissed the Rothschild carriage and walked up the steps of Sheringham House. The porter who answered his knock stared at his disheveled state in speechless bewilderment. Jean ignored the man, brushing past him to go up the stairs to his bedchamber.

It was impossible to ignore Curtis. The valet took one all-encompassing look at Jean's stained breeches, laddered stockings, crumpled cravat and ripped coat and said with wounded dignity, "Really, sir, this is not at all what I'm accustomed to. I expended a great deal of time and effort and, yes, skill to turn you out properly tonight. May I ask, sir, if you intend to indulge frequently in the activities that have brought you to such a pass?"

But Jean had had enough of a disastrous evening. "I intend to indulge in any activities I see fit," he snapped. "If you don't approve, Curtis, feel free to find another employer."

Chapter Nine

On the morning after Lady Ellington's ball, Camilla's abigail said solicitously, as she was dressing her mistress's hair, "You don't look well, ma'am. Didn't you sleep well last night?"

Camilla peered into the mirror at the dark circles under her eyes. "No, I didn't sleep very well, Becky," she admitted. As a matter of fact, she wanted to deny sleeping at all, though she knew she must have dozed off periodically during the night. When she'd arrived home from Lady Ellington's ball, she'd felt exhausted, but her overly active mind had kept her awake by reviewing, repeatedly, the incidents of the evening, from her encounter with Aubrey Elvaston to that last shattering quarrel with Jean.

Aubrey Elvaston. His appearance at the ball had been such a shock. It shouldn't have been, she acknowledged. At some point, it was inevitable that Sir Aubrey would return to England from abroad, but she'd willfully blocked that realization from her consciousness. As long as she didn't have to see Sir Aubrey, or hear news of him, she could also block from her mind the terrible memories of the night that Philip died.

Camilla's thoughts shifted to Jean. After her unsettling meeting with Sir Aubrey, she'd felt such warmth, such comfort in Jean's arms. A few minutes later, she'd panicked, not so much because he'd kissed her, but because of her own swift, instinctive response to the pressure of his lips and arms. She was as much to blame as Jean for what had happened. Granted, he shouldn't have broken the pledge he'd made only days before, to keep their relationship within the bonds of friendship, but would any man have failed to misinterpret the shameless way she'd pressed against the hard contours of his body? What would happen now? Stiff-necked and independent as he was, would Jean be able to forgive the blow to his face and the affront to his pride? Did she want him to?

A light tap sounded at the door, and the abigail reported that Lord Sheringham had called to see Mrs. Rayburn.

Camilla sighed. She couldn't turn away Uncle Nigel, although, on this particular morning, she'd much prefer not to see him. She brushed a dusting of powder over the dark areas beneath her eyes, hoping for the best, and started down the stairs.

In the drawing room, the earl rose at her entrance. "My dear," he said in quick concern, "you don't look well."

"It's dissipation, not illness," said Camilla cheerfully. "Lady Ellington's ball lasted until all hours, and then Dorcas and I chatted until dawn." The last statement was an outright lie, of course. After a long look at Camilla's ravaged face, Dorcas had crept off to bed immediately after their return from the ball. "Do sit down, Uncle Nigel. Will you have some coffee, or a glass of wine?"

"Nothing, thank you. I called to inquire how you enjoyed your evening. You've already answered my question," said the earl, his eyes twinkling. After a moment, he added casually, "How about Jean? Did he enjoy the occasion, too? I saw him last night as he was leaving. He looked very impressive. Since you took him in hand, Camilla, I don't think there's a man in London who can match him for looks. Manners and poise are something else again, naturally, but I think he's learning. You don't agree?" he added, when Camilla didn't answer immediately.

"Oh—yes. Jean has a very quick mind. Uncle Nigel, there's something I think you should know. Jean and I quarreled last night."

"So?" The earl smiled indulgently. "What was it about this time? Some new aspect of the *ton* that he doesn't approve of?"

"It wasn't just another one of our tiffs. Jean was really angry. He left Lady Ellington's ball midway in the evening, and didn't come back, leaving poor Miles to escort both Dorcas and me home. Uncle Nigel, you know about my pact with Jean. He agreed to stay in England for the Season if I promised to guide him through what he calls the pitfalls of society. Well, now he may decide to break the pact. He may decide to return to Canada. I thought you ought to be prepared."

"I see." Lord Sheringham eyed Camilla thoughtfully. "Would you mind telling me what you quarreled about?"

"I—no." Camilla could feel her face growing hot. "It was—it was a personal matter."

"I see," said the earl again, compressing his lips. Apparently understanding the situation perfectly, he just as obviously swallowed his disappointment. He rose, hat and stick in hand. "Well, my dear, I won't keep you any longer this morning. Don't fret about what happened. What will be, will be. Either Jean will recover from his bad temper, or he won't. No blame attaches to you, in any event. I know you tried your best to be—ah—friendly with him."

After her godfather had left, Camilla wallowed in a slough of guilt. Of course she hadn't "tried her best." Otherwise she wouldn't have struck Jean with all the force of which she was capable. She doubted very much that he'd want to renew their "friendship" after that kind of humiliation, even if she apologized. And she wasn't sure she could, or should, apologize. Last night her emotions, which she'd guarded so carefully, so desperately, over the years, had been dangerously touched.

Her head was splitting. She went up to her bedchamber, where she amazed her abigail by returning to bed, with instructions that she was not to be disturbed. Camilla had never been one to take naps, but now all she wanted to do was to pull the coverlets over her head and escape the world.

She awoke several hours later, feeling considerably refreshed, and went downstairs to catch up on her correspondence. Nearing the bottom step of the staircase, she heard the sound of voices and a desultory series of chords from the pianoforte. Miles and Dorcas, she thought resignedly. With his usual tact, Miles hadn't asked any questions last night, when she'd been in such obvious emotional distress, but he'd have been less than human if he hadn't felt curious about Jean's sudden departure from Lady Ellington's ball.

Camilla squared her shoulders. Miles was an old friend, and she owed him some kind of explanation. She walked into the drawing room, and stopped short. "You!" she exclaimed in dismay. It wasn't Miles at the pianoforte, looking up at Dorcas with a charming smile as his long fingers stroked the keys.

At the sound of Camilla's voice, Aubrey Elvaston rose from the bench of the pianoforte and walked over to her. As she watched him approach her, she noticed, in a detached corner of her brain, that, though he limped badly, he was still oddly graceful in his movements. He reached for her nerveless hand and raised it to his lips.

"My dear Mrs. Rayburn, I was desolated to hear from your abigail that you were indisposed. I'm delighted to find you feeling more the thing."

"Thank you. I feel very well," said Camilla woodenly. Dorcas's presence prevented her from snatching her hand too demonstratively from Sir Aubrey's grasp.

"You can imagine my disappointment when it appeared I wouldn't have the pleasure of seeing you," Sir Aubrey went on in the blandly pleasant tones that were so at odds with the chilliness of the gray eyes. "I think we both felt that our talk last night at Lady Ellington's ball was too brief and unsatisfying. However, I very nearly forgot my disappointment when your sister made me feel so welcome." He smiled at Dorcas. "I'm ashamed to admit I'd quite forgotten about your existence, Miss Vernon. After all, you were still a schoolgirl when I knew Mrs. Rayburn."

"Oh, Camilla, it must bring back such wonderful memories to see Sir Aubrey again after all these years," exclaimed Dorcas. "He's been telling me about his friendship with you and Philip, how close you all were, how much time you spent together." Her eyes filmed with moisture. "You and Sir Aubrey were the two people who loved your husband the best in all the world, and I was so touched to hear how you comforted each other when poor Philip died so tragically."

Sir Aubrey said cheerfully, "Fortunately, Miss Vernon, most of my memories of Philip are happy ones." He turned to Camilla. "Do remember the time he challenged me to a point-to-point race for two? We nearly broke our necks, the both of us."

"I also remember you won a very handsome sum from Philip that day," said Camilla coolly. "Five hundred guineas, wasn't it?"

"Alas. Poor Philip." Sir Aubrey shook his head. "He had so many wonderful traits, but he wasn't a very lucky gambler, was he?"

"Camilla!" said Dorcas excitedly, as if she'd been holding her tongue for some time while the others chatted. "The most interesting coincidence! Sir Aubrey is as great an admirer of Mr. Mozart as I am. He's invited us to the Italian Opera House on Saturday to hear Mme. Catalani sing in *Così fan tutte.* Do say we can go!"

Camilla looked closely at her sister. Normally so quiet and sedate and lacking in self-confidence, to the point of appearing actually colorless, this Dorcas was an entirely different person. Her eyes were sparkling, her face was animated, and she was speaking without a trace of her usual shyness. Camilla felt chilled. She'd forgotten how magnetically charming Aubrey Elvaston could be when he chose to exert himself, especially when the object of his attentions was an inexperienced young girl.

Camilla took a deep breath. "No, we can't go to the opera," she told Sir Aubrey coldly. "We have another engagement for Saturday. And no," she added, as he opened his mouth to speak, "we can't accept your invitation for any other evening. Our social calendar is completely filled. But thank you very much for thinking of us."

"Oh, come now, Mrs. Rayburn," Sir Aubrey said with an easy confidence. "Surely you can find time for a single evening at the opera. I know you wouldn't wish to disappoint Miss Vernon."

He was forcing her hand, or trying to. Spurred by a growing anger, Camilla said, "Listen to me very carefully, Sir Aubrey. I won't attend the opera with you, nor will I accept any other kind of invitation from you. What's more, I don't wish to see you under any circumstances. If you call on Park Street in the future, you'll be turned away."

"Camilla!" Dorcas protested. "How can you be so rude to an old friend?"

"Dorcas, please leave the room. I wish to speak to Sir Aubrey privately."

Dorcas gasped, turning a bright red, and rushed blindly from the drawing room to the muffled sound of sobs.

"That wasn't very kind of you, Camilla," Sir Aubrey observed. "Or very wise, either. How are you going to explain to your sister why you treated an old friend like me so cavalierly?"

"That's my affair," said Camilla curtly. "Please go, Sir Aubrey. I made it perfectly clear to you last night that I wanted nothing to do with you."

"And I thought I'd made it perfectly clear to *you* that we had a score to settle," snapped Sir Aubrey. "You owe me, Camilla. You can pay your shot quickly and easily by granting me one assignation, at a time and a place of your own choosing. You can be as discreet as you like. I promise you that would be the end of it. You see, my dear, whatever attraction you once had for me is gone. Now all I want is simple justice."

"The answer is no. And please go. I never want to see you again."

"You really think you can get rid of me so easily? In the end, you'll give me what I want."

"You must be mad," said Camilla contemptuously, "if you think you can force me to sleep with you."

"Mad? No, not at all. Don't forget, there are many different varieties of 'force.' For example, I fancy you'd react quite strongly if rumors of past sexual misconduct with me started surfacing among your friends."

Stiffening, Camilla exclaimed, "You wouldn't—no one would believe such rumors."

"No? Are you so sure? At the very least, there'd be questions, whispers, innuendos."

"Don't forget, the rumors would affect you, too."

Elvaston laughed. "Why should I care if I'm labeled a loose fish? It certainly wouldn't affect *my* social life. But you, my dear. Ah, that's a different story. You're so proud of your reputation, aren't you, Camilla? The always virtuous Mrs. Rayburn." Elvaston laughed again at the sudden pinched expression on Camilla's face. "Well, we'll see. Scandalous rumor-mongering isn't the only arrow I have to my bow. I have other ideas, also. You'll come around, my dear. Count on it."

"Get out," Camilla said in a strangled voice. "I'm sorry now I didn't kill you that time in—"

She broke off at the sound of a familiar voice in the hallway.

"That's all right, Lizzie, I'll announce myself," Jean told Camilla's maid of all work as he strolled into the drawing room. He paused, glancing from Camilla to Elvaston with narrowed eyes. At last he said with a dangerous politeness, "I trust I'm not intruding?"

Elvaston lifted his quizzing glass to stare at Jean with the same supercilious contempt he'd displayed the night before. " 'Pon my word, Camilla, have you hired yourself a bodyguard? Isn't this the same fellow who interrupted our conversation at Lady Ellington's ball?"

Jean made a quick, instinctive forward movement, and Camilla caught at his arm. "Jean, please. No, you weren't intruding. And Sir Aubrey is just leaving."

Elvaston repeated thoughtfully, "Jean . . . Jean . . ." He snapped his fingers. "Ah. I have it. This is Hilliard, Lord Sheringham's Colonial heir." He remarked to Camilla with a sneering smile. "Light dawns. Not a bodyguard. Oh, very definitely, not a bodyguard. More of a domestic convenience, shall we say?" He bowed. "We'll meet again soon, my dear. Be sure of that. My compliments to your pretty little sister." He limped to the door, passing by Jean without a glance.

Jean's body was rigid, and his dark eyes were shooting sparks. He muttered a phrase under his breath.

"What did you say?"

Jean relaxed, grinning. "You wouldn't want to know. It would offend your delicate ears. That was Montreal street French. Fur traders' French. Camilla, what did that fellow Elvaston want? And don't tell me he was just paying you a visit."

Looking away, Camilla said, "There's no need for you to be concerned, Jean. The situation is quite simple. Sir Aubrey would like to renew our old acquaintance. I've refused his request. Unfortunately, he's a very persistent man. However, I think I may have convinced him at last. I've just informed him that under no circumstances will I ever receive him in this house again."

Clenching his fists, Jean exclaimed, "Just say the word, I'll beat him to a pulp. I've never seen you so distressed . . ." He caught his breath, looking suddenly guilty. "Yes, I *have* seen you that distressed, and it was my doing. Camilla, I've come to apologize for last night. Not for kissing you," he added defiantly. "That was an accident. I never planned it, but when it happened I enjoyed every second of it. No, I'm apologizing for what I said to you. I was stupid and boorish and unkind, and I didn't take into account how much that Elvaston court card had overset you."

Camilla said impulsively, "I'm sorry, too. I shouldn't have slapped you." For the first time, she noticed the purpling contusion on his right cheekbone. "Jean," she exclaimed in horror. "Your face is all bruised. I couldn't have hit you that hard."

"No, you didn't," he said hastily.

"But, then, how — ?"

"It's of no consequence. Camilla, does this mean we can be friends again? Just friends. Friendly friends," he added awkwardly, when she hesitated to reply.

"Yes," said Camilla at last, and wondered why she felt such a surge of reassurance and contentment.

"Bon. Grâce à Dieu," murmured Jean, reverting, as he so often did in moments of emotion, to his native French. His face lighted up with a smile. "Now we can be comfortable again. What shall we do today to celebrate making up our quarrel?"

"Oh, Jean, I can't go anywhere today. Dorcas and I have calls to make, and after that we'll be preparing for Mrs. Armbruster's rout this evening. You're invited to that, too, you know."

"Zut," said Jean inelegantly. "You can call on all those ladies tomorrow, or next week. Do you know what I'd really like to do today? I'd like to take you to a village fair. Something ordinary and common, like me. Henry—he's one of Lord Sheringham's footman, and a very good sort, too— has been telling me about the annual fair at Blackheath, which is being held now. Henry says it's always well worth attending. I tell you what, Camilla, if you won't go to this fair with me, I do believe I'll take Henry."

Camilla burst out laughing. "Oh, well, I can't allow myself to be cut out by Henry, can I? Very well, Jean, I'll go to the fair with you."

After Jean had left, looking smugly pleased with himself, and promising to return early that afternoon, Camilla reflected with considerable amusement how like him it was to strike up a friendship with one of her godfather's footmen. Probably Jean had never given a second thought to the difference in rank between "Henry" and the heir to an earldom.

Her amusement died away as her thoughts shifted to her problem with Aubrey Elvaston. She still felt chilled by his threats to force her into an assignation with him, but her fears, and her revulsion, were gradually fading. What, after all, could he do to make good on those threats? If he spread scandalous rumors about her, the stories might possibly be believed by some people, although she fancied her social credit would carry her through the worst of such gossip. However, once the rumors had been circulated, and either believed or disbelieved, that weapon would be useless to Sir Aubrey. After that, what further harm could he do? Very little, she told herself reassuringly, provided she stayed on her guard and avoided all contact with him.

More pressing, she decided, as she started up the staircase, was her problem with Dorcas. She must mend fences with her sister, whose feelings had probably been severely wounded. Camilla tapped lightly on the door of Dorcas's bedchamber.

"Yes?"

"It's Camilla. May I speak with you?"

After a considerable wait, Dorcas called, "Come in."

When Camilla entered the room, Dorcas was sitting in a chair by the window. Her eyelids were puffed and swollen.

"Dorcas, I'm very sorry if I was rude to you. I shouldn't have ordered you out of the drawing room like that."

"Well, it's your house, isn't it? I daresay you can do as you like in it," said Dorcas bitterly. "I must say, though, that it's one thing to treat me like a naughty child, even though I'm a grown woman. After all, I'm merely your sister. It's quite another to order your dead husband's oldest friend out of your house, as if he were no better than a — a tradesman, or a pedlar! Camilla, how could you do such a thing?"

Camilla mentally counted to ten. Dorcas wasn't a little girl any more, inclined to accept everything her older sister said at face value. And yet Camilla couldn't possibly tell her the truth. Camilla said cautiously, "It's true, Sir Aubrey was a close friend of Philip. However, I never cared for him, and now that Philip's gone I see no reason to continue the friendship. You'll agree, won't you, that I have a right to choose my friends?"

"Oh, of course, but there's also such a thing as common courtesy. Why was it necessary to be so unpleasant to Sir Aubrey? Did he do something to offend you all those years ago? If so, it couldn't have been a very serious matter, since he seems to have only the most pleasant memories of those times. Camilla, Sir Aubrey wants so much to remain your friend. Couldn't you meet him halfway? At least allow him to call?"

"No," snapped Camilla. "I don't like Sir Aubrey, and I won't have him in my house."

Dorcas tossed her head. "Well, I *do* like him. I think he's utterly charming. And you'll agree, won't you, that I, too, have a right to choose my friends?"

Reining in her temper, Camilla said, "Dorcas, let's not quarrel, certainly not about Aubrey Elvaston. Look, Jean Hilliard has asked me to go to the fair in Blackheath with him this afternoon. Wouldn't you like to go with us?"

"No, thank you," replied Dorcas stonily. "And I must say, in view of your treatment of Sir Aubrey, that I'm surprised you can excuse Mr. Hilliard's behavior so readily. He left us at Lady Ellington's house last night without a word of explanation. Miles says that no other gentleman of his acquaintance would have been guilty of such rudeness!"

Throwing up her hands, Camilla left the room before she could say something she'd later regret. Never in their lives had she and Dorcas been more out of charity.

She was still feeling depressed from her set-to with Dorcas when Jean arrived several hours later in his curricle, with one of Lord Sheringham's smaller and younger grooms acting as the customary tiger.

"What's the matter?" Jean asked casually, as he put the team in motion. He turned his head slightly to glance at the groom, sitting stiff and immobile behind them on his perch. Lowering his voice, he said, "You look a trifle blue-deviled. You haven't changed your mind about us, have you?"

"Oh, no. I had a little tiff with Dorcas, that's all."

"Is that all?" Jean looked relieved. "Oh, well, don't worry about it. Dorcas will come around." He settled down to his driving.

As they passed along Piccadilly toward Westminster, Camilla took a long look at Jean's left cheekbone, which was now changing from purple to black, and said, also keeping her voice low, "How *did* you bruise your face, if I'm not responsible?"

"Well—uh—if you must know, I drank blue ruin until I was castaway, and then I got thrown out of a gaming establishment," said Jean sheepishly. "Not White's or Boodle's. A hell that Wingate warned me not to go into. He was right, confound him."

"Jean! You could have been killed, or robbed, at the very least."

"I *was* robbed, actually. And then the oddest thing happened." Jean's voice quickened with interest. "A complete stranger bundled me into his carriage, took me to his home and pushed coffee and food into me until I started to feel more the thing. Not foxed any more, just a bit on the go. Camilla, you'll find this hard to credit, but the man was Nathan Rothschild!"

"The merchant banker? I've heard of him. He came to England from Germany some years ago, I believe. Isn't he supposed to be fabulously wealthy? I've heard he's made loans to important people like the Prince of Wales."

"Good God, Camilla, he's not merely a banker, he's a financier. The man, or his brothers, have made loans to royalty all over Europe! He's a fascinating person, the most interesting man I've ever met since I came to England. And would you believe it, he's asked me to dinner next week!"

Jean looked so pleased and impressed at the invitation that Camilla suppressed the remark that had been on the tip of her tongue. She and Jean had just made up their differences. There'd be time enough later to suggest to him—oh, discreetly, of course—that he should cultivate friends from among his own class, not among foreigners of Jewish extraction, no matter how wealthy or successful such people might be in business.

Jean drove across Westminster Bridge and along the London to Dover road until he reached the vicinity of Shooter's Hill, where he turned off, at the groom's direction, into a road leading to a large open tableland. The normally empty hearth was crowded with people and lined around its perimeter with a bewildering variety of booths. Leaving the curricle in the care of the groom, Jean and Camilla strolled arm in arm through the crowd, which seemed to be a mixed one, composed mostly of soberly dressed farmers and townspeople, with a sprinkling of rougher and more sinister-looking elements.

Rather to her surprise, Camilla found herself enjoying the fair. The rope dancers and jugglers and puppet shows revived memories of her childhood, when her father, on his infrequent shore leaves, had taken her and Dorcas to itinerant carnivals. Even the booths selling toys and gimcracks were fascinating, simply because they were so different from the fashionable shops she normally patronized. At one booth Jean bought her a knot of ribbon to match one of her gowns, and he insisted on buying her a particularly ugly doll, a "Blackheath doll," which, according to the vendor, was an absolutely necessary purchase for everyone attending the fair.

Camilla was vastly amused to watch Jean as he flung himself into the festivities. Showing her a side of himself that she'd never seen before, he was like a child, uninhibited in his enjoyment. He laughed until the tears ran down his cheeks at the antics of the puppets in the Punch and Judy show. He was fascinated by the conjuror who miraculously produced red apples from a desiccated branch. He kept muttering, "It's a trick—I know it's a trick," as he stared, mesmerized, at the educated horse that could distinguish the value of one bank note from another. Camilla had to remind him of the lateness of the hour more than once before he reluctantly agreed it was time to go.

The crowd was still so dense that Camilla was jostled several times by inebriated adults or boisterous children as she and Jean walked toward the outer reaches of the heath and the waiting curricle. It was also difficult to see more than a few feet ahead into the crowd, so it came as a complete surprise, when they finally reached the curricle, to find their groom sprawled unconscious beside the carriage and a roughly dressed individual in the act of driving off the vehicle.

With an oath, Jean rushed forward. He reached up a long arm to drag the would-be thief from the driving seat, and chopped such a tremendous blow to the man's jaw that he dropped motionless to the ground.

"Jean! Behind you," screamed Camilla.

Instantly Jean whirled. He was a split second too late to avoid the knife in the hand of the man who had crept quietly up behind him. The glittering weapon slashed against Jean's arm as he lurched desperately to the side, trying to avoid his opponent. Then, in one quick, violent movement, Jean turned and smashed his booted foot into his attacker's groin. The man doubled up, groaning in agony, as his knife slipped out of his hand.

Jean stood poised, waiting for an offensive move from either of his assailants, but it was obvious that both men were out of action for the immediate future. After checking on the injured groom, who was already sitting up, groaning, Jean turned to Camilla, saying cheerfully, "Well, Miles Wingate and Gentleman Jim Jackson wouldn't approve of my tactics in that fight, I daresay. They're always talking about something called 'the Marquess of Queensberry' rules. No kicking, especially in — er — sensitive spots. Neither of them would survive five minutes in a Montreal street brawl, let me tell you. Why, Camilla, what is it?" he asked in alarm, as he noticed her ashen face. "Those thugs didn't touch you, did they?"

She pointed at his arm, saying in a shaking voice, "Your sleeve is cut. And you're bleeding."

Glancing quickly at his torn sleeve, Jean laughed. "It's just a graze. Nothing serious. But my eye and Betty Martin, that valet of mine will have my hide for this. It's the second coat I've ruined in two days. Curtis takes a very dim view of gentlemen who engage in fisticuffs."

Weak-limbed with relief, Camilla slumped against the side of the curricle. "Jean, you could easily have been killed."

Jean caught her up in his arms and held her tight. "You shouldn't ever worry about me, *ma petite,*" he murmured against her hair. "I'm indestructible. I'm a French Canadian, remember?"

Camilla felt the familiar shiver of delight at Jean's touch, and for a moment she leaned against him. Then, as she made a halfhearted effort to push him away, he released her instantly. He looked down at her, his dark eyes glinting with amusement. He didn't say a word. He didn't have to. But she knew he was perfectly aware that she'd responded once again to the pull of the powerful sensual current flowing between them.

Chapter Ten

Jean, and Nathan Rothschild rose politely from their chairs at the dining table as Mrs. Rothschild, a dark, quietly pretty woman, prepared to leave them to their port.

"It was a wonderful meal, Mrs. Rothschild," said Jean. "I especially enjoyed those triangle-shaped sweets with the poppy seed filling."

His hostess smiled gravely. *"Hamentaschen,"* she said. "I'm happy they pleased you."

"It's such a pleasure for us that you were able to join us for an informal meal, Mr. Hilliard," said Rothschild, seating himself after his wife had left the room. He poured Jean a glass of port. Gazing at his guest over the rim of his glass, he commented, "You appear more at peace with the world than you did at our last meeting."

Jean broke into a grin. "At least I can say I haven't been thrown out of any more gaming hells."

"That's an improvement, certainly. What about your tentative plans to return to Canada? Have you come to any decision about that?"

"Well . . . No. I promised Cam—I promised a member of the family that I'd remain in London until the end of the Season. It's possible, I suppose, that I might decide to stay on after that. That is to say, I might do so if my personal—er—wishes come to anything."

"I see," said Rothschild, politely ignoring the befuddled ambiguity of Jean's reply. "I did wonder about your future plans, because I recently made it a point to inquire into the affairs of the Hudson's Bay Company. I've learned that their solicitors have advised the directors of the company to change their tactics against their competitors in Canada. The solicitors have suggested that, instead of suing companies like yours for breach of monopoly of the fur trade, the Hudson's Bay Company should prosecute for trespass of their territory. Personally, I believe this change in tactics will be very successful. For what my opinion is worth, Mr. Hilliard, I'd say that all the small fur trading companies in Canada will soon be out of business."

Jean drew a deep breath. "I'd begun to suspect as much," he confessed. "Well, I'll have to look into other business opportunities, won't I?" He began to laugh. "What a shame it is that smuggling, by its very definition, is against the law! Doubtless I could make a very good thing of it, taking a boat across the Channel from the fishing village near Lord Sheringham's Kentish villa, coming back with a profitable load of brandy or silks or tobacco, everything made easy for me on the other side by my cousin in the French customs. Oh, if I had a criminal bent, I could make a fortune!"

Jean paused as he noticed how intently Rothschild was staring at him. "Is something amiss, sir?"

"No, no," said Rothschild hastily. "It was just that I didn't realize you had relatives in France. I thought your people had lived in Canada for generations."

Having explained about his scapegrace Uncle Pierre and his enforced move from Canada to France, Jean added, "Apparently my uncle and his family have prospered in France, which has put my poor mother, who's very strait-laced, into a dilemma. On the one hand, she can't but rejoice that her brother has done well, but she also thinks he ought to have suffered a little bit of punishment, at least, for his ne'er-do-well behavior."

Rothschild burst into a hearty laugh. "Mothers! Oh, I know all about mothers. Mine is the most redoubtable lady in all of Frankfurt." He added casually, "What put the idea of smuggling in your head?"

Looking blank for a moment, Jean said with a laugh, "Oh, I was visiting Lord Sheringham's villa near Folkestone not long ago, and someone mentioned that most of the local fishermen were also smugglers. I suggested to my friends—just as a joke, you understand—that I might try to take passage with one of the smugglers in order to visit my French cousins."

Pulling out his watch, Jean glanced at it and rose, saying, "I mustn't keep you from your bed until all hours. Thank you for the supper and the good conversation, Mr. Rothschild. Perhaps you'll allow me to return the hospitality? I don't have a house of my own, but I do belong to White's and Boodle's. Will you have dinner with me one night soon at either of those clubs?"

"I'd be delighted, Mr. Hilliard." Rothschild gave Jean a quizzical glance. "Have you considered, however, that I might not be especially welcome to your aristocratic friends in those clubs? I'm in trade, you know. Even worse, I'm Jewish!"

Jean's face turned cold. "I can only say, Mr. Rothschild, that if *you* aren't welcome as my guest at White's, then they've seen the last of me, also."

Camilla resolutely kept her eyes away from the clock on the mantel. She couldn't give offense to Mrs. Tolliver by hinting that the hour was late, even though all her other callers had left a good ten minutes ago. *Why* was Mrs. Tolliver lingering, making meaningless small talk?

The Honorable Mrs. Augustus Tolliver, a handsome, stolid woman whose husband had inherited a substantial fortune, and whose eldest daughter was making her coming out this year, finally started nibbling around the edges of her concern, which turned out to be, to Camilla's astonishment, the person of Jean Hilliard.

"You've been seeing a great deal of Mr. Hilliard, I understand," said Mrs. Tolliver in an offhand tone that didn't deceive Camilla in the least.

"Why, yes, my godfather has asked me to introduce Mr. Hilliard to my friends. He arrived here from Canada a complete stranger, you know."

"Oh, of course. He *is,* truly, Lord Sheringham's heir?"

"Truly," said Camilla solemnly.

"Mr. Hilliard is a fine-looking man. So handsome. So distinguished in appearance."

"Yes, isn't he?"

Mrs. Tolliver coughed. "I – ah – some of my friends and I have heard rumors that Mr. Hilliard is – er – not entirely of English blood."

"That's quite true. His father was English, but his mother was French Canadian." Camilla was quite enjoying herself now. Mrs. Tolliver was digging for information, and Camilla was going to make her work to obtain every last shred of it.

"Oh, but I believe I've also heard that Mr. Hilliard is – er – related to – to natives of Canada?"

"Indeed. His grandmother was a Cree Indian. The daughter of a tribal chief, I believe."

Mrs. Tolliver brightened. "In effect, a native princess, one might say?"

Camilla considered the question. "Yes, I think one might say that. Like the Indian Princess Pocahontas, you know, so long ago."

Mrs. Tolliver doggedly pursued the subject. "I've heard that Mr. Hilliard is the last of his line."

"That's true. Mr. Hilliard is Lord Sheringham's only remaining heir. If Mr. Hilliard were to die tomorrow, the earldom of Sheringham would become extinct on the death of my godfather."

"Ah." Mrs. Tolliver breathed deeply. "So Mr. Hilliard must have issue. He *must* marry." She shifted her gaze, looking down at her fingers, toying with the beaded

149

fringes of her reticule. "Dear Mrs. Rayburn, one doesn't wish to pry, but, according to the *on dit, you* might be considering marrying Mr. Hilliard."

The sheer vulgarity of the remark made Camilla temporarily speechless. After a moment, she said coldly, "The rumors are quite false. Mr. Hilliard and I have never discussed marriage."

A gleam of gratification faded from Mrs. Tolliver's face as she realized, dimly, that she'd made a social gaffe. Shortly afterward, she took her leave.

Camilla remained in her chair in the drawing room, gazing down at her clenched hands, wondering why she was so annoyed. Obviously, Mrs. Tolliver was on the prowl in the marriage mart. It would be a great feather in her cap if her eldest daughter succeeded in snaring the heir to an earldom, an earldom, moreover, which was one of the oldest in the kingdom, and which carried with it an immense fortune. Few in the *ton* would question Mrs. Tolliver's interest in Jean as a possible husband for her daughter. That being the case, why would she, Camilla, care if Mrs. Tolliver was out to capture Jean as her son-in-law?

Unless . . . But no, that was ridiculous. She was *not* jealous. Jean was welcome to marry anyone he wished. She'd certainly made it clear enough to him and to everyone that *she* wasn't interested in a romantic relationship with him.

"You're looking very thoughtful today, Camilla."

She looked up in confusion to find Jean standing in front of her. She'd been so lost in her reverie that she hadn't heard the maid announce him. He smiled at her, but he didn't take her hand in greeting. In fact, since their latest reconciliation, he'd gone out of his way to avoid any physical contact. But now, as always, there was a gleam in his dark eyes when he looked at her, a gleam that signaled his feelings quite plainly.

"Did I look thoughtful? I fear I was only woolgathering," Camilla said hastily, ruing the quick flood of color she could feel spreading across her cheeks. "Do sit down, Jean."

As he took a chair, he said in a bemused tone, "I just had the queerest experience. I was handing my reins to my groom in front of your house when I noticed a lady who was about to get into her town carriage. She came right over to me, greeting me like an old friend, and mentioning how much Dulcie had enjoyed her dances with me. I don't recall ever meeting the woman. And Dulcie! Who on earth is Dulcie?"

Camilla felt an incomprehensible little bubble of joy explode inside her. "That was Mrs. Tolliver," she told Jean. "I believe you met her at Lady Middlemarch's ball last week. Dulcie is her daughter."

"Oh." Jean looked puzzled. "What has that to say to anything?"

"Jean, I must tell you that you're about to become the prime catch in this season's marriage mart. Every fond mama of a pretty daughter—and some that aren't so pretty!—will soon have her eyes fixed on you! You'd best prepare your defenses, if you don't choose to be leg-shackled."

Jean's dark brows drew together in a frown. "Why would anyone think I was looking for a wife?"

"Oh, Jean! With your prospects as Uncle Nigel's heir, with your good looks . . ." Camilla's words remained frozen on her lips at the sudden flash of anger that crossed Jean's face.

"Lord Sheringham, ma'am."

Camilla looked up with relief as her godfather entered the drawing room. The air in the room had suddenly become charged with strong emotion.

If her ever-perceptive godfather noticed any constraint in the atmosphere, he chose to ignore it. "I'm sorry to be a little late," he apologized. "I've just come from Montague House. As you probably remember, Camilla, I'm a trustee of the Museum. Well, now, my dear, if you'll produce pen and paper, we can get down to planning our dinner."

A few minutes later, Camilla sat staring in dismay at the long list of names on the sheet of paper in front of her. "Uncle Nigel, is your heart set on hosting a dinner? Your dining room's an enormous one by any standard, but you can seat only thirty at the most. How can we possibly choose from among all those people which guests to invite? We'll risk offending some of your oldest friends. Wouldn't it be better to entertain at a rout, or possibly a musical evening, so that we could have a larger guest list?"

"No," said the earl firmly. "I want this dinner to be an exclusive affair, to introduce my heir to the cream of London society. A few members of the Cabinet. The leading hosts and hostesses, of the *ton*." He smiled at Jean. "Several directors of the East India Company and the Hudson's Bay Company, to reflect your interests, my boy. And"—the earl's voice became dramatic—"I have hopes that the Prince of Wales will attend. I talked to His Royal Highness several days ago. He assured me he would do his best to clear his engagement calendar for that date."

Looking acutely uncomfortable, Jean broke into Lord Sheringham's remarks. "Sir, I had no idea you were planning such a grand occasion. When you told me you were giving a dinner to introduce me to your friends, well, that was one thing. But cabinet ministers! The Prince of Wales! Next you'll be telling me that the king himself is coming! Please reconsider. I'd feel like a fish out of water at such an affair. You seem to forget I'm just a Canadian fur trader."

"You're the heir to the earldom of Sheringham, and I want everyone to know the importance I attach to your presence here," said the earl sharply.

Jean subsided, though still looking extremely disgruntled, and Lord Sheringham and Camilla settled into a marathon scrutiny of the preliminary guest list.

"Uncle Nigel, if we have Lord and Lady Jersey, I don't

think we need invite the Lievens," said Camilla at one point. "It isn't necessary to include *all* the hostesses of Almack's, after all! And besides, I've never liked Countess Lieven. I'd as lief not be in her company for an entire evening!"

An hour later, the earl rose from his chair, saying, "Thank you, Camilla. Our final list seems quite satisfactory. You'll attend to the invitations, then?"

Before Camilla could answer, Jean broke a lengthy silence. "I say, sir, I'd like to invite two of my friends to this dinner."

Appearing slightly surprised, the earl answered with his customary polished politeness, "Why, certainly, Jean. Camilla and I will simply remove two names from our list and substitute the names of your friends. Er—who are they? Do I know them?"

"I have no idea. Are you acquainted with the merchant banker, Nathan Rothschild? And his wife, of course."

Lord Sheringham's fabled sangfroid showed sign of cracking. "Er—no. I haven't had the pleasure."

Without stopping to weigh her words, Camilla said quickly, "Jean, do you think Mr. and Mrs. Rothschild would fit into the company? Perhaps we could invite them another time—" She broke off at the sudden frozen look that appeared on Jean's face. At the same time, she observed her godfather's warning shake of the head.

"I think it's a splendid idea to invite your own personal friends to my dinner, Jean," Lord Sheringham said suavely. "I look forward, as a matter of fact, to meeting Mr. Rothschild. I've heard a great deal of him. I believe he's actually had dealings with the Prince of Wales."

"Sir, won't you try once more?"

Jean glanced at the piles of crumpled neckcloths that littered the floor around his dressing table. "In the fiend's name, Curtis," he said to his valet, "I've tried at least a dozen times to tie your blasted—what do you call it?—oh, yes, the Mahratta knot, and I'm at a stand. Why is it so important to you? And another thing." Jean looked down at his waistcoat of striped marcella. "Where did this thing come from? I don't recall ever seeing it before."

Curtis coughed delicately. "I took the liberty, sir, of ordering a new waistcoat from your tailor in honor of the occasion. As for the Mahratta knot, I do believe it will add the crowning touch to your toilet. It's not everyone, I assure you, sir, who can tie a Mahratta knot."

Jean darted a truculent look at his valet. "Enlighten me, Curtis. Why should I take special pains with my appearance tonight?"

"Why, sir. Tonight his lordship is officially introducing you to London society as his heir at a *very* exclusive dinner."

Muttering a curse under his breath, Jean turned his attention back to the mirror of his dressing table as he renewed his struggle with his cravat. He'd long suspected that the valet knew more about the doings of the *ton* than the people who were part of it, but he was still baffled by Curtis's concern for his master's social status. Inured to his own sturdy, independent belief that he should make his own way in the world, Jean understood only dimly that Curtis's sense of personal identity depended on the importance of his employer's status.

Finally succeeding in tying the difficult knot, Jean stepped back from the dressing table with a sigh of relief.

"Perfect, Mr. Hilliard. Quite perfect," said the valet. "I have no doubt, sir, that tonight will be a triumph for you."

Jean felt considerably less confident about the outcome of the evening as he made his way down the stairs to the drawing room. There was a hollow knot in the pit of his stomach at the thought of being the center of attention by the noblest names in England. He felt as if he were about to cross a patch of quicksand, where the slightest misstep would result in disaster. He also felt a simmering sense of

154

resentment. By officially introducing his heir at so impressive a function, Lord Sheringham undoubtedly hoped to make it extremely awkward for Jean if he should ever decide to carry out his intention to return to Canada.

Lord Sheringham and Camilla, who was acting as his hostess tonight, were already present, ready to receive their guests, when Jean entered the drawing room.

"You look lovely," Jean told Camilla, with an admiring glance at her gown of sea-green crepe worked with gold spangles. "Is that a new dress? I don't recall seeing it before. And I like that gold tiaralike ornament you're wearing. It doesn't hide your hair."

Camilla squirmed inwardly. Jean was fast becoming an expert at touching on forbidden topics without ever mentioning them directly. She knew he'd made his remark about her tiara with the deliberate intention of reminding her of the incident on the beach at the Kentish villa, when he'd removed her little lace cap because it was hiding her hair. And then he'd kissed her . . . Suddenly, to her own astonishment, she blurted, "Jean, did you take my cap?"

Looking puzzled, her godfather said, "What's this about a cap, my dear?"

"Nothing. Uncle Nigel. It was a joke."

Jean turned a bright red.

The butler appeared in the doorway. "Mr. and Mrs. Rothschild."

After only a few moments in the Rothschilds' company, it was clear to Camilla that her fears about the wisdom of inviting the merchant banker to this affair were probably well founded. Unprepossessing in appearance, with his short, stocky body, flattish nose and protruding blue eyes, Nathan Rothschild spoke with a thick German accent, and he seemed to have few social graces. By contrast, however, his wife was, mercifully, pretty, elegant and well-mannered.

155

Lord Sheringham remarked pleasantly, "I'm pleased to meet you at last, Mr. Rothschild. I believe we have a great deal in common. We're both Mancunians."

Nathan Rothschild smiled. "You flatter me, Lord Sheringham. Yes, in some sense we're both citizens of Manchester, but I doubt the people of the city would put us on the same level. For some years I was engaged in the cotton industry in Manchester. You, I understand, own most of the city and the land around it."

The earl laughed. "Oh, come, sir. You underestimate yourself, and vastly overestimate me."

Observing the faint pleased smile on Jean's lips, Camilla was glad that her godfather had exerted himself to make Nathan Rothschild feel welcome.

The rest of the guests began arriving, and soon the drawing room was comfortably full. It was a glittering assembly. Parliament was represented by Lords Liverpool and Castlereagh, among others, and by the Prime Minister himself, Mr. Perceval. The great society hostesses of the day were there, Ladies Jersey, Holland and Melbourne. The guests included, as the earl had promised Jean, directors from the East India Company and the Hudson's Bay Company. And only a few minutes past the hour when dinner should have been announced, the Prince of Wales himself walked into the room, accompanied by his secretary, Colonel MacMahon.

"Lord Sheringham, I almost changed my mind about attending your dinner this evening. I have a bone to pick with you," said the Prince genially.

Camilla reflected that His Highness's easy charm was still intact, despite the years of self-indulgence and the obesity that had blurred his once handsome features.

The earl's eyes twinkled. "May I ask in what way I've offended Your Royal Highness?"

"Why, you bought that Chinese urn I wanted for my collection, right out from under my agent's nose," said the Prince reproachfully.

"Indeed, sir, I had no idea I was bidding against you. I'd be very happy to make amends by selling the piece to you—at a handsome profit, of course," said the earl, cocking his head at the Prince.

The Prince laughed so hard he was in danger of choking. "You dog, Sheringham," he gasped. When he regained his breath, he turned to Jean, saying "You're the heir, are you? I'm very pleased to meet you, Mr. Hilliard. You're from Canada, I hear. Very interesting country, I believe. M'brother Kent spent some time there a while back."

Well over an hour later, as she left the dining room with the ladies, leaving the gentlemen to their wine, Camilla thought with satisfaction that the dinner had gone off very well indeed. The menu, which she and Uncle Nigel had planned so carefully, had been lavish, delicious and exquisitely prepared without being overly ostentatious. Not for the fastidious earl the excessive number—thirty-six and twenty-four, respectively, as an example—of *entrées* and *entremets* that so often graced the Prince of Wales's table.

While the coffee was being served, Camilla made it a point to talk to Mrs. Rothschild, who, though she didn't seem uncomfortable in the company, was a stranger to the other women in the room.

"We like Mr. Hilliard so much," she told Camilla. "My husband sees Mr. Hilliard as a kindred soul, both so interested in business. Then, too, my husband finds Mr. Hilliard's lack of pretension so refreshing, so unlike the manners of other—" Mrs. Rothschild paused, biting her lip. "Oh, dear. I didn't mean to suggest . . ."

Camilla laughed. "I agree with your husband. Jean isn't the least bit toplofty, like so many gentlemen of the *ton*. He's always simply himself."

The gentlemen began trailing into the drawing room. The earl informed Camilla quietly that the Prince of Wales had departed for another engagement. She greeted the news gratefully. The Prince's presence could sometimes have a subduing effect on social gatherings.

157

Observing Jean standing near the door of the room, well apart from his fellow guests, Camilla walked over to him. "Come have some coffee," she began, and stopped short at the expression of sullen rage on his face. "What's the matter?"

"It's that fellow from the Hudson's Bay Company," Jean muttered. "Allyson, I think that's his name."

"Lord Allyson, yes. He's a director of the company. What about him?"

"He's been baiting my friend Rothschild. Frankly, I think it may have been mostly the port talking. Allyson drank down half a bottle before the rest of us finished our first glass. But because he's foxed, that doesn't excuse what he's been saying."

Looking quickly around her, Camilla lowered her voice. "How do you mean, baiting?"

"Oh, I think he's like all the rest of your aristocratic friends. Despises anyone who 'smells of trade.' Allyson's been making remarks like, 'I hear you're no longer doing business in the cotton trade, Mr. Rothschild. Now you deal exclusively in money.' Or again, 'Mr. Rothschild, I understand that you not only know the price of every stock on the Exchange, but you also know infallibly whether each stock will go up or down. Such a skill must be so convenient for you in your business dealings.'"

Camilla stared at Jean, appalled. "I wouldn't have believed a man in Lord Allyson's position could be so rude. It *must* be the wine that's responsible. How is Mr. Rothschild reacting to such insulting behavior?"

"Like a perfect gentleman—so far," Jean growled. "Just tosses off Allyson's thrusts with a 'You do me too much credit, my lord.' I don't know how much longer he'll turn the other cheek, though. *I'd* like to darken Lord Allyson's daylights."

Camilla clutched at Jean's arm. "Please, please, don't make a scene. We'll just have to keep Mr. Rothschild and Lord Allyson apart for the rest of the evening."

But it was too late for Camilla's scheme. When she and Jean came up to Nathan Rothschild, they found him confronted by Lord Allyson, a short, spare man with sharp, angular features and a decided tic in his left cheek. A strong smell of port wafted from his person. He was saying in a slurred voice, "Will you join me in a game of whist, Mr. Rothschild?"

"No, thank you, my lord. I don't play cards."

"Really? How very odd, sir. I thought all gentlemen played cards. What — er — what do you do, then, to occupy your leisure moments?"

There was the faintest emphasis on the word "gentlemen," and Camilla, standing close to Jean, felt his body stiffen. Rothschild, however, merely shrugged, saying stolidly, in his heavy German accent, "Essentially, I don't have any leisure moments, Lord Allyson. I don't play cards, I don't read books, I don't go to the theater, I don't hunt. My only pleasure is business."

The tic in Lord Allyson's face became more pronounced. He raised his quizzing glass, looking at the merchant banker with the air of a scientist examining a specimen under the microscope. "That, if you'll allow me to say so, is a most un-English way of life," he sneered. Then he struck his forehead in a mock gesture of chagrin. "But then, I was forgetting. You're *not* English, are you, Mr. Rothschild?"

Rothschild no longer sounded quite so stolid. "As a matter of fact, I'm a British subject, Lord Allyson," he said evenly. "Of course, I'm also an Ashkenazic Jew from the Rhineland."

"Ah, doubtless that explains your devotion to business."

Before Camilla could stop him, Jean stepped forward beside Rothschild. His dark eyes glittering like black diamonds, he said, "Are you implying, Lord Allyson, that foreigners *and* businessmen are somehow unworthy of English regard?" His own accent was more pronounced than usual. Camilla wondered fleetingly if it was anger or deliberate intent that made him suddenly sound so French.

The drawing room had turned very quiet. Guests who had been drinking their coffee or making up tables for whist fell silent. Jean's truculent remarks had been clearly audible to everyone in the room, and it seemed to penetrate, at least temporarily, the fumes of port clogging Allyson's brain. With a glance at Lord Sheringham, standing nearby, Allyson said with a placating smile, "Why, no, Mr. Hilliard. I had no intention, I assure you, of maligning foreigners."

"I'm happy to hear it," Jean snapped. "Because, if you had such an intention, I'd be obliged to remind you that 'foreign businessmen' in Canada have made you and your company look like rank amateurs in the fur trade. In fact, if you hadn't had an unfair monopoly of the Hudson's Bay Territory, you'd be out of business by now!"

Allyson slowly turned a dull red. He also seemed to have sobered up considerably. "Oh, we have competitors in the Canadian fur trade, Mr. Hilliard, but I was unaware that they were foreigners. Are not residents of French Canada also British subjects? As you are, sir, I believe. Of course, the criminals who killed our factor and two of his men and burned our factory on the Assiniboine weren't citizens at all. They were Indians, or part-Indians, employees of a minor Montreal fur trading company. But what can you expect from such savage brutes? They're not really human, after all."

Every muscle in Jean's body seemed taut with rage. "You're either lying, or you've been badly informed about that attack on the Assiniboine, Lord Allyson. In any event, you need a lesson in what savages are really like. If you'll be patient for a few minutes, I'll be happy to show you."

Jean stalked out of the drawing room, leaving behind him some thirty people who stood in frozen silence, carefully avoiding each other's eyes.

Forcing herself to move, Camilla went to her godfather's

side. She whispered, "Uncle Nigel, this is a frightful coil. What could Jean be planning to do? What should *we* do?"

His face grim, Lord Sheringham didn't reply, merely squeezing her hand. He walked over to Lord Allyson. "My dear sir, I fear this has been a distressing experience for you," the earl said to the Hudson's Bay Company director. "Perhaps you'd prefer to retire."

"With my tail between my legs?" Allyson snarled. "No, Lord Sheringham. I'll wait to see what Mr. Hilliard has in mind."

The earl bowed. "As you wish."

After that exchange, the embarrassed silence remained unbroken until Jean reentered the drawing room a few minutes later. A collective gasp arose. Camilla's heart seemed to stop, and then began thumping erratically.

He was barbaric. He was threatening. He was dangerous. He was beautiful. He was magnificent. Camilla longed to throttle him with her bare hands.

Jean was wearing the costume of his Cree ancestors. He was virtually naked except for tight-fitting fringed deerskin leggings and a bright red wool breech cloth, both of which were supported by a leather belt decorated with colored quills and purple and white wampum beads. The leggings didn't quite meet the belt, so that generous amounts of smooth bronze flesh were visible at his thighs. He wore a brief leather vest, also beaded and decorated, which exposed most of his chest. Around his neck he'd hung a necklace of some kind of animals' teeth and an intricately worked silver gorget, and long silver earrings dangled from his ears. Confining his dark curls was a beaded headband, from which two large feathers dangled down his back. He'd painted slashes of green and red paint across his cheekbones.

Jean remained posed in the doorway for several long seconds, presumably, Camilla thought bitterly, to allow the assembled guests to have a thoroughly good look at his exotic costume. Then he walked slowly into the room.

Even his walk was different. He moved with a catlike, gliding grace, as if he were stalking a deer, or possibly an employee of the Hudson's Bay Company.

He stopped directly in front of Lord Allyson. "This is what those 'savage brutes' look like, my lord," he said softly. "And this is what we can do, if we put our minds to it . . ." With a lightning-swift movement, he pulled a long, wickedly sharp-looking knife from the sheath at his belt. The knife glittered in the candlelight as he swung it high over his head and then pressed it against Lord Allyson's neck. To Camilla's horror, she saw a tiny dot of bright red appearing on the white stock at Allyson's throat. After a moment Jean pulled back the knife and stepped away from his victim, smiling. "But, of course, my lord, even a savage brute is too civilized to slit your throat in front of your friends."

Allyson had turned a ghastly shade of greenish white. He was visibly trembling with shock. His voice, when he at length managed to force his words out, was thready, almost unrecognizable. Bowing jerkily, he said to the earl and Camilla, "If you'll excuse me . . . I must go."

Seemingly mesmerized, the roomful of people watched Allyson's slow progress to the door. Then the dam broke. The guests crowded against each other in their haste to take leave of their host and hostess. Camilla and Lord Sheringham woodenly accepted the flimsy excuses each guest gave for his early departure. Nathan Rothschild was among the last to leave. His wife by his side, he remarked to the earl, "Thank you for your hospitality. This has been, without doubt, the single most interesting evening of my life, if a trifle catastrophic." He glanced at Jean, standing still and silent off to the side with his arms clasped across his chest. "Pray, Lord Sheringham, that you don't experience too many evenings like this."

It was over. Camilla whirled on Jean. "How could you do such a thing?" she asked fiercely. "How could you threaten a guest of Uncle Nigel in his own house, and how could you make a spectacle of yourself by appearing in public in those—those scraps of leather, for all the world as if you really were the savage Lord Allyson called you?"

"Perhaps because I really am a savage? That's what some of your friends have been calling me behind my back. Why not satisfy their suspicions?" Jean asked bitterly. "What would you have had me do, Camilla? That poltroon, Allyson, insulted my friend Rothschild not once, but many times. *My* code of honor doesn't allow me to sit back while a guest is insulted in my house." He glanced at the earl, who stood silently by, watching and listening. "You've told me I should consider this my house, sir." To Camilla he added, "Should I have slapped a glove across his face and asked him to name his second, like a proper English gentleman? I think my way is better."

Throwing up her hands, Camilla said, "You're hopeless, Jean. You don't seem to have the faintest notion of how much you've disgraced Uncle Nigel and me. In all these weeks, you haven't learned the first thing about civilized behavior, have you? How can you expect anyone in London to receive you after an exhibition like that?"

Jean winced at the scorn in Camilla's voice. Then he said coldly, "And how can you expect me to care? Remember, you're the one who wanted me to stay in London for the Season. If you want to change your mind about my stay here, just say the word. I'll be happy to oblige." He turned on his heel and strode out of the room, his feet in the beaded moccasins making no sound.

Camilla said forlornly, "Oh, Uncle Nigel, I'm so sorry. He's ruined everything. It's true, you know, what I said to Jean. How can he ever show his face in a London drawing room after an exhibition like that?"

Lord Sheringham spoke at last. "Well, at least the boy speaks his mind," he said in a tired voice.

"Uncle Nigel, you can't possibly excuse Jean!"

"No. No. Though he certainly had provocation . . ." The earl flexed his shoulders. "I see one small ray of hope."

"What on earth could that be?" Camilla asked in surprise.

"My dear, in the *ton* an old title and a large fortune can make up for a multitude of sins."

Chapter Eleven

The aftermath of Lord Sheringham's dinner for his heir sent ripples of gossip through the *ton,* as Camilla soon discovered to her sorrow.

Several evenings after the dinner, Dorcas came into her sister's bedchamber, saying, "Camilla, are you wearing your pearls tonight? And if not, may I borrow them?"

Camilla looked up from her dressing table, where her abigail was putting the final touches to her hair. "Of course you may wear the pearls. They'll look lovely with that embroidered gauze gown."

Peering into the cheval glass while she fastened the clasp of the pearls, Dorcas said in a casual tone, "Is Mr. Hilliard going to escort us to Mrs. Sylvester's ball?"

"No," replied Camilla, rather shortly. Then, noticing Dorcas's quick, inquisitive look, she smiled, saying, "We'll have to make do with Miles's company tonight. Do you mind?"

Dorcas colored faintly. "Of course not. I enjoy being with Miles." After a pause, taking a deep breath, she said, "Camilla, we've seen very little of Mr. Hilliard lately. Have—have you and he quarreled?"

"No. Well, not exactly. Oh, the devil, Dorcas, you've heard something. What is it?"

"Well . . ." Obviously Dorcas was torn between curiosity and embarrassment. "Miles says the rumors are flying all over London that Mr. Hilliard tried to kill someone at

165

Lord Sheringham's dinner party," she said in a rush. "Miles says that nothing else is being discussed in the drawing rooms or the clubs."

"Oh, Lord," Camilla groaned. She clapped her hands to her head, disregarding the anguished cry from her abigail, who had spent fifteen minutes arranging her coiffure. "I was afraid of this. There were thirty people at that dinner, and I daresay at least twenty-five of them have been busily prattling the details of what happened there to their friends. What else has Miles heard, Dorcas?"

Turning a sudden bright red, Dorcas hesitated briefly. Finally she blurted, "According to the *on dit,* Mr. Hilliard practically disrobed in public. Something to do with a—a native Indian costume, I believe."

"Damnation," Camilla exclaimed. "Fiends of hell!"

"Camilla! I've never heard you use such language!"

"I'd like to use much worse," said Camilla grimly. "If I knew any really bad language, that is, and for all the good it would do."

"You really hadn't heard any of these rumors? Miles has been in such a taking, wondering if he should talk to you about it."

"No, I hadn't heard. But it's not surprising, now I come to think of it. My really close friends wouldn't speak of it to me, naturally. Or to my godfather, either. Poor Uncle Nigel. He was hoping so much that what happened at the dinner would be an overnight scandal and then die away." Camilla shook her head. "Well, I can't do anything to change the situation, and meanwhile we have a ball to attend tonight." She motioned to her abigail. "Becky, I'm sorry, but you'll have to repair the damage I've done to my hair. Dorcas, I'll see you downstairs in a few minutes."

While the abigail began with deft fingers to rearrange her tumbled curls, Camilla brooded over Jean's fecklessness. It was almost a week now since the disastrous dinner. During that interval, she hadn't seen Jean. He hadn't called on Park Street, though for many days now it had been his invariable custom to visit the house at least once a day, and to escort her to any evening function she cared to attend. She suspected he was sulking because of the scathing set-down she'd given him, and he was probably far too stubborn to admit he'd been at fault.

Her godfather hadn't seen Jean either, she mused, though the two were living in the same house. Apparently Jean had been leaving Sheringham House each day in the early morning, not to return until the late hours. Camilla shrugged. So be it, she thought defiantly. She was sorry for Uncle Nigel, but she herself would as lief not see Jean for the present. Ever since she'd met the man, he'd done nothing but disrupt her carefully organized life.

She came down to the drawing room to find that Miles had already arrived. He broke off his conversation with Dorcas to come over to her. "I'm sorry to be the one to bring you these disturbing rumors."

"I had to know sometime. There's more?" she asked, as Miles looked away, avoiding her eyes.

He shifted uncomfortably. "Oh, nothing of any great significance. I hear that Hilliard's been dipping fairly deep at White's and Boodle's the past few days. Not my affair, of course, but I've always understood that Hilliard came here from Canada with his pockets pretty well to let. I did wonder what he was using for rhino. Didn't like to think he was trading on his future prospects with the Sheringham estates. And besides, it's a bad mistake to fall into the clutches of the cent-per-centers."

"Miles! Has Jean been losing heavily at the tables?"

"Well no, actually. The strange thing is, I hear he's had a tremendous run of luck. The rumor has it that he won a packet off Lord Jerningham last night at White's, for instance. They say Jerningham will have to sell off his stables to pay Hilliard. Pity. Jerny's a member of the Four-in-Hand Club, you know."

Miles looked away again, and Camilla said immediately, "I know you, my friend. You're hiding something."

"Confound it, Camilla, there are some matters a gentleman doesn't discuss with females," Miles protested.

167

"Miles! What has Jean done now?"

"Well, if you must have it—he got into a brawl at Gentleman Jackson's Boxing Saloon the other day. The way I heard it, someone asked him if red Indians used fists or knives when they fought, and Hilliard milled the fellow down."

Camilla's fingernails bit into her palms as she clenched her hands. "Did—was Jean hurt?"

"Why, no," Miles said in surprise. "The fellow who challenged Hilliard didn't fight back, of course. Couldn't. Never moved after Hilliard gave him a leveller." Miles coughed. "There's one more thing. I hear that Hilliard's been fairly haunting the premises of Nathan Rothschild. The Jewish merchant banker. Er—wasn't Rothschild the cause of the quarrel between Hilliard and Lord Allyson at your godfather's dinner? Why in heaven's name does Hilliard associate with such a person?"

"Business," said Camilla bitterly.

"Business," said Miles incredulously. "What do you mean, business?"

"They both like money. How to accumulate it. How to invest it."

Miles said austerely, "I'll tell you what, Camilla. I don't like to criticize Lord Sheringham's heir, but I'm beginning to think that Jean-Étienne Hilliard's no gentleman. He has low tastes."

When Camilla entered the ballroom of Dalrymple House with Miles and Dorcas later that evening, the dancing had already begun. She noted with relief that Lady Dalrymple apparently didn't believe in inviting more people than her ballroom could comfortably hold.

"Camilla, look," Dorcas murmured. "Over there. Just finishing the Scottish reel."

Camilla glanced at the dancers, and stiffened. After a last graceful bow to end the reel, Jean was escorting his very pretty partner off the floor. Clinging to Jean's arm, the young lady gazed up into his face with what Camilla could only consider a calflike, simpering look. As Camilla watched, Jean delivered his partner to an imposing dowager, wearing a towering purple turban, who was sitting on the side of the ballroom. The young lady's mother, apparently. Her face wreathed in smiles, the dowager waved Jean to a chair beside her. With every indication of pleasure, Jean sat down and plunged into an animated conversation with the dowager and her daughter. At one point, looking up, he noticed Camilla standing near the door of the ballroom. The smile faded from his face, he nodded briefly, and he immediately returned to his conversation.

"Camilla, I certainly wouldn't have expected to see Mr. Hilliard here tonight," said Dorcas in a low voice. "You'd think that no hostess would care to receive him in her house after—after, well, you know . . ."

"I presume he received his invitation to the ball well before Uncle Nigel's dinner party," Camilla replied shortly. "For some reason, he's chosen to brazen out the rumors by attending this affair tonight."

"Well, but Camilla, that's Lady Wainwright that Hilliard's talking to," said Miles, frowning. "A real Gorgon of a woman, I've always heard. A stickler for the proprieties. But there she is, having a cozy *tête-à-tête* with Hilliard in full view of everybody. Doesn't seem to me as if she considers him to be mired in disgrace. Odd."

Not so odd, perhaps, Camilla thought bitterly. She remembered her godfather's comment at the end of that catastrophic dinner party. "My dear, in the *ton* an old title and a large fortune can make up for a multitude of sins."

"Dorcas, a new set is forming," said Miles. "This is my dance, I trust?" At Dorcas's dimpling smile, he reached out for her card, scribbling his name opposite several other dances. "There. Now, at least, I'm ahead of the trampling hordes of my rivals!"

As Dorcas and Miles went off to join the set, Camilla sat down in a chair at the side of the ballroom. She smilingly refused several requests from old acquaintances to partner her in the country dance. Moments later, she regretted her refusals. Aubrey Elvaston sank into a chair beside her.

Camilla looked at his handsome, fine-boned face, topped by the flowing mane of dark blonde hair, and felt nothing but loathing. She said in a low voice, "I've told you what I think of your attentions, Sir Aubrey. Any gentleman . . ."

Elvaston looked at her with a long, slow, insulting glance. "I thought you were a woman of much greater intelligence, Camilla. You've forbidden me your home. Surely you don't think, because I haven't tried to crash your gates, that I've given up on my intentions? Do give me credit for a little more subtlety of action. I certainly don't want the *ton* to suspect that I'm trying to intrude where I'm not welcome. No, no, I'm simply biding my time. As I've told you on several occasions, Camilla, you owe me something. I intend to collect."

"Go away, Sir Aubrey. I want nothing to do with you. You can't force me to associate with you."

"No? My dear girl, I'm 'associating with you' at this very moment. Unless you rake my face with your fingernails, and jump up from your chair with an expression of outrage on your beautiful face—and you're not going to do any such thing, are you?—people will simply assume we're renewing an old friendship."

Elvaston rose slowly as the country dance ended and Miles approached them with Dorcas on his arm. "My dear Miss Vernon, what a great pleasure to see you again," Sir Aubrey said to Dorcas with a beaming smile.

Camilla's heart sank. Dorcas's expression reminded her of a delicate flower, opening its petals to the first gentle rays of a spring sun. "Sir Aubrey," breathed Dorcas, "I'm very pleased to see you again, too."

With a lazy grace, Elvaston reached out for Dorcas's dance card. "I see, by some extraordinarily fortunate coincidence, that no one has claimed this dance, Miss Vernon. Alas, I no longer dance, but I'd much appreciate the opportunity to continue the delightful conversation that was so rudely interrupted the last time we met. Dare I ask you to sit out this dance with me? Oh, in full view of your chaperon, naturally," he added, nodding to Camilla.

"I'd like that," Dorcas said shyly. "To tell the truth, I'm a little weary of dancing."

Short of creating a scene, Camilla could only acquiesce with a wooden smile as Sir Aubrey sat down beside Dorcas. After a moment, Miles said stiffly, "Excuse me, Camilla, Dorcas. I've asked Lady Emily Dorset for this dance."

Sir Aubrey deftly proceeded to captivate Dorcas. Looking deep into her eyes, he said, "Now, Miss Vernon, tell me everything you've been doing since the last time we met." He seemed completely absorbed in Dorcas's account of her activities, asking a question here, making a comment there. "I'm so glad you enjoyed Mrs. Siddons's performance as Lady Macbeth as much as I did," he told Dorcas at one point. "One more thing we have in common!" When she asked him about his diplomatic duties in Constantinople, he held her spellbound with his tales that made the Ottoman court seem like something out of the *Arabian Nights.* "Oh, yes, the Sultan really does have a harem, a very large one, I hear," he assured Dorcas, his eyes twinkling. "Alas, the seraglio was the one place I wasn't allowed to go!"

Left out of the conversation, Camilla sat numbly by, remembering her own first encounters with Elvaston. It had taken her some time to penetrate to the real man behind that curtain of practiced charm. How could she expect Dorcas, with her youth and inexperience, to see Sir Aubrey as he really was?

The country dance ended, a new set began forming, and a young man came up to claim Dorcas as his partner. Sir Aubrey rose slowly — by now Camilla had realized that he habitually assumed a practiced slowness in all his movements in order to disguise his lameness — and bowed to her, saying, "Until next time, my dear, and that will be very soon, I promise you." He walked languidly away.

As she watched him go, Camilla observed Jean standing nearby, talking to his hostess. He looked impossibly handsome in his perfectly tailored evening clothes. Camilla noticed that he'd tied his cravat in an intricate new knot. Lady Dalrymple was looking up at him with much the same bemused expression that Camilla had already glimpsed on the faces of several of Jean's dancing partners. His lips wreathed in his familiar quirkish smile, Jean seemed to be telling Lady Dalrymple an amusing story. After a few moments, Lady Dalrymple burst into a laugh and playfully tapped Jean on his cheek with her fan. Camilla could almost hear her saying, in a teasing, forgiving tone, "Naughty boy!"

Lady Dalrymple moved off to speak to another of her guests, and Jean, turning his head, met Camilla's eyes. He hesitated, his expression suddenly wary. Then, giving his shoulders a barely perceptible shake, he sauntered over to her. "May I?" he asked, indicating a chair.

"If you wish," Camilla said coolly. She tried to ignore a telltale quiver of excitement as Jean settled his lithe powerful body next to her. Unwillingly she admitted to herself that his absence during the past week had created a void in her life.

They stared at each other in an uneasy silence for several seconds. Unspoken questions and reproaches stirred the shards of their shattered relationship. From the glint of anger in his dark eyes, Camilla knew Jean was remembering the flaying remarks she'd made to him at her godfather's dinner. Jean broke the silence by observing casually, "That's a lovely gown. You always look well in blue."

"Thank you."

Another short silence, and then Jean remarked, again with the air of snatching a topic of conversation out of the air, "I saw Elvaston doing the pretty with Dorcas. Not very wise, do you think, to allow him to associate with an innocent like your sister?"

Camilla suppressed a stab of anger. What right did Jean

172

have to question her supervision of Dorcas, especially after his outrageous behavior at Uncle Nigel's party? "Dorcas is simply being pleasant to Sir Aubrey. He introduced himself to her as a friend of my late husband. Dorcas adored Philip."

Jean cocked his head at her. "I wonder why I find that remark so hard to believe? There's something about this Elvaston fellow you're not telling me."

"I'm not obliged to tell you anything," Camilla snapped. She paused, biting her lip. In his own way, Jean was as infuriating as Sir Aubrey. She changed the subject. "I was very surprised to see you here tonight," she said offhandedly.

His expression hardened. "Why? Did you think I'd be afraid to show my face in public after what happened at Lord Sheringham's dinner?"

"I thought you'd feel somewhat embarrassed, at least." Something — jealousy? chagrin? — prompted Camilla to add, "I also thought the ladies of the *ton* would be shocked by the rumors of your behavior. Apparently I was wrong. Your hostess was extremely cordial to you a moment ago, and earlier Lady Wainwright was positively doting." Camilla paused, then added, "Of course, both those ladies have marriageable daughters."

A muscle twitched in Jean's cheek, but his voice was elaborately casual as he said, "You know, I suspected I might be pitched right out of the *ton* after my set-to with Lord Allyson. Not that I'd have minded all that much. *You* know what I think of most of your aristocratic friends! But would you believe it, I'm being inundated with fresh invitations to this and that."

Camilla looked her surprise.

Jean nodded. "Yes, indeed. Now, it may be that the fond mamas do have their eyes on me as possible marriage fodder." He smiled in self-derision. "After all, I *am* a future earl! However I must say the ladies are asking me some very intelligent questions about Canada and the fur trade. Our hostess wished to know if I could construct a canoe! But the young ladies—!" Jean rolled his eyes. "They seem most interested in my Indian costume. A number of them have asked me to model the garments. Doubtless they want to see what a real Canadian Indian looks like."

Unbidden, an image of smooth bronze naked flesh flashed before Camilla's eyes. At the same time, she found herself wondering how it would feel to be clasped against a tautly muscled bare body clothed only in a breech cloth and vest and scanty deerskin leggings. Her cheeks flamed, and she looked away. Then anger restored sanity. She knew quite well what Jean was up to. He was being deliberately provocative, trying to throw her off balance. Evidently her outburst at the end of Uncle Nigel's dinner had struck him in the most sensitive corner of his being.

She looked him straight in the eye, willing her voice to sound indifferent. "What a splendid idea, Jean, to model your Indian costume. So educational for this year's crop of eager young females."

Jean's smile didn't reach his eyes. "Perhaps you'd like a private showing, Camilla."

"No, thank you. I've already seen you in all your glory, remember?"

Lord Sheringham pounded his stick on the floor, digging into Camilla's Aubusson carpet. "I don't understand the boy, Camilla. What's in his mind? He avoids me. Leaves in the morning before I rise, doesn't return until I'm abed. He avoids your company, too, though he sees you virtually every evening, at whatever function you attend. He was even invited to the Duchess of York's *soirée*, which I understand was a most exclusive affair." The earl shook his head. "This is the same man who's told us, more times than I can recall, how much he despises the doings of the *ton*."

"Jean's trying to show us up, Uncle Nigel," Camilla said rather wearily. She could understand her godfather's concern for his erratic heir, but she was tired of bearing the brunt of persuading Jean to observe his commitments to his family lineage.

"But Camilla, what will happen? Do you think Jean intends to return to Canada?"

For the first time she could remember in her relationship with her godfather, Camilla lost her temper. "Uncle Nigel, I'm not a mind reader. I don't know what Jean intends to do."

Lord Sheringham rose. "My dear, I'm sorry. I've placed too heavy a burden of responsibility on your shoulders. I can't expect you to solve all the problems of the succession to the earldom of Sheringham."

"Uncle Nigel—"

"It's all right, Camilla. What will be, will be."

After Lord Sheringham had left, Camilla sat racked by guilt and regret. She felt like a complete failure. She'd promised her godfather to persuade his heir to remain in England, and here, scant weeks after she'd made that promise, her only contacts with Jean were the stilted greetings they exchanged when they encountered each other at social events. And she'd promised Jean to introduce him to the *ton*, and, without the slightest help from her, he was rapidly becoming the lion of London society. She gritted her teeth at the thought of the dowager who'd approached her recently, wanting to know if Mr. Hilliard's Indian grandmother had indeed been the heiress to half of the North American continent.

Without bothering to have himself announced, Miles strolled into the drawing room. "Good morning, Camilla." He pulled out his watch. "I'm a trifle early. Will Dorcas be ready soon?"

"What?" Camilla tried to gather her thoughts. "Oh, you and Dorcas are driving to Kensington this morning."

Miles turned a keen eye on her. "You look a trifle blue-deviled, Camilla. Anything wrong?"

"Oh, no. Well, perhaps I'm a little tired. Dorcas and I have been going from one event to another from morning to night for weeks now, and the Season is only half over. You know, Miles, I fancy I'm getting too old for the social whirl."

"Old!" Miles scoffed. He grinned. "You'll never be old, not even in your shroud!" He settled into a chair, looking suddenly serious. "Camilla, please don't think I'm criticizing you, but . . . Do you think it's wise to allow Dorcas to spend so much time in Aubrey Elvaston's company?"

Her brows drawing together, Camilla stared at Miles. "What do you mean?"

"Well, you must have noticed. Last night at the Eddystones' she sat out two dances with him. She did the same thing two nights ago at Mrs. Crawford's ball, where she also went into supper with him. The thing is, people will soon start to talk. Elvaston's a libertine. He's compromised more females than I care to count."

Camilla bristled, even thought Miles was only echoing her own worries. She'd barred Sir Aubrey from the house on Park Street, but, with his charm and his social connections, he'd managed to obtain invitations to most of the events that she and Dorcas had attended recently, and he'd made a point of seeking out Dorcas at every one of them. Attempting to mask her misgivings, Camilla told Miles, "You make too much of this. Dorcas is never out of my sight when we go out in public. She's certainly in no danger of being compromised. The fact is, Miles, that Dorcas likes Sir Aubrey because he was such a close friend of Philip, and Philip was her idol when she was growing up."

"I know all that," Miles replied quietly, "but Dorcas is too young and too innocent to be so much in Elvaston's pocket, even in full view of a roomful of people. At the risk of offending you, Camilla, I must insist you warn Dorcas that Elvaston isn't a safe friend for an unmarried young girl."

Camilla's temper flared. "For your information, Miles, I *have* warned Dorcas against becoming too friendly with Sir Aubrey." She paused, biting her lip. "Don't let's quarrel. You're probably right. I should speak to her again."

She rang for the maid. When the girl appeared, Camilla said, "Lizzie, please tell Miss Dorcas that Mr. Wingate is here."

Several minutes later, the maid reappeared. She sounded puzzled as she said, "Ma'am, Miss Dorcas ain't in her bedchamber."

Camilla stared at Lizzie. "Where can she be, then? Did you check my room? The morning room?"

"Yes, ma'am." The maid hesitated. "There's one thing p'raps I ought to tell ye . . . Last night, Miss Dorcas said I warn't to bring her tea to her this morning. She said she was tired and wanted to sleep a bit late today."

Camilla was silent for a moment. Then she said calmly, "Thank you, Lizzie. Don't worry about it. Miss Dorcas probably took it into her head to go for an early morning stroll."

When the maid had left, Miles expostulated, "Good God, Camilla, what madness is this? Dorcas must know she shouldn't go out walking without at least one of the servants to accompany her. And why would she go for a stroll before breakfast?" He glanced at the clock. "It's nearly ten o'clock. Why isn't she back from this stroll? Something must have happened to her."

"I don't think Dorcas went for a stroll," said Camilla in a tight voice. "I think she—" She paused at the sound of voices in the hallway. In a moment, Jean entered the drawing room, dragging by the arm an exceedingly angry and frustrated Dorcas.

"Camilla, Miles," wailed Dorcas. "Tell Mr. Hilliard to let me go."

"See here, Hilliard, what's the meaning of this?" said Miles angrily.

Jean removed his hand from Dorcas's arm and stepped back from her. Ignoring Miles, he said to Camilla, "Perhaps you'll tell me it was none of my affair, but I didn't think you'd approve of an assignation between Dorcas and Aubrey Elvaston in the Green Park before nine o'clock in the morning. Or, indeed, at any hour. So when I drove past

177

the park and saw them strolling along together, I got out of my curricle and tried to persuade your sister to allow me to drive her home."

"Persuade!" said Dorcas bitterly. "He abducted me! And when Sir Aubrey tried to stop him, Mr. Hilliard shoved him aside so violently that he staggered and almost fell!"

Miles seemed utterly bewildered. "Hilliard *abducted* you, Dorcas? He scuffled with Aubrey Elvaston? In the Green Park? What on earth were you doing in the Green Park, and how did you get there? Camilla doesn't keep a carriage."

Camilla interrupted him. "Miles, I think you should go. I'd like to talk to Dorcas alone."

The dazed look left Miles's face. He said stiffly, "If you want me to go, of course I'll go, Camilla. Dorcas, you seem a trifle indisposed. Perhaps we can arrange to drive to Kensington another day." He jerked a bow and left the room.

With a spitefulness that was unusual in her, Dorcas snapped, "I think you should leave, too, Mr. Hilliard."

Jean shrugged and turned to go. Camilla followed him into the foyer. "Jean, I quite agree with you that Dorcas should never have arranged to meet Sir Aubrey secretly in the park. I know you meant well, and I thank you for the way you tried to handle the situation, but . . . Was it really necessary to be so—so cavalier?"

Jean's brows drew together. "Cavalier?"

"Well, I gather you forced Dorcas into your curricle as if she were a naughty child. Couldn't you have been, well, less physical, less public? Did you really try reasoning with Dorcas? Were there many people about? If so, and anyone recognized her, or you, or Sir Aubrey, for that matter, I shudder to think of the scandal."

Jean said, grim-lipped, "It's the old story, isn't it? I should have been more of an English gentleman, less of a French Canadian brawler. I must remember that, if I should ever have the occasion to rescue your sister again."

178

Swinging on his heel, he made for the door.

Her feet dragging, Camilla walked back toward the drawing room. She was angry at Jean, even angrier at herself. She'd handled the situation very badly. Jean had made a real, if misguided effort to help, and she'd rebuffed him.

Her voice was still tight with anger when she confronted her sister in the drawing room. "Well, Dorcas? I'd like an explanation of your conduct."

"I haven't done anything wrong," said Dorcas defiantly.

"Let me be the judge of that. *Did* you arrange to meet Sir Aubrey in the Green Park this morning?"

"No. Well, not exactly. I walked to the end of Park Street, and Sir Aubrey met me there in his carriage. Then we drove to the Green Park, got out of the carriage and went for a short stroll. I intended to be back here, of course, before it was time to go driving with Miles. And I would have been, if Jean Hilliard hadn't interfered. Camilla, he made me feel like a — a criminal! And he could easily have injured Sir Aubrey."

Trying hard to control her temper, Camilla said, "You're an intelligent girl, Dorcas, and you were well reared. I give my stepmother credit for that, at least. You must have known you were risking your reputation by making an assignation with Sir Aubrey. Why did you do it?"

"Because I like Sir Aubrey, and I enjoy his company, and you won't allow me to see him," Dorcas flared. "You won't let him come to the house, you shoot daggers at us with your eyes if I sit out a dance with him. So when he suggested we'd have a little privacy to talk in an early morning walk in the park, of course I agreed to meet him. And I repeat, Camilla, I didn't do anything wrong."

"Dorcas, I've told you this more than once. Sir Aubrey isn't a safe friend for you. I want your promise that you won't see him again."

"But *why?* You never give me a reason why I shouldn't be Sir Aubrey's friend, or why you're so unfeeling and so vindictive toward a man who was so close to Philip."

179

Camilla hesitated. At last she said, "There are certain—certain incidents in Sir Aubrey's life that make him an unsuitable acquaintance for a young girl."

"What incidents?"

"You'll have to take my word for this. I can't discuss the matter."

"Same old story," sneered Dorcas.

And now Camilla's patience snapped. "Enough of this. I'm your guardian, remember? While you're in my care, you'll do as I say." As she watched the mutinous cloud spread over Dorcas's face, Camilla knew she'd taken the wrong tack. Her voice softening, she said, "Dorcas, there's an expression gamblers use. Vowel. Do you know it? To vowel someone means to pay him with an I.O.U. You've voweled me, you know."

"What do you mean?" asked Dorcas, her interest caught in spite of herself.

"Well, several months ago you sent me a desperate call for help. I rushed down to Bath and rescued you from Mama and her scheme to marry you off to that odious Mr. Stinchcombe. Later I asked Uncle Nigel for twenty thousand pounds to pay Mama for the privilege of becoming your guardian. Now I'm sponsoring you in your coming out season. Don't you think you owe me something? I'm calling in your I.O.U.'s. I want you to promise me that you won't see Sir Aubrey Elvaston again."

Dorcas's struggle with her emotions was clearly visible on her face. After a long silence, she said reluctantly, "Very well, I'll do as you ask. I'll stop seeing Sir Aubrey. You're quite right, I do owe you a great deal." She shuddered. "If you hadn't helped me, I'd be Mrs. Stinchcombe by now. I'd rather be dead!"

Chapter Twelve

As she took one last look at her image in the cheval glass, Camilla said over her shoulder to her abigail, "Becky, please see if Miss Dorcas needs any help with her toilet. Tell her it's getting quite late. Mr. Wingate will be here soon."

"Yes, ma'am." Returning several minutes later, the abigail reported, "Miss Dorcas ain't dressed, ma'am. Says she ain't feeling well."

Camilla walked down the hallway to Dorcas's bedchamber and pushed open the door. She peered through the gloom of the darkened room at the prostrate figure swathed in a cocoon of bedclothes. "Dorcas, Becky says you're ill."

The bedclothes stirred slightly. "I have the headache," Dorcas muttered. "It feels as if someone is pounding my head with a hammer. I'm sorry, Camilla. I don't think I can go with you tonight. I should have told you sooner, but I kept hoping the headache would go away."

"Of course you can't go out tonight if you're not feeling well. Don't worry about missing the Chatterley's rout, which I suspect will be another frightful bore!"

A faint giggle sounded from the bed. "Camilla! You told me Mrs. Chatterley was such an important hostess."

"So she is, but she still gives boring parties. Goodnight, Dorcas. Try to get some sleep. Becky will bring you a cup of tea."

A little later, sitting beside Miles in his carriage, Camilla said with a sigh, "I wish I could stay at home with Dorcas. You know, I can't imagine why I used to think a coming out season was so exciting. I can't wait for this one to end. I can't wait to get back to my old peaceful way of life. Small dinner parties. An occasional musical evening. Taking tea with my friends."

Miles reached over to pat her hand. "Amen to that. I think I'm a little past this nightly round of engagements myself. However, I think Dorcas is gloriously enjoying her coming out season. That's what's important." Miles was silent for a moment. Then he added, "Although I must say, I've thought Dorcas has been a bit subdued this past week or so. Perhaps she's beginning to feel a little fatigued. She's not especially strong."

"No." Camilla's thoughts wandered. Dorcas had indeed seemed subdued during the past few weeks, but Camilla doubted that fatigue was the reason. Keeping to her promise, Dorcas had been scrupulously avoiding Aubrey Elvaston's company, merely greeting him briefly when they met in public. She hadn't sulked, she hadn't reproached her sister for interfering in her life, she hadn't once mentioned Sir Aubrey's name, but Camilla sensed that, behind Dorcas's quiet, smiling facade, resentment still festered.

Entering the Chatterley's townhouse, Camilla surreptitiously examined the faces of the guests as she moved from room to room. Jean wasn't there. She told herself she was glad. These days they never exchanged more than a nod and a bow when they met, but it was much better for her peace of mind not to see him at all. Aubrey Elvaston wasn't among the guests, either, though his absence, for once, was immaterial. Dorcas wasn't here tonight, so she wouldn't be exposed to the temptation of seeing Sir Aubrey.

Soon Miles went off to hobnob with a crony from the Four-in-Hand Club, leaving Camilla momentarily to her own devices. She glanced around, catching the eye of a rather dumpy-looking young woman with whom Dorcas had formed one of those quick friendships so common in any coming out year. "Good evening, Miss Arbuthnot."

"Er—good evening, Mrs. Rayburn."

"I'm sorry to tell you that my sister isn't here with me tonight," Camilla said pleasantly.

"Oh, dear. I hope Dorcas isn't ill."

"She has the headache. I daresay she'll be fine tomorrow."

"Oh, I'm sure she will. Dorcas is a *very* healthy person. Healthier than most people. Oh, yes, I fancy she'll be right as a trivet before the cat has time to lick behind his ears."

Camilla's eyes sharpened as she studied Kitty Arbuthnot. There was something very strange about the girl's manner. For one thing, she was practically babbling. For another, she seemed both oddly excited and at the same time apprehensive, and she avoided Camilla's eyes. What's more, she hadn't seemed in the least surprised to learn that Dorcas wasn't present tonight.

"Pray tell Dorcas I hope she feels well soon," said Kitty with a nervous titter. "Would you excuse me, Mrs. Rayburn? I think Mama is looking for me." She turned on her heel with the relieved air of one escaping a deadly peril.

"Oh, I'm sure your mama can spare you for a few moments while we have a little chat," Camilla said with a friendly smile, seized by a sudden conviction that Kitty's odd behavior had something to do with Dorcas. Speaking at random, she said, "I like to get better acquainted with Dorcas's friends. You and she have become quite close, I believe. She told me how much she enjoyed her ride in Hyde Park with you yesterday. It was very kind of you to offer her a mount. As you may know, I don't keep my own stables."

At the mention of the ride in Hyde Park, Miss Arbuthnot became agitated. "Oh, the ride in the Park. It was nothing, really. I was happy to oblige Dorcas. Our head groom says the mare was eating her head off in the stables and doing no work for it. Mrs. Rayburn, I really must go."

"In a moment." Camilla fixed a gimlet eye on the unfortunate Kitty. "My dear, I think you're hiding something from me. About Dorcas. Something I should know. Tell me about it. Or perhaps I should speak to your mama."

Kitty Arbuthnot's plump face twisted with anguish. "Oh, no, you mustn't do that. Mama would be overset to think I hadn't told her about—she likes to know all my concerns, you see. And yet . . . Mrs. Rayburn, I *can't* tell you about Dorcas. She'd be so angry with me."

Camilla felt sorry for the girl—at the mercy of a mother who allowed her no privacy—but not sorry enough to drop the subject. "You've gone too far, but not far enough, Miss Arbuthnot. Tell me."

Wringing her hands, Kitty gave in. Her words came out in an incoherent jumble. "I don't actually *know* anything. It was just that Dorcas was so full of herself. She kept giggling, and saying I wasn't to be surprised if she didn't come to the Chatterleys' rout tonight, because she had a *much* more interesting invitation from someone else, and she was going to pretend she was ill so that you wouldn't insist she should come with you. And that's all I know, Mrs. Rayburn. Truly."

Keeping her expression carefully unconcerned, Camilla said, "Thank you, Miss Arbuthnot. I won't keep you any longer. I'm sure this is just a tempest in a teapot. Nothing at all important. In any event, Dorcas won't be angry with you, I promise."

Camilla went straight to Miles, standing close by with his friend from the Four-in-Hand Club, and touched his arm. She said in a low voice, "Miles, will you take me home immediately?"

"Certainly." Excusing himself to his friend, Miles moved off with Camilla. "What is it? Are you ill?"

She shook her head. "I'm fine. It's—I'm worried about Dorcas."

"What's the matter with Dorcas?" Miles asked in quick alarm.

"I'm not sure. Nothing, perhaps. Please, Miles, call for your carriage."

As they drove to Park Street, Miles renewed his questions. Camilla would only say, "Wait until we reach the house. Then we'll talk."

The housemaid, Lizzie, answered the door. She seemed very surprised to see her mistress. "Ye're home very early, ma'am."

Camilla pushed past the maid and raced up the stairs and down the hallway to Dorcas's bedchamber. Opening the door, she peered into the room. In the dim light coming from the single lamp in the hallway she could see the mounded heap of coverlets on the bed. Purposefully she walked to the bed and pulled back the coverlets.

A gasp sounded behind her. Her abigail's low, worried voice said, "Oh, ma'am, I'm sorry I didn't catch you before you came in here. Miss Dorcas *will* be in a taking. She asked me to tell you not to look in on her when you returned from your engagement. She said she hoped to be able to sleep soundly through the night . . ." The abigail's voice trailed away. From her position on the threshold, Becky could see as clearly as Camilla that the bed was empty.

In silence, Camilla lit a candle and marched over to the wardrobe, where she quickly scanned the numerous garments hanging there. "You're more familiar with Miss Dorcas's clothes than I am, Becky. See if I'm right. I think Miss Dorcas's rose and silver gown is missing."

A few minutes later Camilla walked slowly into the drawing room. Miles jumped up from his chair. "Well?"

"Dorcas is gone, Miles. She pretended to have a headache so she wouldn't be obliged to accompany us tonight. Then, immediately after we left the house, she apparently dressed and went out without being observed. I think we'll find that she pushed back the bolt of the scullery door before she left, so she'd be able to slip into the house in the early hours without arousing the servants."

Miles stared at Camilla disbelievingly. "But — why? Where could she have gone?"

"I can only guess, of course, but I think she's with Aubrey Elvaston."

"No!" Miles's face was livid with anger and denial. "Oh, granted she met with Elvaston that morning in the Green Park. But that was merely ill-advised. Dorcas has so little social experience. But you can't tell me she'd make an evening assignation with him. She'd never be so lost to propriety. And another thing. Even an innocent like Dorcas would surely realize how easily she might be recognized in Elvaston's company. He lives at the Albany, doesn't he? People coming and going at all hours. Her reputation would be blasted."

"Miles, I'm not accusing Dorcas of making an assignation with Sir Aubrey at his rooms in the Albany. We both know she wouldn't do such a thing. Dorcas probably thinks she's been invited to attend a supper party with Sir Aubrey's friends at his villa on the Thames."

His face troubled, Miles said slowly, "That sounds like more than a guess. You seem to know a great deal about Aubrey Elvaston and his way of life."

"I do, yes. I've known Sir Aubrey for a long time, to my sorrow. Miles, we haven't a moment to lose. We must go after Dorcas, to save her from —" Camilla swallowed hard. "We must get to her before something happens that will scar her for life. But first we need help."

"Well, my friend, I hear you've been busy on 'Change," said Nathan Rothschild, pouring Jean another glass of wine. His wife had left them to their port some time before.

Jean looked up from the walnut he was cracking. "You hear everything, don't you?" he said, his voice

186

rippling with amusement.

"I certainly try. So you bought a block of Midlands Colliery stock and sold it a week later for a handsome profit. Very good. You also dabbled a bit in bullion, also at a profit. Even better."

"I was merely following your advice, NM" The initials came easily to Jean's lips now. During these past weeks, his unlikely friendship with Nathan Rothschild had flourished to the point where he was using the nickname employed only by the merchant banker's closest associates. "I'd acquired a little capital, you see—"

"Excuse me, my friend, that's not how I'd refer to the proceeds of a stunning run of luck at the hazard table," said Rothschild dryly. "Hardly my idea of the best method of raising investment funds. Personally, I never gamble. I like a sure thing."

"You *do* hear everything! Well, for your information, I've stopped gambling. I know I'd eventually come a cropper." Jean glanced challengingly at Rothschild. "Some folk would say that what we're doing on 'Change is a form of gambling."

Rothschild gave a snort of disgust. "More fools they."

Jean laughed. "All the same, NM, I know you've taken some enormous risks."

"I'm still solvent, my boy."

Jean laughed again. Then, becoming thoughtful, he said, "I've been thinking over your warning about the future tactics of the Hudson's Bay Company in regard to their competitors. I thought you might be interested to learn that I've advised my partners in Canada to sell out to the Northwest Fur Trading Company. Northwest has been making offers to us for over a year now. I believe it's time for me, at least, to leave the fur business."

"A wise decision." Rothschild cleared his throat. "Does this also mean you've decided against returning to Canada?"

His face darkening, Jean aimlessly pushed walnut shells

around on the tablecloth. "No. That is, I'm not sure. I promised—"

"I know," finished Rothschild. "You promised a certain somebody you'd stay in London for the Season. None of my affair, naturally. The reason I asked you about your plans for your future is that I remembered what you told me about your relatives in France. They live in the Calais area, as I recall. Now, I have certain—er—financial connections in France." He paused, as if he were considering how to phrase his next words.

Jean smothered a grin. In his brief career in the London business world, he'd heard the rumors that Nathan Rothschild had made a small fortune running contraband goods into European ports in defiance of Napoleon's Continental blockade. Jean was about to ask why Rothschild was so interested in his French relations when a servant entered the dining room with a note on a tray.

"Message for Mr. Hilliard, sir," said the servant.

"For me?" Jean exclaimed. "But no one knows I'm here." He opened the note and quickly scanned the few scrawled lines it contained. He rose, pushing back his chair so violently that it crashed against the wall. "Sorry," he muttered. "I must go, NM. Thank you for your hospitality."

"You seem distressed, my friend. Can I help?"

"No. Thank you. Please excuse me. My—friend—is waiting outside for me."

Jean raced out of the door of the Rothschild house. He came to an abrupt stop at the sight of the tall figure standing beside the carriage which was waiting in front of the house. "Wingate!" he exclaimed, as he recognized Miles in the flickering light of the street lamp. "I didn't expect to see you. Her note said that Camilla—"

"Camilla's in the carriage," said Miles curtly.

Jean jerked the door of the carriage open and peered inside.

Camilla leaned forward and held out her hand. "Jean!

I wasn't sure you'd come," she said with relief.

"You weren't sure?" he exclaimed incredulously. "Why weren't you sure?"

Camilla moved over on the cushions to allow Jean to sit beside her. Immediately she was conscious of a surge of confidence and hope at the nearness of that powerful muscled body. Miles settled himself on the opposite seat. As the carriage moved off, Jean asked, "How did you find me?"

"First we tried White's and Boodle's," said Miles. Camilla caught the distinct note of resentment in his voice. He hadn't wanted her to send for Jean. "I'm quite capable of dealing with Elvaston," he'd growled. "Why waste time chasing after Hilliard?"

"Because we can use reinforcements," she'd retorted. "And Jean is a street fighter. He won't allow the slightest degree of polite compunction to interfere in our rescue of Dorcas. That is, if he agrees to come with us," Camilla had added, in an onset of uncertainty. Her relations with Jean had been going from bad to worse. Why should he rush into a possibly dangerous situation for her sake?

Miles's voice brought her back to the present. He went on to explain to Jean how they'd discovered his whereabouts. "When we didn't find you at your clubs, we went to Sheringham House. The earl was out, but your valet said you'd mentioned having supper with Nathan Rothschild."

Jean chuckled. "For the first time since I hired him, I'm grateful for Curtis's nosiness. He *always* knows where I'm to be found. He makes it his business to know." The amusement faded from Jean's voice. He turned to Camilla, "You said in your note that you needed my help. What do you want me to do?"

After listening attentively to Camilla's hurried story, Jean was silent for a few moments. At last he said, "It's a

189

stab in the dark, Camilla. You must know that. You don't have any real evidence that Dorcas is with Elvaston, other than the fact that she felt friendly toward him, and he wasn't present at the rout tonight."

Camilla said tightly, "Take my word for it, Jean. Dorcas is with Sir Aubrey at his villa."

Without a moment's hesitation, Jean said, "All right, Camilla. I believe you. Where are we going, exactly?"

"Sir Aubrey's villa is on the river's edge in Chiswick. Miles's coachman knows where to go."

They drove in silence from the city in the swiftly darkening June twilight to Hyde Park Corner, past St. George's Hospital and then along the Knightsbridge Road for several miles to Hammersmith.

Camilla sat huddled against the squabs, a prey to growing anxiety. She wasn't really angry at Dorcas. She knew all too well how charmingly persuasive Sir Aubrey could be, how easily he could make black seem like white. She was certain that Dorcas thought of her escapade tonight merely as a lark, made even more exciting by a touch of the forbidden. Camilla shivered and pulled her fringed silk scarf more tightly around her, though the night air was quite warm. What if she and Miles and Jean arrived at the villa too late? What if Aubrey Elvaston had already accomplished his purpose?

As if he was completely attune to her feelings, Jean instantly wrapped his arm around her. "Hold on, *petite,*" he murmured. "We must all be strong for Dorcas."

For a moment Camilla relaxed against him, feeling oddly reassured, feeling also an overwhelming urge to transfer all her apprehensions and insecurities to his broad shoulders. Then she straightened, saying in a low voice, "I'm sorry to be so missish. It's just that I'm so worried . . ."

He took her hand in a warm, vital grasp. "I know."

They had left Hammersmith and were approaching Chiswick, surrounded on three sides by a wide loop of the

River Thames. Though it was only six miles from Hyde Park Corner, it had remained an area of large estates and farms and market gardens. As they drove into Chiswick along the Mall, passing the old Red Lion Inn, Miles stirred on his seat opposite Camilla and Jean, saying, "We must be almost there. Hilliard, we should be making some plan of action beforehand."

Jean replied, "We can't make a plan until we've seen the house and grounds. How much farther, Camilla?"

"Not far. The coachman is driving toward the river now. When he reaches the church, he'll turn into a side lane leading to Sir Aubrey's villa."

Jean nodded, lapsing into silence until they arrived at an ancient and dilapidated church building. Then he signaled to the coachman by rapping on the roof. When the vehicle stopped, he explained, "I don't think we should take the carriage any farther. No point in advertising our presence. Camilla, I gather you've been to Elvaston's villa as a guest. Tell me something about it. Is the property walled, and does it have a gatehouse?"

"Yes, the house and grounds are completely surrounded by a wall, except for the riverside frontage, and there is a gatehouse." A hard note crept into Camilla's voice. "Sir Aubrey likes complete privacy when he entertains."

"I see." After several moments' thought, Jean said to Miles, "Well, Wingate, this is what I think we should do. You and I will go down the lane to the gatehouse, check to see if a gatekeeper is present, and, if so, dispose of him. Then we'll proceed up the driveway — by the way, Camilla, how far is the gatehouse from the villa itself?"

"It's a very short driveway, not over an eighth of a mile long, I should say. But what do you mean, Jean, by saying that you and Miles will go to the gatehouse? You're not leaving me behind."

"Camilla!" exclaimed Jean and Miles in unison.

"You're staying here," said Jean with finality.

"Hilliard's right" Miles chimed in. "This could be dangerous. After all, we'll no doubt be breaking and entering. If one of Elvaston's servants were to catch you, he might try to manhandle you."

"Tell me how you two propose to stop me from going with you," said Camilla sweetly. "Are you going to tie me up? Of course, you have no rope. Or perhaps you'll order the coachman to hold me fast with my arms twisted behind my back. Vastly uncomfortable for both of us, if you're gone for any length of time. Not to mention I'd be out of my mind with worry, not knowing what was happening!"

"Camilla, be reasonable," Miles protested.

"I'm being very reasonable," Camilla retorted. "Think about it. I know the floor plan of the villa. You don't. And I could act as your lookout if you need one."

Jean threw up his hands. "You win, Camilla." He added grimly, "but you'll do as you're told, and you'll be careful."

A few lights shone in the handful of cottages around the church, but nothing was stirring, not even a stray mongrel, as Camilla and Miles and Jean got out of the carriage and began walking up the tree-lined lane leading to the villa. The twilight had merged into full darkness. A half moon was rising on the horizon, but, even so, Camilla had difficulty seeing ahead of her. She marveled at Jean in the lead, moving swiftly and steadily along the driveway, as if he were traversing a forest path in his Québec homeland. Perhaps his Indian grandmother had bequeathed him the ability to see in the dark.

Near the end of the driveway, Jean stopped abruptly. A faint light showed in the gatehouse. "Camilla," he whispered. "Do you think you could act like a strumpet?"

"What—?"

"Sh-h-h. I want you to rouse the gatekeeper, telling him that Sir Aubrey has invited you to visit him. If possible, persuade the gatekeeper to come outside to talk to you. Act and talk as vulgarly as you can. The gatekeeper may or may not believe you have a rendezvous with Elvaston, but while you're keeping him occupied, Miles and I may be able to come up behind him and put him out of action."

"Coming it too strong, Hilliard," muttered Miles. "I can't allow Camilla to do this. Why, the fellow might lay a hand on her!"

"Oh, do be quiet, Miles. I think it's a famous scheme." Camilla removed her satin evening toque with its nodding plume and coaxed her hair to lie in flirtatious curls around her forehead and ears. She trailed her shawl negligently from her elbows, and pushed her brief sleeves down on her arms to expose an enticing expanse of bosom. "How do I look?" she murmured.

"Like a strumpet," breathed Jean. She could hear the choked laughter in his barely audible tone.

Camilla stepped out into the open area in front of the gatehouse and walked purposefully toward the gates. She pulled vigorously on the bell rope. A lighted window in the upper story of the gatehouse opened, and a rough voice called out, "Yes? Who is it?"

Placing her hands on her hips and cocking her head provocatively, Camilla called, "I'm 'ere to see 'is lordship. Sir Aubrey, I mean."

"Sir Aubrey, 'e didn't tell me 'e was expecting a female visitor." The rough voice merged into a cackle. "Which is 'ardly surprising, since 'e's already *got* a female visitor."

Camilla's heart missed a beat. She forced herself to laugh, hoping she sounded properly lascivious. "Recken ye must be a real innocent. Don't ye know these 'ere gentry morts, they likes to entertain more'n one female at a time? Sir Aubrey, now *'e's* a proper man wif the ladies, the more the merrier!"

For the first time, the voice sounded uncertain. "Well, that's as may be, my pretty, but Sir Aubrey, 'e didn't leave no message 'e was expecting another female. So ye kin jist go away, an' leave a man to take 'is rest."

"Sir Aubrey jist fergot to tell ye I was coming, that's all," said Camilla impatiently. "I'm sure ye wouldn't wish to git into Sir Aubrey's bad graces by turning away an invited guest from 'is door, now, would ye? An' fer 'eaven's sake, must ye stay in there where I can't see ye? Come out 'ere where I kin talk to ye properly."

After a pause, the voice said, "Oh, all right, then. I'll come down."

As Camilla waited for the gatekeeper, she glimpsed in the faint moonlight the swift passage of two shadowy figures from the lane behind her to positions on either side of the gate.

In a few moments the gate opened, and an unprepossessing individual in rough clothes appeared. He peered at Camilla in the dim light with a distinctly approving gaze. "Blimey, I cain't see why Sir Aubrey wouldn't be content to entertain jist ye, lass," he said with a leer. A split second later, he fell to the ground with a leaden thud as Jean slipped up behind him and chopped a powerful blow on the back of the man's neck with the side of his hand.

"See if the fellow has a wife or other appendages in his cottage," Jean instructed Miles as he began tearing off his cravat.

In a few moments, Miles returned from the gatehouse to say wryly, "Fellow must be a bachelor. No wife or children in residence."

"Good. So far we're in the clear." Jean ripped off a piece of his cravat, which he tied as a gag around the gatekeeper's mouth, and used the rest of the linen strip to secure the gatekeeper's hands behind his back. He held out his hand. "You'll have to make the supreme sacrifice, Wingate. I need your cravat, too."

With a morose look, Miles removed his cravat and handed it to Jean, who promptly tied the gatekeeper's ankles together. "There, that should keep the fellow out of mischief for a while," Jean said with relief. "Give me a hand, Wingate. We'll put him inside his cottage, out of the way of any curious eyes."

When he and Miles returned from disposing of the gatekeeper's unconscious body, Jean said to Camilla with a grin, "That was a tremendous performance you gave. You were a doxy to the life. Perhaps you've mistaken your calling. You should go on the boards."

"For God's sake, Hilliard, this is no time for jokes or other pleasantries," Miles said impatiently. "Let's get on with it!"

The grin left Jean's mouth. "You're right." He headed for the gates in the wall that surrounded the property. Miles and Camilla followed after him. Keeping their steps slow and cautious, they walked up the short driveway, which led straight to the rear of the villa and then curved around the building to the porticoed front entrance, which faced a graceful sweep of lawn sloping down to the river. Motioning Miles and Camilla to silence, Jean paused in the shadow of a large tree near a front corner of the house to examine the building. Lights shone in several rooms on the ground floor and the first floor and in one room on the second floor. Camilla's stomach twisted. That second floor room was probably Sir Aubrey's bedchamber.

"Tell me about the floor plan, Camilla," Jean whispered.

"Dining room and drawing room facing each other across the foyer, library and billiard room behind, kitchens and scullery on the ground floor."

"We'll try the kitchens." Jean began moving back to the rear of the villa. Despite the gravity of the situation, Camilla felt a flicker of amusement. Without a conscious decision on anyone's part, Jean had coolly taken charge of the situation tonight.

Reaching the rear of the villa, Jean peered into a window of the kitchens. "There's just one servant in there," he reported back in a whisper. "Looks like a scullery maid. She's sitting half asleep at a table." He put out his hand to the door handle and cautiously turned it. The door wasn't locked.

Before the drowsing scullery maid was aware that intruders had entered the room, Jean had swept through the door and across the room to clap his hand across the girl's mouth. He picked up a knife from the table and held it in front of her eyes. "In a moment, I'm going to take away my hand from your mouth," he said, in a low, menacing tone. "If you utter one sound, I'll use this knife to cut your throat. Do you understand? Nod your head if you do."

Her eyes bulging with fright, the scullery maid nodded her head frantically.

"*Bon.*" As he so often did in moments of stress, Jean had reverted to his mother tongue. He slowly removed his hand from the girl's face, keeping the point of the knife lightly pressed against her neck. She sat in frozen shock, scarcely daring to breathe. Camilla felt sorry for her. The girl couldn't know that Jean had no intention of slitting her throat.

"Now, I want some answers from you," Jean growled. "How many servants are in the house tonight?"

"Jist me, sir, and Sir Aubrey's valet, o'course," said the scullery maid in a shaking voice. "The master, 'e told the rest o' the servants they was to have the night off. Cook, after 'e served dinner, 'e went off, too. I'm 'ere jist to clear the dining room and wash up the dishes when Sir Aubrey finishes 'is meal."

A familiar ploy, Camilla thought bitterly. Sir Aubrey wanted as few witnesses as possible to his gallantries. However, she was glad he was acting in character. It would be much easier to rescue Dorcas if Sir Aubrey was unable to call on his staff of servants.

Jean continued, "Sir Aubrey's still in the dining room, then?"

"Why, yes. Leastways, 'e ain't rung fer me yet."

Jean thought for a moment. "Where's this valet?"

"Why—upstairs in Sir Aubrey's bedchamber, I reckon."

The scullery maid gasped in fear as Jean suddenly ripped the voluminous apron from around her waist.

"Wingate, I need you."

Silently Miles moved forward to help Jean tear the apron apart and gag and tie up the scullery maid. When they had finished, Jean said quietly to the girl, "Don't worry. No one will harm you. I'll see you're released soon." He turned to Miles and Camilla. "Let's go."

Silently they filed out of the kitchen, up the staircase and into the hallway. From under the doorway of a room to the left, the subdued light of candles gleamed. Jean raised his eyebrow to Camilla. She nodded. They were outside the dining room. A low murmur of voices was barely audible. Camilla felt an overwhelming sense of relief. They weren't too late.

Jean slowly turned the handle of the door and opened it a crack. Apparently no one in the room noticed, but now the listeners in the hallway could hear the low voices more distinctly.

Dorcas was saying, "Sir Aubrey, I'd like to go home now. It's very late." Knowing her sister so well, Camilla recognized the note of panic in Dorcas's voice.

"Oh, come, now, my dear, the evening's young," said Sir Aubrey. His tone, soft and caressing and intimate, made Camilla feel sick. "There's no reason to be concerned about the time, you know. Your sister thinks you're safely tucked in your bed, and I'll see that you arrive home before anyone misses you. Relax. Have another glass of this champagne. Really a very decent vintage, thanks to our efficient English smugglers."

"I don't want any more wine. Please, Sir Aubrey, I want to go home." Dorcas's voice became shrill. "I'd never have come here if I'd known I was to be the only guest. You told me you were having an intimate supper party for all your most amusing friends."

Sir Aubrey chuckled. "A mere shading of the truth. I'm hoping that *you'll* become my most intimate friend. I invited you here because I wanted us to know each other better."

Jean wrenched the door completely open and strode

into the dining room, followed by Miles and Camilla. Seated at either end of the dining table, Sir Aubrey and Dorcas stared at them in stupefaction.

"Dorcas knows you quite well enough, Elvaston," said Jean curtly. "We've come to take her home."

Recovering from her momentary paralysis of surprise, Dorcas jumped up from the table, her face flooded with a joyous relief. "Mr. Hilliard, Camilla, Miles, oh, I'm so happy to see you," she exclaimed.

Sir Aubrey rose from his chair more slowly. Casting an especially venomous look at Jean—Camilla remembered that it was only a few days ago that Jean had shoved him to the ground in the Green Park—Sir Aubrey said sharply, "What are you three doing in my house? I never asked you here. You're trespassing, and I'm ordering you to leave immediately."

"That's exactly what we intend to do," said Camilla, "and we're taking my sister with us."

"Wingate, you go on ahead with Camilla and Dorcas," said Jean. "I'll stay here long enough to make sure that Elvaston doesn't try to make mischief."

"I'll thank you not to give me any more orders, Hilliard," said Miles in a voice quivering with rage. "*You* go on ahead. Before I leave, I intend to give this miserable loose screw a beating he'll never forget. I'll see to it that Dorcas is the last innocent he tries to seduce." He strode purposefully toward Sir Aubrey, who backed away from the table toward a sideboard set against the wall. Keeping a wary eye on Miles, he opened a drawer in the sideboard and produced a small pistol.

"Don't come an inch closer, Wingate," Elvaston warned.

Miles laughed and kept on advancing. "You're a loose screw, but you're not stupid. You'd never try to murder me in cold blood in front of three witnesses," he jeered.

Elvaston fired, and Miles fell to the floor, clutching at his shoulder. Jean leapt across the room like a huge cat and smashed his fist into Elvaston's jaw.

Sir Aubrey dropped like a stone.

On her knees beside Miles's prone form, frantically trying to remove his coat so she could examine his wound, which was bleeding profusely, Camilla muttered to Jean as he threw himself down beside her, "Oh, God, Jean, Sir Aubrey could have shot you, too."

"Not with a single-barreled dueling pistol," Jean retorted. "Give me your shawl, Camilla." He took the garment and pushed it under Miles's coat, holding it firmly against the shoulder. "This pressure should slow the bleeding. Camilla, go as fast as you can to fetch the carriage. Have the coachman drive to the front entrance. We must get Wingate to a surgeon as soon as possible."

As Camilla, without questioning, started instantly for the door, Jean glanced up at Dorcas, standing still as a statue, in such a state of shock that she seemed unable to comprehend what was happening. "Dorcas," he said sharply. "Get hold of yourself." In a moment her eyes cleared. She took a long look at Miles's white face and bloodstained coat and she fainted dead away.

Camilla turned back to care for her sister. "Leave her be," Jean growled. "She'll soon come around. *Mon Dieu,* I'd hoped she could make herself useful—stand over Elvaston and hit him over the head if he showed signs of reviving, some such thing." His voice sharpened. "Camilla, will you do as I say? Fetch the carriage before Wingate bleeds to death."

Chapter Thirteen

"Dorcas, please try to stop crying," Camilla pleaded, holding her sister close in the darkness of the carriage. "You'll make yourself ill."

Dorcas shuddered. "I deserve to be ill," she said tearfully. "If Miles dies, I deserve to die, too. It's all my fault that he was shot."

Her nerves on edge, Camilla looked out the window of the carriage at the tall, narrow building that housed the home and surgery of Miles's doctor, in a quiet cul-de-sac off Harley Street. Desperately she willed Jean's tall form to appear in the doorway of the house. Half an hour before, he and the coachman had carried Miles's body into the surgery. The coachman had returned to sit on his box, but Jean was still inside, waiting, as Camilla and Dorcas were waiting in the carriage, to find out if Miles would live or die after being shot by Aubrey Elvaston.

The minutes dragged leadenly by, and Dorcas continued to weep. Finally the door of the house opened, and Jean stepped out. Camilla's heart began to pound. Jean hurried to the carriage and opened the door. "Good news, Camilla," he said jubilantly. "The surgeon's removed the bullet. He says it was a clean wound, and Wingate will be himself in no time at all. Dr. Hancock is keeping him in the surgery overnight, merely as a precaution, in case Wingate's wound starts bleeding again, or he becomes feverish."

Dorcas gave a great gasp, and burst into a storm of hysterical sobbing that racked her slender body. Jean ordered the coachman to drive to Park Street and climbed into the carriage. Staring at Dorcas, he said helplessly, "Confound it, Camilla, why is Dorcas crying now, when she's just found out that Wingate will recover?"

"Oh, for heaven's sake, Jean, have a little compassion. She can't help herself," Camilla burst out. She paused, biting her lips. "I'm sorry. I shouldn't have lashed out at you like that. It's just that everything that's happened tonight has been too much for Dorcas. She needs to be put to bed with a sedative." She put her arms around her sister, murmuring soothing phrases that Dorcas didn't seem to hear. She continued to sob hopelessly.

Dorcas was very near collapse by the time they reached Park Street. Jean carried her up the staircase and deposited her on her bed. "I'll wait for you downstairs," he told Camilla.

"That's not necessary," Camilla said quickly. "I can manage now. Why don't you go home and get some rest yourself?" She swallowed hard. "Oh, God, Jean, what must you be thinking of me? I haven't even thanked you for saving Dorcas, and getting Miles to a doctor before he bled to death."

"There's no need to thank me," Jean said quietly. "I wanted to help. But Camilla, I'm worried about you. I've never seen you so distressed. You're very close to the breaking point yourself. There's more to this situation than you've told me, isn't there? I think you need to talk. I'm ready to listen."

Camilla shook her head. "No. There's nothing. I can't . . ."

Jean put out his hand, gently stroking her cheek with his strong, work-roughened fingers. "I'll be waiting for you, if you do want to talk."

Half an hour later, Camilla entered the drawing room

with a slow, dragging step. She hadn't wanted to come downstairs. She felt so tired, so drained of emotion, that the effort of putting one foot in front of another was almost beyond her. And yet her conscience wouldn't allow her to leave Jean waiting vainly for her in the drawing room. At the very least she should go down, if only to tell him to go home.

"Dorcas is sleeping soundly," Camilla told Jean with a weary sigh. "She was utterly exhausted. I gave her a dose of laudanum. She'll sleep until morning."

"Good." Jean placed his hand under her chin and looked deeply into her eyes. "And how are you?"

The note of warm concern in his voice, added to the accumulated strains of the evening, broke down Camilla's defenses. The tears began streaming down her face in an uncontrollable flood. Guiding her to a settee, Jean sat down beside her. He folded his arms around her and held her closely against his chest, murmuring, "Cry it out, *petite.*"

At last the tears stopped. Reluctantly Camilla lifted her head from the comforting haven of Jean's shoulder and sat up. She took the handkerchief that Jean silently handed to her and mopped her eyes vigorously.

"Better now?" he asked, looking at her closely.

She nodded, not speaking, pulling the handkerchief nervously between her fingers.

Jean said softly, "Do you know what I think, Camilla? I think you've kept something hurtful bottled up inside you for a very long time. You don't speak of it, you try not to think of it, but it's there. Whatever that something is, it will only go on festering and growing more hurtful, until you bring it out into the open."

For a long moment, Camilla hesitated. Then, with a great sigh, she began to talk . . .

* * *

Carrying a glass of wine in his hand, Philip Rayburn walked into his wife's bedchamber. "Good God, Camilla, you've not begun to dress," he exclaimed in a tone of acute displeasure, eyeing her silk dressing gown.

Seated in a chair by the window, Camilla looked up from the book she was reading. "I don't intend to dress," she said calmly. "Nor do I intend to go to Aubrey Elvaston's villa for the weekend. I have the headache. Go on without me, if you like. I shall be quite all right here by myself. I have several new books from the circulating library."

His face reddening with anger, Philip drained his wine and hurled the empty glass at the fireplace. "Damnation, Camilla, don't you try to bubble me. You're never ill. This so-called headache is just a trumpery excuse to avoid keeping our engagement, and I won't have it. Elvaston invited us both, and both of us will go."

Camilla glanced at the broken shards of glass glittering on the floor in front of the fireplace and back to her husband's face. She and Philip had been married for almost a year now, and she'd become accustomed to his violent rages. In point of fact, she'd realized within a month of their wedding that her marriage was a mistake. Philip was a deeply flawed human being.

They'd met in Bath, on one of his periodic visits to an ancient aunt who might, or might not, be inclined to leave him her money. Philip proposed at their second meeting, and she accepted him at their third. She wasn't madly in love with him, though she liked him very much, and she enjoyed his company. He was handsome, with his chestnut curls and bright blue eyes and infectious smile. On the surface, at least, he was lighthearted and infinitely amusing. Above all, he was her passport to freedom. She'd have seized almost any opportunity to escape from Bath and from the constricting bonds of her stepmother's jealousy, which had grown steadily worse since Camilla had turned eighteen and inherited her mother's small fortune.

"Well?" Philip demanded truculently.

Camilla studied her husband's face as he stood glaring at her. He was only twenty-five, but already the marks of dissipation were beginning to blur his handsome features. He drank too much, he gambled his nights away, he took too little exercise. Camilla knew he must be deeply in debt, judging by the dunning bills that poured across her desk. Certainly the income from her modest inheritance, combined with Philip's small allowance from his family, had never been sufficient to support their style of living, quite aside from Philip's excesses. She suspected they might soon be evicted from their fashionable rooms in this substantial house on Jermyn Street.

Philip said harshly, "Did you hear me, Camilla? I won't accept your excuses. I insist you come to Elvaston's villa with me. He's gone to a great deal of trouble to arrange this party. He told me just the other day that he'd invited people he knew would be congenial to you."

Shrugging, Camilla turned her attention back to her book. "I've made up my mind, Philip. I'm not going. I don't like Aubrey Elvaston, and I don't like his friends."

With a sudden swift movement, Philip snatched the book from her hand, tossed it on the floor and ground it beneath his heel.

Camilla raised her eyebrows. "Did you enjoy that? I can't imagine why."

Philip's face seemed to crumble. He sank into a chair opposite her. "I'm sorry. It's my cursed temper. Camilla, I beg you to come to Elvaston's villa with me. I'll go down on my knees to you, if you like."

Although Philip's harsh words and threats had made no impression on her, the note of desperate appeal in his voice reached Camilla. She asked, "*Why* is it so important to you that I go to the villa?"

Philip said reluctantly, "I — I've lost a lot of money to Elvaston. Faro, whist, piquet. He has the devil's own luck. He's not pressing for payment, not yet, but I can't afford to get into his bad graces. You see that, don't you? Please, Camilla. Do this for me."

Her mouth dry, Camilla asked, "How much do you owe Sir Aubrey?" Her eyes widened in shock at his reply. "Ten thousand pounds? How can you ever hope to repay such a sum? And you owe more than that, don't you? Much more, at a guess. To tradesmen, to our landlord. To other gambling friends, no doubt. Philip, what are we going to do? We can't go on this way."

Philip stared down at his clenched hands. "I know. I haven't given you a very good life, have I, Camilla? But I'll change, I promise you. I'll stop gambling. I won't drink so much. I'll go to my father, ask him for money one last time. Once we're out from under this load of debt, we can start over. But for now, I can't antagonize Aubrey Elvaston. He could have me blackballed all over London. We'd be ostracized by everyone. I couldn't show my face on St. James's Street. Please, Camilla, come with me to the villa. I won't ask you for anything, ever again."

Her lips tightening, Camilla gazed at Philip's bowed head. She knew better than to believe in his promises to reform, to stop drinking and gambling. He'd made promises before. She was sure his long-suffering father wouldn't advance his wild younger son another shilling. No, she and Philip would go on as they'd been going, sliding deeper and deeper into debt, with the prospect of debtors' prison for Philip a real possibility. For the moment, though . . .

Her heart lurched in pity. He was so unhappy, so desperate. And he was her husband. What did it matter, one weekend spent at Aubrey Elvaston's villa with him and his rakish companions? She heard herself saying, "Very well, Philip, I'll go."

They arrived at the Chiswick villa in late afternoon of a Friday, drawing up in front of the graceful front portico in a carriage that wasn't paid for, driven by a coachman whose wages were in arrears, with an abigail and a valet and their luggage following behind in a hired hackney. As she stepped out of the carriage, Camilla looked admiringly at the building, with which she was familiar from previous visits. Much as she disliked Sir Aubrey, she'd never been able to fault his taste. The house was an exquisite miniature copy of a Palladian villa, transplanted from northern Italy.

Servants swarmed out of the house to take their baggage, direct the coachman and the valet and the abigail to their proper places and escort Sir Aubrey's guests to the drawing room, where he waited to receive them. As Camilla and Philip entered the room, Sir Aubrey advanced toward them with outstretched hands. "You're in very good time," he beamed. "If only all my guests were as prompt." He took Camilla's hand, touching his lips to her fingers in the exaggerated Continental fashion of the foreign diplomats with whom he associated.

Camilla suppressed the urge to snatch her hand away precipitously. Elvaston's touch repelled her. It was strange, in a way. With his flaxen hair and spare classical features, he was a handsome man, tall and slender and graceful. His manners were impeccably polished, and he'd always treated her graciously. So why, then, did she dislike him so intensely? It's his eyes, she thought suddenly. They were like gray icicles, without the slightest trace of warmth. And also, for the first time in their acquaintance, it dawned on Camilla that, whenever Sir Aubrey looked at her, he was mentally undressing her with a chilly, clinical passion.

With a mental shudder, she withdrew her hand from his grasp and stepped back from him. "Philip hasn't told

206

me who our fellow guests will be," she said, with a false appearance of interest.

Sir Aubrey laughed. "Well, now, I hope you won't be disappointed, Mrs. Rayburn, when I tell you there will be no fellow guests."

Camilla gazed at him blankly. "Philip said this was to be a house party."

"That's what I originally had in mind. But then several people I'd planned to invite told me they had previous engagements, and Mme. Valetta—whom I'd asked to be my hostess—was unexpectedly asked to substitute for Catalani at the Royal Opera. So I decided, why not just ask the Rayburns? It will be an opportunity for us to become better acquainted." Sir Aubrey slapped Philip on the back. "Isn't that so, Rayburn?" he said jovially.

"What? Oh, yes, to be sure," Philip replied. He seemed curiously abstracted. Paying no attention to the conversation, he gulped down the Madeira that Elvaston offered him, and immediately held out his glass for a refill.

Camilla felt disquieted, as if the atmosphere was charged with a vague menace that she could sense but not see. Later, in their bedchamber, as she and Philip dressed for dinner, she said, "I'm uncomfortable with the thought of the two of us being Sir Aubrey's only guests. I'd like to leave in the morning after breakfast."

To her surprise, Philip made no objection. "As you wish," he said curtly. He added, "I don't care to stay, either. There's be no point to it." It was such a strange remark, and his mood seemed even more strange. It persisted into dinner. He ate very little, merely pushing his food about on his plate, but he drank heavily, consuming the better part of a bottle of wine.

Camilla's heart sank. At this rate, after he'd drunk his after-dinner port with his host, Philip would probably be half seas over. He might even collapse in a drunken stupor, leaving her alone in Sir Aubrey's company. She took a quick decision. When she rose to leave the table after the second course, she said, "Sir Aubrey, I'm sure you won't object if I don't wait for you and Philip to join me for coffee in the drawing room. I'm not feeling quite the thing. I believe I'll go straight to bed."

Elvaston gave her a charming smile. "But of course, Mrs. Rayburn," he said sympathetically. "Shall I ask my cook to bring you a *tisane?* A very effective remedy for any indisposition, I've found."

"No, I thank you. Sleep is the only remedy I need." She made a hasty retreat, sighing with relief when she closed the door of her bedchamber behind her. Philip would be angry with her, she knew, for cutting short the evening—if he weren't too foxed to remember what had happened, that is—but under no circumstances would she risk engaging in a cozy session alone with Sir Aubrey.

Her abigail helped her undress and brushed out her hair. Camilla smiled at the girl, saying, "Thank you. You may go now. Do you have a comfortable place to sleep?"

"Yes, ma'am. I'm sharing a nice room over the stables with the scullery maid."

"Over the stables?" Camilla said in surprise.

"Yes, ma'am. Cook sleeps there, too. Most o' the servants, though, they lives in the village."

Camilla's lips tightened. Sir Aubrey's desire for privacy must be acute, indeed, if he refused to house his servants in the villa itself. Once again she felt a strong sense of disquiet. She was glad she was leaving tomorrow.

After the abigail left, Camilla sat down in a comfortable chair with a book, too restless to sleep. She glanced with distaste at the bottle of champagne in its silver ice bucket on the commode at the side of the room. Had Philip ordered it? By the time he stumbled up to their bedchamber later tonight, he'd surely be too castaway to consume the champagne.

Her eyelids were beginning to grow heavy when the door of the bedchamber opened. She sprang up, her book dropping to the floor unnoticed. "You! What are you doing here?"

Sir Aubrey smiled, closing the door behind him. "Isn't it self-evident? I'm paying you a little visit."

"Where's Philip?"

"I have no idea. He's left the house, in any event, leaving me a clear field. He won't be back this evening."

"What do you mean?" A powerful vice seemed to have closed around Camilla's chest, making it difficult for her to breathe.

Sir Aubrey didn't answer her question. He advanced slowly into the room, looking about him with a pleased expression. "It's a pretty room, isn't it? I hoped you'd enjoy staying in it." His gaze settled on Camilla. "That's a very pretty dressing gown, too. Not that you'll be wearing it very long, of course."

Keeping her voice steady by a supreme effort of her will, Camilla said, "I want you to leave this room immediately, Sir Aubrey. Then find Philip and tell him to order our carriage. I won't stay in this house another hour."

Sir Aubrey's lips curled with amusement. "You'll stay the night at least, my dear. You see, your husband has made a bargain with me. A fair one, all things considered. I'm to cancel his I.O.U.'s in the amount of twenty-five thousand pounds. In return, he's agreed to loan me his wife for an evening."

Sir Aubrey's calm, matter-of-fact statement bludgeoned Camilla with the force of a giant hammer. Her first instinct was to deny the monstrous implications of what he'd said. Momentarily, when Sir Aubrey had first entered the bedchamber, she'd thought that Philip had drunk himself into insensibility, and Sir Aubrey had taken advantage of the opportunity to attempt to seduce her. Now, a few seconds later, knowing Philip and his weakness of character as well as she did, she didn't doubt that Sir Aubrey was telling the truth.

All the pieces fit together. Philip's desperate insistence that she accompany him to the villa. The absence of other invited guests. Philip's tense, abstracted manner during dinner. Perhaps he'd been feeling an intolerable guilt. She wanted to think so. But, guilt feelings or no, he'd deliberately lured her out here in order to hand her over to Sir Aubrey, in return for the remission of his debt of honor.

However, even as she acknowledged the truth of Philip's ghastly betrayal, a new horror crept into Camilla's consciousness. "Twenty-five thousand pounds?" she repeated stupidly. And then she felt sick. Philip had even lied about how much he owed Sir Aubrey. In some cruelly illogical way, it made what he'd done infinitely worse.

"I confess I've been anticipating this evening with considerable relish," said Sir Aubrey, advancing leisurely toward her. "You're an uncommonly handsome creature, my dear. I've had my eye on you for a long time. You didn't notice? Odd. I could have sworn you were attracted to me, a little. Anyone with half an eye could see you didn't care a fig for that havey-cavey husband of yours."

"Don't come a step closer. I'll scream if you touch me," warned Camilla, backing away from him until she came up against the commode at the side of the room.

"No one will hear you. The servants are all gone, except for my valet, and he's conveniently and selectively deaf. Don't be missish," Elvaston begged. "You can't get away from me, you know. Why don't you relax and try to enjoy the experience? I've been told, by a number of discriminating females, that I'm a very adequate lover."

"Discriminating? I'd call them queer in their attic,"

snapped Camilla. Out of the corner of her eye she glimpsed the bottle of champagne in its silver ice bucket on the commode. She snatched the bottle out of the bucket and held it in front of her. "I meant what I said. Don't come closer."

"What? You're threatening to hit me with a bottle of champagne?" Elvaston doubled over with laugher. Then, still laughing, he made a lightning-swift lunge and twisted the bottle out of her hand. "My dear Camilla, this is vintage champagne. I couldn't allow you to waste it," he said. "Here, let me open it."

While his attention was momentarily occupied with disengaging the wire from the cork, Camilla rushed past him and out the door of the bedchamber. He caught up with her at the head of the staircase. She struggled frantically to escape from his rough, hurting grasp, raking at his face with clawing hands, kicking out at his legs and ankles.

"Enough of this," he muttered between clenched teeth, lifting his hand in an involuntary gesture to brush away the blood flowing into his eye from a deep scratch on his forehead. At that moment, with his hold partially broken, Camilla freed herself by pushing violently against his chest. Losing his balance, Elvaston plummeted down the stairs, waving his arms grotesquely in an attempt to break his fall.

Trembling with reaction, Camilla tore her eyes away from the sight of Elvaston's crumpled, unmoving form at the foot of the stairs, and stumbled back into the bedchamber. There she tore off her dressing gown, and with fumbling fingers put on a dress and shoes and pelisse. She ran out of the room and down the servants' stairs at the other end of the corridor, without sparing a glance or a thought for the still figure at the bottom of the main staircase . . .

* * *

"I believed Sir Aubrey was dead," said Camilla dully. "I thought he'd struck his head when he fell. Later I learned he had only a slight concussion. The main damage was to his thigh. He was permanently crippled."

Having listened in intent, unmoving silence while Camilla told him about that earlier terrible encounter with Aubrey Elvaston, Jean now stirred, saying fiercely, *"Mon Dieu,* Camilla, if I'd known what Elvaston had done to you, I'd have killed him with my bare hands tonight." He paused, breathing hard. Then he took her hands in a warm, comforting grasp. "What about your husband? Can you talk about him? What did he say when you saw him the next day?"

"I never saw Philip again," Camilla whispered, her eyes darkening with remembered horror. "They found him the following morning, lying dead of a broken neck beside a hedge on Sir Aubrey's property. They said it was an accident, that he'd gone out riding alone after dinner and failed to jump the hedge. I knew better. Philip was a bruising rider, but even if he'd been dead drunk, I knew he'd never have attempted to jump a hedge as high as that. I knew he'd committed suicide. He couldn't live with himself after what he'd done."

"Oh, Camilla." Jean wrapped his arms around her and hugged her close. "Now I understand why you didn't want to marry again, why you didn't want me to kiss you. You couldn't give your trust to a man again, after what Elvaston and Philip had done to you."

"I swore I'd never give a man power over me again. And I couldn't bear to have a man touch me," Camilla said in a low voice. "It made me feel sick." She burrowed her head into his shoulder. "You've never made me feel sick."

"I know, *ma mie,"* Jean said softly. For a few moments longer, he cuddled her against him. Then he gently disen-

212

gaged himself. "I want you to go to bed now, *petite*. You're exhausted."

Camilla clutched at his arm. "Jean, don't go. I don't want to be alone tonight."

"You're not thinking straight, love. You know I can't stay." Jean chuckled. "What would the servants say? What would your neighbors say, if they glimpsed me leaving the virtuous Mrs. Rayburn's house in the wee hours of the morning? My reputation is bad enough already!" He brushed his lips across her cheek and stood up. "Get some rest, *chère*. I'll see you tomorrow."

The next morning Camilla came down the stairs and headed for the dining room with a springing step. She couldn't remember feeling so full of energy so early in the day. She sat down at the dining table and rang the bell. When Lizzie appeared, Camilla said, "I'm starved. I'd like a rasher of bacon, please."

Lizzie looked at her doubtfully, "Ye never have more'n a cup o' tea an' a bite o' toast fer breakfast."

"Well, this morning I could eat my weight in tigers, Lizzie. Bring an egg, too. No, two of them."

Having finished her unprecedently hearty breakfast, Camilla wandered into the morning room, where she sat down with the *Morning Post*. However, she soon tired of reading about births and marriages and deaths among the *ton*. Her own thoughts and feelings interested her far more. For the first time in many years she was at peace with herself, and she knew why. By revealing to Jean the terrible secret that she'd concealed for so long, she'd been able to free herself from the bondage of the past. She could think of Philip now less with blame than with pity for his weakness, and her festering fear of Aubrey Elvaston had largely disappeared. He could no longer cast a pall over her life. If it proved necessary in the future, she could deal with him.

"Camilla, can I talk to you?"

Camilla looked up to see Dorcas hesitating on the threshold. "Why, of course, love. Come in and sit down."

Dorcas settled herself onto a settee opposite Camilla. Instead of speaking, she sat with downcast eyes, crumpling and uncrumpling a fold of her muslin skirt.

At last Camilla said gently, "Did you want to talk about what happened last night?"

Another long hesitation, and then the words came in a rush. "Oh, Camilla, I've been such a fool. You warned me about Sir Aubrey, and I wouldn't listen to you. He fascinated me. He was so elegant, so much a man of the world, and yet he seemed so kind, too. I thought he really liked me, and I was so flattered. But he was only interested in one thing from me . . . Oh, Camilla, I can't bear to think of what would have happened to me if you and Mr. Hilliard and Miles hadn't come to the villa." She cut herself short, turning deathly pale. "Miles. Oh, God, if Miles dies, I'll be a murderer!"

Camilla left her chair to sit beside Dorcas on the settee. Clasping her sister's hands, Camilla said, "Shush. Miles will recover, I'm sure of it. And you mustn't blame yourself for his injury, any more than you should blame yourself for being deceived by Aubrey Elvaston. If anyone's at fault, I am. I'm convinced that Sir Aubrey lured you out to his villa in order to revenge himself on me."

Dorcas gasped. "What do you mean?"

"Remember how you kept asking me to give you a reason why you should avoid Sir Aubrey, and I always refused? I was ashamed, Dorcas. You see, when I was first married, he inveigled me out to his villa for a romantic rendezvous."

Dorcas's eyes widened. "You were in love with Sir Aubrey?"

"No, no. He tricked me into that rendezvous, just as he tricked you. I rebuffed him. In fact, I pushed him down the stairs. I'm responsible for his lameness, Dorcas. He's never forgiven me for it."

"I can understand why you didn't care to tell me about this," Dorcas said slowly. "You must have been concerned about the harm to your reputation if it became known. But — ashamed? Why should you be ashamed? It's Sir Aubrey who should be ashamed!"

Camilla swallowed against the hard lump in her throat. She'd liberated herself from her guilt and fears by talking to Jean. Now she must tell the truth to Dorcas. "What I couldn't bring myself to tell you was that Philip secretly arranged for me to spend the evening with Sir Aubrey in order to settle a gambling debt."

Dorcas sat paralyzed with shock for a moment. Then she threw herself into her sister's arms, exclaiming tearfully, "Oh, how I wish I'd known this before I allowed myself to turn into a selfish little monster!"

"Mr. Wingate, ma'am," announced Lizzie.

"Miles! You're not dead!" shrieked Dorcas joyfully, her tearful contrition vanishing on the instant. She jumped up from the settee to rush to Miles, who stood in the doorway, pale and weak-looking and with his arm in a sling, but very much alive.

Swaying slightly, and turning suddenly a light shade of greenish white, Miles said in a thready voice, "My dear Dorcas, I think I should sit down."

Taking charge, Camilla said briskly, "Of course you should sit down, you idiot. More to the point, you should still be in bed." She guided him to a chair, telling her sister, who had turned as pale as Miles, "Dorcas, bring Miles a glass of brandy."

Several minutes later, after Miles's color had improved

215

and he was speaking normally, Camilla scolded him. "What possessed you to get out of your sick bed and come here?"

"I blame your doctor, Miles," declared Dorcas, still pale and overset. "He should never have allowed it."

"Dr. Hancock couldn't help himself," said Miles with a grin. "I just walked out of his surgery. I knew you'd both be worried about my condition, and . . ." He looked at Dorcas with his heart in his eyes "I was worried about you."

Her voice trembling, Dorcas said, "Miles, how can I ever make it up to you for putting you in such danger?"

"Well . . . I know one way you can make it up to me."

Dorcas gazed at him questioningly.

"You can marry me at the end of the Season. I love you, Dorcas."

Dorcas's pallor turned to a rosy pink. "Oh, Miles. Oh, Miles." She sank down beside his chair, looking up at him with a tremulous smile. "Yes," she breathed. "I'd be very happy to marry you at the end of the Season. I love you, too, so very much."

"Then we're engaged," said Miles in a glow of happiness. He glanced at Camilla. "I know I promised I'd wait to propose to Dorcas—"

"Never mind, future brother-in-law. Welcome to the family." Camilla walked over to Miles and entwined her arms around him and Dorcas.

"Mon Dieu," came a voice from the doorway. "Is this a minor orgy? Am I expected to participate in this group embrace?"

Camilla laughed, rising to greet Jean. "You may certainly kiss Dorcas, to congratulate her on the occasion of her betrothal."

"Mes félicitations," beamed Jean. "I wish you both very happy. You're a lucky man, Wingate."

"And a very weary one," said Dorcas with an unexpected firmness. "You must go straight home to bed, Miles, before you collapse on us. Mr. Hilliard, will you help Miles to his carriage?"

"But I don't wish to go home, Dorcas," protested Miles. "We just became engaged . . ."

"*Mon ami,* you'll learn soon enough that the gentler sex is always right," Jean told him. "Here, let me help you out of that chair."

"And," said Dorcas, with that same newfound firmness, "I'm going with you to your lodgings, Miles, to make sure your valet is taking proper care of you."

"No," Miles declared, looking appalled. "I'll not permit you to do anything so unseemly. Young unmarried females don't visit bachelors' lodgings." When Dorcas stared at him in mulish silence, Miles appealed to her sister. "Camilla, *you* tell her."

"I will, but you won't approve of what I say," said Camilla. "Dorcas, since Miles has no family, I quite agree that you should accompany him to his lodgings. Make sure his valet puts him to bed and keeps him there. I also agree with Miles that you shouldn't give the prattleboxes any food for gossip. So take Lizzie with you, and mind you don't stay above fifteen minutes."

A little later Jean returned to the drawing room. "They're off," he said, laughing. "Miles is still arguing with Dorcas about the propriety of her accompanying him, and she's paying him no heed." He gave Camilla an inquiring look. "You're *such* a proper lady. I marvel at your permissiveness. Even *I* know that genteel young ladies don't pay visits to bachelors' lodgings."

She shrugged. "After what happened—or nearly happened—last night, the *convenances* don't seem quite as important to me as they once did."

Looking at her closely, he said, "You're different today."

"Oh? In what way?" Camilla's heart started to pound.

The atmosphere had suddenly become charged with emotional intensity.

"Your defenses are down." Swiftly Jean crossed the few feet that separated them and put his hand lightly on her shoulder. "Look at me, Camilla. Did I do the right thing, advising you to tell me about you and Elvaston?"

"Yes," she said, forcing herself to meet his eyes. "I feel as if a terrible burden has been lifted from me."

His eyes shone. "I'm glad." Slowly he bent his head, claiming her lips in a warm, clinging kiss. Gradually the pressure of his mouth became harder and more demanding, and his hands slipped from her shoulders to her waist and pulled her close against him. Releasing her mouth at last, he loosened his embrace slightly so that he could look down at her. His breathing had turned rough and uneven, and black diamonds were blazing in his eyes, but he was keeping a tight control over himself.

"You liked that, didn't you, Camilla?"

"Yes," she said breathlessly. She felt curiously warm, as if a fiery stream were cascading through her body.

"And for the first time, you'd didn't pull away from me when I kissed you."

"I didn't want you to stop kissing me," she blurted before she could stop herself And now, in addition to the heat in her body, she could feel the hot embarrassed flood of color in her cheeks.

"Oh, Camilla," he said with a smothered laugh. He cupped her face in his hands and brushed a brief butterfly kiss across her lips. "I wanted so much to kiss you last night," he muttered, a tender smile curving his mouth, "but you were so vulnerable after you told me about Elvaston and your husband, you wanted and needed comfort so much . . . I didn't want to take advantage of your feelings when you weren't quite yourself." His voice changed, became matter-of-fact. "So I decided to wait until this morning to propose to you."

Camilla gasped, feeling as if she'd been doused with a bucket of cold water. She took a quick step back from him.

"No, you don't." Jean seized her arm. "We're having this out. Camilla, I love you, and I want you to marry me."

"Jean, I've told you so many times that I don't wish to marry again . . . "

"Why not? Because you're afraid your next husband might be another Philip?" He gave her a little shake. "Camilla, you ninnyhammer, you know I'm nothing like Philip." He pressed a quick, hard kiss on her lips. "And you like me to touch you. Don't try to deny it. I can feel your response in every nerve of your body." He shook her again. "What's more, you love me."

"I—"

He swept her into his arms. "Camilla, I know you love me. Admit it."

She struggled to free herself. "Please, I can't think when you're so close to me," she whispered. "Yes, I love you, but I can't bear the thought of losing my independence. I lost it once, and it was disastrous."

"Oh, the devil, Camilla," Jean said impatiently. "You can be as independent as you want to be when you're my wife. You can walk all over me if you like. Just marry me."

The tension drained out of Camilla, and she began to laugh. "Jean, you're the last man in the world to allow a mere female to walk all over you."

Jean kissed her again. "Try me," he murmured against her lips.

Surrendering at last, Camilla said, "Oh, very well, I'll marry you, on one condition."

"Which is?"

"I'll marry you if you promise to stay in England and groom yourself to be the next Earl of Sheringham!"

For a long moment, a very real expression of doubt clouded Jean's face. Then, bracing his shoulders, he said, forcing a smile, "Done! I'd do much more than that to win you, if I had to. Slay a dragon. Walk on water. Take on the whole Hudson's Bay Company." The dancing lights were back in his eyes. He said quizzically. "I told you that you could stay independent, that I'd allow you to walk all over me. Have I proved my case? I'll do anything you ask. You can wind me around your little finger, and I'll love every minute of it."

Chapter Fourteen

"An engagement is announced and a marriage will shortly take place between Miss Dorcas Samantha Vernon, daughter of the late Thomas Vernon, Royal Navy, and Mrs. Vernon, of Bath, Somersetshire, and Mr. Miles Wingate, son of—"

Camilla stopped writing and gazed around the morning room for inspiration as she chewed on the end of her pen. *What* was the Christian name of Miles's father? She must have known Mr. Wingate's name at one point. Why couldn't she remember it now?

Strong arms encircled her from behind in an exuberant hug? "Were you writing to me, love?" Jean said softly as he nuzzled her throat. "I hope so. Because, if I find you're writing to another man, I'll break the poor fellow's neck."

"Bloodthirsty rogue," Camilla declared, as she twisted in his hold to look up at him with a smile. "There's no need for you to be jealous. I was writing an announcement for the *Times* and the *Morning Post* about Dorcas's engagement."

Jean pulled her out of her chair and into his embrace. Eagerly he sought her lips in a lingering kiss that deepened as his arms closed more tightly around her. "Your mouth tastes so wonderful," he murmured, breaking the kiss momentarily. "Your body feels so wonderful against mine. Oh, Camilla, darling, we've wasted so much time, when we could have been doing *this* from the first moment we met." His mouth closed down on hers again, demanding, enticing.

Before she drowned in the sweet languorous tide of passion flooding through her, Camilla managed to push Jean away. "Darling, someone might see us," she said breathlessly. "Dorcas, or Lizzie, or Cook!"

"*I* don't care if everyone in the whole world knows I love you." Jean reached for her again, and she evaded his grasp.

"But I do care," she said firmly. "Jean, behave yourself."

Stepping back from her, he stood at attention, his arms folded across his chest. "Your wish is my command," he said, grinning. "I told you last night I'd do whatever you wanted me to do, and I meant it." He added, softly, insinuatingly, "So when you want me to kiss you again, just tell me. I'll be happy to oblige."

"Jean, you wretch, what am I going to do with you?"

"Keep loving me, I hope." He glanced at the unfinished engagement announcement on Camilla's desk. "When are you going to send our betrothal announcement to the newspapers?"

"Not until Uncle Nigel knows about our betrothal. I couldn't let him learn about my marriage in the pages of the *Morning Post*. Jean, let's go see him now. He'll be so happy to hear our news."

The laughter died out of Jean's eyes. "As you wish," he said curtly. In his curricle on the drive to Hanover Square, he was silent to the point of taciturnity. Camilla thought she knew why. He'd accepted Lord Sheringham's presence in his life very unwillingly, and only up to a point. And, though he'd agreed to live in the earl's house to please Camilla, she knew that Jean still felt a strong animosity toward her godfather. Standing between the two men was Jean's conviction that the earl had deliberately exiled and ruined his father.

Knowing that Lord Sheringham's single-minded aim from the beginning had been to keep his heir in England, Jean might now be feeling he'd been forced to give in because of his love for Camilla. Last night she'd given him a laughing ultimatum: I'll marry you if you'll stay in England as Uncle Nigel's heir. A man deliriously in love, he'd accepted the ultimatum. Had he now begun to regret his decision?

Half an hour later, as Camilla and Jean were ushered into his library, the earl put down his newspaper and rose to greet them. "My dear Camilla, I'm delighted to see you." To Jean he said politely, "You, too, my boy. I'm sorry we haven't seen a great deal of each other since my—er—unfortunate dinner party." His gaze sharpened. "Far be it for me to pry, but do I gather, since you're here together, that you two have made up your differences?"

Camilla walked up to the earl and kissed his cheek. "Uncle Nigel, wish us happy. Jean and I are betrothed."

His eyes sparkling, Lord Sheringham hugged his goddaughter joyously. "Wish you happy? Better wish *me* happy!" Turning to Jean, he held out his hand. "My heartfelt congratulations. As Camilla's husband, you'll be second only to her in my regard."

Jean's handshake was brief and perfunctory. The expression on his dark face was remote and unresponsive.

The earl said, rather hesitantly, "I don't wish to rush my fences, but—dare I hope this means that you and Camilla will be living in England rather than in Canada?"

"Yes, it does," said Jean shortly. "You've won, sir. I stay in England. Not because of any regard for your wishes. I want to make that clear. I'm staying for Camilla's sake. I'm simply not willing to take her away from her family and friends to live in an alien land. In many

223

ways, Québec is still a primitive country."

"Well, whatever your reasons for staying in England, Jean, I'm grateful," said the earl quietly. "You've made a dream come true."

Camilla said impulsively, "Uncle Nigel, I think you should tell Jean about his father."

The earl's brows drew together in a frown. "That subject is closed," he said coldly.

Jean's frown matched the earl's. "What about my father?"

"Jean, I know you've always believed Uncle Nigel treated your father unjustly—"

The earl's voice cut like a whiplash. "Camilla, that's enough."

"It's more than enough," snapped Jean. Confronting the earl, he said, "I don't just believe, I *know* what you did to my father. You were always jealous of him, you tried for years to turn his family and friends against him. Finally, you persuaded an elderly aunt not to leave him her small fortune, money he'd been counting on to build an independent life for himself, in the Army, perhaps, or in Parliament. What's more, you spread the rumor that Father had in some fashion cheated his aunt. He was finished in England. He had to emigrate to Canada, where, without skills or connections or money, he might have starved if it hadn't been for the kindness of my mother's family."

When Jean finished speaking, he stared truculently at the earl. "Well?" he demanded, as if he expected a rebuttal.

Lord Sheringham merely stared back at him in silence, his face registering no expression. It was left to Camilla to reply. "Your father lied to you, Jean."

Flinching as if someone had struck him a heavy blow, Jean said in a choked voice, "Don't say any more, Camilla. I won't listen to such filth, even from you."

224

Pale and distressed, the earl exclaimed, "Jean's right. Camilla, stop this at once."

Disregarding both men, Camilla rapidly described to Jean how her godfather had twice paid John Hilliard's gambling debts, and then, when he discovered that his cousin had embezzled money from an elderly aunt in order to cover yet another debt of honor, the earl had replaced the stolen money on condition that John Hilliard go into permanent exile in Canada.

Jean heard her out. Then, white to the lips, he said, "That's a damned lie."

"Uncle Nigel can prove it, Jean. Your father signed a confession."

"That's another lie."

Gazing into Jean's furious, desolate eyes, Lord Sheringham gave a long sigh and bowed his shoulders. "Oh, Camilla, you've raised the devil this time. Why didn't you stop when I asked you to?"

"Uncle Nigel, I think it's time for the truth, no matter how much it hurts."

"Do you really think so, my dear? Sometimes the truth hurts too much." Slowly, reluctantly, the earl opened a drawer in his desk, from which he removed a metal box. He flicked through the documents in the box. Abstracting a sheet of paper, he silently handed it to Jean, who rapidly scanned the thirty-year-old admission that branded his father as an embezzler.

"God!" Jean's hand, holding the confession, fell limply to his side. He said to the earl in a dull, flat voice, "Why didn't you show me this before?"

Shrugging, Lord Sheringham said, "You loved your father. With good reason, apparently. He must have been a good father to you. Why should I spoil your memories of him?"

Obviously fighting a difficult inner battle, Jean kept his eyes fixed on the floor while the moments of silence were punctuated by the ticking of the clock over the mantelpiece. At last he raised his head. "Sir, the father I knew wasn't the man who signed that confession. Obviously he changed after he came to Canada. I'd like you to believe that."

"I'd already guessed as much," said the earl quietly. He walked toward Jean, extending his hand. "Shall we let the past stay buried?"

A sudden smile transformed Jean's troubled face. He grasped the earl's hand warmly. "Gladly, sir."

Visibly relaxing, the earl rang for a footman, saying, "I think we need something to drink to celebrate the cessation of hostilities. And then we must plan a wedding!"

A little later, over a glass of Madeira, Jean said, "Speaking of planning a wedding, sir, I'd like to get married as soon as possible."

"Oh? How soon?"

"Tomorrow," said Jean promptly.

"Jean!" exclaimed a startled Camilla.

"Well, in three weeks' time, then," he amended with a grin. "That's how long it takes to post the banns, isn't that right? Unless I could persuade you to let me apply for a special license," he added hopefully. "Then we could get married almost immediately."

"A special license!" Camilla began to laugh. "Next thing I know, you'll be suggesting we should elope. Jean, why all this hurry to get married?"

He reached out to clasp her hand. "Because I love you. *Mon Dieu,* I fell in love with you the moment I first saw you!" He made a face. "Of course, it took you a while longer to appreciate me!"

"Jean . . ."

"Ma mie, we're adults, we love each other, we know our own minds. Why should we wait to begin our life together? Marry me now, Camilla."

Looking faintly embarrassed to witness such an open

226

show of emotion, the earl put in, "People might talk, you know. They might question such haste to get married. You've known each other for such a short time."

"*Tant pis,*" said Jean rudely. "I don't give a—I don't care a fig what the prattleboxes might say." He paused. "But Camilla, if you—"

She heard the note of uncertainty in his voice, and saw the longing in his eyes, and came to an instant decision. Leaning over to kiss his cheek, she said, "I don't care a fig for the prattleboxes, either." She looked at her godfather, her eyes twinkling mischievously. "I agree with Jean, Uncle Nigel. I think we should get married as soon as possible. Look at it this way: Jean and I have had so many quarrels that we'd best get married while we're still speaking to each other! Our next quarrel might be the end of us."

The earl laughed. "I won't argue. As Jean says, you're two grown adults, after all. Let's see, now. I hope it's not too late to reserve St. George's Hanover Square, for the wedding. So convenient for a reception at Sheringham House! What a pity the seating at the church and the size of my public rooms limit the guest list to about four hundred people. But then, I do hate a squeeze. I always want my guests to be comfortable.

"Now, wait," Jean exclaimed in alarm. "Are you talking about a large, lavish wedding?"

"As large and as lavish as I can possibly make it," replied Lord Sheringham calmly. "It will be the wedding of the year, of any year."

Camilla looked at Jean's apprehensive face, and said, "Uncle Nigel, perhaps we could plan a smaller wedding. Smaller doesn't mean less fashionable or less suitable, after all. Last year, you'll recall, when the Duke of Devonshire's daughter was married, only her father and her stepmother and her brother were present."

The earl said austerely, "I hope you aren't implying

that I must follow the example of the Duke of Devonshire. We Hilliards are an even older family, I'll remind you. I want to give you and Jean a lavish wedding because it's not just any day that my heir marries the most beautiful and accomplished woman in England!"

"La, Uncle Nigel, you mustn't say things like that. You'll make me blush," Camilla said with a mock modesty. She smiled at Jean. "We'll have to give in, my love. Uncle Nigel has made up his mind." She drew a quick breath. "Oh, Lord! Do you realize we'll be obliged to invite my stepmother to the wedding?"

"Must we go that far?" asked the earl, grimacing. His expression became resigned. "Yes, we must. People really would gossip if we didn't invite her." To Jean, he said, "I hope you won't think Camilla and I are uncharitable, discussing her stepmother in this way."

"Not at all, sir," said Jean gloomily. "You forget that I've met the lady. It was on the Bath road. She was trying to scratch my eyes out."

"Miles, you're not wearing your sling," said Dorcas, looking at her fiancé with a worried frown, as he walked into the drawing room of the house on Park Street on an afternoon a week later.

Miles kissed Dorcas lightly on the cheek. "My love, I can manage perfectly well without a sling. Besides, the confounded thing spoils the fit of my coats." He grinned at Camilla, sitting over an embroidery frame in a chair near the window. "Tell Dorcas I must be fashionable at all costs!"

Glancing out the window, Camilla said dryly, "That's your town carriage out there, I believe. Could it be that you don't feel up to driving your curricle yet? In which case, perhaps, you should reconsider wearing your sling—" She broke off. "Dorcas, a post chaise has just stopped in front of the house, and—wait a moment, now—yes, the postilion is helping Mama down the steps."

"Oh, Camilla . . ." Dorcas's voice was almost a wail. "I know I should be glad to see my own mother, but I'm not."

Turning away from the window, Camilla said with a sigh, "I know. I'm not especially pleased to see her myself, but, you know, I had to invite her to my wedding."

Miles put his sound arm around Dorcas in a brief hug. "It will be all right, my dear. Remember, Camilla is your legal guardian now. Your mama can't interfere with your life in any way."

Three pairs of eyes were glued on the doorway of the drawing room when Lizzie announced, "Mrs. Vernon."

Francine Vernon swept into the room, more modishly dressed than Camilla had ever seen her—the clothes, Camilla cynically thought, had undoubtedly been purchased with part of Uncle Nigel's twenty thousand pounds—and trailing a cloud of expensive scent. She rushed to embrace her daughter and her stepdaughter. "Darling Dorcas, I'm so happy to see you. I've missed you so much. My dear Camilla, I vow, you're more beautiful than ever in your happiness. And what a charming little bandbox of a house."

Despite her stepmother's determined vivacity of manner, Camilla sensed an underlying nervousness. Obtuse though she was, even Francine had to feel a certain amount of guilt. She had, in effect, sold her daughter for Uncle Nigel's twenty thousand pounds, and she must have been uncertain about the warmth of the reception she would receive on Park Street. But Francine had always yearned to be a part of the London social scene, and she hadn't been able to resist accepting Camilla's invitation to her wedding.

As Francine turned to Miles with an expectant look,

Camilla said, "Mama, I must present to you Mr. Miles Wingate."

Francine's gaze sharpened. "Mr. Wingate! Camilla wrote to me that you were betrothed to my little girl. Come, sit down with me, so we can have a comfortable coze. If I'm to be your future mama-in-law, we must get to know each other better!"

Exchanging speaking glances, the two sisters watched Francine go after her prey. Although Camilla had given her stepmother a brief account of Miles and his family circumstances, Francine wanted to know more. A great deal more. Ruthlessly she pinned Miles by her side, questioning him about his family, on both the paternal and maternal sides, and the size and location of his ancestral estates. She even probed for details of his education and his clubs. Submitting with his usual polished grace, Miles was beginning to look distinctly harassed when a welcome interruption occurred. Without bothering to be announced, as was his custom since his engagement, Jean walked into the drawing room.

"Hallo, darling," he said with a radiant smile, and bent over Camilla's chair to give her a thoroughly satisfying kiss. In the family circle, Jean had no inhibitions about displaying his unabashed affection for Camilla, and she, to her own surprise, didn't mind in the least, however much it had shocked her godfather, Dorcas and Miles at the outset.

"Camilla!" The choked cry turned all eyes in the room on Francine. She rose from her seat on the sofa, pointing a trembling finger at Jean. "What are you about, Camilla, allowing this man to kiss you? For that matter, what's he doing in your house? Don't you realize this is the villain who threatened me at that inn on the Bath road?"

Camilla was torn between anger and a wild desire to laugh. Controlling herself, she said, "Mama, this is Jean-

Étienne Hilliard, the Earl of Sheringham's heir and my fiancé."

A ludicrous blend of emotions played across Francine's face. At last she said, a hopeful note in her voice, "I was mistaken, wasn't I, Mr. Hilliard? You're not the man from the inn on the Bath road?"

Poised like a rapier in the hand of a skilled fencer, Jean replied with a silky politeness, "Alas, I fear I'm that very same man, *madame*. And you, of course, are the very same woman I met at that inn. Neither of us seems to have changed in the least."

Spots of color burned suddenly on Francine's cheeks. She opened her mouth to speak, and changed her mind. Camilla almost felt sorry for her. Her stepmother would have been stupid not to realize she'd been subtly insulted, and Francine wasn't stupid. At the same time, however, she knew better than to strike back at her stepdaughter's fiancé, possibly causing an open feud and thereby endangering her cherished opportunity to take part in the London season.

Tossing Jean a repressive glance, Camilla said lightly, "I fancy we were all three of us quite up in the boughs that night on the Bath road, Mama. Shall we put it behind us?"

Francine exclaimed in relief, "Oh, yes, darling. A famous notion!"

Flashing Camilla a teasing smile, Jean murmured, "I promised to do whatever you wanted me to do, love. Just tell me what to remember and what to forget."

"*Ma mie,* we're here."

Camilla jerked herself awake. She'd fallen asleep during the short drive with Jean from Park Street to the Marsdens' residence in Grosvenor Square. Dorcas and Miles and Francine were following in another carriage.

231

"I'm worried about you, Camilla," Jean muttered as they walked from the carriage toward the canopied entrance of the Marsden mansion, where a double row of impassive-faced footmen in elaborate liveries and powdered wigs lined the steps. "You look so tired. You've been overdoing. Planning a large wedding at such short notice. Chaperoning Dorcas to all her coming out parties. It can't help, either," he added with a touch of malice, "to be in your stepmother's pocket day and night."

Camilla suppressed a yawn. "The days *are* rather full," she admitted. "But Uncle Nigel's secretary is being very helpful. He's sending out the invitations and contacting the tradesmen about the food and flowers for the reception. He's also making arrangements with the orchestra. And Mama isn't quite the trial I thought she'd be. She's on her best behavior, you know. She doesn't want to miss any of the balls and parties."

They walked past the footmen and started up the long sweeping staircase to the ballroom. "I'm giving you fair notice, love," Jean growled in her ear. "After our wedding it'll be goodbye to balls and routs and dinners for a very long time, and yes, to your stepmother, too. I don't intend to share your company with anyone."

Camilla was still smiling in amused appreciation at Jean's muttered remark when they entered the ballroom, where their hostess promptly pounced on them. "My dear Mrs. Rayburn, Mr. Hilliard, I was so delighted to hear of your engagement," Lady Marsden gushed.

"Not half as delighted as I myself was to hear it," declared Jean, smiling down at her ladyship. "I trust you plan to dance with me at our wedding?"

As Camilla watched Jean reduce his hostess to simpering jelly, she marveled at the changes a few short months had made in him. With his magnificent dark good looks and his claim to an ancient earldom, he'd doubtless have won acceptance by the *ton* eventually, in spite of his rough edges. But, miraculously, the rough edges had vanished. He now had the poise and the effortless charm that men like her godfather and Miles had spent years acquiring.

Jean interrupted her train of thought. "My love, will you excuse me? Lady Marsden would like me to speak to her great-uncle, Sir Montague Dacre, who has made a study of ancient languages, about the aboriginal Indian dialects of Canada."

Camilla caught the faint tremor of amusement in his voice. She hoped Lady Marsden hadn't noticed it. "Why, of course, Jean," she said solemnly. "I daresay you'll be a fount of valuable information to Sir Montague."

As a matron and an officially affianced lady, Camilla felt she had sufficient excuse to refuse the numerous requests she received to dance. She sat contentedly at the edge of the ballroom, watching the dancers. Soon Francine joined her.

"Oh, Camilla," breathed Francine, "I've heard so much about the London season, but I never dreamed it would be as grand as this. Dorcas tells me that you often have two or three invitations for the same evening."

"I daresay you'd soon tire of the social round, Mama," said Camilla dryly. "One ball is very much like another, after all."

"Not to me, my dear," said Francine simply. After a moment she said with a trace of hesitancy, "I just heard something—I was talking to a very nice lady, though, unfortunately, I can't remember her name—who told me—who told me . . ."

"Mama, what on earth are you trying to say?"

Lowering her voice to a strained whisper, Francine said, "This lady told me that Mr. Hilliard was a—red Indian!"

Camilla looked at her stepmother coldly. "Jean's grandmother was an Indian woman, that's true. She was

233

a chieftain's daughter, as a matter of fact."

"But Camilla . . . How is it, then, that Mr. Hilliard is accepted by the *ton?* How can you bear to—to be touched by a—a man of tainted blood?"

Camilla's fury boiled over. "Because he's the heir to the oldest earldom in England," she snapped. "Because he's the most handsome, most attractive man I've ever met. Because I love him to distraction. Because he has more charm in his little finger than—" She stopped short. "Oh, my God," she breathed, as she stared at Jean, standing some ten feet away from her in an animated conversation with a spare, middle-aged woman.

"Camilla, what is it?"

Camilla rose. "Mama, please excuse me." She walked over to Jean and his companion.

"Camilla, you remember Lady Montfort?" said Jean smoothly.

"Oh, indeed. How do you do, Lady Montfort." Camilla had a hollow feeling in the pit of her stomach. She hadn't seen Lady Montfort, the wife of the ever-so-influential director of the Academy of Music, since the disastrous occasion when Jean had disrupted her musical evening, the evening that she'd hoped might lead to a public performance of her sonata. The evening when an inebriated Jean had fallen asleep and snored loudly during the performance, and had later scandalized Lady Montfort with that vulgar story. One would have expected Jean to avoid the lady's company at all costs. And yet here he was, apparently on the best of terms with her.

"I've just been making my belated apologies to Lady Montfort for my behavior at your musical evening," Jean told Camilla. "She was quite right to regard me as a musical moron. I've explained to her that I knew nothing about music when I arrived here. Real music, that is. Oh, we have fiddles in Canada, of course. Drums."

"Tom-toms," said Lady Montfort, nodding wisely. "Mr.

234

Hilliard's been telling me that his—er—relatives not only use these drums for musical purposes, but actually send messages with them. Quite fascinating."

"Yes, isn't it?" Camilla murmured. Suppressing an impulse to giggle, she avoided looking at Jean. She knew his black eyes were snapping with a wicked amusement.

"My dear Mrs. Rayburn, I was so interested to learn from Mr. Hilliard that you'd very much like to have your sonata performed publicly," said Lady Montfort. "Now, as I'm sure you know, my husband is a director of the Academy of Music." She paused, smiling archly. "Mind, I don't quite know how much influence I have with my husband, but I'd be happy to drop a tiny hint in his ear."

"Oh, I'm sure you have all the influence in the world, Lady Montfort," Jean assured her. "Who could resist your appeal? Now, may I escort you to a chair, and will you permit me to fetch you a glass of ratafia?"

As Jean moved away with Lady Montfort, Camilla stood watching them, too stunned momentarily to move. What bold, unconventional move would Jean decide to make next?

A familiar drawl interrupted her thoughts. "My dear Camilla, I'd ask you to dance, since we're at a ball, but that would be rather futile. As you of all people know, I'm no longer able to dance. Perhaps we could talk instead."

Camilla turned to look into the glacier-cold gray eyes of Aubrey Elvaston. She repressed a shudder, reminding herself that she'd at last exorcised her fear of him. "I've talked to you for the last time, Sir Aubrey. I don't intend to have any further contact with you, ever again, and I've no need to tell you why."

He took her arm in a talonlike grip that she couldn't attempt to break without calling attention to herself. He guided her to a pair of vacant chairs at the side of the room. "Sit down, Camilla. You'll hear me out. Surely

235

you didn't think I'd overlook breaking and entering, trespassing, assault and battery, and the various other crimes you and your friends committed against my person and my property? I could have had you and your friends up before the magistrates—"

"And admit to attempting to seduce an innocent girl?" Camilla said bitterly.

Elvaston ignored her jibe. "As I was saying, I could have lodged a complaint with the magistrates, but I prefer to conduct my affairs privately. I've approached you tonight, Camilla, to make sure you realize that your account with me isn't settled."

"You've done your worst to me. I'm not afraid of you. Not any more."

Elvaston fixed Camilla with a chilling reptilian stare. "You should be, my dear. You should be."

Chapter Fifteen

Nathan Rothschild glanced around the elegant coffee room of White's Club and remarked to Jean, "I'm much impressed, my friend. I never thought I'd actually be dining one day at the most prestigious gentleman's club in all of London." He added with an impish grin, "I do hope I haven't damaged your social credit. Your acquaintances nod to you as they pass by the table, but they don't stop to talk to you. Perhaps they're afraid my presence is contagious?"

"You're baiting me, NM," said Jean, tossing a frosty glare at a fellow member who had, indeed, just passed the table with a mere smile and a nod. "You know you don't care a damn about hobnobbing with the *ton*."

Rothschild smiled his acknowledgment of the thrust. After the waiter had poured their wine, he observed, "So, it's really true. You'll soon join the ranks of the benedicts. Your wedding will take place next week, I believe. As a Jew, I heartily approve. We like our young men to settle down early to family life."

Jean chuckled. "So they can concentrate on business, NM?"

"Exactly," Rothschild replied imperturbably.

Jean sipped his wine. "I hope you're planning to attend the wedding, sir," he remarked.

"I'm no great hand for the social scene, as you well know, but Mrs. Rothschild informs me that your wed-

237

ding is one event she will not allow me to miss." The merchant banker looked at Jean thoughtfully. "My sources tell me you're still investsing in the stock market."

"Yes, sir. You sound a little surprised."

"Well, you've now decided to remain in England as your cousin's heir. Your aristocratic friends look down their noses at trade."

"I like trade. I like business. I like making money." Jean tossed Rothschild an impudent grin. "One day soon, I hope to inform Lord Sheringham that I've acquired by my independent efforts a fortune as large as his own."

Rothschild burst out laughing. "I've told you this before, my friend, but I'll say it again. I like you."

A club porter stopped beside Rothschild with a sealed note on a tray. "For me?" the banker said in surprise. He tore the note open and read its contents quickly. He nodded a dismissal to the servant and sat in frowning silence.

"Anything wrong, NM? Mrs. Rothschild, the children—?"

The banker shook his head. "They're very well." He hesitated. At last he said, "We had a rather interesting conversation several weeks ago. You told me you still had relations in France. I informed you I had business interests there. Now I'll tell you that I employ . . ." Rothschild paused, choosing his words carefully. "I employ couriers who occasionally travel between my offices in London and my—er—contacts on the Channel coast. I've just received word that a trusted courier will be unable to undertake a highly important mission across the Channel for me tonight. As it happens, I've no one else to send . . ."

"You've got me, NM."

"I should warn you, it could be a dangerous journey." Jean laughed. "You forget, I'm a veteran of the fur

238

trade wars in Québec. Life's been rather tame since I arrived in England. I fancy I'll enjoy a little excitement."

Miles Wingate lifted his hands from the keys of the pianoforte, and the audience in the salon of the Crown and Anchor Tavern on Arundel Street burst into applause.

Camilla stood to receive the congratulations of the friends and acquaintances who had attended the special afternoon presentation of her sonata by the Academy of Music.

"My dear Mrs. Rayburn, that was lovely," said Lady Montfort.

Her husband followed close behind her. "Lovely!" he snorted. "My dear wife, it was wonderful! Mrs. Rayburn has a real future as a composer."

Camilla smiled her appreciation to the influential director of the Academy of Music.

"But where is Mr. Hilliard?" inquired Lady Montfort. "I certainly expected to see him here today. He was so excited about the prospect of having your sonata publicly performed."

"He was so sorry to miss the occasion," said Camilla. "He asked me to thank you both for your efforts on my behalf." She lowered her voice confidentially. "Lord Sheringham asked Jean to attend to a problem on the family estates in Northamptonshire."

"Ah." Lady Montfort nodded approvingly. "Lord Sheringham is getting somewhat on in years, I believe. How splendid that Mr. Hilliard can relieve the earl of some of his duties."

"Well!" said Lord Sheringham a few minutes later, as he walked with Camilla to her carriage. "Getting on, am I? I fancy I could give both the Montforts a few years." He smiled a little sheepishly. "My vanity's catching up with me. Now, what's this about my sending Jean on an errand to Northamptonshire? What a bouncer! Where is he, by the way? I haven't seen him in days."

"I don't know where Jean is, Uncle Nigel," said Camilla, a throb of fear in her voice. "I last saw him five—no, six days ago. We'd gone driving in Hyde Park at the usual hour of promenade, and he told me then he'd invited Mr. Rothschild to dine with him at White's that evening. Next morning I received a brief note from him, saying he had to attend to a pressing matter and would be back in two days. I haven't seen or heard from him since then. I'm afraid something's happened to him."

About to hand Camilla into her carriage, the earl stood transfixed on the trottoir. "Good God," he said. "How extraordinary! We must do something, Camilla. Your wedding is in three days' time. I daresay the first thing I should do is to make inquiries at Bow Street. But surely, if Jean was waylaid about a week ago, someone would have found . . ."

He broke off, leaving unspoken any thoughts of bodies lying abandoned in the gutter. He added hastily, "Come now, I daresay there's some good reason for Jean's absence. And no doubt he'll put all your worries to rest by coming back in time for my gala at Vauxhall Gardens tonight."

"I hope so. In any event, we'll know about Jean, one way or another, in three days, won't we, Uncle Nigel? If Jean is well, and at liberty, he'll surely attend his own wedding."

Camilla climbed into the carriage and the coachman drove off. As she rode along, she wondered at the strangeness of real life. Who could have imagined that the realization of her fondest dreams, to have her sonata performed publicly, would mean so little to her? She'd scarcely listened to the performance. All her thoughts had been on Jean.

Dorcas said nervously, "Camilla, it's after seven o'clock."

Turning away from the window, where she had been staring unseeingly out into the street, Camilla gazed at her sister's troubled face, and said, "Yes, it's time to go, Dorcas. Mama, are you quite ready? Miles, since Jean isn't here, we won't need more than the one carriage."

"But Camilla," objected Francine, "Lord Sheringham is giving this gala at Vauxhall Gardens in honor of your wedding. Won't it look very strange if Mr. Hilliard isn't present?"

"Please, Mama," said Dorcas quietly. "I don't think you should badger Camilla. You know quite well, even though we've agreed not to talk about it, even among ourselves, that Camilla is worried about Mr. Hilliard. She's had no word of him for almost a week."

"I wouldn't dream of badgering her," Francine retorted, "and I'm as concerned as everyone else about Mr. Hilliard's whereabouts. But really, Camilla, you must be practical. What will you tell Lord Sheringham and his guests to explain Mr. Hilliard's absence from the gala?"

"What absence?" came a voice from behind them.

Camilla whirled to face Jean, standing in the doorway. He was dressed impeccably for the evening. Advancing into the room, he said, "I've no intention of missing the gala. Camilla, are you ready to go? If so, the carriage awaits."

Taking a long look at Camilla's strained face, Miles said to her with great presence of mind, "Dorcas and I and Mrs. Vernon will go on ahead to Vauxhall. I'll inform Lord Sheringham that you and Hilliard are on the way."

Waiting until the others had left the room, Camilla burst out, "Jean, where have you been for almost a week? I've been half out of my mind, worrying about you."

"Camilla . . ." Jean cleared his throat. "I'm very sorry.

241

I didn't mean to be gone this long, and I had no way of getting a message to you. The fact is, I took it into my head to go down to Kent, to your godfather's villa—"

"You what?"

"Well, you see, since we'll be spending our honeymoon there, I thought I should just check to see if the house was ready for occupancy."

Camilla said, startled, "Uncle Nigel's houses are always ready for occupancy."

"Yes, well, I didn't realize that. At any rate, I intended to come back that same day, but then one of the local fishermen invited me to go out on his boat, and I accepted. Shortly after we sailed, a terrible storm came up. I was convinced we'd sink, but instead the winds drove us to Jersey in the Channel Islands. We were forced to stay in port there until the winds abated and we could sail back to Lynharbor."

Camilla stared at Jean. She didn't believe him. Oh, the bit about being weather-bound in Jersey, that had the ring of truth. Not the rest of his story. He was lying to her. Her nerves on edge from days of frantic worrying, she said contemptuously, "You must take me for a tremendous gull. Shall we start again? Where did you really go, and why won't you tell me the truth of it?"

Jean reddened. After a moment, he said, "I should have known I couldn't lie to you, Camilla. I can't tell you the truth, either, unfortunately. I'd be betraying a confidence. I swear to you, though, that where I went and what I did had nothing to do with you and me and our relationship."

Camilla's lip curled. "Believe it or not, I wasn't concerned about a possible rival for your affections, only about your safety." She picked up a gauzy silk scarf embroidered in silver thread and draped it around her shoulders. "Shall we go? I don't wish to be late to Uncle Nigel's gala."

Jean put out his hand as she walked past him.

"Camilla, don't be angry with me," he pleaded. "Can't we talk about this?"

She looked down at the long slender fingers on her gloved arm. "Will you tell me where you've been these last six days?"

"I can't. I gave my word."

"Then I don't think there's anything to talk about. Can we go, please?"

During the drive across Westminster Bridge and along the Kensington Road, Camilla sat pressed against her side of the carriage, as far away from Jean as she could get. She replied only in monosyllables to his remarks, and finally he gave up the attempt at conversation.

She knew she was being a little childish. Eventually she'd have to swallow her anger and hurt and begin talking normally to Jean, unless, that is, she was prepared to cry off from her engagement. That, she knew in her secret heart, was an impossibility. Jean was a part of her inmost being now, and she could never let him go. Yes, at some point, she'd have to ignore or forget the mysterious errand which, with that granitic stubbornness that was becoming so familiar to her, he refused to tell her about. But not yet. Her heart still felt too sore for her to forgive him too readily for putting her through six days of torture.

The carriage stopped in front of an inconspicuous porched door in a wall bordering a lane off the Kensington Road. As soon as Camilla and Jean stepped through the door, they entered a brilliantly lighted fairyland. Ahead of them was a rectangle formed by four graceful colonnades, which enclosed a large open space, the Grove, interspersed with trees. The colonnades were illuminated by thousands of lamps and hanging lanterns. In the middle of the Grove was a lofty orchestra pavilion, glittering in the glow of innumerable colored lights.

On any given evening during its season, Vauxhall Gardens would normally be swarming with thousands of patrons from every station in life. Tonight its clientele was limited. Lord Sheringham had reserved the entire premises for his guests, who occupied the supper boxes in the colonnades surrounding the pavilion, where an orchestra was softly playing the latest popular airs.

Lord Sheringham received his heir amiably, with no reference to Jean's recent absence. "I decided against a receiving line, Jean. I'd like you and Camilla to go from box to box, greeting our guests. The main concert will begin at nine o'clock. Catalani will be singing."

During the next half hour, Camilla walked with Jean along the line of supper boxes, pausing at each box with a smile and a brief word of appreciation. Jean appeared completely carefree, displaying all his newfound poise and grace. He especially charmed Lady Montfort, who reproached him flirtatiously for not being present at the performance of Camilla's sonata. Camilla found herself smoldering with resentment. He had no right to be so unharried after what he'd just put her through.

Her temper didn't improve when, after they'd greeted the last of their guests, Jean took her arm in an iron grip and marched her out of sight behind one of the colonnades and back toward the entrance of the gardens.

"Jean, where are we going?" she protested. "Uncle Nigel expects us to take supper with him."

"I don't want to spend the rest of the evening being ignored by you while you make small talk with your godfather," Jean retorted. "You and I are going to Richmond, where we can have supper in private and put an end to this quarrel."

"No!" She dug in her heels, attempting to slow their progress. "Have you gone queer in your attic? We're the guests of honor at this gala. We can't repay Uncle Nigel's kindness with such rudeness."

"I'll leave a message for him at the gate. He'll understand, I hope. If not . . ." Jean shrugged. His voice hardened. "Camilla, either you'll walk with me to the

244

carriage, or I'll carry you there. It's up to you."

Camilla glared at Jean in helpless rage. Faced with the loss of her dignity, she had no choice. Yielding to Jean's insistent hand on her arm, she walked toward the entrance of the gardens. Later, in the carriage, she sat in frozen silence as the coachman began the drive along the Thames through Wandsworth and East Sheen to Richmond.

After making several futile efforts to induce Camilla to answer him, Jean asked, "Are you going to sit mumchance like that until we get to Richmond?"

She glanced at him fleetingly in the dim light of a street lamp, but didn't reply.

"Perhaps we can communicate in another way, then." Suddenly Jean wrapped a long arm around her, claiming her mouth in a hard, insistent kiss. Camilla stiffened, willing herself not to respond to the leaping flame his lips had ignited. After a long moment he released her.

Twisting away from him, Camilla said scathingly, "What do you think that proved, Jean? That you're physically stronger than I am? I don't deny that."

She heard his sharp intake of breath. Then he settled back against the squabs, his arms folded across his chest, lapsing into a grim silence that lasted until the carriage drew up before the Star and Garter Inn on the summit of Richmond Hill, near the entrance to the park.

Though Camilla had never previously visited the Star and Garter, she knew of it as a comfortable inn-hotel, resembling a country mansion, which had become increasingly popular with Londoners as a place where one might enjoy a leisurely dinner outside the city.

Still not speaking to Jean, Camilla allowed him to hand her down the steps of the carriage, and then walked with him through the entrance of the inn, where an attentive waiter showed them to a table. First ordering a bottle of champagne, Jean asked, "Is there anything special you'd fancy for supper, Camilla?" She shook her head. Shrugging, he ordered a lavish meal.

When the food arrived, Camilla sniffed the aroma of a well-browned capon and suddenly realized she was ravenously hungry and quite thirsty. At Vauxhall Gardens she'd been too occupied with greeting the guests to sample a morsel of the famous thin-sliced ham, or even to sip a glass of punch. If she followed her original plan, to sit stiffly at the table, disdaining to share a meal with Jean, she'd be cutting off her nose to spite her face. She decided she was going to eat the food he'd ordered, which looked and smelled uncommonly delicious, but there was no necessity to talk to him, or even to acknowledge his presence, and she had no intention of doing either.

Several glasses of champagne and generous helpings of capon, ham and boiled eels had a mellowing effect on Camilla. A little later, when Jean reached across the table to seize her hand, she made only a halfhearted attempt to release herself.

"Camilla, darling, are you ready to talk to me now? I love you, I'm sorry I've hurt you, I'll do anything to make it up to you—"

"Except tell me the truth." But there was little venom in Camilla's voice, and she left her hand clasped in both of his.

His fingers tightened. *"Ma mie,* if I could, I would. It's a matter of honor." He scowled, adding in sudden annoyance, "If it hadn't been for that damnable storm that kept me penned up in the harbor on Jersey for four whole days, you wouldn't be as angry with me."

"That was the only part of your story I believed. You're a terrible liar, Jean," Camilla observed before she could stop herself, and then, as she met Jean's eyes, she started laughing.

"Then you've forgiven me?" he said hopefully.

"Yes. I'm weak-minded."

A smile of relief lifted the corners of Jean's lips.

246

"Grâce à Dieu," he breathed. "Oh, Camilla, I missed you so much while I was gone. Every minute that I was away, I dreamed of holding you in my arms." He suddenly looked beatific. "I can't quite believe that in only three more days I'll never have to let you go again." Keeping his eyes fixed on hers, he raised her hand to his lips and slowly kissed each finger one by one.

Camilla snatched her hand away. Her cheeks burning, she muttered, "Jean, the waiter!"

Jean looked up into the fascinated eyes of the young waiter who had just brought a second bottle of champagne to the table. "Leave the bottle," Jean said calmly. "I'll open it later." He rose, saying to Camilla, "Shall we go for a stroll in the gardens? I understand the view is unforgettable. This is the highest point in the Thames valley, you know."

"Jean, you're so transparent," Camilla murmured, as they walked out of the inn and turned into the large garden, illuminated faintly by hanging lanterns. "Why didn't you just say you wanted to be alone with me? Precious little we'll see of that famous view in the middle of the night!"

But in this she was mistaken. She gazed in wonder and delight at the spectacle far below of a necklace of lights outlining the course of the river as it wound in sinuous curves through the hamlets and villages of the Thames valley.

"How lovely," she sighed. Glancing around her, she observed, "I'm surprised none of the other guests are out here admiring the view. But perhaps it's too chilly for them tonight."

Jean wasn't looking at the view. He was looking at her in the dim light of the swaying lanterns. "You're not chilly, are you, love?" he muttered, gently pushing back her silver-embroidered scarf, and bending his head to brush his lips lingeringly across the bare flesh of her throat and shoulders. "You're warm and desirable, and

247

just the touch of you fills me with such heat . . ." He swept her against him, kissing her with a hungry intensity that grew insatiable as he parted her lips with his tongue and plundered the inner recesses of her mouth.

When at last he lifted his head, his voice and his breathing were uneven. "Oh, Camilla, I want you, I need you," he whispered. "We'll be married in three days. We're as good as married now. Stay with me tonight. The Star and Garter rents rooms to overnight visitors."

Camilla clung convulsively to Jean, every nerve in her body clamoring with a fiery desire to consummate their love. The moments crept by, and finally she murmured, "Jean, I want so much to stay, but . . ."

Jean took a deep breath. Looking down at her tenderly, he said, "I know, love. I understand. If you don't come home until morning, Dorcas and your stepmother and your servants will all know you've spent the night with me."

Camilla whispered, "I'm sorry, Jean, to be such a coward."

"Sh-h-h." He held her close. "I told you I understood. I can wait." He gave a sudden chortle of laughter. "After we're married, though, don't think you can ask me to wait for anything!"

Chapter Sixteen

The weather on Camilla's wedding day was perfect. She woke up to brightness and warmth and unclouded blue skies, which continued into late afternoon, when she began dressing for her wedding.

"Camilla, you look so beautiful," Dorcas said softly, as she gazed at her sister's gown of gossamer silk crepe in a deep shade of blue that almost exactly matched her eyes, worn over a slip of white satin. A wreath of multicolored flowers circled the dark-gold curls piled high on the top of her head.

Camilla turned to look into the cheval glass, noting the excited brilliance of her eyes, shining like twin sapphires. She smiled at Dorcas. "Thank you, but if I look beautiful today it's because I'm so happy."

Francine, who with Dorcas had been helping Camilla to dress, darted forward to adjust a gauzy fold of crepe. "I must say, my dear," she observed with a faintly disapproving note in her voice, "that you don't appear in the least nervous. In my experience, all brides are nervous. Well I recall how all-to-pieces I was on *my* wedding day. But of course, you're not really a young girl any more, are you? And you *are* a widow."

Camilla bit back a retort. Francine's presence on Park Street was beginning to be a trial. Seemingly she never tired of delving into every aspect of the families and backgrounds of her two future sons-in-law. She had a particularly avid curiosity about Jean's "savage blood." And in recent days she'd shown signs of reverting to her old ways in Bath, when she'd tried to manage every aspect of her daughters' lives.

Looking distressed at her mother's latest embarrassing comment, Dorcas quickly changed the subject. "I was talking to my friend Sukey the other day, Camilla, and she says that her mother says that your wedding will be the largest and grandest event London has seen in years."

Camilla laughed. "I fear Sukey's mother is right. There was no stopping Uncle Nigel. It's a mercy that Jean wasn't frightened off by all this pother."

There was a knock on the door of the bedchamber, and Lizzie poked her head around the doorway. "Lord Sheringham is here to take ye to the church, Mrs. Rayburn—oh, ma'am, ye do look lovely."

"Lovely," her godfather smilingly echoed a few moments later when she entered the drawing room. He offered his arm. "My dear, it's time to go to your wedding."

During the short drive to St. George's Church, Camilla noted with amusement that she was the most composed person in the carriage. Her godfather held her hand tightly, and she knew that, despite his mask of imperturbability, he was feeling an inevitable letdown of tension now that his fondest dreams were about to come true. Dorcas had turned pale and fidgety; Camilla suspected she was dreading the prospect of being the center of attention when she preceded her sister down the aisle. Francine was faintly flushed, and an unmistakable smile of triumph wreathed her lips; it wasn't hard to imagine that she was reveling in the thought of taking part in one of the most prominent social events of the London Season.

But Camilla, although she was fully aware of her surroundings and of what was going on, was conscious only of a dreamy calm. She had only one thought in her mind. She was thinking of Jean. When the wedding party arrived at the church, she walked down the aisle on her godfather's arm, behind Dorcas's slender pink-clad figure, looking neither to right nor left at the packed pews in the vaulted nave and in the galleries, her eyes fixed on Jean's tall lithe form as he stood at the altar with Miles Wingate at his side.

As she approached Jean, an incandescent smile lighted his dark face, and his lips moved silently to say "I love you," and "You're beautiful." His hand enfolded hers in a warm, vital grasp, and his deep voice repeated the responses quickly, almost impatiently, as if he couldn't wait for the ceremony to end. And then it was over, and she was walking with him to the vestry to sign the register. As he scrawled his name, he peered at her with an impish grin, murmuring, "There, *ma mie*. You can't ever get away from me now."

Emerging under the huge portico of the church with Camilla on his arm, Jean impatiently waved away the footman who was holding open the door of the waiting carriage. "Good God, it's only a few yards to your godfather's house, Camilla. We'll walk," he said firmly.

The laughing guests, some of them appearing a little shocked, also abandoned their carriages and trooped behind the bridal pair in the late afternoon June sunshine, following them along the short length of the curiously funnel-shaped George Street into the broad expanse of Hanover Square.

"I love you, I adore you, I'm the happiest man in the world," Jean said softly as they approached the entrance to Sheringham House. He squeezed her arm against his side. "But I've had enough of wedding ceremonies and wedding parties. How long will it be before we can be alone, so that I can kiss you into a state of helpless passion and do all the things to your beautiful body that I've been longing to do since the first moment I met you?"

Her face flaming, Camilla whispered frantically, "Jean! Someone will hear you!"

"So? Everyone knows I'm a coarse Canadian," he murmured with a teasing smile at her discomfiture. Then, relenting, he said, "I'll behave, word of honor. But, to get back to essentials, how long will these nuptial celebrations last?"

Camilla shot him a mischievous glance, happy to get back at him. "Quite a long time, I fear. Let me see, now. First there'll be a receiving line, then a ball, then a supper."

"Oh, God," said Jean morosely. "It's all your godfather's doing, and I daresay he'll enjoy every moment of it. You'd think it was his wedding. He should remember that it's not *his* honeymoon that's being delayed!"

Camilla burst out laughing, and after a moment Jean grinned back at her. "I know, I know, my dear love," he said. "There's nothing for it but to endure. And I promised you I'd behave, and I will, if it kills me."

He was a model of propriety in the receiving line, he dutifully danced every dance during the ball, he gracefully replied to Lord Sheringham's toasts at the supper table, but as he and Camilla were leaving the dining room, he muttered in her ear, "Enough is enough. Now is *our* time. Go change your clothes, or whatever it is you must do before we can leave, and *hurry*."

A few minutes later, as she helped Camilla into a cream-colored sarcenet carriage dress, Dorcas said blissfully, "It was a *perfect* wedding. I only hope mine will be half as lovely."

Looking up from a large box into which she was carefully depositing Camilla's wedding gown, Francine said sharply, "Why shouldn't you have as grand a wedding as Camilla, Dorcas? I vow, it wouldn't be seemly of Lord Sheringham to allow you to marry a man of Mr. Wingate's standing in some sort of havey-cavey ceremony!"

"Mama!" Red-faced with embarrassment, Dorcas exclaimed, "Lord Sheringham has no obligation to pay for my wedding. In fact, he's already been far too kind to me. Even if he offered to frank my wedding, I couldn't allow him to do so."

"My dear Dorcas, surely you can't expect *me* to give you a wedding like this," Francine began, when a knock sounded at the door.

"Come," called Camilla, glad of the interruption.

Her godfather entered the room. Glancing briefly at Dorcas's strained face, he smiled at Camilla, saying, "I came to say a little private goodbye, my dear."

"Mama and I were just leaving, Lord Sheringham," said Dorcas quickly. She threw her arms around Camilla in a quick hug. "Goodbye, darling. I know you and Jean will be happy. Come, Mama."

Neither Camilla nor the earl noticed that, in her haste to leave, Dorcas left the door slightly ajar.

Camilla crossed the room to the earl and kissed him on his cheek. Stepping back, blinking against a sudden sting of tears at the back of her eyes, she said softly, "Thank you for my beautiful wedding, Uncle Nigel. And thank you for loving me all these years."

"My darling Camilla, I don't deserve any thanks for that. Loving you has been as natural as enjoying God's sunshine. You've been my daughter as much as if you'd been born to me. You *should* have been born to me. Your mother . . ." He paused, his eyes filming. After a moment, he said, "Your mother was the love of my life, you know that. If things had been different . . ."

"I know, Uncle Nigel." Camilla knew her godfather must be greatly moved. He'd never before spoken quite so frankly about his youthful romance with her mother.

Looking faintly embarrassed, the earl cleared his throat, saying, "Great Jupiter, we're being much too solemn on so joyful a day!" He shook his finger at her playfully. "I'll tell you what, Camilla. That was the best work I ever did, bribing you with twenty thousand pounds to charm Jean Hilliard into remaining in England!" His eyes twinkling, he added, "I must admit, though, that I never really expected you'd be obliged to resort to marriage to keep him here! Rather an extreme measure, wouldn't you say?" He added with an exaggerated concern, "Just to relieve my conscience, you do like him, don't you, at least a little?"

Camilla laughed. Entering into her godfather's joking mood, she said, "Oh, yes, I like Jean well enough, thank goodness. It would be quite dreadful, being married to a man I couldn't abide at all."

Lord Sheringham replied, still with a mock gravity, "I'm glad to hear it. In a good marriage, a wife should have *some* feeling for her husband." He held her close for a moment. "Goodbye, my dear. It's time for you to join your new bridegroom. All my love goes with you."

Something was wrong.

Glancing sideways, Camilla studied Jean's profile, etched against the lamplight streaming into the carriage windows as they crossed Westminster Bridge and turned into the Old Kent Road. He turned his head to observe, "The weather's holding. We'll have a fine day for our run down to Kent tomorrow."

It was a perfectly normal, straightforward remark, the same kind of remark that Jean had been making ever since he and Camilla had slipped quietly down a rear staircase at Sheringham House to enter the carriage taking them on their honeymoon. The problem was that it didn't sound like the remark of an ardent bridegroom, alone with his new bride for the first time.

Camilla felt chilled. Jean simply wasn't himself. So far, during the drive from Hanover Square, he'd made no attempt to put his arm around her. He hadn't kissed her. And this was the same man who'd found it so difficult to keep his arms and his lips to himself during the last few days of their betrothal.

Unable to keep her concern to herself any longer, she burst out, "Jean, what's the matter? Why are you acting so—so cold?" When he didn't reply immediately, she added involuntarily, "Why don't you kiss me?"

There was no emotion in Jean's voice. "I don't make love in public places, Camilla. A carriage is a public place." After a slight pause, he added casually, "We'll be at Shooter's Hill in half an hour."

Camilla felt an initial surge of relief. Of course. For

once in his life, Jean was being circumspect. If the coachman had to halt the carriage for any reason, Jean didn't want to be interrupted at an embarrassing moment. He was waiting to make love to her until they arrived at Shooter's Hill, where they'd arranged to spend their wedding night at the Bull Inn. Tomorrow they would resume the long journey to the Kentish villa.

Doubt set in almost immediately. It wasn't like Jean to restrain his emotions, especially where she was concerned. She'd expected him to crush her in a passionate embrace the moment they were alone together after the wedding, and hang the consequences if anyone should observe them. A thought struck Camilla. Was it possible that Jean, like many a newly married bachelor, was temporarily regretting the loss of his freedom?

The conflicting ideas chased each other around in Camilla's mind like captive squirrels in a cage, and she hadn't reached any firm conclusion about Jean's behavior by the time they reached the summit of Shooter's Hill and the Bull Inn.

Despite the lateness of the hour, the hotel staff was prepared for their arrival. A manservant conducted them to a tastefully appointed bedchamber with an adjoining dressing room, overlooking the hotel gardens. After the servant left, Jean remained near the door, arms crossed over his chest, his black eyes staring at her out of his expressionless face.

A knife twisted in Camilla's vitals. Behind that blank stare, where was the impetuous, passionate man she'd married? The start of her honeymoon had gone so tragically wrong, and she didn't have the faintest notion of what had caused the problem, or what she could do to remedy it.

The two portmanteaus that the hotel manservant had deposited in the center of the bedchamber caught her eye. Grasping at straws, she said with a provocative little laugh that sounded hollow in her own ears, "Darling, it was so clever of you to insist on sending my abigail and your valet

255

ahead of us to Kent with most of our luggage. Now you'll be obliged to valet me yourself! These tiny buttons on the back of my gown, for example. I can't reach them, love. I need your help."

"You can stop pretending, Camilla. I know what you really think of me. I know how you've had to steel yourself to let me touch you all these weeks since we became engaged. Well, in future, you need have no qualms. I haven't the faintest intention of touching you, ever again."

Camilla gasped. "Jean, what is it? Why are you acting this way? I love you. I thought you loved me. We were married only a few hours ago . . ."

Jean cut her off. "As I said, you can stop pretending. You see, Camilla, I overheard your conversation with your godfather earlier tonight, when he came to your bedchamber to bid you a fond goodbye before you went off on a honeymoon with his oaf of a Canadian heir. I'd gotten impatient, you see. I wondered what was keeping my beautiful bride from joining me on the first stage of our honeymoon. Your bedchamber door was slightly ajar. Very careless of you and the earl. I hesitated to interrupt you—can you blame me?—when I heard Lord Sheringham mention that he'd offered you twenty thousand pounds to persuade me to remain in England."

Camilla turned limp with relief. It was all a ridiculous misunderstanding. "Jean, you can't believe that Uncle Nigel paid me to—to seduce you!"

"Oh, but I do believe it. I was listening to you and your godfather very attentively. I heard Lord Sheringham tell you quite plainly that it was 'the best work I ever did, bribing you with twenty thousand pounds to charm Jean Hilliard into remaining in England.' Then he added, 'I never expected you'd be obliged to resort to marriage to keep him here.'"

"But Jean, Uncle Nigel was *joking!*"

"Really? Was he also joking when he asked you if you liked me, at least a little, and you replied, 'Oh, yes, I like him well enough. It would be quite dreadful, being married to a man I couldn't abide at all.' "

Jean's voice was no longer expressionless. Hearing a throbbing note of raw hurt, Camilla realized how cruelly he'd been wounded by her godfather's lightly amusing remarks, which Lord Sheringham had made to cover his own emotional state. She said urgently, "Please listen to me. I can explain about the money—"

"Oh? Then I didn't imagine the twenty thousand pounds?"

"No, of course not. Jean, you know that my stepmother tried to force Dorcas to marry that dreadful man in Bath, and that I spirited her away to London to live with me. What I never told you, because Dorcas felt so humiliated she didn't want anyone to know about it, was that Francine demanded money to give up Dorcas's custody. Twenty thousand pounds, to be exact. Uncle Nigel offered to give me the money, on condition that I attempt to persuade you to stay in England. One favor in exchange for another is the way he put it. But I knew he had no intention of enforcing such a bargain. If I'd refused to cultivate your acquaintance, Uncle Nigel would still have given me the twenty thousand pounds to buy off my stepmother."

"But you didn't refuse to cultivate my acquaintance, did you? You sent me invitations. You offered to introduce me to your friends. You promised me your friendship. You did all that, even though you and your friends considered me an uncouth Colonial."

Thrown on the defensive, Camilla said, "Well, yes, at first I did make friends with you for Uncle Nigel's sake. He was so desperately eager to keep you in England, and he'd been so infinitely kind to me over the years. But later . . . You surely don't doubt that I came to care for you for your own sake?"

With a lightning-swift lunge, Jean crossed the room and seized Camilla by her shoulders. He glared down at her, his eyes like chips of obsidian. "Yes, I doubt that you care for me. I doubt everything you've ever said to me, everything you've ever done. I remember how, when I first met you, you couldn't bear to let me touch you. It was only when you realized that the only sure way to keep me in England was to marry me that you became more generous with your favors."

Suddenly he bent his head to crush her lips in a grinding, hurtful kiss. When he finally released her mouth, he said, "That proves my point, I think. The only emotion you felt then, if any, was lust. I can get that from any whore on the streets of London. I didn't need to marry for it." He pushed her away from him with contemptuous, offhand violence.

"Jean, you're mistaken," Camilla said desperately. "I swear to you that Uncle Nigel never bribed me to marry you. I love you. I want to be your wife. I want to live with you for the rest of my life."

A hard glitter in his eyes, Jean said, "That wish I intend to gratify, Camilla. You'll live with me until the day you die, but not in England. According to English law, you're my property now, my chattel. I can do anything I like with you. I'm taking you back to Canada with me as soon as I can get my affairs in order. Let's see how much the next Countess of Sheringham will enjoy queening over those uncouth Colonials in Montreal, or presiding as hostess in a log cabin in the wilderness in the middle of a Canadian winter!"

He picked up one of the two portmanteaus in the middle of the floor. "Don't worry about playing the part of a loving bride on her wedding night," he gibed. "I'll be sleeping in the dressing room. Goodnight, Camilla."

Stunned into a momentary apathy, Camilla watched Jean disappear into the dressing room. The sound of the door slamming behind him roused her. She raced to the door, trying to wrench it open. It was locked. She pounded on the door. "Jean, please open up. We must talk. We can't leave the situation like this. Jean, it's our *wedding* night . . ."

He didn't answer. Listening through the door, she could hear a boot dropping to the floor, and shortly afterward another, followed by the characteristic small rustling noises made by a man preparing for bed, and finally the sound of a long lean body settling onto the hard cushions of the small settee in the dressing room.

Camilla gave up the attempt to talk to Jean and walked away from the closed door. Tomorrow his mind, and hers, too, would be clearer. They could talk then.

Struggling with the tiny buttons on the back of the sarcenet dress, Camilla finally succeeded in unfastening them. She removed her short corset and her petticoats and put on a nightdress of fine white embroidered linen lavishly trimmed with lace. Her heart constricted. She'd chosen the nightdress because she thought Jean would find her attractive in it. Now she wondered if he would ever see her in it. That thought, and the others swarming through her brain, didn't linger long. Unutterably weary both in spirit and body, Camilla fell asleep almost immediately after she climbed into the high tester bed.

On the morning after her wedding, the mellow sunshine of a perfect June day poured across Camilla's bed and touched her face. She sat up abruptly, fleetingly unsure of where she was. Then, instinctively, she turned to the space beside her on the bed. It was empty. She looked toward the dressing room. The door was open. "Jean?" she called. He wasn't there, as she discovered a few moments later when she jumped out of bed and rushed to the dressing room. His portmanteau was gone, too.

Slowly Camilla crossed to the bell rope and rang for a servant. When the hotel maid appeared, Camilla ordered tea and toast, and then, hesitating, she asked, "Has my husband had his breakfast?"

An avidly curious look crossed the maidservant's face. "Oh, yes, ma'am. Mr. Hilliard, 'e's long since 'ad 'is breakfast, 'e 'as. 'E left a message for ye, 'e did, ma'am."

"Oh? And what was the message?" Camilla inquired, pretending to an indifference she didn't feel.

"Ma'am, Mr. Hilliard, 'e left word that 'e 'ad decided to travel to Kent by 'orseback."

"I see. Thank you," said Camilla with a frozen calm. "Please bring my tea as soon as possible."

After the maidservant had left, Camilla paced the floor with quick, nervous steps. Jean had deliberately cut off any move toward reconciliation, or, at the very least, a discussion of their problems, by refusing to travel with her in their carriage to the Kentish villa. What was she going to do about the situation?

At the moment, she felt nothing but anger and a burning sense of resentment toward Jean. He'd judged her on the basis of an overheard conversation. He'd refused to listen to her explanations. He'd denied her love, in the most wounding of terms. Her first instinct was to order the carriage for an immediate return to London. Why should she go to the Kentish villa for a renewal of her humiliation? What purpose would it serve?

As she continued to pace the floor, other thoughts, other feelings crowded her mind, vying with each other for her attention. Pride, for one thing; if she returned to London alone, her friends and acquaintances would know that her marriage was over, that it hadn't lasted a day. She and Jean would be the laughingstock of the *ton*.

Nor could Camilla ignore her own sense of fairness. As she went back in her mind over the events of last night, she slowly began to realize how Jean might have felt justified in acting as he did. Reveling in the joy of knowing he could soon consummate his love, he'd learned—or thought he'd learned—that his new wife had married him for money. The shock must have been devastating. Of course he should have trusted in Camilla's love. Of course he should have known in his bones that she could never betray him. However, as he'd listened to that damning conversation in her bedchamber, he hadn't been able to see Uncle Nigel's misty-eyed, wryly deprecating expression, and in his agitation he'd completely missed the jocular tone in the earl's voice. Doubtless the conversation had merely reminded Jean, to deadly effect in his overset state, how desperately important it had been to Uncle Nigel that he stay in England and take his place as the Sheringham heir.

Camilla slowed her restless steps and walked to the window, where she stared blindly down into sun-drenched gardens. Now it was her turn to remember, to relive every moment of the passionate, all-consuming love she and Jean had felt for each other, and she knew she couldn't let it die, for lack at least of an effort on her part. She'd go to Kent. She'd *make* Jean realize how badly he'd been mistaken. Perhaps, she thought hopefully, she'd even find when she arrived that he'd already come to his senses.

When the maidservant brought her breakfast, Camilla drank her tea and nibbled at her toast with more appetite that she would have thought possible a few minutes before. Then, after repacking her portmanteau, she ordered her carriage.

The drive from Shooter's Hill to the coast near Folkestone seemed to take much longer than usual. Always before, she'd driven to the villa with Lord Sheringham, or with friends who had also been invited as guests, and in such cheerful company the miles had flown by. On her last visit, she'd driven down with Jean in his curricle. Smiling reminiscently, she recalled how Miles, his male ego ruffled, had challenged Jean to a curricle race, and how, when Jean had won the race by beating Miles to the turnoff leading to the villa, the two men, by some unfathomable male logic, had become fast friends.

It was late afternoon when Camilla's carriage came to a stop under the portico of Lord Sheringham's pretty villa on the Kentish coast. The earl's well-trained servants came out to welcome her and to take charge of her luggage. First asking the housekeeper for a tea tray, Camilla trudged wearily up the staircase, glad to be finished with the interminable drive. In the hallway she met Curtis, Jean's valet.

"Mrs. Hilliard, ma'am, I'm happy to see you. You had a

pleasant journey, I trust?" Curtis's polite, masklike face betrayed not a hint of the intense curiosity he must have felt when his master arrived at the villa without his new bride.

"As pleasant as possible, under the circumstances," Camilla replied coolly. "I was feeling vilely ill, as Mr. Hilliard probably informed you. I often become ill during long carriage rides. I believe the constant swaying motion of the vehicle is responsible." She added casually, "It was so considerate of my husband to suggest that I drive down by myself. Privacy is so important when one is feeling indisposed."

"Ah." A mingled expression of instant understanding and approval crossed the valet's face and disappeared. "Mr. Hilliard is a most considerate man."

Without words, Curtis and Camilla had exchanged a message. She knew the valet didn't believe in her tale of illness caused by the swaying motion of her carriage. After all, he'd observed her state of blooming health after she'd driven with Jean in that wild curricle race with Miles. She also knew that Curtis would assiduously spread the story among the servants at the villa. The valet was a snob, far more concerned about scandal in his master's household than Jean himself was. Undoubtedly, it hadn't suited Curtis's notions of propriety that Jean and Camilla had arrived separately at their honeymoon destination.

"Where is Mr. Hilliard?" Camilla inquired.

"I believe he went down to the fishing village on the shore, ma'am. Most interested in the angler's art, is Mr. Hilliard."

Most interested in avoiding me, too, Camilla thought resentfully. Well, this was a small estate. Jean couldn't avoid her forever.

After changing her clothes and drinking her tea, Camilla went walking in the garden behind the house, where the early summer flowers were in full bloom, sweetening the air with their intoxicating scents. Restless, concerned about Jean, and failing to find the peace she normally felt in the garden, Camilla wandered down the path leading to the beach. She paused at the spot under the spreading old tree where she and Jean had picnicked during their visit to the villa several months ago. Dreamily she remembered how he'd plucked off her little lace cap and buried his face in her hair and tried to kiss her.

At the sound of a pebble being dislodged, she looked down the path, to see Jean making the steep climb from the beach. When he reached her, he glanced at the old tree, his lips tightening momentarily, and she knew he was remembering, too.

That was his only show of emotion. Giving her a level look, he said, "So, you decided to come down to the villa."

Camilla lifted her chin at him. "You didn't think I would?"

"Frankly, I wasn't sure. I thought you might return to London."

Camilla couldn't prevent a tremor of hurt from sounding in her voice. "And you didn't care, one way or the other?"

He shrugged. "Not particularly."

Camilla said pleadingly, "Jean, I know you're hurt, I know you feel deceived and betrayed, but I can make everything right if you'll only let me explain about Uncle Nigel and the twenty thousand pounds—"

He cut her off. "I don't want your explanations. I understand the situation perfectly. You see, I've had a little time to think since I left you last night, and I now believe you when you say your godfather didn't bribe you to befriend me."

Her eyes widening, Camilla exclaimed, "But then why, Jean—"

He cut her off again. "It's the rest of your story I don't believe," he said brutally. "From the very beginning, our relationship has been one vast lie. It wasn't necessary for Lord Sheringham to bribe you. You'd have done anything to please him, and that included bedazzling a country clod from Canada. Time and again I sickened you with my

263

gaucheries—my behavior at your musical evening, my initial encounters with the fashionable dowagers and the Pinks of the *ton*, my outburst at your godfather's dinner party—and time and again you overlooked my sins. Then, with the Season drawing to an end, I still hadn't given you a definite commitment to stay in England, so you made the supreme sacrifice. You agreed to marry me."

"Jean, you're wrong. I married you because I love you. In any case, Uncle Nigel would never have asked me to 'sacrifice' myself for him."

"It wasn't necessary for him to ask. You'd have done anything to make him happy. Because, after Elvaston raped you—"

"What are you saying?" Camilla said in a trembling voice.

"You lied about that, too, didn't you? Or perhaps, to give you the benefit of the doubt, you may have argued that if you denied it, even to yourself, it wouldn't be true. But it was true, nothing else explains how you acted. And so, after Elvaston raped you, and your husband committed suicide, Lord Sheringham helped you put your life back together again. You owed him a tremendous debt, and finally you paid it at my expense." Jean paused, looking at Camilla out of cold, empty eyes. "I told you I understood the situation, Camilla. Now there's no need for us to discuss it again." Turning on his heel, he strode up the path to the gardens and the house.

Too shocked to move, Camilla stood staring after Jean's retreating form for several moments. It was worse, much worse, than she'd imagined. Jean had completely misinterpreted every incident, every aspect, of their relationship since they'd first met. What's more, given that he believed the horrible fantasy that Aubrey Elvaston had succeeded in raping her, she could understand, at least in part, the twisted but persuasive illogic that had brought Jean to this pass. And she wasn't at all sure she could think of any fact, any argument that might make him change his mind.

She dressed for dinner without seeing any more of Jean,

wondering if he would see fit to join her for the meal. He did so, sitting at the opposite end of the table in Lord Sheringham's graceful baroque dining room. However, he didn't open his mouth to speak except to ask the butler to decant another bottle of wine.

Leaving the table at the end of the second course, Camilla said in a low voice, "Jean, I wish to speak with you. After you've had your port, please join me in the drawing room for coffee."

She waited in the drawing room for fifteen minutes, half an hour, forty-five minutes, drinking a second and third unwanted cup of coffee. Then, slowly, she mounted the stairs to her bedchamber. Although it was still early in the evening—the twilight hadn't completely melded into darkness—she had her abigail prepare her for bed, and then, dismissing Becky, she sat down in an armchair beside the opened window, breathing in the soft night scents. Her spirit felt bruised and desolate. She hadn't been at such a low ebb emotionally for years, not since she'd learned of Philip's death, and realized he was a suicide.

The door of the bedchamber opened. Jean stepped into the room and closed the door behind him. Her heart clamoring with a sudden hope and excitement, Camilla rose from her chair.

"I came to congratulate you," said Jean. His voice was slurred. Camilla wondered apprehensively if he'd been drinking port since she'd left him at the dinner table. He went on, "Curtis told me your ingenious explanation for our separate arrivals at the villa. You want to avoid scandal at all costs, don't you? Well, yesterday, I didn't care a whit about scandal. Today I've had second thoughts. I have a certain amount of masculine pride, and as long as I stay in England, I'd as lief not be the subject of gossip by the *ton*. I don't want your toplofty friends speculating about my private affairs, wondering why I couldn't please my new wife—or why you couldn't please me—for even one night. So I'll make you a promise, Camilla. From now on, until we leave for Canada, I'll play the happy bridegroom in public."

Camilla felt a rush of relief. The specter of gossip, though not her greatest concern in this crisis in her marriage, had weighed heavily on her spirit. "Thank you," she began in very real gratitude, and paused, her heart pounding, as Jean walked across the room.

Stopping in front of her, he gazed down at her, his dark eyes kindling with a familiar intense heat. "That's a pretty robe," he said softly, reaching out to push the pale blue silk from her shoulders. It fell in a shimmering heap to the floor. He fingered the lacy frill at her neck. "It's an even prettier nightdress. Did you buy it for your wedding night, Camilla?" His voice became a husky whisper. "Did you buy it for me?"

"Yes," Camilla breathed, trembling as his fingers slowly unfastened the buttons of her nightdress. He inhaled sharply. "God, but you're beautiful," he murmured. He brushed the exposed creamy flesh with lips that burned a fiery trail to her mouth. After a long, hard, devouring kiss that bruised her lips and left her half fainting with desire, he muttered, "I've changed my mind, Camilla. I told you I had no intention of touching you again. But why should I be such a fool? You've killed my love, but there's no reason why I shouldn't enjoy your body. A man has needs, and you're not only attractive but accessible."

The brutal words hit Camilla with the force of an icy deluge, destroying every vestige of physical longing. She felt only a powerful consuming anger. Wresting herself from his grasp, she said with a cold scorn, "Go ahead and take what you want from me. You're stronger than I am, and I won't fight you. But it will be no better than rape, nonetheless. Because you were right about me all along, Jean. I cultivated you solely for Uncle Nigel's sake. You were a dolt, a ruffian I had no desire to know. You had no manners, no conception of what it meant to be a gentleman, and I hated every occasion when I had to appear with you in public. My flesh crawled every time you touched me. I had to nerve myself to keep from shuddering when you kissed me, and I dreaded the time when I'd be obliged to allow you into my bed—"

"That's enough," Jean snapped. The smooth bronze of his face had an underlay of grayish white. "Now that you've admitted the truth at last, you needn't fear I'll ever disturb you again. I'd rather sleep with a snake."

Desperately clinging to her composure until the door had closed behind Jean, Camilla sank to the floor, her face buried in her hands. What Jean had tried to do, using her body with no more compunction than if she'd been a common street tart, had been cruel and unforgivable. She'd struck back at him with the first weapon at hand, and the lies she'd told had been equally cruel and unforgivable. If there had ever been the slightest chance that she and Jean could find their way back to each other, it was gone now, destroyed by their mutual anger and wounded pride.

Chapter Seventeen

From the courtyard of the Bull Inn, Camilla stood looking down at the hazy panorama of London far below, eight or nine miles in the distance. Under the heavy pall of smoke lying over the city, she could catch glimpses of crowded masts in the river and a forest of church steeples rising above the brick buildings.

Jean walked up to her. "The carriage is ready," he said briefly.

She followed him back to the carriage, where he silently handed her up the steps and climbed in beside her. As the coachman drove out of the courtyard of the inn, Camilla said a mental prayer of thanks. In little more than an hour, they would be in London. They long, trying journey from the Kentish villa was almost over. For over nine interminable hours, she and Jean had been cooped in enforced proximity in the carriage, not speaking to each other, but with the echoes of past anger and estrangement and resentment almost palpable in the atmosphere.

At the foot of Shooter's Hill, the carriage lurched as it made a sharp turn around a curve in the road, sending Jean sliding across the seat against Camilla, locking their thighs together. Reacting instantly, as if he'd touched a burning coal, Jean scrambled back against the opposite side of the carriage. He looked away from her, staring out the window. This is what they had come to, thought Camilla. Jean couldn't bear to touch her, he could barely bring himself to speak to her.

The ten days of her "honeymoon" had been the most difficult period of Camilla's life, even more difficult than that dreadful time following Philip's death. To be fair, she thought their stay at the villa had been an agonizing strain for Jean, also. They'd both observed the rules of the agreement that Jean had proposed just before their final shattering quarrel: they would keep scandal at bay by pretending to be happily normal newlyweds. In public, in front of the servants, they'd been polite and pleasant to each other. In private, during those times when they couldn't avoid being alone together, they were silent and distant.

They didn't speak now, during this final stage of the drive from Kent, until the carriage drew up in front of Sheringham House in Hanover Square. When Jean jumped to the pavement and extended his hand to Camilla, he said, jibingly, "Welcome home." Immediately he clamped his lips together. She knew that the words had slipped out involuntarily, from a fount of bitter resentment.

The butler opened the door as they walked up the steps, and a small, slender figure raced like a whirlwind down the staircase from the floor above to greet them in the foyer. "I was looking out my window and spied your carriage stopping in front of the house," said Dorcas happily. She threw her arms around Camilla. "Oh, I'm so glad to see you!" She turned to kiss Jean heartily on his cheek. "Jean, I refuse to call you Mr. Hilliard ever again," she said with a grin. "We're brother and sister now."

Forcing a smile, he replied, "Of course you must call me Jean. And I'm delighted to have a sister. I was an only child, you know." To Camilla he said, "You'll want to talk to your sister and rest after the journey. I'll leave you to it."

As she accompanied Camilla up the stairs, Dorcas kept up a constant round of chatter. "I love living in Sheringham House," she declared. "I'm so glad the house on Park Street was too small for you and Jean *and* a younger sister! Of course, the earl's secretary is busily looking for a suitable house for you. The earl says there's no hurry, however; your new house must be exactly right for the amount of entertaining you and Jean will be obliged to do."

"You sound as if you and Uncle Nigel were becoming bosom friends," Camilla said, with a gaiety she was far from feeling. She and Dorcas had entered a large sunny bedchamber, part of a suite consisting of two large rooms connected by a dressing room, that Lord Sheringham had offered to her and Jean until they found a home of their own. This was the same bedchamber in which she'd changed her clothes on the night of her wedding, the same room in which she'd had the fatal conversation with Uncle Nigel that had changed her life forever.

"I love Lord Sheringham," said Dorcas simply. "I think he must be the kindest man in the world. He wants to give me my wedding." She hesitated. "Camilla, can I possibly accept his offer, when he's already done so much for me? Mama keeps insisting I'd be a fool not to accept. She says Lord Sheringham is so wealthy he could afford to pay for the weddings of a hundred of your sisters, supposing you had that many!"

Lost in her bittersweet thoughts, Camilla had been paying only an absentminded attention to Dorcas's prattling. Now she said sharply, "Mama? She planned to return to Bath immediately after my wedding. Is she still in London?"

A hunted expression crept over Dorcas's face. "Yes. She's staying at Fenton's Hotel. She came here to visit the day after your wedding, and hinted to the earl that she'd like to stay at Sheringham House, to take your place as chaperon while you and Jean were on your honeymoon. I was so mortified. Mama already knew, for I'd told her, that the earl had arranged for his cousin, Mrs. Frame, to go about with me until you came back from Kent. The earl politely refused Mama's offer, of course, so then off she went to take a room at the hotel. She comes here every day to visit," Dorcas added bleakly.

Camilla repressed an urge to scream. The last thing she needed in her life right now was the intrusive presence of her stepmother. Francine was not only incurably inquisitive; she had a knack for prying out other people's secrets. All

Camilla said to Dorcas, however, was, "Perhaps Mama will soon become bored and go back to Bath. The Season is nearly over, you know."

But Dorcas's mind was no longer on her mother. Blushing furiously, she asked, "Camilla, can I ask you something? I haven't anyone else to talk to . . . Are you truly happy? Is marriage as wonderful as you thought it would be? Do you think Miles and I . . . ?"

Hugging her sister, Camilla said firmly, "Yes, I'm happy, you goose. Can't you tell? And of course you and Miles are going to be even happier than Jean and I!"

When Dorcas left to dress for dinner, Camilla thought back over their conversation and wondered apprehensively if her sister had sensed her estrangement from Jean. But no, that was hardly possible. Dorcas had seen Jean and Camilla together for only a few moments. More likely than not, her questions had been prompted solely by a growing nervousness about her own coming marriage, Camilla reassured herself. Provided she and Jean observed the terms of their pact, there was no reason for anyone to suspect that their marriage was a sham.

Later that evening at the dinner table, however, Camilla felt less confident. Several times she caught her godfather's eyes fixed on her with a faintly questioning glance. She and Jean were trying hard to act naturally. Perhaps they were trying too hard. The earl's keen eyes missed very little. Moreover, he knew her very well.

As the meal progressed, Camilla grew more grateful by the minute that her godfather had asked Miles to join the family in welcoming her and Jean home. Miles's cheerful exchange of chatter with Dorcas covered any awkward pauses that occurred, and made it easier for Jean and Camilla to conceal the strain they were under.

First glancing questioningly at Miles, who smiled and nodded, Dorcas cleared her throat, saying, "I have important news. Miles and I have set our wedding date. September the fifteenth. Miles sent the announcements to the newspapers this morning."

"By Jove, what capital news," declared the earl.

"Yes, wonderful," Camilla agreed. Her eyes twinkled as she said to Miles, "You sly rogue, you waited until I was out of town to do this. We agreed that you and Dorcas could marry in the autumn. I thought in terms of October, or possibly early November. You've stolen a march on me, Miles. You should be ashamed of yourself. Now Dorcas and I will be obliged to scramble to complete our preparations for the wedding on time."

Dorcas giggled, and the usually unflappable Miles looked faintly sheepish. Happily, preliminary planning for the ceremony and reception occupied everyone's attention for the remainder of the meal, giving Camilla a respite from the need to watch every word she uttered. The conversation about the wedding continued after the men joined her and Dorcas in the drawing room for coffee. At the end of the evening, however, after Miles had taken his leave and Dorcas had retired to bed, her respite ended.

"Camilla, Jean," said Lord Sheringham pleasantly, "could I talk to you for a few moments in the library?"

Camilla and Jean exchanged glances. Then, shrugging, Jean replied, "As you wish, sir."

Leaning back in a chair behind his desk in the library, the earl gazed at the two figures sitting in front of him. At last he observed, "Something's amiss. Can I help in any way?"

"Uncle Nigel, I've often suspected you could read minds," said Camilla with an unconvincing little laugh. "The fact is, Jean and I have had a spat. Nothing important, and no, we don't need any help, but thank you for offering."

Jean ripped out an oath. While Camilla and the earl were still looking at him in shock, he said, "Let's put an end to this balderdash, Camilla. Lord Sheringham will know soon enough what's happened. Why not tell him now?"

"But—I thought we'd agreed . . ."

"We agreed to pretend to be happy newlyweds in public. Sheringham House isn't public. It's our home, at least for the time being. I'm damned if I'll act the part of your loving husband in private, too. A man needs a little relief from playing the buffoon." Jean smiled thinly. "Besides, you really should have a little consideration for your godfather. He was telling me before dinner that he has his secretary scouring the West End for a suitable house for us. Surely you'll want to spare him such a useless effort."

"Jean." The earl's voice held a dangerous calm. "I'd like an explanation, please."

"Yes, sir. To put it briefly, I've discovered the real reason why Camilla married me. Not for love, but to fulfill your request to charm me into staying in England. Oh, there's also the little matter of the twenty thousand pound bribe, but I'm inclined to believe Camilla when she says you'd have given her the money even if she hadn't promised to seduce me."

Lord Sheringham looked at Camilla helplessly. "My dear . . ."

Jean continued doggedly. "Obviously I can't continue in this farce of a marriage. I daresay my simplest course would be to sue for divorce or annulment, and then return to Canada to wait for you to die, sir. As to the divorce, I don't relish the thought of the *ton* tittering at me over the juicy details of my marriage, and I also think I'm entitled to get a bit of my own back. So this is what I've decided, Lord Sheringham: I'm returning to Canada, *and* I'm taking Camilla with me, and there's not a damned thing you can do about it."

The expression of helpless shock was fading from the earl's face. "Jean, listen to me," he said sharply. "Camilla never schemed against you. No one did. But if there's any fault in this muddle, it's my doing. Camilla loves you. She's also a woman of enormous integrity. She wouldn't have married you simply to gratify my wish to have you stay in England."

His face cold and grim, Jean replied, "Naturally, you'd support Camilla's story. I don't believe you. I don't believe Camilla's holier-than-thou ranting, either. Nothing you say will make me change my mind. Camilla goes with me to Canada."

"Not if I can help it," Lord Sheringham snapped. "What

will you live on in Canada? I won't allow you a shilling. You'll be going back to a bankrupt fur trading business. I have some influence in the financial establishment. I'll see to it that not a reputable banker in the city loans you a penny on your 'expectations' of my estate. That leaves the money-lenders. See how much the cent-per-centers will give you. And at what interest. You'll starve in Canada, and you'll starve Camilla along with you."

"I think you're overestimating your influence with the London bankers," Jean said coolly. "I don't doubt I could easily obtain a loan on my 'expectations' from your estate. However, I don't anticipate any problem in raising money by other means." He smiled mockingly. "I have hidden talents, sir." Rising, he looked down at Camilla. "My dear wife, I've been a dutiful husband since early this morning. I've endured an hellish day in your company, trapped with you in a carriage. I've spent an intolerable evening with your family and your about-to-be brother-in-law. I've more than fulfilled my marital obligations, so now I'm going out in search of a blessed relief from all of you, at White's, or possibly Boodle's." He swept Camilla and the earl an exaggerated bow, and left the room.

Lord Sheringham said dully, "Oh, Camilla, what have I done?"

She shook her head. "Don't blame yourself, Uncle Nigel." She explained about the conversation that Jean had overheard on her wedding night. "After that, Jean apparently went back in his mind over every incident, every word that you and I had spoken to him since he arrived in England, and misinterpreted every one to fit his theory." She was silent for a moment. Then she said, "Does Jean really have the legal right to force me to go with him to Canada?"

"Yes, I fear so. A husband has the choice of domicile, and his wife must go with him," the earl said somberly. "But Camilla, surely it won't come to that. When Jean has had the opportunity to reflect on the situation, he'll realize his accusations are untrue."

"I wish I could agree with you. Jean's a very proud man,

274

and an obstinate one. His pride is in the dust now. I don't think he'll ever forgive us for the humiliation." Rising, Camilla looked at her godfather with a sad, crooked little smile. "No, I believe I should start reviewing my French, and lay in a supply of warm winter garments. I may soon be living in a log cabin in the wilderness. Goodnight, Uncle Nigel."

Later, after she'd dismissed her abigail, Camilla walked into the dressing room that connected her bedchamber with Jean's, and tried the door of Jean's room. It was locked.

Several days later, as she sat at her desk in her bedchamber, catching up on her accumulated correspondence, Camilla reflected with a twinge of surprise that it was almost the end of July. Why the date should have surprised her was, of course, illogical. The wedding had taken place at the end of June, she and Jean had spent ten days in Kent on their macabre "honeymoon," and they'd returned to London more than a week ago.

Opening one letter stamped with a ducal crest, Camilla discovered an invitation for a country house party at the Lincolnshire estate of the Duke and Duchess of Ventnor. The date was for the beginning of October. Where would she be at the beginning of October, she wondered. Still holding the invitation in her hand, she stood up, hesitating for a few moments, then walked into the dressing room and knocked on Jean's door.

After a short delay he opened it, standing looking at her with the cold, impersonal politeness she'd learned to dread. "Yes?"

"Good morning, Jean. Can I speak to you for a moment?"

"Certainly."

"I wanted to remind you of the Cathcart ball tonight."

"I hadn't forgotten. I'm surprised you thought it necessary to remind me. I'm not aware of missing any of our social functions recently. Is there anything else?"

Camilla bit her lip. It was so obvious that Jean considered her reminder about the ball that night merely an excuse to talk to him. He was quite right, of course. He didn't need reminders of his social obligations. Since their return from Kent, he'd faithfully escorted her and Dorcas to all their engagements, and had done so with a grace and charm — in public — that had successfully concealed their marital rift.

"Yes, there is something else, Jean. You've told me you intend to return to Canada, and to take me with you. Is that still your intention?"

"It is."

The total absence of emotion in his voice chilled her. Trying for a composure to match his own, she motioned to the invitation in her hand, saying, "I'm already receiving invitations for the autumn. Can you give me a date for our departure, so that I can begin making my own plans?"

After a brief pause, Jean replied, still in that cold, impersonal tone, "I haven't decided on a date yet. When I do, I'll inform you. Now, if you'll excuse me, I must go. I've arranged to meet a friend at Manton's Shooting Gallery."

Camilla went back to her desk, swallowing against a lump in her throat. Was this cold hostility, this complete disregard for her wishes, all she could expect from Jean in the years to come? She shivered. Her situation would be infinitely worse in Canada, where she didn't know a soul, where she would lack the support of friends and family.

"Camilla? Are you ready to go?"

Lost in her thoughts, Camilla hadn't heard the tap on the door. She looked up to find Dorcas standing in the doorway. "What?"

"Camilla! My wedding gown!" exclaimed Dorcas reproachfully. "You promised to go with me to Mme. Labelle's shop this morning."

"I forgot. I'm sorry. I can be ready in a moment. Just let me fetch my bonnet and pelisse."

As she and Camilla walked to their carriage a little later, Dorcas said blissfully, "Sometimes I can't believe my good fortune. Imagine, Lord Sheringham insisting that I buy my gown at the most expensive *modiste* shop in London!" After a pause, she added with a trace of dejection, "And mind, after we've shopped for my gown, we must go visit Mama at her hotel."

After their shopping excursion, during which, as a result of considerable soul-searching, they had selected the design for Dorcas's wedding gown, Camilla and Dorcas made a reluctant stop at Fenton's Hotel on St. James's Street. Gazing around the tastefully appointed private sitting room that Francine had engaged for receiving her visitors, Camilla speculated idly on the cost of her stepmother's protracted stay in London. Apparently Francine had been considering the question, too.

"Camilla, dear," she began pensively, "before I came here, I had no idea that London was so expensive. This hotel, for example. Very nice, of course, but . . ." She shook her head. Then, as if the idea had just occurred to her, she said, "Your little house on Park Street is vacant now, isn't it? Perhaps you'd allow me to stay there for a few weeks?"

Once Francine was ensconced in free lodgings, Camilla reflected, it was unlikely that her stepmother could be pried out of London.

"I'm so sorry, Mama," she said with a total lack of sincerity. "Uncle Nigel has suggested that I rent the house. I don't quite like to go against his wishes, you know, because, as you may recall, he bought the house for me in the first place."

Francine looked unhappy with this decision, but she was far too much in awe of Lord Sheringham to persue the subject. Instead, she went on to talk of her latest social triumph. "I took tea yesterday with a Spanish *contessa* who's staying at the hotel," she announced proudly. "The *contessa* has invited me to a small evening party she's giving next week." At the sound of a knock on the sitting room door, she called out, "Come in."

Aubrey Elvaston entered the room with his graceful dragging limp, saying, "My dear Mrs. Vernon, I fear I'm intruding. You already have visitors—" He broke off with a convincing show of surprise, lifting his quizzing glass to gaze at Camilla and Dorcas. "Camilla—Mrs. Rayburn! I beg your pardon, it's Mrs. Hilliard now, isn't it? And Miss Vernon. What a pleasure to see both of you again."

Dorcas had turned very pale. She looked at Sir Aubrey like a trapped creature. It was the first time she'd seen Elvaston, except for brief glimpses from a distance, since his attempt to seduce her.

Camilla's first impulse had been to leave immediately, to get away from Sir Aubrey's presence, but now she doubted that Dorcas's legs would support her as far as the door. To cover Dorcas's numb, stricken silence, Camilla joined with pretended interest in the conversation between Francine and Elvaston. At one point, Elvaston said to her, "Camilla—I mean Mrs. Hilliard—I was desolated that I wasn't able to attend your wedding. But you understood, I'm sure."

"Oh, I understood perfectly, Sir Aubrey," Camilla replied, resisting the urge to slap her reticule across his handsome, smiling face.

His expression turning thoughtful, Elvaston went on, "In one sense—and in one sense only, I assure you—I was glad I couldn't be among your wedding guests. I fear that Philip's memory would have intruded . . ." He interrupted himself, looking horrified. "I'm so sorry. I shouldn't have said that."

Hypocrite, thought Camilla viciously. Villain. You never miss an opportunity to bait me, do you? Aloud she said coolly, "But then, you and Philip were *such* good friends."

In a few minutes, to her immense relief, Sir Aubrey seemed to tire of the underground warfare he was waging with her, and rose to take his leave. He told Francine, "As a mere man, I know I can't compete for a beautiful lady's attention when her two equally beautiful daughters are present. Do I have your permission to call again—and soon?"

Francine bridled with pleasure. "Please do, Sir Aubrey. You're always welcome." After Elvaston left, she said, "What a perfectly charming gentleman. So distinguished. From such a fine old family, and with a high post in the dip-

278

lomatic service, too. I vow, I'm privileged to know him."

Noting thankfully that Dorcas's color was returning, Camilla asked in a carefully casual tone, "I wasn't aware that you knew Sir Aubrey, Mama."

"Indeed, yes. He came up to introduce himself to me one evening in the hotel dining room. He apologized for his informality, but he said he'd seen me several times in your company at various parties before your wedding, and he felt he already knew me! Since then, he's come to take tea with me several times, and only yesterday he invited me to drive with him in the Park." Francine fixed an inquisitive eye on Camilla. "Sir Aubrey told me how friendly he was used to be with you and Philip in the old days, and then he hinted at some sort of a misunderstanding."

"Sir Aubrey was Philip's friend, more than mine," Camilla said curtly. "I really don't feel that I know him at all any more. I recall, he's been out of the country for some years."

"I see. Well, that's as may be, but I fancy Sir Aubrey would like to renew his friendship with you, Camilla. He thinks so highly of you, he's so interested in your affairs, and Mr. Hilliard's. Really, he was quite fascinated when I talked of Mr. Hilliard's relatives in France, and his friendship with Mr. Nathan Rothschild, and that time a few days before your wedding when Mr. Hilliard simply disappeared—" Cutting herself off short, Francine said in a small voice, "I daresay I shouldn't have told Sir Aubrey about *that*. I remember you didn't want the subject discussed outside the family."

"What's done is done, Mama," Camilla replied, her thoughts churning furiously beneath her assumed calm. Why was Aubrey Elvaston cultivating her stepmother? Certainly he could have no personal interest in a fortyish provincial widow of small fortune. Whatever his purpose, you could be sure he was up to no good. Camilla opened her mouth to warn Francine against any further association with Sir Aubrey, and changed her mind. Unless she was prepared to tell her stepmother the whole truth about Elvaston—including the circumstances of his crippling injury and of Philip's suicide—she knew she'd never be able to persuade Francine to give up such a dazzling acquaintance. Perhaps the wiser course would be to ignore the connection, and hope that Sir Aubrey would soon tire of Francine's company.

Glancing at Dorcas, who seemed completely recovered, Camilla said, "We must go, Mama. Dorcas and I are attending the Cathcart ball tonight." At the door, Camilla turned, wagging a playful finger at Francine. "Mind you don't turn any more susceptible gentlemen's heads, Mama, or people will begin to consider you just a trifle fast!"

Immediately Camilla felt ashamed of herself. Francine looked positively incandescent with delight.

———

Nathan Rothschild gazed at his young guest, sitting lost in thought in his usual place at the dining table. "Another glass of port, Mr. Hilliard?"

Jean roused himself, extending his glass. "Yes, thank you, NM."

"And so, you've decided to return to Canada, my friend," Rothschild continued, ignoring the fact that, moments before, Jean had retreated into some private corner of his mind. "Isn't this rather a sudden decision?"

"Not really. I came to England intending to stay only a short time." Jean flushed as he returned Rothschild's dispassionate, mildly inquiring look. "For a while, before—before my marriage, I'd changed my mind about staying. Now"—Jean shrugged—"I've changed my mind again."

Rothschild didn't probe. "When will you leave?"

"I'm not sure. Certainly not until I've increased my capital to fifty thousand pounds. That should be sufficient to start my own business in Canada." Jean smiled suddenly. "Perhaps my own bank!"

"Which reminds me . . ." Rothschild rose. "Excuse me for a moment, please." He returned to the room shortly with a sheaf of banknotes in his hand, which he handed to Jean.

Rapidly counting the notes, Jean looked at Rothschild questioningly. "What's this, NM?"

Seating himself again, Rothschild replied, "That's payment for services rendered, with a little extra to compensate you for being stormbound in a Jersey port for days on end just before your wedding."

His eyebrows drawing together in a frown, Jean said curtly, "I don't want payment for helping a friend."

One of his rare smiles crossed Rothschild's plump, homely face. "That's a Corinthian speaking, a pink of the *ton,* not the hardheaded businessman I've come to know. Jean-Étienne Hilliard, you not only helped a friend, you enabled him to make a handsome profit. You're entitled to a share of that profit. What's more, I'm about to ask you to help me again."

His somber mood passing, Jean laughed outright. "Is that why you asked me to dinner, NM? I thought you wanted the pleasure of my company."

"That, too," Rothschild said, smiling. "Well, my friend? Will you act for me again? My chief courier is still incapacitated, and I don't like to entrust such delicate business to any of my younger people. Especially when you have such excellent connections on the other side of the Channel! And naturally," he added firmly, "I'd expect to reimburse you for your trouble."

A gleam of excitement came into Jean's eyes. "I'd be happy to oblige. Actually, I welcome the chance to see my French cousins again. For that matter, I'd as lief get out of London for a spell."

"Very good." The merchant banker gazed blandly at Jean, repressing a wave of intense curiosity. This was a business transaction, and the fact that a very recently married bridegroom was eager to leave his residence and his new bride had nothing to do with business.

Consulting the clock on the mantel of the drawing room, Lord Sheringham said, "I fear we can't wait any longer for

Jean. I suggest we go up to the ballroom without him. Our guests will begin arriving shortly."

Rather timidly, Dorcas asked, "Camilla, where *is* Jean? When I talked to him several days ago, he said he was looking forward to dancing with me at my engagement ball."

Before Camilla could reply, Miles said quietly, "I daresay he was simply detained, Dorcas." He turned to the earl. "Doubtless you've sent him on another errand to Northamptonshire on estate matters, sir."

"Yes, that was it," lied Lord Sheringham, without a ripple of expression in his face. "Jean was sure he'd be back in good time for the ball. Possibly there was an accident to his curricle, and he had to stop for repairs. We must all make his excuses."

"And he may still arrive before the evening is over," said Dorcas hopefully.

Camilla glanced at the three people in the room, each of whom, in his or her own way, was attempting to overlook the signs of her rift with Jean. Although she and Jean had, so far as she knew, concealed their situation from the public, she'd sensed in recent days that both Miles and Dorcas had begun to realize that she and Jean were estranged.

The tale that Jean had been detained on estate business in the country would probably pass muster, she mused, as she walked with her godfather and Miles and Dorcas to the ballroom. She'd used that same excuse before, when Jean had disappeared so mysteriously for six days before their wedding. But—echoing Dorcas's question—where *was* Jean, and what had delayed him this time? He'd certainly intended to be present tonight at the ball that Lord Sheringham was giving for Dorcas.

Three days ago Jean had come to her bedchamber with a brief announcement, totally devoid of apology. "I won't be able to escort you to the opera tomorrow night, or to Lady Jersey's rout," he'd said in clipped tones. "I'm going away for several days. I'll return in time for Dorcas's ball."

She'd looked into his chilly dark eyes, knowing her question was futile before she asked it. "Can you tell me where you're going?"

"No. It's a confidential matter."

And then he'd left, without a word of goodbye, closing the door of the dressing room firmly behind him.

At the end of the evening, everyone went home saying that Lord Sheringham's engagement ball for Dorcas and Miles was one of the spectacular events of the waning Season. Camilla remembered it differently. Before the night was over, she was mentally fatigued from repeatedly fending off questions about Jean's whereabouts, and from a harrowing conversation with her stepmother.

Almost immediately after Francine's arrival at the ball—to which her daughter and her stepdaughter had most unwillingly invited her—she launched an inquisition against her stepdaughter. Drawing Camilla aside to some chairs sheltered by a convenient potted palm, Francine had said sternly, "And where, pray, is Mr. Hilliard tonight?" Before Camilla could produce the story of Jean's supposed errand in the country, Francine rushed on. "I feel for you so much, Camilla. Mr. Hilliard's absence from an affair in honor of Dorcas and Mr. Wingate, you must agree, is an open insult to Lord Sheringham and to my daughter and her affianced."

Her temper rising, Camilla said, "Now, look here, Mama—"

Her stepmother interrupted her. "What is even worse is the probable *reason* for his absence." Lowering her voice, Francine added, "My poor darling, I see by your expression that you don't know your husband is gambling away his substance every night until the small hours, not only in respectable clubs like White's and Boodle's, but in the most infamous gaming *hells* in London. You'll be fortunate to have even a few farthings with which to set up housekeeping, unless your godfather is very generous!"

Camilla stared at her stepmother in tight-lipped fury. "Before you say one more word, Mama, tell me the source of this buffle-headed nonsense."

Francine looked wounded. "Truly, I'm not blaming you. I

have my information on the best of authority. Sir Aubrey Elvaston—he has such a delicate sense of honor!—approached me with these dreadful rumors. He was very distressed for you, wondering if you should be informed, fearful that you might consider it an unwarranted intrusion if *he* brought you the news. So, of course, I offered to inform you myself."

Rising from her seat under the potted plant, Camilla looked down at her stepmother. In a shaking voice she said, "If ever, Mama, you come to me with one more word of gossip about my husband, you can consider yourself unwelcome in my house."

She walked away, trying to calm herself. Jean had taken to leaving Sheringham House after he brought her and Dorcas home from social events, and she'd assumed he was going to the gambling clubs. However, she strongly doubted he was losing heavily. According to Miles, Jean was a canny and a very lucky gambler. In any case, whether the rumors were true or false was immaterial. Aubrey Elvaston was pouring his venomous reports into Francine's willing ears, knowing they would get back to Camilla, for one reason only: to remind Camilla that he was still a threatening factor in her life.

At the end of the evening, Camilla watched the last of their guests straggle down the stairs from the ballroom with a vast feeling of relief.

"Camilla, you look ill," said the earl with a worried frown.

She managed a smile. "Not ill, Uncle Nigel. Weary. I'm beginning to think one must be eighteen years old or younger to survive the rigors of a London season!"

A little later, after saying goodnight to the earl and Dorcas, she was walking slowly to her bedchamber at the far end of the corridor when the door of Jean's room opened. Jean's valet emerged, narrowly avoiding a collision with her. Curtis apologized. "I'm very sorry, indeed, Mrs. Hilliard."

"What on earth are you doing with those?" Camilla inquired with a distasteful look at what appeared to be a bundle of old clothes in the valet's arms. "They smell like fish."

"So they do, ma'am. Very damp they are, too. Mr. Hilliard must have been most uncomfortable wearing them."

"Mr. Hilliard has returned, then?" said Camilla quickly.

"Oh, indeed, ma'am. An hour and more ago. Very tired he was, and his clothes!" Curtis rolled his eyes. "I'll do my best with them, but I doubt very much if Mr. Hilliard can ever wear these garments again."

As the valet shifted the pile of clothing away from his own fastidious person, he and Camilla could hear a clinking sound. Curtis reached into the pocket of a coat to pull out several coins. "That's odd, ma'am. These don't look like proper English money, would you say?"

Accepting the coins, Camilla peered at them in the dim light of the corridor lamps. "No, they don't, Curtis. I believe these are French coins. *Napoléons d'or.*"

"Is that a fact, now? Well, perhaps you'll give them to Mr. Hilliard. Goodnight, ma'am."

After Curtis had left, Camilla stood in the corridor, staring down at the coins in her hand, her mind a maelstrom of confused thoughts. Had Jean gone to France? Certainly he'd been a passenger on a boat, judging by the condition of his clothes. And he still had relatives in France. He'd told her that on several occasions. But why would he cross the Channel in wartime? If he were apprehended by the French authorities, he'd face prison, or even death. Unless . . . Camilla drew a deep breath. Could Jean possibly be a spy?

She dismissed the thought almost immediately. Jean had been in England for only a few months. What could he possibly know about vital English concerns that would interest the French government? Her lips tightened. Spy or no spy, she was convinced Jean had gone to France on some mysterious errand, and this wasn't the first time he'd done so. She recalled those six dreadful days when she hadn't known if Jean was alive or dead. He'd claimed he'd been caught in a storm at sea while on an excursion with some Kentish fishermen.

Suddenly so angry that she failed to consider the consequences of what she was doing, she wrenched open the door of Jean's bedchamber and stalked into the room. She was tired of Jean's lies and evasions. She was tired of their sterile life together. It was time to have it out.

Jean's torso was submerged in a tub of steaming water, and he was holding a glass in one hand and a half emptied bottle of wine in the other. He turned his head to look at her. Sounding both unsurprised and unimpressed to see her, he uttered one word. "Yes?"

Camilla's heart began pounding at the sight of the naked bronze flesh of Jean's powerful chest and shoulders. Confused and embarrassed, momentarily distracted from the cutting edge of her anger, she blurted, "Where have you been? You promised to be here for Dorcas's engagement party."

"Where I've been is nothing to you. I did try to get back here for Dorcas's party, but I was detained." Jean leisurely poured himself a glass of wine and set the bottle on the floor next to the tub.

The total indifference in Jean's voice and manner struck Camilla with a cold dash of reality. "Jean, can't we put an end to this farce?" she asked suddenly. "We don't have a marriage. It was over before it even began. You say you intend to return to Canada. That's your right, but why insist on taking me with you? Oh, I know you have some idea of revenging yourself on me and Uncle Nigel, but haven't you already done that? Why don't you simply file for divorce? No, annulment. Then we could take leave of each other with some dignity, and get on with both our lives."

Quite deliberately, Jean put down his glass beside the tub and reached for a towel. He stepped out of the tub, apparently oblivious to the possible effect his nakedness might be having on Camilla, and wrapped the towel around his dripping body. He walked over to her, coming to a stop inches away from her.

Her senses reeled at his closeness. The overwhelming power of Jean's sexuality was almost irresistible. A wave of desire swept over her. She longed to caress the magnificent

286

bronze flesh, and to feel the hard muscled body beneath the flimsy towel pressed close to hers.

She knew he was physically aroused also. His nostrils widened, and the familiar hot leaping flame appeared in the depths of his dark eyes. But he didn't lay a finger on her, and then his voice, uncaring, brutal, shattered her mood. "This marriage will end—if it ever does—when I decide it will. Make no mistake about it, Camilla. You go to Canada with me."

Chapter Eighteen

Camilla looked out the window of the drawing room, noting with dismay how wind-driven sheets of rain had nearly obliterated her view of Hanover Square. She was dressed for the street in a carriage dress, pelisse and bonnet, and she'd had the forethought to carry an umbrella, but an umbrella wouldn't be of much use in protecting her from this downpour, even during the brief walk from the front door of Sheringham House to her waiting carriage.

Perhaps she and Dorcas should postpone their shopping expedition until another day. But no, it was already the end of August, and Dorcas's wedding was scheduled for the fifteenth of September. Her trousseau was virtually complete, but Miles wanted Dorcas to select and order, before their wedding, all the furnishings for the townhouse on Bruton Street on which he'd taken a lease. Camilla sighed, resigning herself to a very wet morning.

"May I speak to you for a moment, Camilla?"

Camilla turned away from the window. Jean was standing in the doorway of the drawing room. He was dressed in breeches and top boots and an ankle length driving coat with a multitude of capes.

"Of course. What did you wish to talk about?" she said, the cold politeness of her tone matching the iciness in his voice. Each time they met like this, like hostile strangers, she couldn't help wondering how all the blazing passion they'd once felt for each other could have vanished so completely.

Jean said, "I just wanted to tell you that I'll be unable to be your escort tonight."

Glancing at his clothes, she observed, "I gather you're off on another of your mysterious trips." Moved by a sudden impulse, she reached into her reticule. "Here," she said, tossing several golden napoleons in his direction. "You may need these."

Catching the coins automatically, Jean gave them a cursory look. Then he drew in his breath sharply. "How did you — ?" He cut himself off, clamping his lips together. After a moment he muttered, *"Il n'importe pas."*

Camilla felt a flicker of satisfaction. For once, in all these dreary weeks since their wedding, she'd made some kind of an impression on Jean. Her triumph was short-lived.

Recovering his composure, Jean said coolly, "I had something else to say to you. I've decided on a date for returning to Canada. We'll set sail for Montreal on the *Indomitable* on October the fifth. I trust this advance notice will give you enough time to plan your packing. Don't forget, we have frigid winters in Canada."

By evening of that day the rain had abated to a raw drizzle.

"What a miserable night. I'm thankful indeed that I'm not obliged to venture out," said Lord Sheringham, grimacing. He'd come to join Camilla in the drawing room, as he often did before she went out in the evening. "When this infernal war is over, I plan to escape our hellish English climate and spend every autumn and winter in Italy." He added casually, "I understand Jean went off in his traveling chaise today. Another of his secret journeys?"

Camilla nodded.

"Where does he go, my dear? Do you have any idea?"

"I suspect he goes to France, Uncle Nigel."

"The devil he does," exclaimed the earl in surprise. "What makes you think that?"

Camilla told her godfather about the *napoléons d'or* that Jean's valet had found in the pocket of a coat which Jean had obviously worn on a sea voyage. "And do you remember that first time Jean went away, Uncle Nigel? Only a few days before our wedding? When I was so concerned about his safety? He told me then he'd been marooned in a harbor on Jersey during a severe storm, while he was out on an expedition with some of the fishermen from Lynharbor. I think now he'd been to France for the first time."

Lord Sheringham frowned in intense concentration. "What a strange thing for Jean to do. Why would he want to go to France?" The earl asked suddenly, "Could he possibly be a spy for the French? He's always considered himself a Canadian, first and foremost. He's never made any bones about his dislike of the English. And he does have relations in France."

Camilla shook her head. "I've thought of that, but I dismissed the idea immediately. It's not that Jean isn't capable of spying for the French, but what does he know about English affairs that could possibly interest Napoleon? No, Uncle Nigel, I think there's a more prosaic explanation for Jean's secret trips. Don't you remember the friends he made among the Kentish fishermen during our visit to your villa? And isn't it an open secret that these fisherman are also active smugglers? I think Jean has taken to some lucrative smuggling with his fisherman friends. Recall, he needs money to establish himself in Canada."

"Good God, you may be right." The earl looked horrified. "If Jean were caught . . ." He pulled himself together, saying grimly, "We must hope and pray that he isn't caught. I don't relish the prospect of seeing my heir in the dock."

"Amen," said Camilla quietly.

Lord Sheringham lapsed into a frowning silence. At length he said, "Jean's possible career as a criminal isn't our only problem. Forgive me for prying, Camilla, but have matters between the two of you improved at all?"

"No. I doubt they ever will. Jean and I are a lost cause, Uncle Nigel. I do have some news, however. Jean told me this morning that he'd arranged our passage to Montreal on a ship sailing the fifth of October."

"Oh. I never really thought . . . that is, I hoped . . ."

"You hoped Jean would never carry out his threat to return to Canada," Camilla finished.

"Yes. Oh, God, Camilla, this is all my fault. How I wish I hadn't meddled in your affairs. Jean is your husband now, and there's nothing I can do to prevent him from taking charge of your person and your assets."

Camilla leaned over her godfather's chair to kiss him on his forehead. "It's *not* your fault, Uncle Nigel. You never meant anything but good for me, and I'll always be grateful."

Dorcas came into the drawing room just then, followed shortly afterward by Miles, and soon the three young people left Sheringham House to attend an engagement party hosted by an elderly Vernon cousin, Lady Elizabeth Vane. During the carriage ride, Camilla's thoughts were on her godfather. Tonight the earl had looked suddenly older and unwell. The news that Jean had set a definite date for leaving England, finally crushing any slim hopes Lord Sheringham still had for his heir, must have been a staggering disappointment, and he was also suffering immense guilt for his part in her own predicament.

Miles's remarks to her sister interrupted Camilla's train of thought. "And so, is it really true, Dorcas, that your mother has decided to return to Bath?"

"Yes, Mama told Camilla and me yesterday that she planned to go home to Bath right after our wedding."

Miles said wryly, "Forgive me for saying so, my love, but I can't quite believe our good fortune!"

"Miles! You shouldn't say things like that!"

Ignoring his fiancée's halfhearted protest, Miles observed, "I thought Mrs. Vernon adored London. What made her decide to leave?"

Camilla thought she knew the reason. Several weeks ago, Aubrey Elvaston had dropped her stepmother as suddenly as he'd taken up with her. It had been a decided shock to Francine to lose her most distinguished admirer. "I must have offended Sir Aubrey," she'd said anxiously to Camilla, "but I simply cannot imagine how."

"Sir Aubrey's always been fickle, Mama," Camilla had said. "You're well out of it." Her remark had, of course, been small comfort to Francine.

Dorcas said demurely, "I think Mama's returning to Bath because of the letter she received several days ago from Mr. Stinchcombe. He wrote that he missed her company very much."

In the darkness of the carriage, Camilla stared incredulously at her sister. Then she burst into helpless laughter. Mr. Stinchcombe, fat and pompous and elderly and rich, who had tried so hard to get himself engaged to Dorcas. Who was, in fact, responsible for Dorcas's stay in London, and even, indirectly, for her marriage to Miles. Was it possible that he was now angling after Francine? And would Francine accept him? Not a doubt of it, Camilla decided. As the wealthy queen of Bath society, Francine would cease to pine for a place in the London sun.

She was still wearing an amused smile when she entered Lady Elizabeth Vane's house a short time later. The ludicrous thought of Mr. Stinchcombe as Dorcas's new stepfather lightened her spirits and kept her mind off her problems with Jean. Though she'd expected to be bored, she found herself enjoying Lady Elizabeth's party.

Midway through the evening, she looked up from a conversation with her hostess to find a footman at her elbow with a note on a tray.

"My dear, what is it?" asked a concerned Lady Elizabeth. "You look so pale. Is it bad news?"

"Yes, I fear so. My godfather's been taken ill. His butler, Mason, writes that Uncle Nigel collapsed in a dead faint and is still very weak. I must go, Lady Elizabeth. Mason has sent a carriage for me."

"I'm so sorry. Of course you must go. Shall I ask the servants to find your sister and Mr. Wingate?"

"No. I won't ask them to leave a party in their honor until I learn how serious Uncle Nigel's condition is. I'll send word as soon as I've talked to the doctor."

Camilla hurried down the steps of the house to the waiting

carriage. The rain had started up again, and in her haste to avoid being drenched she failed to notice that the footman who handed her into the vehicle was unknown to her. She also failed to notice that the carriage, though it was similar in style and color to her godfather's town chariot, did not display the Sheringham crest on the door.

As the footman closed the door of the carriage, a rough hand clamped itself across her mouth, and the hatefully familiar voice of Sir Aubrey Elvaston said, "Good evening, Camilla. I regret disrupting your evening, but I have more important plans for us."

Putting up her hands to wrench Sir Aubrey's hand from her face, Camilla realized immediately the hopelessness of her predicament. Besides Elvaston, there was a second shadowy person in the carriage, who in moments had deftly bound her hands and her feet. Sir Aubrey, sitting next to her on the cushions, removed his hand only long enough to whip a strip of some kind of soft cloth across her mouth and bind the gag behind her head.

"My dear Camilla, pray excuse such drastic measures," said Sir Aubrey. "I'm doing my very best to avoid scandal. After all, we can't have you screaming as we drive through the streets of London, now, can we? Even if it's only those woefully inept Charleys who might hear you, let us preserve the amenities at all costs. Incidentally, I'm happy to relieve your mind about your godfather. To the best of my knowledge, Lord Sheringham is in perfect health."

Unable to move or to speak, Camilla settled back awkwardly against the seat, wasting neither mental nor physical energy in a useless attempt to escape her bonds. She was grateful, at least, that her hands had been tied in front of her, rather than behind her back. In the intermittent light from the street lamps, she glimpsed, sitting on the seat opposite her and Sir Aubrey, the man who had tied her up. He didn't say a word during the journey, nor did Aubrey Elvaston. Biding his time, thought Camilla bitterly.

The carriage rolled smoothly along the rain-drenched streets. Camilla didn't bother to check for familiar landmarks, or to guess at the direction they were taking. With a sense of agonizing inevitability, she knew where Elvaston was taking her.

The motion of the carriage changed as it left the turnpike and moved off onto a rougher road. Soon it stopped beneath the dimly lit portico of a small Palladian house—Aubrey Elvaston's Chiswick villa.

"Willis, untie the lady," muttered Sir Aubrey. Using an unseen knife, the shadowy figure on the opposite seat quickly snipped the ropes that bound Camilla's hands and feet. At the same time, Elvaston pulled the hood of Camilla's cloak closely around her face. A footman opened the door of the carriage. Sir Aubrey waved the man away, saying, "Willis will help the lady down the steps." Willis jumped to the pavement, extending his hand to Camilla. In a moment Sir Aubrey himself emerged from the carriage, which immediately moved off in the direction of the stables.

"Come along, my dear," said Sir Aubrey.

Camilla walked numbly up the steps and into the foyer. Sir Aubrey pulled the hood from her head and deftly removed the gag from her mouth. "You can scream all you like now," he jeered. "I've dismissed all my servants for the night. No one will hear you except Willis, and he doesn't count. He knows he wouldn't last another minute as my valet if he opened his mouth about my affairs."

Glancing at the valet, a small thin man with dead eyes and a carefully wooden face, Camilla felt her heart sink. She could count only on her own ingenuity to free herself before Sir Aubrey accomplished his purpose with her. As usual, he'd covered his tracks perfectly. He'd dismissed the household servants. His coachman and his footman, whatever they might have suspected, had merely seen a lady enter Sir Aubrey's carriage, apparently of her own free will. They hadn't observed the ropes that tied her hands and feet, and the hood of her cloak had concealed the gag on her mouth.

With a taunting smile on his lips, Elvaston said, "This is reckoning day, Camilla. Don't worry. I'm not going to hurt you. Not physically, at least. Not unless you force my hand. I simply want what's owing to me. Remember that little bargain I made with Philip, all those years ago? Once you've fulfilled that bargain, you'll be free to go. First, however, we'll observe the occasion properly, with an intimate champagne supper in my rooms. Willis, show Mrs. Rayburn — I beg your pardon, Camilla, I keep forgetting you're Mrs. Hilliard now — to her bedchamber. She'll wish to make her toilet before supper. You'll remain outside the door, of course."

Perfectly aware that Elvaston was toying with her, hoping to increase her apprehensions, Camilla fought against the wave of sick terror that threatened to overwhelm her. Her only course was to remain calm, to stay on the alert for the slightest opportunity to extricate herself from this web of evil. Without a word or a glance to Sir Aubrey, she started up the staircase, followed closely by Willis.

She entered the bedchamber indicated by the valet, and stopped short, as the door closed quietly behind her. She glanced around her, filled with revulsion as she recalled her last sight of the room. Every detail of the luxuriously furnished bedchamber was familiar to her. Nothing had been changed since a servant had shown her and Philip into it on that night three years before. By putting her into the same room tonight, Aubrey Elvaston was indicating his determination to extract the last drop of blood from his pound of flesh.

Camilla drew a deep, ragged breath, fighting for composure. She couldn't allow herself to be affected by Sir Aubrey's latest gratuitous cruelty. Deliberately she moved to the dressing table and sat down in front of it. Her coiffure was disheveled from being confined under the hood of her cloak. She picked up the silver-backed brush on the dressing table and smoothed her hair. Peering into the mirror, she saw that her face was very pale. She looked like death warmed-over. The dressing table was equipped with every toiletry a lady might need. She opened a pot of rouge and carefully brushed a film of color across her cheeks. If she possibly could, she'd prevent Aubrey Elvaston from realizing how frightened she really was.

A voice came from the other side of the door. "Mrs.

Hilliard, are you ready to join Sir Aubrey?"

Camilla walked to the door and opened it. Willis, the valet, stood in the corridor. In a colorless voice, he said, "Please follow me, Mrs. Hilliard."

"Wait, Willis. Please come inside. I want to talk to you."

Slowly the valet advanced a foot or two beyond the threshold of the room. His face was expressionless. "Yes, madam?"

Speaking rapidly, keeping her voice low, Camilla said, "You know full well that I'm not here of my own free will. Sir Aubrey kidnapped me. I'll pay you any amount you ask, if you'll help me escape from this house. *Any* amount. I can get the money from my godfather, Lord Sheringham. You must know of him. He's one of the wealthiest men in England."

Camilla detected a faint, momentary flicker of sympathy in Willis's face. Then it disappeared. "I'd like to help you, but I can't," he said flatly. "It would be as much as my life is worth. Sir Aubrey holds proof that I once tried to embezzle money from him. Please come with me, Mrs. Hilliard."

Camilla's shoulders sagged. She hadn't had much hope that her appeal to Willis would succeed, but now even that faint hope was gone. Dejectedly she followed the valet down the corridor to Elvaston's bedchamber. She found him sitting at a table set for a meal, with candles, white linen, silver and china. He was wearing a elaborate dressing gown, and he was engaged in opening a bottle of champagne.

"Do sit down," he said, motioning to a chair opposite him. "Willis will begin serving our meal shortly. I went to a great deal of trouble choosing a menu I thought you would like."

Wordlessly Camilla sat down. She'd made up her mind to do as she was told, avoiding the indignity of being forced to do so, until — if — she discovered an opening for escape. Soon she was caught up in a feeling of unreality. Pressing food and wine on her like a solicitous host, Sir Aubrey chatted about books and the theater and the doings of the *ton*, quite as if he were entertaining at an ordinary dinner party.

He was playing cat and mouse with her, of course. At first she refused to allow herself to be drawn, although she quickly refused the food that was offered to her, and she made no reply to Sir Aubrey's remarks, which soon became a monologue.

The interminable meal dragged on. Finally Willis removed the dishes from the second course and piled them on a tray. "Will there be anything else, sir?" he asked in his colorless voice.

"No, that will be all. Consider yourself free for the rest of the night, Willis."

After the valet had left the room, Sir Aubrey opened a second bottle of champagne and waved it in her direction, saying, "Drink up, drink up. I'm already far ahead of you. I assure you that the evening will be much more relaxing and pleasurable if we're both — er — a trifle castaway." Elvaston's face was faintly flushed, and his voice was slurred. He was more than a trifle foxed. He was already half drunk.

Camilla's carefully maintained calm shattered. She exclaimed, "I think you must be mad. Perhaps you can force me to sleep with you, but you must know that won't be the end of it. I'm no servant girl or shop assistant that you can force into your bed and rape without suffering any consequences."

Elvaston gulped down another glass of champagne. "What consequences?" he said with a leer. "Are you threatening to complain to the magistrates? No, no, I think not. You'd never do that. You value your lily-white, ladylike reputation too highly to accuse me of raping you. In any case, it's your word against mine. There are no witnesses to what's happened tonight, except Willis, and I've already told you *he* won't talk."

Camilla clenched her hands together so tightly that her knuckles cracked. Elvaston didn't believe in her threat to seek legal redress, and he had good reason to think so. Even if she went to the magistrates, even if they believed her story, even if they put Sir Aubrey into the dock, her reputation would be permanently, hopelessly tarnished.

Trying one last desperate ploy, she said, "Perhaps you're right. Perhaps I *am* too much of a social coward to admit to the world that you lured me here and raped me. But don't think you'll escape scot-free. My husband will track you down and take his own private revenge. And don't forget he's part Indian. Indians scalp people, I understand. Jean will probably remove that blonde hair you're so proud of."

"Oh, I think my scalp is perfectly safe," said Elvaston with a sneering smile. "After tonight, your loutish Colonial husband will be rotting in a French jail."

"What do you mean?" Camilla asked in a low, trembling voice. "What have you done to Jean?"

Elvaston laughed. "It's not what I've done, it's what the French police will *do*. And I should remind you that French jails are notoriously unpleasant places. I wouldn't care to be in Jean-Étienne Hilliard's shoes tonight."

Her mouth dry, her nerves stretched taut with apprehension, Camilla said, "Tell me about Jean."

Sir Aubrey laughed again. "As far as I'm concerned, that's an unimportant subject. It's time for us. It's time for you to pay your debt to me." He pushed back his chair and slowly rose from the table.

Camilla jumped up from her chair and gazed frantically around the room for something, anything, she could use as a weapon. She dashed toward the fireplace. As she passed Sir Aubrey, he put out his hand to stop her and succeeded only in ripping the bodice of her gown. Whirling away from the fireplace, Camilla brandished a heavy poker in front of her.

"Don't be ridiculous, Camilla. Put that thing down."

Moving with surprising speed despite his lameness, Elvaston lunged at Camilla. For a split second she stood frozen. Then she lashed out with the poker and struck him with all her force on the thigh of his crippled leg. Uttering a cry of agony, he sank to the floor.

Standing over him, poker poised for another blow, Camilla snapped, "Doubtless I've broken your thighbone again, Sir Aubrey, just as I did the last time you tried to attack me. If you force me to hit you again on that leg, you know as well as I do that you'll probably never walk again. Not without crutches. It's your choice. You can risk permanent deformity, or you can start talking. Tell me about my husband." She raised the poker in a threatening gesture.

Elvaston's eyes widened with fear. "Don't — please don't," he begged. "I'll tell you anything you want to know, but not while I'm lying here on the floor. Help me into a chair."

"Do you take me for a fool? I'm not coming anywhere near you. Here." Camilla pushed a chair close to Sir Aubrey. "That's the most I'll do for you."

Gasping with pain, Elvaston slowly pulled himself up into the chair. He leaned back against it. His face was a grayish white and drenched with perspiration. "I think you did break my thighbone again," he snarled. "You'll pay for this."

"I don't care about your leg. Talk."

Suddenly, surprisingly, an expression of pure vitriolic pleasure spread across Elvaston's face. "Oh, I'll talk. I'll tell you everything. I hope you enjoy it. You see, Camilla, I not only had to settle my score with you, I had to find a way to get back at your dolt of a husband. I don't allow any man to invade my house, interrupt my assignation with a lady and assault me. I could have challenged him to a duel, I daresay. However, I've heard he's a crack shot, and besides, a duel seemed a little crude. So, some time ago, I began casting about for information I could use against Hilliard. Your stepmother was very useful to me."

"So that's why you were so friendly with Mama. You were picking her brains about Jean."

"Exactly so. She told me about Hilliard's family connections in France, and about his friendship with Nathan Rothschild. I was particularly interested to hear about Hilliard's periodic mysterious disappearances. Now, I'd also been making inquiries among my friends in the government. There were rumors, for example, that certain people were smuggling gold out of England. Strictly forbidden by the English government, of course, and with good reason, in view of our precarious wartime financial situation. One of the names mentioned as being involved in illicit gold dealings was Nathan Rothschild."

Though he was obviously still in great pain, Elvaston managed a gloating smile. "So I put two and two together, Camilla, and decided that your husband was acting as a courier to transport Rothschild gold to France. My guess is that Hilliard probably enlisted the help of his French relations. So I reported your husband's activities to the French government."

"You reported Jean to the *French* government?"

"Indeed. The authorities in the Calais-Gravelines area are keeping a strict watch for Hilliard. The next time he crosses the Channel with Rothschild's gold, the French police will be waiting for him." Elvaston flicked Camilla a malicious grin. "Hilliard left today on another of his little trips, did he not? Count on it, my dear. By tomorrow morning, your husband will be in a French jail."

Camilla said angrily, "I don't believe a word of this. You're trying to bubble me, to frighten me senseless. Why would you report Jean to the French? Why not to the English authorities, since you claim he's breaking English law? For that matter, how is it that you, an English diplomat, have any access to French police channels? Unless . . ." She stared at Elvaston, her mind beginning to churn with terrifying possibilities.

Apprehension battled with vanity in Sir Aubrey's expression. After a long moment of hesitation, vanity won out. "There's no harm in telling you, I suppose. If you ever repeat what I say, I'll simply deny I said it. It will be my word against yours. The fact is, Camilla, that I've been in the pay of the French for years. My involvement began when I was a secretary at the English embassy in Paris during the Peace of Amiens in 1802. I started gambling heavily. Soon I was so deeply in debt that I knew I could never recover. The French secret police came to me then, offering me an enormous sum for a copy of one of the British ambassador's confidential reports to Whitehall. I gave them the copy. I've been their agent ever since, which explains, obviously, why I was able to contact them about Hilliard."

Camilla looked at him with loathing. "And so, in addition to every other filthy thing you've done, Aubrey Elvaston, you're also a traitor to your country. And now you've trapped my husband in your slimy coils." She walked over to his chair and stood over him, lifting the poker again. As he shrank back in sudden fear, she said urgently, "You claim to know so much. Then tell me how Jean crosses the Channel. Where does he take ship? With whom? Talk! Talk right now, or . . ." She raised the poker a trifle higher.

His face turning pale again, Elvaston said in a choked voice, "Rothschild has arrangements with several fishermen in the Folkestone area. He's been employing them for years to smuggle contraband across to France. One of them is a Captain Allen, in the village of Lynharbor. That's all I know. I swear it." Apprehensive though he was about the possibility of reinjuring his leg, his natural viciousness got the better of him. "If you're thinking of dashing down to Kent to warn Hilliard off, forget about it," he sneered. "You'd never catch up to him. He's already well on his way to France."

A stricken Camilla stared at Sir Aubrey. Could he be right? Could she really do nothing to help Jean? In her uncertainty and preoccupation, her hand holding the poker dropped to her side. Seizing his chance, Elvaston suddenly leaned forward, reaching for the poker. Instinctively Camilla jerked away from him, barely avoiding his grasp. Caught off balance by his forward lunge, Elvaston toppled from his chair, his crippled leg doubled under him at an unnatural angle. He uttered an agonized scream and then slumped into unconsciousness.

Wasting neither glance nor sympathy on him, Camilla dashed out of the bedchamber into the corridor and started down the staircase, still holding the poker. She had only one thought in her mind, to get to Jean and warn him of his danger. In spite of Sir Aubrey's taunts, she refused to believe it was too late to help Jean. True, he'd left London today. He was already hours ahead of her. But perhaps he wasn't scheduled to sail for France until tomorrow. Or he might have been delayed for some reason. In any event, hopeless though it probably was, she had to try to reach him. But first she had to get away from Sir Aubrey's estate.

In the foyer, remembering the plan of the house from her last visit, when she and Jean and Miles had rescued Dorcas, she ran down the corridor in the direction of the kitchens.

From the rear entrance of the house it would be a shorter distance to the stables and the exit from the park.

As she neared the kitchens, a door opened and Willis, the valet, stepped out into the corridor. He was carrying a bottle of wine and a glass, and a powerful odor of spirits clung to his garments. "Mrs. Hilliard!" he gasped. It took several seconds for his liquor-fogged brain to respond to the situation. Then he dropped bottle and glass and launched himself at her, hands outstretched.

Without a moment's hesitation, Camilla rapped the poker across the valet's skull. He sank to the floor. Looking down at his unconscious form with a curious lack of feeling, she paused, frowning. She couldn't simply leave Willis here. He might revive and come after her, raising the alarm, before she could escape from the estate. On the other hand, she knew it wasn't in her to kill a defenseless man. After a moment's intense thought, she hurried into the dining room, where she pulled the corded ties from the elegant brocaded draperies. Returning to the valet, she trussed him securely with the drapery ties, and, as an added precaution, took a towel from the kitchen and gagged him as well. Now, with Elvaston incapacitated, and his valet tied up, there was no one left in the house to follow her.

About to bolt out the kitchen door, Camilla had a flash of fugitive memory, and ran back to the dining room. With shaking fingers, she pulled open a drawer in the sideboard, the same drawer from which she'd once seen Aubrey Elvaston snatch a duelling pistol and shoot Miles Wingate. She exhaled a sigh of relief. The pistol was back in the drawer.

The rain had started up again. There was, of course, no moon to light her way, and as Camilla stumbled down a sodden path shadowed by trees, leading toward the stables, she fell several times. Finally she reached the stables and stood uncertainly just inside the door, trying to decide what she should do next. In their stalls the horses, aware of her presence, made small rustling noises. The interior of the building was very dark. The grooms' quarters must be on the floor above. She could just make out the dim outline of a staircase on the right-hand wall.

Moving cautiously, trailing her hand along the wall to keep her balance, Camilla climbed the stairs. A closed door separated the servants' living area from the stable area below. Breathing deeply to calm a sudden burst of fear, she pounded on the door, shouting, "Open up!" She repeated her pounding and her shouting until the door opened.

A half-dressed groom, holding a lantern high, said angrily, " 'Ere, wot d'ye fink ye're up to now, tell me that! Wakin' a man from 'is well-earned rest, disturbin' the 'orses . . ."

The groom grasped as Camilla raised her pistol and leveled it at him. She said curtly, "How many grooms and household servants are sleeping in the loft?"

"Jist the two o' us," the groom stammered. "The master, 'e said as 'ow everybody else could 'ave a free evening."

She might have known, thought Camilla. Sir Aubrey's behavior was thoroughly predictable. He wanted no witnesses to his villainies. Aloud she said, "I want a team of horses harnessed to Sir Aubrey's carriage immediately. Bring the other groom down with you. If you make one misstep, I'll bore a hole in your head. Now, hurry."

It was only afterward that she realized what an astonishing sight she must have presented to the groom in the swaying light of his lantern. Her bodice was ripped, her gown was wet and muddy from the rain and her several falls on the path, her hair was drenched and falling in wild elflocks around her face.

Camilla kept her pistol fixed steadily on the frightened grooms as they crept down the stairs, harnessed a team of horses and led them out of the stable.

Camilla followed the grooms to the carriage house, where they hastily hitched a team to Sir Aubrey's town chariot. Brandishing the pistol, she said to the grooms, "One of you will drive, the other will sit inside with me. If the driver doesn't obey my instructions exactly, I'll shoot the man sitting inside the carriage with me. Is that understood?" They nodded dumbly.

During the forty-five minute drive through the rain from Chiswick to London, keeping her pistol trained on the unfortunate groom who shared the carriage with her — the man was obviously frightened out of his wits — Camilla feverishly made her plans. She'd quickly abandoned her original impulse to order Sir Aubrey's driver to take her to Kent. She was wet through, her dress was torn, she had no cloak or pelisse, and, above all, she had no money to pay for changes of teams at the posting stations. The sensible course would be to return to Sheringham House, where she could change her wet garments, obtain money for the journey and make use of her godfather's carriage and servants.

She jumped down from the carriage when it reached Sheringham House. "I don't need you any more," she told the driver curtly. "You can go back to Chiswick." His face blazed with delight, and he drove off.

Pounding on the door of the house, she was admitted almost immediately by a footman who gaped at her wildly disheveled appearance. Hardly had she entered the foyer when Dorcas and Miles Wingate hurried out of the drawing room to gaze at her with relief and delight.

"Camilla, thank God you're here. We were so worried about you," exclaimed Dorcas. She looked more closely at her sister, and gasped. "What's happened to you? Where have you been?"

Miles cut in, "And why in the fiend's name are you carrying a pistol?"

Chapter Nineteen

At Miles's question, Camilla blinked, looking down at the pistol in her hand. She'd forgotten she was still holding it. Her abduction by Sir Aubrey, and her discovery that Jean was in mortal danger, had driven out of her mind any other considerations. She'd completely forgotten that she'd left Dorcas and Miles at Lady Elizabeth Vane's party earlier in the evening to go to Sheringham House to check on her godfather's illness. Later that night, when Miles brought Dorcas home from their engagement, the two would naturally have expected to find Camilla waiting to talk with them about the earl's condition. Instead, they'd have learned from the servants that Lord Sheringham was perfectly well, and that Camilla herself had never returned to the house. No wonder they were frantic with worry.

Camilla looked at the concerned faces of Dorcas and Miles, and realized that she had to tell the truth. Some of it, at least. "Sir Aubrey abducted me," she said baldly. "I got away from him in his own carriage before—before anything happened. I hit him with a poker," she explained with relish. "I doubt he'll ever walk again, even with crutches. I also stole his pistol. So you see, there's nothing to worry about."

His face set grimly, Miles snapped, "Nothing to worry about? For God's sake, Camilla. Give me that pistol. I intend to blow Elvaston's brains out."

"Miles!" Dorcas cried in alarm.

Camilla said forcefully, "You'll do nothing of the kind,

305

Miles. I don't want a scandal. I don't want to see you in the dock on a capital charge, either. Leave it be."

"But damnation, Camilla . . ."

"It's not your affair," she said with finality. "If Jean, when he comes home, wants to pursue the matter—" She shrugged. "And now, Miles, please go home. I've had a dreadful evening, and I want to go to bed."

After Miles, still protesting, had left the house, Dorcas followed Camilla upstairs to her bedchamber.

"Camilla, are you sure you're all right?" asked Dorcas with a troubled frown. "You weren't just putting Miles off when you said nothing happened with Sir Aubrey? You look so—oh, I don't know—so strange. So *distracted*."

"I'm just tired, Dorcas. Sleep is all I need. Goodnight."

After Dorcas rather unwillingly had left the room, Camilla hurriedly stripped off her wet clothes and put on dry undergarments, gown and slippers, a pelisse and bonnet. Carrying an umbrella, she slipped down the stairs to the library, where she rang for a footman. She told the servant, who could scarcely contain his curiosity, to order a carriage and team brought around immediately. She scribbled a note to Dorcas and her godfather, telling them she would be gone for at least two nights, and handed it to the footman when he returned. Then, opening a drawer in the desk, she removed a thick stack of the bank notes that she'd known her godfather always kept in the desk. Ten minutes later she was sitting in a carriage, riding swiftly out of Hanover Square.

It was still raining. Camilla felt a pang of sympathy for the coachman and footman, who would be thoroughly drenched before the night was over, but she had no thought of delaying her journey.

As the carriage sped through the dark, wet streets, she wished momentarily that she'd asked Miles to come with her. His presence, his cool common sense and strong right arm, would have been so reassuring. But she'd already decided, on the drive from Chiswick to Hanover Square in Elvaston's carriage, that she had to attempt Jean's rescue by herself. Jean and Nathan Rothschild had broken the law by smuggling gold out of England. They were both subject to very serious penalties if they were caught by the authorities. Despite his long friendship with Camilla, Miles might have been unwilling to become embroiled with the law by helping her to rescue Jean from the consequences of his crimes. Miles was a very conventional man, and he had a strong aversion to smuggling. No, it was better not to involve him. She could perfectly well travel down to Kent and do what was necessary by herself.

The carriage tore through the night, taking the familiar route across Westminster Bridge to Shooter's Hill and on through the succeeding posting stops on the route to Folkestone. The pace was as swift as a well-sprung carriage and superior teams would allow, but to Camilla the miles dragged interminably. Bexley. Dartford. Rochester. Maidstone. Ashford. Sandgate.

Camilla knew in her heart of hearts that she was pursuing a useless quest. Logic told her that Jean must have long since embarked on his journey across the Channel. She couldn't hope to save him, and yet, given the slightest excuse to believe that he might have been delayed, she couldn't give up. She couldn't face the prospect of never seeing him again. Which method of execution did Napoleon prefer? The firing squad? The guillotine? Her heart began to beat so hard that her chest felt sore.

It was raining even harder now. Past Ashford, as dawn began to break, the storm winds increased with such velocity that the carriage was buffeted violently from side to side. Suddenly the vehicle gave a violent lurch and collapsed. Camilla slid across the seat, coming to a stop at the right side of the carriage against the door.

Her drenched, bedraggled coachman opened the door on the opposite side and peered in at her. "Ma'am, we've lost a wheel. We're in the ditch. I'll ride one o' the horses to the next posting stop to get help. The footman, Jack, will stay wi' ye."

Huddled against the side of the carriage, Camilla became increasingly uncomfortable. The vehicle seemed to be listing more to the side with each passing second. Rain or no rain,

Camilla decided she'd be better off in the open. Taking her umbrella, she climbed laboriously up the steeply inclined floor of the carriage and jumped down to the road, hastily unfurling her umbrella against the wind-driven downpour.

"Terrible weather, ma'am, not fit fer man nor beast," said the footman who'd been left to guard her. His teeth were chattering, and in the faint light from the carriage lamp he looked utterly miserable. Suddenly, a split second after a vague shadowy form loomed up behind him, he collapsed in front of her with a stifled groan.

"Jist 'and over that purse o' yourn, missus," exclaimed a rough voice, "or I'll be obleeged to 'it ye be'ind yer ear, the same as I did that there cove alyin' on the road."

Camilla could make out very dimly a tall shambling figure. Instinctively, she reached into the pocket of her pelisse and pulled out Sir Aubrey's dueling pistol. Cocking the weapon, firing blindly, she heard simultaneously a shrill scream of pain, followed immediately by the sound of dragging, receding footsteps. Waiting a few moments longer, until she was sure the would-be thief had gone, she knelt down in the pelting rain beside the fallen footman, who had already regained consciousness and was struggling to stand up.

"I 'eard a gun goin' off," he muttered, as Camilla helped him to his feet. "What 'appened, ma'am? Are ye all right?"

"I shot the thief, or highwayman, or whatever he was," said Camilla, shivering. Reaction had set in. She was beginning to realize that she'd actually shot a man. "I hope he doesn't die," she murmured.

"No more'n the thief deserves," said the footman stoutly.

Pacing nervously up and down beside the carriage in the driving rain, Camilla felt her spirits sinking, and not just because she might have killed another human being. The accident to the carriage had caused one more delay in her breakneck race to reach Jean before he took ship for France. And she must still be almost ten miles from the coast.

Half an hour passed, and then she spotted the bobbing side lanterns of a carriage coming toward her. Her coachman was returning with a substitute carriage and team. Camilla didn't allow the coachman and footman more than a moment or two to discuss the interesting tale of how she'd shot the highwayman. "Hurry," she urged the coachman. "I can't waste any more time. I must get to Lynharbor as soon as possible."

An hour later, in the cold, dank grayness of a storm-swept dawn, Camilla's carriage rolled into the tiny hamlet of Lynharbor, less than a mile from Sandgate and her godfather's villa. It was the fishing village that Jean had so often visited. No one was stirring in the town, and as Camilla looked at the mountainous waves breaking on the shore, she could understand why. No fishing boats would be venturing out today in such high seas.

The coachman stopped before a cottage, and the footman jumped down from his perch at the rear of the carriage to dash to the entrance of the building. He knocked until a reluctant-looking individual finally opened the door. A few moments later the footman returned, opening the door of the carriage to say hastily to Camilla, "The cottage o' that fishing captain ye wanted to see is jist up the way, ma'am. We'll have ye there in a trice."

Shortly afterward, grimly holding her umbrella above her head, though it afforded little protection from the slanting sheets of rain, Camilla opened the gate of Captain Allen's trim cottage, rather larger than most of the others in the hamlet. She walked to the door. After she'd knocked several times, a burly, gray-haired man, who'd obviously thrown on his shirt and breeches in considerable haste, answered her knock.

"Yes?" The man's tone was noncommittal.

"Captain Allen?"

"That's me."

"I—I'm looking for my husband. You may know him. Mr. Jean Hilliard. I believe he's visited Lynharbor several times. I understand he was planning to sail to France. If possible, I must reach him before he takes ship."

Camilla thought she detected a flicker of recognition on the man's face. However, all he said was, "I don't understand, ma'am. Why did ye come to me?"

"I was told my husband might have arranged to sail with you. Or that possibly you could tell me the name of the boat he hired."

The captain's face had turned as hard as stone. "An' who might that be, ma'am, who's been telling ye tales that I sails my boat to France?"

"It doesn't matter who told me," replied Camilla hastily. "I assure you I have no intention of talking to anyone about your affairs."

"Wouldn't make no sense if ye did, missus. I'm a plain fisherman, that's what I am. Every man jack in this village, we're all fishermen. Ain't none of us got no reason to cross the Channel. We happens to be at war with the Froggies, or p'raps ye've forgotten."

Camilla's heart sank. According to Aubrey Elvaston — and she had no reason to disbelieve him — Captain Allen was one of Nathan Rothschild's trusted agents for transporting contraband goods across the Channel. She was morally certain that Captain Allen, or one of his neighbors in the village, had taken Jean to France on several occasions in the past. But — and why hadn't this occurred to her previously? — the captain, or any of his fellow fishermen, was not going to reveal to a complete stranger like herself that he was engaged in the smuggling trade. Of course Captain Allen wouldn't admit that he even knew Jean Hilliard.

Camilla tried once more. "Please, Captain. I'm not interested in your — er — business activities, but I simply must find my husband. It could be a matter of life or death."

The captain looked back at her, not a flicker of expression on his stolid face. He said indifferently, "I'm that sorry, ma'am. I'm afeard I can't help ye."

It was a stalemate. Her shoulders sagging, Camilla turned away from the door that had closed so decisively in her face, and trudged back to the carriage. "Go to Lord Sheringham's villa," she told the coachman.

During the short drive to the earl's villa near Sandgate, Camilla sat hunched against the cushions, weary, wet and utterly defeated. Her attempt to save Jean had been hopeless and illogical from the very beginning. She'd been too stubborn, and too filled with anguish about Jean's safety, to admit the possibility.

When she arrived at the villa, one of her godfather's efficient servants answered her knock immediately. "Mrs. Hilliard!" the man gasped, as he stared at her sodden garments. "We weren't expecting ye."

"No, I came down on a whim," said Camilla as she entered the foyer. She took off her soaked bonnet and pelisse and handed them to the footman. "Ask the maids to dry these as best they can. And please send breakfast up to my bedchamber. I'd also like a hot bath."

"Yes, indeed, ma'am. Er — shall I inform Mr. Hilliard that ye're here?"

Camilla's heart missed a beat. "Mr. Hilliard is here?" she asked incredulously.

"Why, yes, ma'am." The servant's tone was carefully polite. He knew his place. It was none of his affair if Lord Sheringham's newly married heir went off on a journey without informing his wife of his destination. "Mr. Hilliard arrived yesterday," the man continued. "He told us he was going out on a boat with one of the local fishermen, same as he's done several times before. But of course the weather turned bad."

Camilla didn't hear the last part of the footman's remark. Torn between disbelief and explosive joy, she was already halfway up the stairs. She raced down the corridor to Jean's bedchamber and wrenched open the door. Jean was indeed in his bed, peacefully sleeping.

"Jean, oh Jean, you're really here. You're safe. You're not sitting in chains in a French jail," Camilla screamed in a great outburst of relief. Startled awake, Jean had only a scant moment to toss his blanket aside and make a move to rise before Camilla threw herself on his prone body. He slept in the nude, she belatedly noticed, as she wound her arms around his neck.

"*Mon Dieu,* Camilla, what — ?" Jean's halfhearted protest, or whatever he had intended his remark to be, died away in a smothered groan as Camilla pressed eager lips to his mouth and wriggled her soft curves blissfully against the hard planes of his body. Instantly he swept his arms around her and crushed her mouth in a savagely passionate kiss that sent fiery arrows of desire coursing through her bloodstream. Gradually he forced her lips apart and ravaged the interior of her mouth with his tongue, bringing her to a high pitch of longing. At one point he muttered incoherently, "Why are you so damp? Let's get rid of this damned dress."

"Yes, let's do," murmured Camilla, equally incoherently. For good measure, she also removed her tiny corset and shift and her petticoats. And then she relaxed in a wave of pure pleasure as bare flesh met bare flesh, and Jean's knowing hands explored her body while his lips plundered the sweetness from her mouth.

"Darling, darling, that was wonderful," Camilla sighed. Supporting herself on her elbow, she gazed down at Jean's dark face, relaxed and sated in the afterglow of passion.

"Um," he murmured drowsily, without opening his eyes. "Wonderful." He smiled faintly. *Très magnifique. Très, très magnifique.*"

Camilla chuckled. Gently running her fingers across his bare chest, she smiled as she noticed the instant response of his hardening nipples to her touch. Bemused, responding to a vagrant thought, she asked suddenly, "Darling, why don't you have hair on your chest?"

Her artless question jerked Jean back into reality. He opened his eyes and sat up. "Because I'm an Indian," he snapped. "Indians have hair on their heads, where it belongs." He stared at her, his eyes hard and unfriendly. "Camilla, why did you come here? Why did you—?" He bit off his words, flushing deeply.

"Why did I entice you to make love to me? Because I love you. Because I think you still love me, if only you'll stop letting your pride get in the way." She reached out her hand again, her fingers trailing caressingly along his cheeks, brushing against his mouth, dropping lower to the sensitive skin on his chest.

"Camilla, don't do that. I can't . . ." He grabbed her hands, holding them firmly. "Don't lie to me like this. You never loved me. You married me to please your godfather."

"I married you because I loved you with all my heart and soul, and because I wanted to live with you for the rest of my life. Why can't you believe me?"

His voice grew harsh with desperation. "Camilla, I *heard* you. I heard your godfather boasting about paying you twenty thousand pounds to persuade me to stay in England. I heard you saying, with that laugh in your voice, that you 'liked me well enough.' And then later, when I confronted you, you admitted I was right, that your godfather had bribed you to marry me."

"Darling, I've told you so often that Uncle Nigel and I were joking. No amount of money could have bribed me to marry a man I didn't love. And yes, later, I did admit your suspicions were correct. I have a little pride, too. I was just getting back at you." Suddenly Camilla broke the clasp of Jean's hands and threw her arms around his neck, pulling him down on the bed beside her. Her lips fluttering against his throat, she whispered, "Didn't I prove to you tonight how much I love you? Couldn't you tell how I felt, by the way I kissed you, by the way I touched you?"

The tension drained from Jean's body. "Oh, Camilla, if you really mean what you're saying . . ." With a great sigh, he gathered her into his arms. His face buried in her hair, he muttered, "I felt so rejected when I heard you talking like that. I believed that everything you'd ever said to me, everything that had passed between us, was a lie. I thought you didn't have it in you to love any man, except perhaps your godfather."

"I know, darling. I understand." Camilla nestled closer against him. "Jean, everything is all right now? You're sure of me and my love?"

He raised his head, looking down at her with a radiant smile. "Very sure. You're far too much of a lady, my dear wife, to make love with such abandon unless you really cared for me. You were really shameless!"

Camilla chuckled. "I'm relieved. If I'm going to spend my winters in a frigid Canadian cabin, I want a warm body in bed with me."

"Well, as to going to Canada, I'm not so certain now that we should do that—" Jean sat bolt upright in bed. "Camilla! I've just remembered what you were shouting when you burst into the bedroom. Something about me being safe, something else about me sitting in chains in a French jail. What did you mean?"

Camilla's eyes widened. In her happiness, she'd almost forgotten the circumstances that had brought her here. She scrambled out of bed, snatched up a sheet and wrapped it around her, and sat down on Jean's side of the bed.

"It was Aubrey Elvaston's doing," she began, and briefly described to Jean her abduction by Elvaston and his boasts that he'd betrayed Jean to the French for smuggling Nathan Rothschild's gold.

"I'll kill Elvaston," said Jean between his teeth. "I'll kill him by inches. I'll take his scalp first. I'll—"

"You'll consider my reputation and leave him strictly alone," said Camilla firmly. "I've already left him half dead. I'm convinced he's so badly crippled that he'll never walk again."

Jean struggled with his feelings. At last he said, "You really hit him with a poker?"

"I did. And his valet, too."

Jean laughed. "Oh, very well. Perhaps the fellow's taken enough punishment. *I'd* hate to have you coming after me with a poker! So I won't kill him. If you'd allow me to scalp him, however, I daresay he'd no longer fancy himself so much with the females."

"Jean!"

Grinning, he threw up his hands. *"C'est fini.* Elvaston's not important, not any more."

Frowning, Camilla said, "No, Jean, we haven't finished with this. Was Sir Aubrey telling me the truth? *Did* you come

314

down here yesterday to smuggle gold to France for Mr. Rothschild?"

Jean hesitated. "Yes," he admitted reluctantly. "I was supposed to sail with Captain Allen, but the storm made it too dangerous to attempt to cross the Channel. The captain thought the bad weather would continue for several days, so I simply returned here to the villa to wait it out."

"You've been acting as Mr. Rothschild's courier for some time, haven't you, Jean?"

"Yes," Jean replied, still more reluctantly. "But you're not to talk about this. I pledged total secrecy to Nathan Rothschild."

"Well, I certainly am going to talk about it, at least to you," Camilla flared. "Jean, you're breaking the law. If you should be caught, you'd be jailed. You might be hanged! And it would be the outside of enough if I were to lose my brand-new husband to a hangman's noose!"

Gazing at her anxious face, Jean said slowly, "I should have been more open with you, *ma mie*. I see that now. It wasn't fair to worry you so. But I'd promised Nathan Rothschild . . . Oh, the devil, nothing is more important than the love and trust between you and me. NM will understand."

Pausing for a moment to collect his thoughts, Jean continued. "It's true that technically I've been breaking the law by transporting Nathan Rothschild's gold across the Channel. However, I've never been in any danger of being jailed, either here or in France. For one thing, my cousin Sylvestre is chief of customs at Gravelines, near Calais; he wouldn't allow the French police to apprehend me, or to interfere with me in any way. Sylvestre — a very fine fellow, by the way; I'm grateful for the opportunity to become acquainted with him! — has been well paid for his cooperation. More important, certain members of the British government are well aware of Rothschild's activities and heartily approve of them, though naturally they can't admit their knowledge publicly."

Dumfounded, Camilla said blankly, "What do you mean, that the English government knows and approves of your smuggling?"

A sudden smile lighted Jean's dark face. "It's really very simple. You know, of course, that an Anglo-Portuguese army under Lord Wellington is fighting the French in the Peninsula. From the beginning of the war, Wellington had had difficulty paying his troops, for which he requires hard cash. Specie. Coins. Well, the blockade makes it impossible to transport large enough sums of gold by sea to pay the army, especially under storm conditions in the Bay of Biscay. So Wellington has been forced to borrow huge sums from Spanish and Maltese bankers at ruinous rates of interest, giving them in return bills of exchange which the British Treasury has been cashing at tremendous loss. Nathan Rothschild decided to make a profit *and* serve his adopted country. He smuggles gold to France, depositing it with Paris bankers who exchange the gold for bills. Rothschild's agents then carry the bills across the Pyrenees to Spain, where Spanish bankers cash them and give the money to Wellington."

"But surely some among the French authorities must suspect what Mr. Rothschild is doing?"

"Rothschild's agents have convinced certain officials in the French Finance Department that England is close to defeat, and that the country's situation can only get worse by a drainage of gold from the kingdom." Jean grinned at Camilla. "So there, my darling. I've never been at risk for my gold smuggling activities. Well, I daresay there was some risk that I might have drowned at sea." Jean interrupted himself. "What's wrong?" he inquired, taken aback by Camilla's indignant glare.

"Nothing's wrong," Camilla exploded, "except that I feel an absolute fool! Here I've been out of my mind with worry about you since last night. I pictured you in jail, or shot dead on a French beach. I chased down here to Kent in a raging storm, hoping I'd arrive in time to warn you against going to France. I might have been badly injured when my carriage lost a wheel. I was attacked by a highwayman, and I was forced to shoot him. Then, when I finally reached Lynharbor your Captain Allen denied even knowing your name. And finally, when I arrived at the villa, drenched and exhausted and convinced I'd failed you utterly, there you were, fast asleep in a comfortable bed!"

Trying to restrain his laughter, Jean said, "Think of the bright side, darling. If you hadn't come down here after me, we might never have discovered how much we love each other."

"Well . . ." Camilla looked at Jean's dark face, and her heart melted.

He put out his hand, tugging gently at the sheet which she'd draped around her. "You're not cold, are you?"

Later—much later—Jean whispered in Camilla's ear, "Tell me again that you love me. I'll never tire of hearing you say it, if I live to be a hundred."

Camilla snuggled closer to Jean, nibbling on his ear. "Of course I love you, you idiot. I loved you even when I thought you were a boor and a ruffian and a savage."

"Don't forget the uncouth Colonial," Jean murmured, as he pulled her closer.

THE ROMANCE OF LORDS AND LADIES
IN JANIS LADEN'S REGENCIES

BEWITCHING MINX   (2532, $3.95)

From her first encounter with the Marquis of Penderleigh when he had mistaken her for a common trollop, Penelope had been incensed with the darkly handsome lord. Miss Penelope Larchmont was undoubtedly the most outspoken young lady Penderleigh had ever known, and the most tempting.

A NOBLE MISTRESS   (2169, $3.95)

Moriah Landon had always been a singularly practical young lady. So when her father lost the family estate over a game of picquet, she paid the winner, the notorious Viscount Roane, a visit. And when he suggested the means of payment—that she become Roane's mistress—she agreed without a blink of her eyes.

SAPPHIRE TEMPTATION   (3054, $3.95)

Lady Serena was commonly held to be an unusual young girl—outspoken when she should have been reticent, lively when she should have been demure. But there was one tradition she had not been allowed to break: a Wexley must marry a Gower. Richard Gower intended to teach his wife her duties—in every way.

SCOTTISH ROSE   (2750, $3.95)

The Duke of Milburne returned to Milburne Hall trusting that the new governess, Miss Rose Beacham, had instilled the fear of God into his harum-scarum brood of siblings. But she romped with the children, refused to be cowed by his stern admonitions, and was so pretty that he had the devil of a time keeping his hands off her.

Available wherever paperbacks are sold, or order direct from the Publisher. Send cover price plus 50¢ per copy for mailing and handling to Zebra Books, Dept. 3912, 475 Park Avenue South, New York, N.Y. 10016. Residents of New York and Tennessee must include sales tax. DO NOT SEND CASH. For a free Zebra/ Pinnacle catalog please write to the above address.

DISCOVER DEANA JAMES!

CAPTIVE ANGEL (2524, $4.50/$5.50)
Abandoned, penniless, and suddenly responsible for the biggest tobacco plantation in Colleton County, distraught Caroline Gillard had no time to dissolve into tears. By day the willowy redhead labored to exhaustion beside her slaves . . . but each night left her restless with longing for her wayward husband. She'd make the sea captain regret his betrayal until he begged her to take him back!

MASQUE OF SAPPHIRE (2885, $4.50/$5.50)
Judith Talbot-Harrow left England with a heavy heart. She was going to America to join a father she despised and a sister she distrusted. She was certainly in no mood to put up with the insulting actions of the arrogant Yankee privateer who boarded her ship, ransacked her things, then "apologized" with an indecent, brazen kiss! She vowed that someday he'd pay dearly for the liberties he had taken and the desires he had awakened.

SPEAK ONLY LOVE (3439, $4.95/$5.95)
Long ago, the shock of her mother's death had robbed Vivian Marleigh of the power of speech. Now she was being forced to marry a bitter man with brandy on his breath. But she could not say what was in her heart. It was up to the viscount to spark the fires that would melt her icy reserve.

WILD TEXAS HEART (3205, $4.95/$5.95)
Fan Breckenridge was terrified when the stranger found her near-naked and shivering beneath the Texas stars. Unable to remember who she was or what had happened, all she had in the world was the deed to a patch of land that might yield oil . . . and the fierce loving of this wildcatter who called himself Irons.